PRAISE FOR *BECOMING HOME*

"I'm grateful for Ben DeLong's creative efforts to help people rethink their faith and rediscover parts of themselves that are so easily lost."

BRIAN D. MCLAREN, AUTHOR OF *FAITH AFTER DOUBT*

"Two engaging stories with a powerful, transformational message!"

KARL FOREHAND, AUTHOR OF *BEING,*
THE TEA SHOP, AND *APPARENT FAITH*

"The best stories are the ones we find ourselves in. In *Becoming Home*, author Ben DeLong weaves a beautiful tapestry of hope through the carnage of tragedy and pain. This is a deconstructionist's *Pilgrim's Progress*, helping guide us from wounding and shame to a place of healing and learning to be comfortable in our own skin."

JASON ELAM, THE MESSY SPIRITUALITY PODCAST

First Edition

Cover design and layout by Rafael Polendo (polendo.net)
Cover image by LUMEZIA (shutterstock.com)

ISBN 978-1-7348234-9-3

This volume is printed on acid free paper and meets ANSI Z39.48 standards.

Printed in the United States of America

Published by Shaia-Sophia House
An imprint of Quoir
San Antonio, Texas, USA

www.ShaiaSophiaHouse.com

BECOMING HOME

A Novel

Ben DeLong

SHAIA-SOPHIA
HOUSE

DEDICATION

To Irene and Michael, who never let me settle for less than who I am.

ACKNOWLEDGEMENTS

This book comes out of immense healing in my life, and this could not have happened without the love and support of so many. My wife Irene is my constant companion and cheerleader. My therapist and spiritual director have been pivotal in my growth. My parents have supported and believed in me my entire life. Countless friends have spoken words of wisdom into my life. This book would not be possible without these wonderful people.

Several friends were pivotal in providing feedback for this book. Lori Fish, Paul Fitzgerald, Susanna Fitzgerald, Jessica Monlux and David Tompkins were my early readers that helped me see the potential in this story. Once again, Janet Chaniot provided invaluable editing feedback and was incredibly generous with her time. Shaia-Sophia House has been a tremendous source of strength and guidance for this book as well. Thank you all so much!

1

BILL COULD NOT REMEMBER HOW LONG HE HAD CALLED this land home. He couldn't recall anything before this land, though he knew he had once lived elsewhere. For all intents and purposes, however, this was the only home he had ever known. He was okay with that. In fact, he was relieved.

This was a calm land, a steady land. That's what Bill appreciated. Not the faintest disturbance could be detected, and so the twigs snapping beneath his boots roared like an avalanche. In turn, birds flapped through the branches to escape the incoming presence.

It was a familiar trek, one Bill could make in his sleep. The river began introducing itself in the quiet roars from across the ridge, filling the air like a distant cry. The days had amassed, and the river had become a close friend and a companion in this land.

This was about as much friendship as Bill could handle. Bill was not one for companionship, so the river's presence was quite sufficient. Well, the river, and the loyal canine beckoning Bill's pace to quicken.

Bill had named his fellow traveler 'Rusty' for the orange fur that covered his body. He had a long snout and partially floppy ears. Rusty looked like he could handle himself, but his bark towered over his bite. Rusty was always looking for the next great adventure, and the next intriguing creature to investigate.

Bill reached the ridge crescendo and peered down at the water. The noise from the moving river was starting to drown everything else out. His heart leapt at the thought of wetting his dry mouth, and at the prospect of catching a few of the creatures darting through the water.

The view was spectacular as always. The coming descent pointed toward a wide open frame of the river and all its accessories. Rocks of all sizes peppered the river's edge. Trees lined the opposite side and pierced the blue sky. One tree had dropped several branches into the river, and they were being carried off in the current. A falcon swooped back and forth, looking to snag breakfast.

Bill chose his steps down the hill with great care, wanting to avoid any chance of taking a tumble down the hill. He had more than a few scars scattered on his body reminding him why.

Rusty darted to the water, eager to continue playing with his scaly friends. He submerged half of his body in the water, jumping up and down and yelling at all the fish. Occasionally he would growl, as though frustrated at being ignored. Bill reached the bottom of the grade and strolled over to his usual spot, amused at Rusty's antics.

The day before, a bear had made an appearance across the river. Bill scanned the area for any sign of it. He made sure to bring his revolver in case he needed to scare it away.

Confident that Rusty was the only furry quadruped in the area, Bill peeled his jacket off, trying to stay ahead of the heat. His forehead was already dripping with sweat, and the back of his shirt was damp as well. The water seemed to demand that he dip his head in, and he gladly obliged. The rippling water felt so good. Bill pulled out his cup and dropped it in the water a few times, guzzling down each scoop. "Time to get to work," he reminded himself.

Bill retrieved his fishing pole from the pack and looked it over to make sure it was primed to function well. He wasn't sure if he was a gifted fisherman, or simply had found a fantastic spot. Nevertheless, he had enjoyed great success in this location, and was ready to keep the tradition going.

Rusty began growling at something from across the water. Bill snapped his head over and saw a familiar sight. A dark figure stood across the river and stared at Bill. Its eyes were not visible, but Bill could feel them. It would have been a disturbing sight and, in fact, used to send chills up Bill's back. He was used to the figure now, and they seemed to have an understanding.

The figure appeared to be blocked by some invisible force from entering Bill's land. He often caught it standing across the river, or stationed in the woods out beyond his cabin. There seemed to be a mutual agreement that the barrier would never be crossed, so Bill carried on with his business, determined to honor his side of the deal. The figure left the area as quietly as he had arrived.

Bill rose up from the ground and began peering in the water, trying to find the best spot to aim his line. Most of the time Bill could see fish roaming around this part of the water with ease, and today was no exception. After a few seconds he found a target and began motioning through a few practice throws. Finally, he released his line and shot it straight to his spot. "Perfect!" He exclaimed.

It only took a few minutes for Bill to get his first bite. Rusty cheered his friend on, just as excited for the prospective catch. He had learned long ago that a fish from the water was tasty food for him as well. Bill tugged and pulled, careful not to lose the fish. The creature rose out of the water, closer and closer to the end of Bill's pole. Bill removed the fish from his line and celebrated with another pat on Rusty's head.

After about an hour, Bill was getting ready to shut down. He had caught several more fish and felt pleased with his progress. Rusty, ever easily entertained, was pleased as well, studying Bill's every move.

Bill finished with his last cast of the pole and retrieved an additional fish from the water. Bill began gathering his supplies to pack them back up. He crouched down to adjust the items in his pack. He soon froze, however, concentrating on a faint sound that seemed to be getting louder. He scoured the area, scanning back and forth to detect the location of the disturbance.

"Another bear?" He wondered.

He continued to stay motionless, attempting to pierce through the landscape with his focused eyes. Through the tree line Bill started to make out the figure of a man hiking.

"Damn it," Bill sighed to himself. He could not remember the last time he had seen a new person in these parts. He was quite happy with that. Now his peaceful abode had been invaded. He crossed his arms and continued eyeing every move the stranger made.

Rusty began making a fuss. Curiously, however, he was neither barking or growling. In fact, he was whimpering, as if the man across the river was a long lost companion. He pawed at the rocks and the dirt, attempting to summon the courage to cross the river. Rusty's cries didn't seem to deter the man, however, who continued along seemingly oblivious to their presence.

The man kept walking and disappeared back into the engulfing woods. Bill gave Rusty an inquisitive look, still confused by his odd behavior.

"Well, let's hope that's the last we see of him," Bill chimed in. He collected the rest of his equipment, grabbed his buckets, and began the hike back to his cabin. He would be returning much less settled than when he had left.

2

LIAM HAD GONE INTO MARKETING FOR THE CHALLENGE
and adventure. Lately, however, something was off. There was no excitement or passion. Instead, there was fear of not being good enough. Liam was always second guessing himself now, and it seemed like his creative juices had dried up. He was sure it was only a matter of time until someone else figured that out.

He laid wide awake in his bed, stuck there for the past forty minutes. He could have just gotten up, but he once again was dreading the first step of his morning. The alarm on his phone blurted out with a sound that made Liam cringe. He snatched it to shut it off.

Rachel's arm swung over and gave Liam an empathetic pat on the shoulder. She squeezed his arm before rolling back over to her sleeping pose. His wife knew that getting up in the morning had been a struggle lately, but she was not aware of how much he dreaded heading off to work. Disappointing Rachel was an underlying fear for Liam. He felt an undying need to be the ideal man in her life, so failing at his career was not something he was itching to discuss with her.

Liam turned and planted his feet on the floor. He leaned over and dropped his head into his hands. After a couple minutes he finally got up and dragged himself to the bathroom. The screech of the shower knobs turning cut into the silence like a razor. Liam tested the water a couple times with his hand to make sure it was the right temperature.

Liam's showers had been getting longer and longer, and the hot water always seemed to be in short supply. Liam used every drop, spending much of the time with his hands against the wall while the water washed over his head. The aquatic massage on his scalp roared in his ears.

He tried as much as he knew how to empty his mind. This was one part of the day that he enjoyed, and he hated the idea that his stress would steal this away from him too. He tried, but to no avail. Thoughts darted through his mind like antelope running for their life. Soon the hot water faded away, and Liam turned the knobs off.

He exited the bathroom while drying off his hair. The cool air from the room engulfed his body. He pulled the towel off his head to find Rachel laying on her side facing him with her arm anchoring her head. She wore a huge smile on her face, the kind one sports when trying to cheer up a loved one. Liam returned the smile, but only halfway.

"Good morning," she greeted him.

"Good morning," he replied. He attempted to match her enthusiasm, but it was apparent that it was labored.

"What are you guys working on today?" she asked.

Liam was a team lead at his company. He had received that promotion a couple years ago after his supervisor began noticing his initiative and creative instinct. He was excited about the new opportunity at first, but his ability felt like it was waning.

"We just got a new account for a toy company that's trying to build their online presence, so we're gonna be focusing on that for a while," he answered as he pulled out his clothes for the day.

"That sounds interesting," she replied.

"Yeah, it'll be a fun challenge," he said, trying to convince himself.

"Are you going to have to work late again?"

"I'll have to let you know. I'm not sure, but I'm hoping not to."

"That'd be great," she commented while running her hand through her morning hair. "Do you want some coffee to go?"

"Yeah, I mean, if you don't mind."

"Sure." She rose out of bed and retrieved her robe. She gave him a reassuring smile as she exited the room.

Liam finished getting dressed. He had always hated dressing up in a suit and tie ever since he was a kid. It didn't seem like that big of a deal at work before when he was enjoying what he was doing. Now it seemed like a heavy burden on top of all the others.

He left for the kitchen with his tie still dangling unfinished over his shirt. He opened the bedroom door and was immediately greeted by his beaming daughter, Lizzy.

"Good morning Daddy!"

Liam couldn't help but smile. He loved that, at sixteen, she still greeted him this way.

"Good morning sweetheart. How are you this morning?" He asked as he gave her his typical quick kiss on the top of her head.

"I'm great! We get to give our presentations in history class today."

"Wow, and you're not nervous?"

"Nah, it's no big deal."

"That's my girl, never phased by anything, huh?"

"Yep," she heartily agreed.

That truly was Lizzy. Liam never felt the need to worry about her, other than the typical dad stuff: boys … and boys. She seemed eager to greet whatever challenge faced her.

Liam followed Lizzy down the stairs and to the kitchen, where Rachel was finishing his coffee and their son Aaron was scarfing down his cereal. Aaron was the more mysterious and challenging child for Liam. He was a great kid with a big heart; he just so often had difficulty believing in himself. Much of the time there seemed to be an invisible barrier between the two males of the house. Aaron's rambunctiousness often threw Liam for a loop and bothered him more than he liked to admit. Rachel had observed on many occasions that they were often just too similar, though Liam had a difficult time seeing it.

"Good morning son, how are you?"

"Hi Dad, I'm good," Aaron replied without looking up from his breakfast.

Liam grabbed the coffee from Rachel's extended hand as he moved toward the front door. "Thanks honey."

"No problem. Be safe."

Liam leaned in to land a kiss. "I will. Love you."

"Love you too."

Liam exited through the front door and hurried toward his car. He took a sip of coffee before placing it in the cup holder and strapped himself into the seat. It would be a good forty minutes before he would pull into work.

Though he didn't enjoy the traffic, Liam had come to enjoy the time he spent in the car. Life had become so labored. The car ride gave him the rare opportunity not to have to focus on what others were thinking and expecting of him.

He loved listening to oldies CD's during his commute. He had long ago memorized the lyrics to all the songs on his discs. There was an upbeat and carefree nature to many of the tunes. It was something he craved for himself.

Liam arrived early to work. He pulled into his assigned parking space--a perk of his team lead promotion. He took a deep breath to prepare himself and exited the car.

Just as he was shutting the door, his phone began ringing. He set his things on top of the car so he could take the call.

"Good morning, Liam, this is Daniel. How are you?" Daniel was his boss's secretary. He was too perky for Liam's taste, and any call from the boss always concerned Liam.

"Oh, good morning, Daniel, I'm fine, how are you?"

"I'm doing great! I just need to let you know that Donald would like to meet you first thing this morning."

"Oh, okay. Did he say what it's about?"

"No, I'm not sure what it is for, but he would like to see you as soon as you get in."

"Okay, thanks."

"You're welcome. See you soon!"

Liam hung up the phone and slid it back into his pocket. This morning was not starting off well.

3

BILL ROLLED OVER AS HE HEARD THE SOUND OF A CHIRP-
ing bird outside his window. He rubbed his eyes a few times to make
sure he was truly awake. He looked toward the window, trying to locate
the sound. He was an early riser anyway, but every so often a critter
would turn him into an overachiever. Usually it was his orange haired
companion that did the waking, but he was still snoozing away at the
foot of the bed.

Bill let his bare feet land on the cold wood floor. He pulled his sus-
penders over his shoulders and walked over to the wash basin. As was
his morning custom, he splashed some water on his face to help finish
the waking attempt. The water stunned his face and ran down to soak
his collar. He lifted his arms and let out a forceful yawn. Rusty's head
popped up and he gave Bill a bewildered stare.

Bill gathered some wood from a fallen tree he had dismembered
earlier that week. He began splitting the wood into smaller pieces with
his axe. He loved feeling the reverberation of the axe in his hands and
up through his arms. As he exerted more energy, the cool morning air
could not keep the beads of sweat from flowing down his face.

He started the fire and watched mesmerized as the flames grew and
overtook the wood. He placed a fish on his skillet and proceeded to
cook his breakfast. He also prepared some eggs he had gathered from
the surrounding woods. Rusty laid out beside him, waiting patiently
for his portion to become available.

The sizzle of the meal filled the air. Bill sat and peacefully took in the
familiar scene around him. Each tree had become a friend, each rock
a companion. He noticed movement out of the corner of his eye as a
squirrel danced around a nearby tree. Rusty darted toward it, growling
ferociously all the way. Soon, he was returning with a confident prance,
sure that his quick reaction had protected them.

The meal was cooked to completion. Bill placed some on his plate and threw another portion on the ground for his canine pal. The two friends scarfed down the food. Of course, Rusty never thought he had enough, and always begged for more. Bill sat back, leaning on his arms, and continued to enjoy the scenery as the air blew across his body.

The fire succumbed to the breeze and began to die down. Smoke rose up, signaling the end of the day's first segment. Bill stood up, stretched his arms out wide, and let out another roaring yawn. "Time to get ready," he instructed Rusty, who whipped his tail back and forth in excitement for the upcoming journey back to the river.

Bill returned to the cabin to retrieve his equipment. He prepared his pack, checking several times to make sure he had everything he required. He called Rusty over, who had become distracted by an intrusive bird, and they began their familiar trek to the place they so enjoyed.

As Rusty sprinted forward with his usual carefree enthusiasm, Bill was still pondering the ramifications of the sighting they had taken in yesterday. He couldn't remember the last time he had run into another person. Was the man they had seen simply passing through? Was he a threat? And the most confusing part of all: Why did Rusty react in such a strange way? Bill couldn't know any of this for certain, but he was definitely more alert than usual. His head ached as he continued to reflect on the situation.

Rusty ran himself exhausted as he would continuously run about fifty feet ahead and circle back to check on his companion. He scolded Bill incessantly, as if he had never been on an outing before. "I'm coming, I'm coming," Bill would reassure him.

They arrived at the pinnacle of the hill. Bill took time to scour the area for any sign that another person had been roaming around. He looked for medium-sized rocks or logs out of place, items left behind, or small branches knocked down. As far as he could tell, nothing seemed out of place. Rusty didn't seem to notice any new scents either. Unfortunately, Bill still wasn't satisfied.

He gathered his equipment and began his descent down the hill. He had a quickened pace, as though he was running late for an

appointment. He soon made it to the bottom, where Rusty was waiting to greet him. Rusty transitioned to his pounce position, tail wagging at full speed, and gave Bill a playful bark.

"I know I know, you impatient mutt," he retorted.

Bill proceeded to follow his usual routine. He drank a couple cups
of water, and prepped his fishing pole. He had not found as many
worms as yesterday since he was preoccupied during the trek. With the
amount of fish he had caught the day before, however, he was not in
need of a big haul.

He found his casting site and started aiming his shot, all while
squinting his eyes to scan the area for any sign of the man. Everything
seemed normal and in its place. After a few casts, Bill settled in and
allowed himself to relax a little.

The fish darted through the water. The ambiance of the river was
hypnotic. The rippling sounds seemed to infiltrate his mind as he lost
himself in the moment. He took a seat on a nearby log, ready to test
his patience against the fish.

Bill leapt up from the log as Rusty took off running to his left, barking excitedly as he went. Bill looked in that direction and saw the man
crossing over the river about fifty yards away. He then proceeded to
turn uphill in the direction of the cabin.

Bill dropped his pole, grabbed his knife, and darted toward the hill.
He could feel the adrenaline flowing through him, enabling his muscles
to push harder and harder. Fear and anger pulsated through his veins.
This was what he had dreaded as soon as he saw the man yesterday. Bill
had worked too hard and too diligently, to let some straggler steal from
him, or to ruin his place on this land.

"Damn it!" He scolded himself as he realized he hadn't grabbed his
revolver. There was no time to go back.

Rusty was nowhere to be seen or heard from, but Bill couldn't worry
about that now. He grasped the nearby trees to keep himself from slipping backwards, gripping onto branches and stalks. His lungs struggled
to keep up with the demand for air, but he kept pushing.

Soon he reached the hill top and angled back as he started down-ward. A branch snapped as he reached out to it for help. He nearly fell, but instead skidded about ten feet on his heels, spreading his arms for balance. He recovered and continued his mission.

He spotted his cabin as he approached the bottom. He took a quick glance to see if the man had arrived yet, but there was no sign of him. He leapt over a protruding log and then over the remains of the morning fire. He turned and darted toward the front door, busted through it, and went straight for his bedside. He slid onto his knees and fetched his shotgun from the floor below his bed.

Bill turned back toward the front door, simultaneously cocking his weapon. He could hear rustling in the trees outside the cabin. He stopped short of the doorway to peek around it. He saw the man closing in, with Rusty strolling beside him.

Bill swung himself out of the doorway and faced the man, who walked with no discernable urgency to his pace.

"Stop right there!" Bill commanded. The man stopped immediately, stunned and speechless. They locked eyes. The man looked bewildered as Bill stared at him with his face shaking. After a moment, Bill finally spoke again. "State your business stranger."

4

LIAM SLOGGED DOWN THE HALLWAY TOWARD HIS DIREC-
tor's office. His feet dragged against the carpet as his mind turned over
and over the possible reasons for this summons. Nothing he could think
of would warrant such an appointment. Liam never enjoyed a visit to
the boss's office. He had a difficult time imagining that such occasions
could come from celebratory origins, and this was no different.

He stopped and pulled out his phone to see if there were any emails
that he had missed from his boss. There must be some hint somewhere.
He shuffled through his emails, lifting his head when needed to half-
heartedly greet someone passing in the hall. He continued searching,
but nothing caught his eye as a possible culprit.

He looked ahead and saw his friend Victor transporting a fresh
cup of coffee into his office. Victor and Liam had joined the company
around the same time. They had become very close, and seemed to be
destined to complement each other. Liam was more of a take charge
personality, always eager to best the next challenge. Victor loved to take
the big ideas and flesh them out. There was no success that Liam experienced in his job that could not be partly traced to Victor, and visa
versa. When Liam was promoted to team lead, Victor was an obvious
choice to be his number two.

"Victor!" Liam called out to his friend in a hushed tone.

Victor kept walking. Liam stood confused. He was sure Victor
would have heard his name called. Nevertheless, Liam called again,
"Victor! Victor!"

Victor turned to Liam, and looked sheepish while avoiding eye contact. He scanned the perimeter and then waved Liam quickly into his
office like he was avoiding surveillance. Liam hurried in, confused and
concerned.

Victor shut the door behind them, and proceeded to station himself behind his desk. He aimlessly shuffled papers while keeping his eyes to the ground.

"What are you doing?" Liam inquired.

Victor stalled for several seconds, continuing to rifle through the items on his desk. "Where are you going first this morning Liam?"

"What?" Liam responded, perturbed at not receiving an answer. "I'm going to Donald's office. I was told to go see him first thing this morning." Victor continued looking down at his papers, and seemed to be unsurprised by the response. "Dude, why are you acting so weird? Do you know what Donald wants to talk about?"

"You should really just talk to Donald."

"Seriously? That's all you're gonna give me?"

"You just need to talk to him first. Just keep an open mind, okay?" Victor finally looked up with a concerned face. "And believe me, this wasn't my idea."

Liam stood stunned. His stomach tightened even more than it already was. He felt as if he was a car engine overheating. He ran his hand through his hair and shook his head in bewilderment. "What's that supposed to mean?" He demanded.

"That's all I can say for now." Victor grabbed a folder from his desk and stuffed it underneath his arm. He retrieved his coffee as he darted toward the door.

"Victor, this doesn't make any sense … and where are you going?"

"I have to get to the team meeting," Victor answered with hesitation, as if he was giving away too much.

"What meeting? I'm the team lead. How can there be a meeting without me?"

"Just … I'll see you there," Victor concluded as he exited the office.

Liam couldn't see straight. His heart was racing. His hands were shaking like maracas. He wanted answers; he wanted to know what was going on, but feared the worst. Maybe he didn't want to know. His next stop was the one place he dreaded going most.

He fought to compose himself before he saw his director. He shut himself inside Victor's office. His eyes heated up. Tears of frustration began rising as he struggled to puff air into his lungs. He swiped the glasses off his face and squeezed the bridge off his nose to keep the tears at bay. He was confused and scared, but shuddered at the thought of letting his boss see it.

His mind backtracked to the day he received his promotion. It was the end of a long, summer day. He was ready to pack up and head home to his family, but Donald had called him into his office just before he was about to leave. It was like it happened yesterday. He could still feel the warmth of Donald's hand grasping his shoulder.

"We've been very pleased with your contributions to this company," Donald encouraged him. "Not just your work, but your passion and integrity. We see a strong leader in you."

"Thank you, Mr. Irving. Thank you so much!"

"You're welcome son. Now, you'll wanna choose yourself a solid number two to assist you. I imagine you already have someone in mind though."

A chuckle escaped from Liam's lips. "Of course, sir. I'll go talk to him right now."

Liam heard a door slam in the hallway; it jolted him present. He paced back and forth, trying to imagine any scenario that wouldn't include what he feared was coming. He turned around and noticed the time on the clock. He knew he couldn't keep delaying without it looking suspicious. He took one last deep breath, creaked open the door, and started down the hall.

Donald's office was in the furthest corner of their floor. Liam held his eyes to the ground, focusing on the square pattern of the carpet to avoid interactions with as many people as possible. It was hard to notice anything anyway. Time felt halted, and an invisible tunnel seemed to draw Liam to his fears.

He approached the office, and was greeted by Daniel. "You can go on in Liam, he's ready for you."

"Okay." Liam stopped short of the doorway. He heard Donald's fingers dancing on his laptop keys. His face was buried in his screen. Liam took one more deep breath and ventured inside.

"Liam, thanks for coming," Donald said without looking up. He motioned with his right hand toward the chairs surrounding the coffee table. "Go ahead and have a seat. I'm almost finished here."

Liam found a chair and sat down. His body sank into the cushion. He crossed his legs and placed his hands in his lap. He squeezed his hands together, trying to release the tension. He gazed outside and fixed his eyes on a tree swaying back and forth in the wind. The tree appeared to be so carefree, content to let the breeze direct it anyway it wanted to. Liam longed for that kind of freedom. He was always on guard, afraid that any moment of lost focus could cost him everything. He did not realize how lost in the view he was until Donald came over and patted him on the shoulder.

"I'm sure you're wondering why I brought you down here, Liam," Donald said as he sat down on the opposite chair. Liam tried his best to appear nonchalant, as if his heart was not about to chisel its way through his chest. "I don't want to keep you in suspense. When you began with this company, I told you that I don't let my employees flounder. I reminded you of that when I promoted you to team lead. We don't throw our people aside when they're struggling, but we also need them to move in the right direction. That's why I've brought you in, Liam. You've been struggling, and I don't just want to let you fall by the wayside."

Liam's thoughts were sprinting laps. He tried to hide that his body was shaking, but it was obvious in the cadence of his words. "I don't think I understand. I haven't missed a deadline. Everything has been completed as you've asked."

Donald extended his hand toward Liam to chime in. "It's not about deadlines. Liam, your work has not had the same inspiration behind it as it usually does. There's a lack of depth to it now, like you're just trying to get it done. And that's not you. That's not what you bring to the table. We know the passion and creative spark you have, and that's what we need."

Liam could feel his body growing tenser. He let his eyes hit the floor. "I wish you had brought this up before."

"That's just it, Liam. I've reached out to you on many occasions. Through emails, and chats in the hallway. I've asked if you're doing okay, if there's something going on, and you just give me the usual perfunctory answers. "I'm fine. I'm great." Now, whatever is going on with you is your business. But I want you to thrive, for your benefit, as well as for the company."

Liam didn't know what to say. He felt as if he was being cornered and feared letting anything else out that could make this worse.

"Look, I get it. I was a young man myself, if you can believe it. I know how hard it can be to deal with difficult stuff that's going on inside us. Liam, I don't know what's going on, but you haven't been yourself for a while. I want to give you space to work on whatever it is so you can be healthy and begin thriving here again. In the meantime, I'm having Victor fill your role as team lead, and you will report to him."

Liam's head snapped up, and his eyes filled with frustration. "You're demoting me?"

"This is not meant to be punitive, Liam. I want you back as the team lead as soon as you can start working through whatever you're dealing with."

"I'm not dealing with anything. I'm fine."

Donald peered into Liam's face, hoping for an elaboration. He did not receive one. "Well Liam, this is the direction we're moving for now. You can report to your team meeting. Victor is prepping them for the next project."

Liam couldn't bring himself to say anything else. Any words now would be coupled with the warm tears piling up behind his eyes. But no one would get to see him cry, not if he had any say in the matter. He sluggishly rose from his chair and turned to exit the office, avoiding any eye contact in the process.

He staggered down the hallway toward the conference room. He was overwhelmed at the thought of facing everyone in the room, knowing he had failed. Halfway down he bailed out into the men's bathroom. He shut the door and ensured it was locked. He crouched down and let the tears escape at last, gasping for breath between the heavy sobs.

5

BILL STOOD AS FIRM AS A STATUE, KEEPING HIS GUN pointed squarely at the stranger. The beating of his heart vibrated throughout his body. He was hoping to scare the stranger off, but it didn't seem to be working.

"You can put the gun away, my friend. Rest assured, I mean no harm to you."

The stranger's casualness caught Bill off guard. He peered at him with confusion. "I'm not your friend, stranger. Now state your business, or get the hell out of here."

Rusty barked angrily at Bill, as though embarrassed by his lack of hospitality.

"I guess my first point of business is to introduce myself. My name is Joshua," he informed as he extended his hand toward Bill, ignoring the weapon pointed at him.

"What do you want, Joshua?"

"Well, I saw you down by the water yesterday, and I thought maybe you needed something. So I'm here to help."

"Help with what?"

"Anything that you need."

"I don't need anything, so just … "

"Oh I highly doubt that," Joshua chuckled as he turned toward the fire pit.

"What?" Bill let out a sigh. He was becoming less angry and more annoyed. Rusty was jumping up on Joshua, like he was experiencing a reunion. "Rusty! Get down! Get down, you stupid dog!"

"I imagine you've been out here by yourself for a while," Joshua continued, unfazed by Rusty's enthusiasm.

"What? Why do you presume to know anything about me?"

"Just a gut feeling I guess. So how long have you been out here?"

"I'm not looking for a friendly conversation. If you have nothing else to do here, then just leave."

"Well, I do have one other thing for you," Joshua elaborated, as he reached into his coat pocket.

"Hey!" Bill screamed, fearing Joshua was reaching for a weapon.

"I brought some coffee over. Thought you might want to have a drink."

Bill was perplexed. He had not seen coffee in years. "Where did you get that?"

"I traded for it a little while back." Joshua lowered his pack and retrieved a couple tin mugs from inside. "You want some?" He inquired, as he offered one of the cups to Bill.

"So that's why you're here? To drink coffee with a stranger?"

"Well, a stranger for now since you haven't given your name yet. But I guess I do have a favor to ask."

"That's what I figured."

"You see, I traded for the coffee, but I'd love to have some sugar to add to it."

"I don't have any. Now, if you'll be on your way."

"Oh shoot. Well, that's alright. The coffee will do. Say, I'm a ways away, I'll just use your fire pit to brew some of this coffee before I go."

"You need to just leave," Bill reiterated. Instead, Joshua seemed to ignore his request, as well as his standoffish attitude, and ventured over to the firepit anyway.

Bill, realizing his company was more of an annoyance than a threat, lowered his weapon and watched flabbergasted as Joshua went on with his business. "Get out of here, will ya?"

"I promise, one cup of coffee and I'm gone. Two if you're gonna join me."

"No, I'm good," Bill sighed as he embraced the inevitable.

"You doing okay? You're pretty reserved," Joshua inquired casually.

Bill shook his head in disbelief. "Quit talking to me like you know me. We've never even met before. Of course, I'm reserved"

"Okay. I get it. But really. You haven't met anyone."

"What?" Bill demanded.

"You said I've never met you before. Well, how could I? You don't meet anyone."

"Yeah, well that's the way I like it. People just mess things up."

"That's a pretty sweeping statement."

"I stand by it."

"Okay, but how would you know if you never meet anyone?"

"Well you're definitely not doing anything to change my opinion. Are you done with your coffee yet?"

"Oh, hold on. You can't rush quality."

Bill sighed and rolled his eyes back. "So how long have you been in the area anyway?" Bill asked.

"Oh, quite a while I suppose. Did you just recently notice me down at the river?"

Bill quietly nodded his head.

"Hmm, that's surprising. I've been down there a lot. Just keeping an eye on you, making sure you're alright."

"You've been watching me?"

"Just checking up on you."

Bill shook his head again. "This is bizarre."

"I noticed you've been here a while, but you never venture out anywhere."

"No, I don't."

"Well, maybe you should. You might like what you find."

"No, thank you. This place is all I want. It's got everything I need."

"Really? How great can it be when you don't have any coffee," Joshua responded, as he laughed to himself.

Bill continued to get frustrated, and finally returned to his original inquiry. "Can you just tell me what you want so we can get this over with?"

"I don't want anything, other than to give you any help you might need."

"I told you, I'm fine."

"Okay, okay. But if you do ever need anything, you can always come across the river to find me."

Bill shook his head at a frenzied rate. "I'm never going over there. There's a darkness in that place."

Joshua had a perplexed look on his face. "Really? I hadn't noticed."

"Then maybe you're part of it?" Bill said with a strong accusatory tone.

"Why do you think it's a dark land?"

Bill didn't want to mention the dark figure. He had no idea who this guy was, and was not even tempted to trust him. "Let's just say it's a hunch."

"Hmm, like your hunch that I was here to hurt you?"

"You haven't left yet, so who knows."

"Well, why don't you have a seat," Joshua suggested as he motioned toward the log across from the fire pit.

"I'm not interested in making a friend."

"Okay, okay. Just give me a few minutes. My coffee will be done and I'll be out of your hair."

Bill paced back and forth and pondered the scene in front of him. He had only ever seen the dark figure across the river before. The fact that this man came from there was concerning. He decided to make a query without being obvious.

"You know, I have encountered one other person from across the river," Bill began.

"Oh yeah, who was that?"

"I never got his name. But we had an understanding that no one would cross to the other side. Were you aware that you were in breach of that?"

"No, I was not aware of any such agreement."

"Well, it was more of an unspoken agreement."

"Hmm, I've never been a fan of those."

"Clearly," Bill remarked, hoping that the dig against Joshua's lack of decorum was obvious. "Regardless, those on their side of the river were meant to remain there."

"Well, I'm sorry to tell you, those neat and tidy borders don't usually work out for very long."

Bill grumbled underneath his breath. His frustration was mounting. He was ready to turn around and let Joshua have it.

"Well," Joshua transitioned, "coffee's done. I guess I'll be on my way."

"I guess so."

Joshua nodded and slowly walked off. "I'll see you around," he closed as he disappeared into the distance.

6

LIAM SQUEEZED HIS EYES SHUT IN A DESPERATE ATTEMPT to get his tears to turn off. He hated crying; he hated showing any sign of weakness. That would never get him anywhere. In fact, it could make things much worse. His dad made sure he knew that when he was young, and Liam had never forgotten.

He wiped his face dry and looked in the mirror to see how much the redness would out him. He dampened a paper towel with cold water and pressed it against his face to make it look normal again. Entering the meeting with Victor as the lead would already be embarrassing enough without his face looking all splotchy.

He took a deep breath, threw the paper towel away, and exited the bathroom. As he turned the corner toward the hallway, he spotted the meeting room. The room was surrounded by glass walls, with a large conference table in the middle. Liam could see Victor standing beside the presentation easel, which was covered with brainstorming thoughts. Liam caught Victor's eye, who soon shook his head as he attempted to regain his train of thought. The others in the meeting turned around to discover what had grabbed Victor's attention.

Liam's heart sank as he felt their eyes piercing through him. Thoughts darted through his head. Did they know why he was not leading the team? Were they going to ask him about it? What had Victor told them? Liam could see Victor redirect their attention back to the board, much to Liam's relief. He turned the corner and opened the door quietly, as to not draw too much attention to himself.

"Hey Liam," Victor greeted him, acting as though this was their first encounter of the day. "Sorry you had to miss the bulk of the meeting. We are mainly just giving a short run down of the company, what they're looking for, and what our attack plan is going to be."

"Okay, I'll catch up; just keep going." Liam's jaw was beginning to clench. He could feel anger piling up inside him.

"The main thing that we need to focus on right now … " Victor continued as he pointed toward the brainstorming notes. Liam couldn't pay attention to anything. His mind was all over the place, and he felt as though his blood was going to shoot right through his skin. He couldn't make sense of everything he was feeling. There was intense anger. Anger at Donald for demoting him; anger at Victor for whatever his part was in all of it. But deep down, in a place Liam couldn't fully articulate, a voice kept repeating, "I knew you didn't have what it takes."

Liam could hear the other members of the team speaking, but he couldn't hear what they were saying. His thoughts and emotions drowned everything else out. He kept his eyes to the table. He couldn't stand to think of what the other members were thinking of him, and he didn't want to face the questions that he was sure were written on their faces.

"What about you, Liam?" He jolted out of his trance and realized everyone was looking at him. "Do you have any thoughts on this?"

"Umm … no, not at this time. I'm still catching up," he replied as he stumbled over his words.

"Okay that's fine," Victor responded. "So I think we have pretty much settled on our roles, at least for the front end of this project. Jennifer and Dale are going to focus on researching the buying patterns of the five metro areas that are targeted. Elizabeth and Ricardo will focus on profiling the company and their product line. Liam, you and I will look into online purchasing trends that could be helpful in our approach."

"What timeline are we working with?" Jennifer asked as she took notes on her phone with diligent focus. She was recently hired out of the company's intern program. She impressed everyone with her drive and attention to detail.

"How about let's come back together on Friday? We can assess our progress and see how much more time we need for this stage."

"That'll give us a chance to brainstorm and work through any logjams we encounter," Ricardo commented.

"Yeah, good point. Okay guys, we'll see you Friday. Liam, if you wanna stick around we can go over what you missed."

The four other team members began gathering their things and pushing in their chairs. One by one, they walked past Liam and gave him a pat on the shoulder. As Elizabeth was leaving, she turned back toward Liam. "You guys will be in our thoughts."

She exited the room. Liam became frustrated with that last encounter. He stared at Victor with a stern look. "What do they think happened?" He inquired to himself. "Do they know I was demoted?"

Victor was shuffling through some papers, trying to reorganize himself. "Alright Liam, let's get started."

"Sure," Liam responded sarcastically. "Let's."

Victor lowered his head and shook it back and forth in frustration. "Look, Liam, let's not make this more difficult than it needs to be."

"What did you tell them? Why are they treating me like I'm sick or something?"

"I didn't tell them anything specific. C'mon, it was gonna come up. I had to say something, so I just told them you had some personal stuff you were dealing with and needed to take a step back from team lead."

"So what? They think I'm losing it? I have issues at home?"

"I just kept it general. I didn't say anything about you meeting with Donald."

"Well you could at least have told me. Given me a head's up."

"I was told not to, Liam. Donald wanted to address it directly with you."

"And what is "it"? What is the big issue?" Liam abruptly stood up from his chair and began pacing back and forth across the table from Victor. "He says I'm floundering. What does that even mean?"

"Liam, I'm really sorry that you don't see it, but you have been, man. You're just not even here most days."

"C'mon, seriously?"

"Your work doesn't have the same substance that it used to. You're short with people. You're just going through the motions."

"Really? Wow. I figured I could expect more loyalty after all I've done for you."

"What are you talking about?"

"I brought you on to this team. Made you number two on this team."

"So what? You just did me a big favor? Screw that! I'm damn good at what I do."

Liam's blood was boiling. "Yeah, well I imagine that's what you told Donald when you went after my job."

"I'm getting really tired of these accusations."

"I don't hear you denying it."

"I'll do you one better," Victor announced as he slammed a folder on the table. "I'll tell you exactly what happened. Donald approached me! He didn't think you could handle the lead position right now."

"Whatever, man."

"No, not whatever. In fact, Donald wanted to remove you from the team altogether and put you on some other assignment. I vouched for you. I told him I thought you could handle not being the lead for now. Apparently, I was wrong."

"You know what? Don't do me any favors either." Liam stepped toward Victor and snatched the folder off the table. "I'll catch myself up. Thanks ... boss."

Liam stormed out of the meeting room and marched back to his office, speaking to no one on the way. He slammed the door behind him and threw the folder on his desk.

7

Twigs fractured as Bill darted through the woods. His lungs burned as they churned the air in and out. Several times Bill had almost lost his balance while looking back at the creature chasing him. He kept bracing himself with the surrounding trees to keep from falling over.

He couldn't make out what sort of being his predator was. It seemed to stand upright like a human, but it also appeared far too large to fit that description.

He could make out his cabin through the trees, which distracted him from a small log in his track. He slammed his leg into the rough bark and tumbled over. His leg screamed in pain, but he quickly rose up and began limping toward his front door.

He could hear screaming swirling around him as he dragged his battered leg through the dirt. His heart thumped inside his chest as he inched closer to the entrance. He took one last giant step and swung the door open. Standing in the way was the creature, and Bill stumbled backwards into the ground, grasping his head in fear.

Bill's eyes jolted open. He slowly lifted the pillow off his head and realized he was still in bed. It was light out, but the morning was not as bright as he had come to expect. Overcast clouds engulfed the sky, much to Bill's disappointment.

A few days had passed since Bill had met Joshua. Bill was hoping it would stay that way. He was still relieved to see Joshua was harmless, albeit chatty and annoying.

Rusty was much less content with Joshua's absence. In fact, Rusty spent most of his time moping around, looking for any sign that Joshua would return.

It was time, once again, to return to the river. It was even more pressing now, actually, as Bill had continued to use much of his water to make more and more coffee. It was a real treat, but not one he was willing to admit he fancied. "No sense in letting it go to waste," he convinced himself.

Bill was packed and ready to begin the trek. Rusty, however, had been a much less willing participant for the past few days. "Are you just gonna sulk again today?" Bill inquired. Rusty could only muster raising his eyes to acknowledge the question, then returned to peering out into the trees. "Have it your way. Dumb mutt."

Rusty moaned in disapproval. Bill was much grumpier than normal lately, and his canine companion didn't much care for it.

Bill started toward the tree line, his steps coming more hastily than usual. The hair on the back of his neck had not subsided from his visit the other day. He dreaded running into other people in the area. It didn't happen very often, but once was enough for him, especially after experiencing Joshua's obnoxious persistence. His unexpected impact on Rusty's behavior only added insult to injury.

Bill experienced a paradoxical dynamic as he scurried up the hill. He was moving faster, fueled by an almost nervous energy. Yet, he also felt drained and weighed down. This had become a pattern over the last few days, one which Bill did not care for very much. It was becoming more and more laboring to complete his daily duties, or even exit his bed in the morning.

After about thirty minutes had passed, Bill was bearing down on the riverbank. He had maintained his nervous pace and proceeded to trip over a protruding tree root. "Damn thing," he muttered to himself. He threw his bag to the ground, desiring to punish someone for his exasperation. A few items popped out of the pack, including his cup, which he jammed into the river. He planted his behind in the dirt to catch his breath. As he took a sip of the water, a crackling sound echoed out from behind him, startling him from his seat. He spun around to see a branch tumbling down to the bottom of a large tree, taking several other branches with it. A strong breeze followed through, displaying its power. His chilled skin put him on more alert. The wind wasn't usually this imposing in these parts, and Bill was startled at the sudden display of power.

Everything had seemed to lose it's appeal since his run-in with Joshua, and his arrival at the river was no different. He collected his equipment from his pack, preparing to complete the task at hand. He dipped his cup into the river once more and downed the water with a quick flick of his wrist.

The wind made every movement more difficult than usual. As he worked on prepping his pole, the line whipped around his torso. He tried pulling it off, but it kept slipping through his fingers. "Knock it off!" He chastised.

He finally got the line removed and attempted to run the worm through his hook, but his eyes were watery from the wind blasting against his face. He tried to wipe the blurriness away, but it never seemed to completely leave him.

After he had been thoroughly frustrated, he got the worm in place and attempted to locate a strategic spot in the water to target. The choppy waters made it especially arduous, but as Bill found, it also stirred the fish up quite a bit. This fishing day was looking to be particularly successful.

Bill was almost having difficulty keeping up with the fish coming in. The wind in his eyes didn't help matters, and the river repeatedly sprayed mist in his face. Yet, he was beginning to enjoy himself.

As his task was winding down, and the fish were piling up, Bill walked over to his pack to start concluding the visit to the riverbank. Curiously, he was still feeling water spraying on his face while facing away from the river. He looked down to his pack and spotted rain drops accumulating on top. Suddenly, water began pouring from the sky, drenching everything in sight within seconds.

"Oh no!" Bill rushed to retrieve his fish. He could not remember the last time it had rained like this, but he knew it would make it difficult to ascend the hill back to the cabin. He was afraid to let anymore time pass.

He packed up his fish, snatched his buckets, and returned to his pack to swing it around on his back. The wind was swirling even quicker than before. He speed walked up to the trail. He attempted to hurry up the ascent, but the ground was already getting soggy. The rain only seemed to increase, pouring over his head.

He soon ascertained he would not be able to scale the hill without using the trees to keep himself upright. He would have to leave the buckets of water behind and retrieve them later.

He clung to the trees each move he made up the hill. His feet slipped in the mud repeatedly, and his arms were screaming in pain as they tried to keep him upright. One by one, he grabbed the trees like stairs to the second level. The wind howled, and the rain beat against the ground. Suddenly. Bill heard a familiar cracking sound and looked up to see a tree limb overhead hurling down toward him. He leapt out of the way and endeavored to grasp another tree, but he could not grip it and began sliding down the hill.

He clawed at the ground as he skated down the mud. He reached out for a twig that snapped and flipped him sideways. The side of his abdomen smashed into a tree.

"Aah!" The pain was excruciating. He was breathing intensely, and scrambling to think of a way to get out of his bind. He surveyed the area. With the pain in his side, he saw no way out. He scanned the area below him to see how far the bottom was. Suddenly he felt something rough land on his face.

"Hey!" A voice exclaimed from above.

Bill snapped his head around and glimpsed Joshua standing at the top of the hill.

"Grab the rope!"

"I'm fine! Just go!"

Bill tried to lift himself up. "Aah! Shit! Shit!" His breaths were fast and labored. He couldn't fall back to the bottom, but that almost seemed bearable compared to taking the help.

"C'mon man! Take the rope!"

Bill glanced down the hill once more, then latched onto the rope, squeezing with both hands. He writhed in pain as Joshua slowly dragged his feeble body through the mud. Each tug pulled on his ribs, and Bill did his best to breathe through the pain. After what felt like hours, he finally reached the top.

He allowed himself to relax for a moment and laid his head on the soggy ground. He glanced over to see Joshua on his knees, exhausted and gasping for air. His hands were red and shaking.

"Th … thank you," Bill muttered as sincerely as he could pull off.

"You're … welcome," Joshua let out between breaths.

Bill pressed on his side, trying to locate the exact source of the pain. He found it and winced.

"You're hurt pretty bad?"

"I'll be fine."

"Well the way down to your cabin isn't gonna be any easier, you're gonna need some help there too."

Bill stayed silent. He wanted to tell Joshua to leave, but he knew he was in bad shape. After they had each caught their breath, Joshua stood up and extended a hand to Bill.

"You ready?"

Bill sighed and grabbed it with one hand, holding his side with the other. "Okay, let's go."

+ + +

Bill and Joshua had finally made it down the hill, but not without difficulty. The two had hardly spoken the whole way down, mostly because of how difficult the stretch was. Before proceeding any further, both men leaned up against a nearby tree to catch their breath.

"Why don't you go lie down. I'm sure you're in a lot of pain," Joshua recommended.

Bill slowly stood up, trying to prove that he was feeling okay. "No, it's okay. It's not that painful. Now that we're down the hill, I'll be fine."

They began hearing leaves and twigs swishing as Rusty emerged from the tree line. He came full speed and lunged toward Joshua. Bill tried to play it off. "Well, at least he's glad to see one of us."

Joshua roared laughing as Rusty showered him with kisses. "I guess so!"

"Rusty!" Bill finally scolded. "Rusty! Get off! Get off!"

"It's fine, uh, you know, I still don't know your name."

Bill hated the idea of sharing anything of himself with someone else, but he figured it was the least he could do in return for Joshua's help. "Bill. The name is Bill."

"Well, Bill, is there anything I can do to help. I imagine it's gonna be pretty laboring to do much with that," Joshua commented as he pointed to Bill's side. "Seems like you might have a bruised rib."

"No really, I'm okay. Look, I know I was pretty abrupt with you the other day. But I do things on my own. Just not much of a people person. It's nothing personal."

"I understand. So what are you gonna do in the meantime with that hill being in the way. Gonna be difficult to get to the river for fish and water."

"Well, I still have some fish, and I'll just gather water from the rain."

"Yeah, that should work. For right now, I have some canteens of water in my pack. You know, I could just stick around for one night, just to make sure your injury isn't too serious."

"Well, I don't have anywhere for you to stay," Bill replied, trying to think of any excuse he could to send Joshua on his way.

"I can sleep on the floor. That doesn't bother me at all."

"I'll be fine."

"Okay, well, take care then," Joshua concluded as he turned to walk away.

As much as Bill didn't want the company, he was worried about how serious his pain was, and how long the rain would last to gather water. "Wait," he reluctantly blurted out. "You know what? One night might be good."

Joshua smiled wide in return. "No problem."

8

—

"I'M HOME!" LIAM SHOUTED AS HE CREPT THROUGH THE front door. He had forgotten to let Rachel know that he would be late. He had worked extra trying to make a dent in the project, but his mind wandered so easily. He finally called it a night and endured his commute home.

Rachel peeked around the corner with disappointment written across her face. "Honey, I was waiting for you to call. Everything okay?"

"Yes I'm sorry. Time just got away from me."

"Okay, well, wash your hands, dinner is ready."

Rachel had not expressed as much frustration as she normally would have. Liam wondered if she was in a good mood, or perhaps holding back for some reason. Either way, he appreciated not having to face her venting.

He entered the hall bathroom and closed the door behind him. The stress of the day was so heavy. He gazed in the mirror and saw how tired his eyes looked. It matched how he felt. He longed to wipe it away and start fresh, but he couldn't shake it. He sighed, flipped off the light, and exited the bathroom.

Rachel and the kids were all seated around the table and digging in. Rachel had made lasagna, garlic bread, and a salad. Liam was relieved to see such a delicious dinner. He loved Rachel's lasagna, and usually ate too much of it.

"How was everyone's day?" Liam inquired, wanting to break the silence.

"Well mine was good," Rachel chimed in. "I got to have lunch with Cassandra today."

"Who is that again?"

"You remember. I worked with her at the dental office. You thought she looked like Sally Field?"

"That's right."

Lizzy chuckled. "She doesn't look like Sally Field, Daddy."

Liam smirked back at her. "Sort of."

She chuckled again and continued eating.

"She's doing pretty good," Rachel continued. "Still working over there."

"That's good."

For a few moments, the only sound was mouths chewing and forks cutting. It was so quiet that the sound of the phone ringing startled them all. Lizzy jumped up to answer it.

"Hello ... who? Umm, just a second," she replied as she covered the phone with her other hand. "They want to talk to a William?"

"That's me," Liam responded.

"Oh yeah, I always forget that's your full name."

"Just hang it up; no one calls me that. They're probably just a telemarketer."

"Oh, okay," she complied as she pressed the end button on the phone and returned to her chair.

The table was silent again for a moment.

"What about your day Aaron? How was it?" Rachel asked, knowing he wouldn't chime in on his own.

"It was fine," he replied. "Oh I forgot!" His eyes grew large with excitement. "Dave said he could help me get a job down at his dad's store."

"That's great sweetie!"

"I thought you were going to intern at the firm with me," Liam chimed in.

"I mean, I thought about it. But this will give me some cash. And plus, I'm not really into marketing. I feel like it wouldn't be worth it."

"Well you don't know that unless you try it."

"Honey, it's up to him, right?"

"Of course," Liam replied begrudgingly. It frustrated him when he felt Rachel stepping on his point. "Just saying."

"Jamie and I made plans for this weekend," Lizzy cut in.

"Cool, what are you guys gonna do?" Rachel inquired.

Before Lizzy could respond, Liam bumped his soda and spilled it all over the table. He quickly stood up as it began dripping onto his pants.

"Damn it!" Liam yelled exasperated.

"Liam, it's okay. No big deal."

"Good one, Dad," Aaron snickered.

"Why don't you mind your business," Liam snidely retorted.

Aaron's eyes grew big. "Dad ... I'm sorry. I was just messing."

"I don't need that."

"Honey, he was just joking."

"Could you back off? I don't need all this criticism. I've had enough of it today."

"Okay calm down."

Liam began wiping himself down with his napkin. "Is it too much, after working all day, to ask for a little respect when I get home?"

"Sorry, Dad," Aaron quietly responded with his eyes to the ground. He slowly stood up and walked out of the room. Lizzy stared at her dad with concern and surprise before she followed her brother.

The dining room went silent, except that Liam could hear Rachel staring daggers through him.

"Seriously?" She began, ending the deafness in the room.

Liam continued eating, seemingly ignoring her inquiry.

She rested her hand on his forearm. "Liam, what's going on with you?"

"I'm fine," he replied, refusing to look up from his food.

"You're not fine." Her eyes were starting to well up. "Will you please talk to me?"

"I said I'm fine."

Rachel sat back in her chair and let out a deep sigh. "Fine. If you're not going to talk, I'm gonna talk to you." She took a long pause, hoping to receive some response from her husband, but her wish went unfulfilled. "I wanted to find a better time to bring this up, but it seems like there's no good time to talk to you anyway."

She waited for Liam to acknowledge her words but continued after he showed no sign of speaking up. "I'm seeing a therapist. I had a lot of things that were piling up inside me, and I didn't know what to do, so I started seeing her."

"Okay."

"I've been seeing her for a couple months."

"A couple months?" Liam probed.

Rachel gave Liam her famous 'are you serious' face. "Now you wanna talk?"

"Why wouldn't you tell me about that?"

"I can't get you to talk; how am I supposed to tell you?"

"I'm sorry, I know I've been busy."

"It's not just that you're busy. You're distant. It's like you're holding something back."

"It's nothing. I'm fine."

"That's what I'm talking about."

"What? There's nothing to talk about. Look, I'm glad your therapist is helping you. I'm happy for you."

"Good. Because I want you to come with me."

"What? To see your therapist?"

"Yes."

"Oh my gosh. How many times do I have to say it? I'm fine!"

"You're not fine, Liam! We're not fine!"

"What's that supposed to mean?"

"What do you think?"

"So you're not happy with me anymore?"

"I don't have you anymore! You're never here, and when you are, you won't talk to me."

"So what? A couple bad weeks and suddenly our marriage is in trouble?"

"Weeks!" She exclaimed exasperated. "Do you really think it's been weeks? We haven't had a decent conversation in months! And you started closing yourself off to me way before that." Rachel paused as her eyes began welling up again. "I don't even feel like I know you anymore."

Liam froze for a moment. He was mad as hell. He hated seeing Rachel cry, but he couldn't hold his resentment in. "So this is all my fault?"

"That's not what I'm saying."

"You know, there are plenty of things you do that drive me nuts. You ever think of that? You ever think maybe you make it hard for me to talk about stuff?"

"Then tell me! Tell me what you're feeling."

"What? So you can have more reason to be mad at me?"

"I'm not mad at you! Ugh!" She grunted with her head in her hands. "Damn it! I'm hurting. And I'm sad. And I just want to talk," she pleaded. "Please, go to therapy with me."

Liam stared at the ground. He wanted to make his wife happy, but he had learned a long time ago that letting his feelings out only brought trouble. "I'm fine," he concluded as he walked out of the room. He went back into the hall bathroom and locked the door behind him. As soon as he looked in the mirror he began quietly sobbing. He held his head in his hands in a desperate attempt to muffle any of the noise he was making. He could hear no sound coming from outside the door for a few moments. Eventually, he heard Rachel stepping closer and closer to the door and knocking quietly.

"Liam, I'm going to bed. Are you coming up soon?"

Liam sucked in all of his tears long enough to respond. "I'll be up a little later. I have some work to do."

Liam waited for a response during a long, painful silence. "Okay," Rachel resigned, and she walked down the hall and began up the stairs.

Liam wiped off his face and waited a couple more minutes to make sure he would be alone. He left the bathroom and went into the office to work.

9

A STRONG VIBRATION ABRUPTLY WOKE BILL FROM A deep sleep. He inhaled quick breaths as his eyes adjusted to the darkness. A flash of light revealed he was indeed in his cabin.

The storm was still raging. He could hear the rain pounding on the roof and the wind screaming through the walls. Another rumble of thunder jolted the cabin. Rusty leapt onto Bill's lap, shoving him backwards. "Oh geez. Ouch!" Bill cried out as he grabbed his side. "Careful. You scared me. Silly dog."

Rusty shook while he nervously licked Bill's face. "Alright, alright buddy. It's alright," he assured as he massaged Rusty's head. "What do you think? Is this rain gonna stop any time soon?" Bill had to admit he was growing concerned, especially as the storm continued to grow in intensity.

He rose from his bed and scooted over to the window. The scene outside did not disappoint. Water was slamming against the glass, and he could make out leaves flying by.

Bill jumped as Rusty began barking toward the back of the cabin and jolted Bill. "Seriously dog! You're gonna kill me." Gradually he began to hear what must have gained Rusty's attention. Something was repeatedly tapping against the wall.

Bill decided to brave the weather and venture out to see what was making the noise. Amazingly, through all the racket, Joshua remained asleep on the floor. Bill slid on his boots and put on his coat and hat. He grabbed his revolver and lit his lantern. He called Rusty over to come with him to alert him to any danger. Bill grabbed the door knob and slowly creaked it open. Rusty took one look outside and ran back to the bed.

"Fine, you coward," Bill muttered, "I'll go by myself."

He stepped outside and immediately felt the weight of the rain pelting his body. He lifted the lantern up to illuminate what was in front of him. Flying leaves began bombarding him, some smacking him in the face. He ripped them off and threw them to the ground. "Well, this is fun," he sighed as he plodded through the mud. He hugged the corner of the house and peeked around it, but nothing out of the ordinary appeared. The tapping from the back of the cabin faintly filled the air.

Bill turned the corner. A blasting wind shoved him back against the cabin. "Damn!" He whispered to himself. He was still dumbfounded by the wind's intensity. He made sure to tread carefully as he continued and approached the back side of the cabin. The tapping grew louder as he approached. He arrived at the next corner and prepared his revolver. He took a deep breath and jumped around the corner.

The source of the noise was quickly ascertained. The wind was blowing so fiercely that a tree was doubling over and smacking the back side of the cabin. "Oh geez," he lamented. "What a waste of time."

Bill lodged his revolver back in its holster and turned around to head back inside the cabin. As he approached the front of the cabin, a huge gust of wind flew in and ripped brush from the ground and stole it away. Bill stood stunned as a flash of lightning illuminated the area around him. He noticed a protruding stone in the area where the brush had been before, a stone he had never noticed. It looked completely out of place.

As he approached it, the object began to resemble a tombstone. "What the?" He inquired to no one in particular. As he came close, it was obvious that his hunch was correct. There was brush and mud remaining over the front. Bill lowered onto his knees and began wiping away all the debris. His pants soaked up the moisture in the ground. After several seconds he had removed it all and brought his lantern close to reveal what the tombstone had inscribed on it. His heart started to race as he read it aloud. "Here lies William 1983-1992."

Bill fell back onto his rear and sat stunned for a moment. "What the hell is going on?" He demanded. Thoughts were darting through his mind. Who would put this here? Was someone playing a trick on him? "Joshua," he grunted to himself.

Bill quickly rose up and stormed to the front of the cabin. He burst through the front door and glared toward the space on the floor where Joshua was still fast asleep.

"Hey!" He yelled. "Get up!" The man remained asleep, so Bill grabbed one of Joshua's boots and whipped it at him. "That was your boot in your face. Get up, or it's gonna be my boot in your ass."

"Okay, Bill," Joshua replied with half-opened eyes. "What's going on?"

"That's what I wanna know! Let's go outside."

"What? Why?"

"Let's go."

"Okay, okay." Joshua put his boots on and threw on his jacket. He followed Bill out the door. Rusty accompanied right behind them, not wanting to be left alone. They traversed to the location of the tombstone.

Bill angrily pointed at the tombstone and stared back at Joshua. "What is that?"

"I think it's a tombstone?" Joshua replied, looking confused.

"I can see that. What is it doing there?"

"Bill, I don't really understand your confusion. It's a tombstone."

"I know it's a tombstone! But what is it doing there, because it wasn't there before."

"Wait, you think I put that tombstone there?"

"Is that why you wanted to know my name? So you could make it more fitting? And how the hell did you know I was born in 1983?"

"Look, Bill, I can see that this has you pretty rattled, but I didn't put that there."

"Well how else," Bill stopped talking as he heard a loud crackling sound.

"Look out!" Joshua yelled as he tackled Bill to the ground. A large tree came tumbling in and smashed through the cabin. Joshua and Bill covered their faces as the crash echoed through the air. After a few moments, Bill uncovered his head to assess the scene and was devastated. He slowly stood up, speechless as he gazed upon the scene before him. Half of the cabin was destroyed, and the tree remained in its place.

He heard Joshua get up and walk over to him. They both stood silently for a few more moments.

"Bill, I'm really sorry."

Bill turned his head toward Joshua and scowled. "Get out of here," he demanded sternly.

"What?"

"Get out of here now."

"Bill, I don't … "

"Ever since you arrived on the scene, terrible stuff keeps happening. The storm. The tombstone. And now this. I don't want you here. Go away now."

Joshua looked back with sadness. "Okay I'll go." He turned and vanished into the dark night.

1 0

"LIAM! WE'RE GONNA BE LATE. YOU KNOW HOW YOUR mom gets when we're late."

"I'm coming," Liam yelled back.

Once a month the family went to Liam's parents' house to have supper and spend some time with them. Liam looked forward to it and dreaded it all at the same time.

Liam and Rachel had not spoken much that week. Their argument around the dining room table took them into deep waters, and there was a mutual understanding that they both needed to come up for air.

The dynamic between Liam and Aaron was much less reciprocal. Instead, there was simply the resignation that the awkwardness was present and seemingly insurmountable. Aaron avoided his dad as much as possible, frightened that one wrong word would trigger another outburst.

Liam hurried down the stairs to meet the rest of the family waiting by the door. Everyone was bundled up, as it was the end of February. Spring was attempting to break through, but to no avail as of yet. Rachel was holding a dish with potholders. She always tried to bring something to the dinner, though Liam's parents insisted it was never necessary.

The four of them piled into their sedan and pulled out of the driveway.

"I can't wait to see Grandma again," Lizzy exclaimed.

"Oh, I know," Rachel agreed. "She's a sweetheart."

"Grandpa's okay, I guess."

"What do you mean?" Rachel asked, regretting her inquiry immediately. Liam's father, Frank, was often a sore subject with Liam. It was obvious to her, and everyone else, that his abrasive personality was a source of stress for the whole family, but for Liam in particular. Liam, however, frequently became defensive when anyone pointed it out.

"He's such a grump sometimes. You know, distant and hard to talk to."

"That's just how people of his generation are sometimes," Rachel explained, trying to concoct the most diplomatic answer.

"Oh … but then how come Grandma isn't like that?"

"I don't know, sweetie."

"I could talk to Grandma all day … too bad we can't just visit Grandma."

"Yeah," Aaron chuckled, but quickly quieted down to avoid stirring his dad's pot.

"Hey, Grandpa's got a sweet side to him, he just doesn't show it very often," Rachel replied. "Liam, are there any big football games on today?" She asked, desperately trying to change the subject.

"Football is over. Remember the Super Bowl?"

"Oh that's right. What about basketball?"

"Yeah there are probably some good college games on today."

It didn't take long to journey to his parents' house. They lived in an older neighborhood, in the same house that Liam had grown up in. They had bought their ranch style house along with a number of other people their age back in the 70's and had no intention of ever moving.

As expected, Bill's mom, Susie, was waiting at the door, eager to greet everyone as they arrived. She was as delightful a woman as Lizzy had conveyed. She was nearly always beaming with joy to meet each person as they arrived at her home.

Lizzy and Aaron leapt out of the car to greet her. "Grandma!" Lizzy squealed as she ran into Susie's arms.

"Hello sweetheart," Susie bubbled as she bear-hugged her granddaughter. "Oh I missed you. And look who it is," she announced as she locked eyes with Aaron. "My favorite grandson."

"Grandma, I'm your only grandson," Aaron smirked.

"Tall and handsome, just like I remember," she affirmed as she embraced him.

Liam and Rachel were still waiting in the car.

"I can carry the dish for you," Liam offered.

"No, I'm fine."

"You two hurry up!" Susie directed as they emerged from the car. "Dinner's waiting on me."

"It's so good to see you mom," Rachel called out as she started up the walkway.

"Oh honey. It's good to see you too. You know you didn't have to bring anything."

"I know, I just can't help myself."

"Well alright then, come on in," she invited as she held open the door with one arm. "And there's my boy."

"Hi mom," Liam responded, pretending to be embarrassed by her affection.

"You're always gonna be my boy, you know. Don't matter how big you get."

"I know," he conceded, as they wrapped their arms around each other.

"Mm mm, I sure missed you."

"Me too, Mom."

"You doing okay, honey? You look awfully worn out."

"Yeah I'm fine. Just tired. Been working a lot."

"Well, you be careful. Don't wear yourself down."

"I know. Where's Dad?"

"Where he usually is. Glued to that television. Watching basketball I think."

"Okay, I'll go say hi."

"Okay sweetie."

Liam traversed the house to the TV room. He could hear his kids laughing and playing with his parents' dog, Missy. She was a playful cocker spaniel that the kids looked forward to seeing whenever they came over.

"Damn it! C'mon guys, what the hell are you doing out there?" Liam could hear the familiar argument Frank was having with his TV as he approached the room.

"Hey, Dad."

"Hey, Son! Come on in," Frank invited as he waved Liam over.

"Sounds like they're not doing very well," Liam surmised as he gestured toward the television.

"Oh, they got their heads up their asses."

Liam chuckled, humoring his dad. "How you guys been?"

"Oh, same old, I guess. Just plugging away."

"How's the shop?" Liam inquired. Frank managed an auto mechanic business in town. He started there in his 20's and had worked his way up over the years.

"It's alright. Pain in the ass sometimes though, just with trying to get the young guys to pay attention to detail. It's alright though. Yeah! There you go!" Frank yelled, distracted by the game. "Great shot!"

"Can I have some of those chips?" Liam asked, pointing to the bowl on the coffee table.

"Help yourself. So how you doing?"

"Oh, yeah, we're doing alright."

"Good, job treating you okay?"

"Um, it's okay ... " Liam hadn't told Rachel or anyone else about how difficult his job was lately. His relationship with his father was complicated, to say the least. He knew sharing difficulties with him never ended well, but he also longed for his father to be the kind of man he would look up to. To top it all off, there was the painful experience from work that he was holding in like a long breath, a breath he could only keep in for so long.

"Actually, it's not going that great."

"Oh yeah? What's going on? Your employees not working hard enough?" Frank asked, keeping one eye on the game.

"No, I um, I got removed." He paused to keep from getting emotional. "They removed me from the lead position."

"What? Why would they do that?"

"I don't know really. I mean they say it's temporary, but ... " Liam leaned forward, with his elbows planted in his knees, and hung his head to the ground.

"Hey, Son. Don't you do that. Don't you let them beat you. You remember what I always told you. You gotta be tough. You gotta be tough."

Frank continued to speak, but Liam couldn't hear it. He was transported to nine years old, on his little league field.

"You ready to start this game, Scott?"

"I'm ready, Coach," Liam confirmed. He had pitched on a couple occasions, but this was his first time starting a game. In reality, he was very apprehensive.

"Liam!" Frank called out from behind the fence. He motioned for Liam to run over to meet him. "You ready, Son?"

"I think so, dad. I'm kind of nervous though."

"Hey, keep it together. Go out there and show 'em how it's done."

"Okay, Dad," Liam nodded.

"Remember, you gotta be tough. Be tough."

Frank returned to the bleachers, while Liam joined his team in the dugout. After a final pep talk, Liam and his teammates grabbed their gloves and ventured out onto the field.

Liam began the game with a lot of command. He kept the pitches down like his coach had instructed. He threw two strikes to the first batter before the third pitch was grounded to the second baseman for an easy out. The next batter took a ball on the first pitch, but proceeded to swing and miss on the next three pitches.

Liam inaugurated the third at bat with a strike down the middle, followed by a curve ball that surprised the batter by bending into the strike zone. Liam was ready to finish off the inning quickly and hurled a fastball that just missed the outside edge of the plate.

"Ball," the umpire confirmed.

Liam caught the return throw from the catcher and decided to throw another curve. He tossed the pitch, which broke too low and hit the dirt.

"Ball."

Liam didn't want to go to a full count, so he decided on a low fast-ball. He threw the pitch, but it stayed high, right in the middle, and the batter crushed it to deep center field.

The hit ended up as a double. Liam was beginning to get more nervous. His pitches were all over the place for the next two batters. He tried to settle himself down, but it only seemed to make him more jittery. He walked both batters, filling up the bases. The coach came out briefly to calm Liam down.

"Sorry, Coach, I'm not sure what's going on," Liam confessed.

"It's alright, Liam, I think you're just getting nervous. Just take a couple deep breaths, okay. Just throw the ball. Don't stress over it, just throw it."

"Okay," Liam complied. His coach turned to walk back to the dug-out, and Liam turned to face the next batter. He eyed the plate and attempted to visualize where he wanted the ball to go. He took another deep breath, wound up, and delivered a fastball. It rose higher than he intended, and the batter belted it. Liam's heart sunk, but as he turned to follow the ball with his eyes, he saw his center fielder slowing down as he approached where the ball was heading. He calmly secured the ball in his glove. Liam got lucky on that pitch and sighed in relief as his first inning of pitching came to an end.

Liam headed to the dugout, relieved but still concerned. His team's time up at bat went quickly, with only one batter getting on base. Soon, Liam was back out on the mound, and his fear was realized. Once again, he couldn't control his pitches. He walked two batters, gave up a single, and walked a third. He battled the next at bat, getting it to a full count, but ultimately let up another double, allowing three runs for the inning.

"Time!" His coach yelled as he approached Liam on the mound. "Liam, I think this is it for today."

"I'm sorry, Coach."

"It's alright son. Every pitcher has games like this."

Liam handed the ball to his coach and slowly trudged back to the dugout. He was really upset and disappointed in himself. He felt as though he had let everyone down, and warm tears began to form from his eyes.

He didn't want to draw attention to himself, so he exited the dugout and headed toward a shaded area to hide in for a few moments. As he was approaching his destination, he glanced over to see his dad barreling toward him.

"What do you think you're doing?" His dad interrogated.

Liam froze as his eyes started to water.

"Don't you dare start crying! That's not gonna help anything. You have to be tough!"

Liam tried to control his tears, but they kept coming.

"Ugh. Stop it. You're embarrassing yourself, and you're embarrassing me," Frank scolded as he turned and marched away.

"You know what I'm saying?" Frank asked.

Liam jolted back to reality and looked at his father watching television. "Yeah, yeah, I know what you're saying." Liam looked down at the floor before he heard his mom from the kitchen.

"Food's ready," she announced.

"Well, better go wash up," Liam remarked. He slowly rose from the chair and headed for the kitchen.

As he walked down the hall, he ran into Rachel coming from the other direction.

"Liam, you gotta see what Missy is doing with the kids; it's adorable."

"Oh, okay," Liam remarked with a terrible fake smile.

"Are you okay?" Rachel could tell something was up. She always could. It was the blessing and the curse of being known by another.

"I, I don't wanna talk about it right now."

Rachel pointed her eyes in the direction of the TV room. "Is it your dad?"

"Yeah," Liam responded, figuring that was the easiest answer to get off the hook.

"Yeah, I figured. Well come in, come see the kids and Missy."

Rachel grabbed Liam's hand and led him to the living room. The touch of her hand was soothing and sent a jolt of energy through his body. He still couldn't understand how she could seemingly love him so easily, even when she was upset. It was her super power.

As they approached, Liam could hear the playful noises from Missy and the roaring laughter from the kids. He turned the corner to find Aaron and Lizzy tossing one of Missy's toys back and forth, while she would leap during each throw, trying to catch it in the air. Each time she missed she demanded that the next participant throw the toy back so she could have another chance. Liam loved hearing his kids laugh, and watching Rachel beaming with joy as she watched as well. But in the same instance, a nagging feeling of despair washed over him. It was as though he was watching what he could never hope to experience. He would never laugh and enjoy life as they did. Something inside him would not allow it. And a thought arose within him, "I don't belong here."

"Okay everyone, let's go," Susie commanded as she peeked around the corner.

Everyone filed into the kitchen to wash their hands.

"It smells wonderful, Mom," Rachel commented.

"Aw, thank you, dear."

"As always," Frank echoed, arriving late into the kitchen.

"Thank you, honey."

Liam relocated to the dining room to find his favorite dish, meatloaf, along with mashed potatoes, green beans, and Rachel's macaroni and cheese.

"Everyone have a seat," Susie directed. "Honey, do you wanna say grace?"

"Yes ma'am," Frank obliged, as he waited for everyone to file in. "God, thank you for this food, and for my wife for making it. Thank you for our family. Amen."

"Dig in folks," Susie invited.

They began passing the dishes around the table. Missy saw people walking in the street and sternly let them know they were far too close to the house.

"Shut up, Missy! Damn dog," Frank grumbled.

"Frank," Susie scolded, signaling toward Aaron and Lizzy.

"Oh, sorry kids."

"It's okay, Grandpa," Lizzy reassured. "We've heard worse than that."

"You sure do look stressed," Susie informed Liam.

"I'm fine Mom, really."

"I don't know. You always did push yourself too hard."

"He's just got some big things he's working on at work," Rachel chimed in as she lovingly patted him on the leg.

"It's okay, Rachel, I told Liam not to let that boss of his get to him," Frank informed her.

"Oh really?" Rachel responded, as she used her eyes to let Liam know just how interested she was in this news.

"Oh yeah. I know what he's going through. Bosses can be a really big pain in the a ... a butt," he corrected himself. "Sometimes all they do is breathe down your neck. But Liam will be fine."

"I'm sure he will," Rachel affirmed, speaking every word deliberately.

The rest of their visit was uneventful. Frank returned to his cave, and Susie talked everyone's ear off. All the while, Liam could feel the hurt and frustration oozing from Rachel. He milked every moment he could there, hoping to avoid the inevitable inquiry from his wife.

After several hours, they all said their goodbyes and headed home. Liam didn't dare say anything on the way, hoping to avoid poking the bear. As they pulled into their driveway and parked the car, Rachel turned to Aaron and offered her keys. "You kids go on in. We'll be there in a few minutes."

Aaron grabbed the keys. He and Lizzy gave each other a look confirming they both knew what was going on. "Okay mom."

They shut the car doors behind them and strolled up the sidewalk. The car was silent for a moment.

"I just don't understand," Rachel lamented. Liam held his head down and remained silent. "I don't understand. Why do you do that?"

"Do what?" Liam knew exactly what she was talking about, but asked anyway to buy a few more seconds to find a good answer.

"Why do you go and tell your dad, the world's worst sympathizer, what's going on with you and refuse to tell me anything? Why do you tell the guy who always has a way of making you feel bad about yourself, and keep it from me when all I want to do is help?"

"He doesn't do that."

"Oh really? That's not how it appears to me. You were in that room with him for two minutes and came out looking beat up on the inside."

"You don't know everything."

"You're right. I know what you tell me, and that isn't much."

Liam stared out the window and refused to respond.

"You won't tell me anything, but you'll go and tell the person who has beaten you up the most," Rachel repeated, shaking her head. "You know, sometimes I think you like to be miserable."

Liam snapped his head back toward Rachel, with confusion written all over his face. "What? What the hell is that supposed to mean?"

"You know what? Nothing. It means nothing," Rachel responded as she unbuckled her seatbelt. "It doesn't matter." She slammed the door behind her.

"Ugh," Liam grunted. He waited until she disappeared into the house and finally exited the car himself. He was not looking forward to following her indoors.

11
——

BILL JOLTED AWAKE AS A FEW BIRDS FLEW OVERHEAD and disappeared into the trees. He had managed to retrieve his tent from the wreckage of his cabin after Joshua had left. The mud proved difficult to set it up in fully, however, so instead he had used it as a sort of sleeping bag about fifty yards away from the cabin.

He couldn't remember the last time he had been so uncomfortable. Mud was caked all over him from the night before. He was wet and freezing. He was exhausted, but there was nowhere dry to sit. Rusty, always the trooper, was nuzzled right next to him, and he didn't seem to mind in the least.

Bill listened to the birds chirping in the distance. Other than that, it was curiously quiet around him. After a moment of reflection, he realized it was no longer raining. This was good for keeping him dry, but it added insult to injury as he would now be unable to collect the water in his buckets.

He sat up and felt the weight of the mud trying to pull him back down. He stood up and wiped himself down as much as he could. He remembered that he had set his buckets out the night before to collect some of the rain water. He walked over to them, curious to see how much water had gathered. He stared with frustration at the measly amount of liquid they had amassed. He resisted the urge to send them flying with an angry kick, knowing that was all he had for now. Later he could work on collecting more off of the leaves of the surrounding trees.

He ventured back into the rubble of the cabin. The devastation remained overwhelming. The home he had come to love sat with a tree running through the middle of it. He still couldn't believe it. He ventured into the wreckage and pushed and pulled on any loose boards, attempting to collect anything he could excavate. He found most of his cooking equipment and gingerly worked on pulling it out, trying to avoid causing any of the debris to fall on him. He pulled his items out and moved them over by the tent. Rusty followed him closely, obviously disoriented by the whole scenario.

Bill proceeded through the tree line to gather some wood for a fire. After a couple trips, he gathered enough wood and started building the fire. As it grew, the warmth slowly began evaporating the moisture from his clothes. He rubbed his hands together above the fire, trying to soak in every ounce of heat.

After warming up a bit, he looked over the food he had. There was only one fish left, and it was too old to try and eat. Instead, he decided to use it to set up a trap to catch an animal. He used a rope and some of the rubble from the cabin to set it up, and hoped to find some food later in the evening.

He returned to the cabin, Rusty continuing to follow him every step of the way. He pulled out everything else he could collect, including his clothes, weapons, some tools, and his pack. He moved it all over to his tent. He went to look for anything else he could find, but as he turned, he caught the tombstone out of the corner of his eye. Anger and frustration grew exponentially within him. He grabbed his hammer and stormed over, determined to bash the tombstone into pieces. He looked at it once more and raised his hammer over his head, but when he swung it down and connected with the stone, he was thrown and landed hard on his back. He shook his head, dazed and confused. He stared at his object of hatred, stunned by what had just happened. After becoming enraged, he jumped up and threw his hammer back toward the tent. "Fine," he lamented, "I guess nothing is gonna work for me around here anymore."

He grabbed a few more items that he could find in the cabin and proceeded to finish setting up his tent. He hammered his pegs deep into the ground to try and reach the part that was dry and firm. Finally, it was finished. It was a shelter, if nothing else.

He decided he was ready to start collecting more water, and went to retrieve his buckets. The ground continued to squish beneath his feet with each step. As he trampled over, however, he started to notice a deep, quiet roar. He stopped and tried to listen and ascertain the noise. As the noise became louder, he began to hear crashes and trees crackling. As the rumbling increased, he looked up and saw a mudslide bearing down on him.

He screamed for Rusty to run, but he had already bolted, terrified of the coming behemoth. Bill took off toward the tent. He was not too far from the perimeter of the slide, and pumped his legs as fast as he could, desperately hoping he could get to the other side. Sweat poured down his face and his heart pulsated furiously in his chest. He pushed his body as hard as it could go. He looked up and was afraid he wasn't going to make it. He bolted for a nearby tree and lunged for it as the slide began to reach him and tried to pull him down with it. He smacked into the tree and grasped onto it.

Rusty, standing about thirty yards away, barked and carried on for his friend to get back to him. Though he was on the perimeter of the slide, it was pushing him hard into the tree, and he was afraid that the tree would soon give way.

Just then, he thought he heard his name in the distance. He looked around, trying to find the source of the noise. There, out behind Rusty, was Joshua, running toward Bill.

"Bill!"

"Joshua!"

"Let me find something to pull you in with."

"About twenty yards behind you is a trap I set up with a rope. Go get it!"

"Okay!" Joshua yelled as he turned and sprinted away.

Bill held on as tightly as he could, praying that the tree would hold firm until Joshua came back.

"Hold on, hold on," he cried out as he scanned the trees, hoping to see Joshua return any second.

He heard a cracking sound from the tree. "Aah!" he screamed.

"Come on, come on man. Come on!" He yelled.

Finally he saw Joshua emerge, carrying the rope around his arm.

"I got it!" Joshua proclaimed as he sprinted back within distance to throw the rope. He launched one end of the rope to Bill. It landed on the other side of the tree out of Bill's reach. He reeled the rope back in and tossed it again, landing perfectly in front of Bill.

Bill reached out for the rope and clung to it with both hands. "Okay, I'm ready!" He yelled.

Joshua pulled as hard as he could. Rusty barked without ceasing, beckoning Joshua on. He fell backward from tugging and carefully got back to his feet without losing the rope. Soon, Bill was emerging from the mud and was back on solid ground. He and Joshua laid sprawled out, huffing and puffing, trying to recover from the immensity of the situation.

After a few minutes, Bill sat up and looked gratefully at Joshua. "Thank you. I'm sorry that I … "

Joshua lifted his hands up in protest, "It's okay."

"No, it's not. You keep saving my ass, and I keep treating you like crap. Thank you."

"You're welcome."

They sat silent for the next several minutes, gazing at the destructive power they had just witnessed. Bill could think of no other words to say.

12

RACHEL PULLED INTO THE DRIVEWAY. SHE HAD DROPPED the kids off at school and ran a few errands while she was out. She grabbed the grocery bags out of the trunk and headed for the front door.

Last night had been tense and difficult. She and Liam hardly spoke a word to each other after the conversation in the car. She heard him get up and ready for work, but had pretended to be asleep to avoid talking to him. She was still very hurt, and didn't know how to address it with him. It was obvious that he didn't know how to talk to her either. Sleep eluded her as she analyzed why that was. Had she done something wrong? She seldom felt listened to or understood. Did Liam feel the same way? The only way to figure it out was to talk, the one thing neither of them felt enabled to do.

She returned to the car to retrieve the last couple of bags and closed the trunk. As she returned inside, she heard the phone ringing in the kitchen.

"Hello," she answered.

"Hi, is this Rachel?"

"Yes it is. Who is this?"

"Hi Rachel, this is Victor. I work with your husband, Liam. We met at the Christmas party a couple years ago."

"Oh hi, Victor. Yes, I remember. What's going on? Is everything okay?"

"Well I was actually calling to ask you. Liam called in to work today. I wanted to check up on him. Been kinda worried about him, but he hasn't answered his phone."

"You've been worried about him?"

"Yeah, you know, with what happened last week."

"Oh yeah," Rachel played along. She was embarrassed about not knowing more, and she hoped to gain more information by pretending to be in the know.

"I know it's hard for him to not be the team lead anymore, but it's not meant to be a demotion. Donald intends for it to be temporary, and for Liam to get his position back after he figures some things out."

"Yeah, he's okay. I'll let him know you called," she assured.

"Okay, thanks Rachel."

She hung up the phone. She was filled with so many emotions she could hardly think straight. She hated feeling like everyone knew more about her husband than she did. The hurt kept piling up. But she tried her best to sympathize with Liam. She could imagine the shame and embarrassment he experienced from being removed as team lead.

She pulled out her cell phone and called Liam. The phone rang several times. "This is Liam. I'm unavailable right now. Leave me a message and I'll get back to you as soon as I can."

"Liam, call me back. I'll text you too, but please call me back."

She ended the call and quickly typed a message to him. She wanted to call his parents' house, but was concerned about making Susie worry. She selected their home number and called anyway.

"Hello."

"Hi Susie, how are you?"

"I'm good. How are you?"

"I'm doing good. Hey have you talked to Liam today at all?"

"No, sweetie. Is something wrong?"

"Oh no, he just misplaced his watch, and I wasn't sure if he had been able to ask you yet if you had seen it."

"Oh, no sorry honey, I haven't seen it."

"Okay. No problem, he probably just set it down somewhere."

"Yeah probably. You doing okay?"

"Yeah, I'm fine."

"Okay. You just sound a little flustered."

"Well I just got finished running some errands. That's probably it."

"Okay. Well, I'll talk to you later. Love you."

"Love you too, Mom."

Rachel was getting more worried and decided to go looking for him. She scurried out to the car and jumbled her keys as she attempted to start it. "Where are you?" She wondered to herself. She decided to check the Starbucks that he went to most often. She headed out and attempted to call Liam again using the car console. "Liam, it's me again. Please call me back."

A few minutes later she arrived and briskly walked into the coffee shop. She looked around but did not see Liam anywhere. Her concern was growing by the second. She turned around and hustled back to her car.

"Oh Liam, where would you be." She remembered that he began looking especially sullen right after he talked to his dad. She wondered if he would be at his dad's shop, but that didn't feel right. Then she remembered how important baseball was to them both, especially when Liam played in high school. She backed out of her parking space and began traveling to the high school baseball field.

She drove rapidly, but not so much to draw attention. She was aching to get to him, but apprehensive at the same time. "He hasn't been talking to me for the past few months. Why would he start now?" She wondered. But her concern and compassion would not let her turn around. She turned the corner toward the school and could faintly see a dark figure sitting in the bleachers. She drove up the long driveway, and the figure appeared more like Liam the closer she came.

She pulled up and parked behind the bleachers. Liam continued to stare out at the field. Rachel wanted to rip into him for making everyone worry, but she knew that wouldn't accomplish anything. She took a deep breath so she could approach him with a calm demeanor.

She exited the car. "Liam? Liam, are you okay?"

He continued to stare out to the field. She was startled by his demeanor, and so moved closer with caution. She climbed up onto the bleachers and sat next to him.

"Liam?"

"Hey."

"What are you doing here?" She asked, but no response came.

"I called and texted you."

"I put my phone on silent."

"Well I talked to Victor earlier … he was checking up on you." Liam lowered his head down. "He told me about what was going on at work."

"Okay."

"Is that all you're gonna say? Why didn't you tell me? Is that what you talked to your dad about?"

"I don't want to talk about my dad."

"Well, what then? What do you want to talk about?"

Liam continued staring out at the field. "I used to be really good at baseball."

Rachel was taken aback by his response. "What?"

"I mean, I was really good."

"Yeah I know. I heard a lot of stories. I've seen video of you playing."

"You know there were scouts that came to watch me play?"

"Wow. No, I didn't know that. What happened?"

"I blew it. I played terribly, maybe the worst I had ever played."

"Oh. I'm sorry, Liam. I had no idea. You didn't play in college."

"No, because I knew as the stakes got higher, I would blow it again. That's what I've learned. That's what I've learned about myself. When the stakes get high, I don't have what it takes."

"Oh Liam, that's not true."

"You'll find out eventually. You're finding out now."

"What? Because of your job? You think I'm gonna be disappointed in you?"

"It's not just work, it's everything."

"What?"

Liam gazed out onto the field. "I don't wanna talk about it anymore."

"We need to keep talking; that's the only way we're going to get through it."

"Why do you want to talk to me anyway? Every time I open my mouth I say something to bring you down. Just go away."

"Liam, please just go to therapy with me. We can do this together," she pleaded as she laid her hand on his arm, but Liam flung it off.

"No! I told you I'm not doing it. Just leave me alone."

Rachel looked out to the field for a moment as drops of heartbreak began sliding down her face. She climbed down from the bleachers and returned to her car. She lowered her head and covered the steering wheel with her tears. She wiped the wheel down with her sleeve, turned the ignition, and drove away.

13

"I KNOW YOU DON'T WANT TO HEAR THIS BILL," JOSHUA
began. They had been sitting together around their fire for hours, and
no words had been spoken. "I think we need to venture east and see
what we can find."

Bill refused to meet Joshua's eyes. "I don't wanna go anywhere. This
is my place."

"There's nothing left here Bill. I know it worked for a time. For a
long time. It's served a purpose. But this place is completely destroyed
now."

"We don't even know what's out there. I've never been away from
here."

"I know what's out there, Bill. You don't have to go alone."

"Look, I'm grateful for all that you've done, and I know I haven't
been as appreciative as I should have been. But I'm not going to leave
the only place I've ever known to follow someone I just met. That just
doesn't make any sense."

"I get it Bill. And it's ultimately up to you. I just don't see how you
can make it here now. The river isn't accessible, so no access to fish. And
when the rain clears you'll have no access to water. But it's up to you."

Bill knew Joshua was right, but he couldn't stand the thought of
leaving. Everything was crashing down around him, and it looked
more and more like the only option he had was to rely completely on
another person. That was one thing he never wanted to do.

It was getting late and the sun was going down. They ate some of
the fish jerky that Bill had left over and shared a few pieces with Rusty.
Joshua made some coffee, and for the first time, Bill enjoyed it with
him.

Shortly after, he laid on the ground and fell asleep.

+ + +

Bill woke early the next morning. It took him a second to remember the mud slide, and that his cabin was buried somewhere underneath it. He turned over to take in the scene again, but was stunned that he could not see anything more than about twenty feet away. A dense fog had settled in all around them.

"Joshua, wake up," he demanded. "Joshua!"

Rusty echoed Bill and bayed. Joshua stirred awake, and his eyes grew big as he observed the scene. "Wow. Well, that's impressive."

"You're telling me, and also not very encouraging for our situation."

"Nope. It is not."

Bill hated admitting it to himself, but he was terrified. He didn't dare venture out alone for fear that he would lose track of Joshua. He needed him, and he hated to admit that too.

"This is so unsettling. This area used to be predictable and steady. Now it's all over the place. How long do you suppose this fog will stick around?"

"It's hard to say, but this kind of fog can be particularly stubborn. I've seen it stick around for weeks or months. Suffice it to say it's probably not gonna go away overnight."

"I guess I don't have much of a choice then, huh?"

"What do you mean?"

"I mean I pretty much have to go with you now."

"You always have a choice. And I know you never wanted to leave here. But the question is: is it going to hurt you more to stay here or to go with me?"

"Well, like I said. Not much of a choice," Bill replied.

"Well, I'll take the company anyway," Joshua said, laughing lightheartedly.

Watching Joshua laugh so effortlessly gave Bill a sense of hope, something he was unfamiliar with. He was used to putting all his effort into controlling his environment and making sure everything went to plan. Here was a man who somehow found joy without any form of security and comfort that Bill always strived for. It was refreshing to see. And as much as he was used to being in control, he felt a sense of relief from following someone else.

"We should start getting our things together. We're going to want to travel light. It could be a while until we get where we need to be."

"Where is that?"

"You never really know. Not at the beginning anyway. You just have a sense of what direction you need to go, and eventually things will reveal themselves."

"That sounds pretty risky," Bill assessed.

Joshua stared off into space, and a look of fondness appeared on his face, as though he was remembering someone close to him.

"It is, Bill. It definitely is risky." Joshua turned around and looked Bill in the eyes. "But the meaningful things in life always require a little risk."

Soon they were all ready to start heading east. Bill looked back in the direction of the cabin, or what was left and buried under the mud, but he could only see the murky mist. Part of him was relieved not to be able to see his land. He wanted to remember it as it once was. They began their journey, with Rusty prancing right beside them.

14

LIAM STARED AT THE SHADOWS ON THE CEILING CRE-
ated from the nightlight in the hallway. He tossed and turned for a
while, hoping to find a comfortable position, but nothing had worked.
He had settled on his back with his eyes wide open, his mind swirling
and his stomach twisted and tangled.

He knew he had hurt Rachel deeply. That much was obvious, even
to a dense, unobservant male like himself. The two of them had hardly
spoken a word since he had returned home that evening. There seemed
to be something in the air, as Aaron and Lizzy stayed fairly quiet as
well.

Liam opted to get up and move downstairs. He had a lot of work
to do and figured he might as well be productive if he was going to be
miserable anyway. He pulled the blankets away from his body and felt
the chill of the night sting his skin. He got up and felt his way through
the closet to get his robe. He slid on his slippers and shuffled into the
hallway, hoping to be as quiet as possible.

Liam grabbed a ginger ale from the fridge and proceeded to his
office. He opened up his laptop and returned to the project he was
working on. He began adding notes to his collection from earlier in the
week. Two years ago, this sort of project would have been a dream for
him, but now there was so much weighing him down. He couldn't stop
experiencing the tenseness that came from his meeting with Donald.
Everything he said was true. Liam had known it for a while, but like
everything else in his life, he figured he could bury it and keep going.
To Liam's great dismay, someone had finally caught him and called him
out. He was completely out of his element for this scenario. Faking it
was where he thrived.

That, of course, was not the only new dilemma facing him at work.
He had been a complete asshole to Victor and had said some truly
hurtful things. He knew, deep down, that Victor would never sabotage

or backstab him. He was just so angry and stunned and lashed out at someone who cared about him. Unfortunately, that was beginning to become a trend in his life

He continued to try and push through and make progress on the project, but the computer screen proved to be just as perplexing and enigmatic as the ceiling was above his bed. No matter how long he stared, nothing seemed to connect in his mind. Frustrated, he shut the lid after several minutes, and just sat there sipping his beverage.

His mind wandered back to that summer day as a nine-year-old. It kept eating at him. "You're embarrassing me," kept creeping up. He heard it in his soul over and over again. Everything became so real. The grass beneath his feet, the sweat dripping down his face, and he could see his father standing right in front of him. It wasn't just the words he was saying. It was the look on his face, like utter disgust and disdain for his son. An overwhelming sense of loneliness washed over him. He doubled over as angst beat at his stomach. Tears were about to flow until noise snapped him out of his trance.

Liam heard a creaking sound in the stairs, and saw a figure moving toward his office. Lizzy approached through the darkness. It appeared she could not sleep either, as her face showed no sign of having been awakened.

"Hey darling, what are you doing up so late?"

"I just couldn't sleep, and I heard you come downstairs."

"Got something on your mind?"

"I don't know. Maybe, I guess," Lizzy replied tentatively.

"Well, I can't sleep either, so we can talk about it if you want." He could tell she wasn't sure what to say. "How about a snack?"

"Ice cream?" she proposed with an ornery grin.

"Good choice"

They transported themselves to the kitchen. Liam grabbed the bowls and spoons while Lizzy went for the ice cream.

"Looks like we have cookies and cream or mint chip."

"How about some of both?"

"You're on a roll," Liam affirmed with a smirk.

Liam dished out the ice cream, and they each took a seat at the dining room table. He started with the mint chip. The mint, combined with the chill of the ice cream, stunned his taste buds. He got lost in the comfort and forgot that Lizzy had something she seemed to need to talk about.

"Daddy?"

"Yeah, Liz."

"Are you going to go to therapy with Mom?"

Liam stared at his bowl for a few seconds, trying to gather what to say.

"Your mom really shouldn't be putting you up to this."

"She didn't, Daddy. I heard you guys arguing the other night."

Liam felt a wave of embarrassment flood over his face. It was all overwhelming. It felt as if he were failing on every front possible.

"You really don't need to be concerned about that."

"What? Why not? You're my parents. Of course, I'm concerned."

"Sweetie, it's just … "

"You know, mom's not the only one who has noticed how down you've been lately. And she just wants to talk about it. I don't really understand why you wouldn't go with her."

Liam took another bite of ice cream before responding. He knew Lizzy was not one to give up, and he needed to come up with a satisfactory response, but no such response came to him. "It's just complicated," he replied, fully realizing how lame a statement that was.

"That's just something adults say when they don't have a good enough reason to tell their kids."

Liam was frustrated and impressed.

"You guys are always telling us not to hold things in," she continued, "that if something is bothering us, we can always come to you to talk about it. I just don't understand why you won't do that with mom."

"How'd you get so smart?"

"Well, I am your daughter."

"Flattery too, huh?"

"Yep," she smiled.

Liam pulled her close and gave her a tight hug. "I love you."

"I love you too, Daddy."

They both sat quietly together for several minutes, the only sound was the spoons tapping against the bowls.

"Daddy?"

"Hmm."

"Promise me you'll go with mom."

"Oh sweetie, I don't … "

"Please, Daddy. Just try. Please."

Liam tried to think of some clever way to meander his way out of this one, but he couldn't find anything. He, like so many girl dads before him, had an excruciating time saying no to his daughter. "Okay sweetie. I'll try."

"Thank you, Daddy," she sighed as she laid her head on her father's shoulder.

They sat for a few more minutes, enjoying their ice cream.

"Do you want me to take your bowl?" She asked.

"I got it. You go get some sleep," he directed as he kissed the top of her head. "Love you, sweet girl."

"Love you, Daddy." She proceeded to amble to the staircase and head up to her room.

Liam rinsed the bowls and spoons and placed them in the dishwasher. He grew tense as he realized the weight of what he agreed to do for his daughter. Honestly, he wondered if the therapy offer still stood considering how he had spoken to Rachel earlier that day. He knew that he loved her dearly and wanted to make her happy. For some reason, though, the path she wanted to walk down was terrifying. The sheer thought of it was exhausting. He decided it was time for him to sleep as well, if only to escape from the tension for a few hours.

15

—

BILL AND JOSHUA HAD HIKED FOR A COUPLE HOURS. They were traversing a mild ascent, though Bill was tiring out much faster than he anticipated. A deep exhaustion tugged at his body. He had lived off the land for years, but somehow this seemed completely different.

The terrain was densely populated with trees and bushes, so much so that Joshua often had to use a machete to make space for them to walk. Bill's lungs were working overtime, and his legs were screaming with every ascending step.

Bill's two companions were faring much better than he was. Joshua never lost a step, never even appeared to be winded. He seemed to be in his element, completely comfortable with the apparent chaos around them. Rusty was thoroughly enjoying himself, breaking off periodically to check out a new smell. He always found his way back to them with ease.

"Hey ... can we ... stop for a bit?" Bill requested between breaths, "I need a break."

"Sure, no problem."

Bill peeled off his pack and dropped it on the ground. He found a log to rest on and pulled his canteen out to get a drink. His hat was soaked from sweat. He removed it and wiped his head with his forearms. He scanned the area around them and started to notice some different types of plants. The density made it feel as if they were the first ones ever to travel this way. Still, Joshua seemed to know what he was doing.

"Do you come this way much," Bill queried.

"I have a few times, yeah. I'm all over the place usually."

"You must have a great memory then."

"Yeah, I think I just soak stuff in, and it comes back to me quickly."

"Do you do this kind of hiking often? I walked to the river every day, but that was nothing compared to this. I'm getting wiped out."

"I've done a lot of different kinds of hiking. I think you've just been rutted into your old way of life for a long time. When you stick to the same patterns for a long time, the rest of your ability and potential can get warped or diminished. You're gonna build new muscles as you go in a different direction."

"I was there for as long as I remember," Bill reflected, still gazing at the scene around them.

"Did you ever think of venturing out, seeing what else was out there?"

"No, not really."

"Why not?"

"I guess I was just comfortable where I was. It felt easy and safe. And there was the dark figure that dominated the outer parts." He immediately regretted mentioning the figure, realizing that he had never spoken of him to Joshua before.

"Oh, I suppose that's why you believed the outer areas to be dark lands."

"Um … yeah. I guess so."

"You haven't mentioned the dark figure before."

"Well, I wasn't sure that I could. He and I had an understanding that I would stay in my area, and he would stay in his. To be honest, I'm pretty concerned about the ramifications of leaving my allotted land."

"I wouldn't worry too much about him."

"You know the dark figure."

"I'm familiar with him, yes. And he's not as daunting as you might think he is."

"I have a hard time believing that," Bill confessed. They were quiet for a moment, enjoying the peaceful sounds of birds chirping around them. Rusty sat close to Bill and leaned up against him while having his ears scratched. Suddenly, a few birds darted into the deep brush, and Rusty rushed after them. Bill and Joshua both chuckled at his spontaneity. "Honestly," Bill continued, "I was comfortable there. Everything was so simple."

"I see. Well, when you stay in one mode of being for too long, you start to think that's all you'll ever be capable of. This trek is really gonna push you, but that's not a bad thing." Joshua peered up the hill as much as the fog would allow. "We're gonna want to keep going. We need to find an area to squat for the night before it gets dark."

"Okay," Bill complied as he stood up with a grunt. He lifted his pack and swung it across his back. It felt far heavier than it had when they started. The straps tugged his shoulders back. He stumbled a few steps, attempting to readjust to the weight.

"You good?"

"Yeah I'll be alright. Just really feeling it," Bill admitted.

"Yep, that'll happen."

Bill returned his cool, wet hat to his head. Rusty leapt out of the brush and startled him. "Oh geez! Well, at least he's having fun," he commented.

The three of them continued on their trek.

"Would you like to take the lead this time, Bill?"

"Take the lead? I have no idea where I'm going?"

"That's alright, I'm not gonna let you get too far off track."

"That's okay. I'll just follow you."

"Okay, let's go then."

It turned out they had stopped to rest at a good spot as the incline was about to get steeper. Joshua cut out a crisscrossing path to make it easier, making Bill thankful he had declined to go first.

Bill wrapped his arms around some of the trees as he sought to keep up with Joshua. His muscles burned as he ping ponged from one tree to the next. The view down below would surely have been spectacular had the fog not continued to mask it from them.

After a couple more hours, they were reaching the next ridge. It could not come soon enough as far as Bill was concerned. He felt as though he would pass out from the pain and exhaustion. Once they arrived, Bill fell to all fours, and soon laid out flat across the ground.

Joshua let out a hearty laugh. "Well done, Bill. You made it through your first day."

"I wasn't sure ... I was ... gonna make it." Rusty licked his face several times, as if in an attempt to comfort him.

Joshua stood and looked around at the surroundings they could see in the fog. "This should do well for tonight. I'm gonna go track down some firewood. I'll be back in a bit."

Joshua slowly disappeared into the fog, with Rusty following behind him. Bill continued to lie on the ground, giving his muscles a much-needed rest. The cool ground felt good on his sweltering face. This day had been quite taxing. Physically, it was exhausting, but he also couldn't stop thinking about his old land. He hated leaving it behind, and every step felt like increasing tension and regret.

Bill tore his pack from his back. He rolled over and sat up, arms hugging his knees. The fog was still immensely disorienting to him. He had never encountered this kind of haziness before. He stared into the abyss and longingly reflected on a familiar site by the river. The comforting sound of the charging water washed through his mind, but, as he was losing himself in memory, Rusty darted through some shrubs and jolted Bill from his daydream. Joshua was close behind.

"Got us some wood; you want to help me get this arranged and get the fire going?"

"Sure," Bill replied, as he stood up with a grunt.

They arranged the wood together and produced some sparks for the fire.

"Get this stoking. I saw some berries out there, I'm gonna go back and collect some for us, be back in a few."

Joshua and Rusty disappeared again as Bill worked on the fire. He was still trying to cool off from the hike, but knew that the fire would soon be a welcome guest as the sun was falling from the sky and stealing away its warmth and illumination. Bill studied the red hue spread from one log to another, projecting its heat onto him.

A few moments later Joshua returned with a small bucket full of black berries. They looked bright and delicious. They snacked on the berries and some of their dried fish. They lounged around the fire as the light above them diminished.

"First day is over," Joshua reflected. "I wish I could say the hard part is over, but you're probably gonna be pretty sore tomorrow."

"Oh, I'm sure of it. Today was exhausting. I just keep thinking about my land, my cabin, the river. It was such a wonderful place, and I just don't know if I'm ever gonna find another place like that."

"Well, it's certainly understandable to feel the loss of a place like that. Although I wonder what it is that you miss about it?"

"What do you mean?"

"It was certainly a beautiful place. But as you mentioned before, it was also comfortable and easy. Maybe a part of you misses not being challenged, and not having to challenge yourself. Like I said, sometimes we get stuck in patterns that we don't realize are gripping us."

Bill nodded, less in agreement, but more to humor Joshua. He was far too tired from the hike to think deeply about what was being said. Right now, he was content just to rest. He laid his head back for the night.

16

LIAM HAD MADE IT TO WORK THE NEXT DAY, BUT HE wasn't sure how. Everything seemed so daunting. The next step seemed to be the only thing he could see, as if he was in the middle of a dense fog. He had sneaked into his office to avoid having to chat with anyone. He had his phone laid out on his desk to see text messages as they popped in. None yet, but he was hoping to hear from Rachel soon.

That morning he had risen from bed as quietly as he could. Rachel was still asleep and he didn't want to wake her. He also didn't want to get drawn into a deep conversation. It was far too early in the day for that. Instead, he left her a note letting her know he would get off work early that day to attend therapy with her. Everything within him wanted to run away from that, but he had made a promise to Lizzy, and he was determined to keep it.

It was closing in on 10:00 AM, and Liam had made some good headway on his project. The work felt daunting as he got started, but once he got going, it seemed to calm him down. The challenges he was facing in his life were forcing him to focus only on what was right in front of him, anything more than that was overwhelming. That strategy was paying dividends for his project.

Liam heard a knock on the door.

"Come in."

"Hey, man," Victor greeted him as he entered, holding a cup carrier that was gripping two coffees.

"Hey, Victor."

"How's your day going?"

"You know, okay I guess. You?"

"Yeah I'm okay," Victor answered before he took a long pause. "Listen, man, I'm really sorry about last week. I knew it was gonna be hard for you, and I just lost my cool."

"Dude, I'm sorry too. I had a bad attitude, and I didn't mean those things I said. You are great at your job, and you absolutely deserve the recognition you've received."

"We're good, then?"

"Yeah man, we're good."

"Okay good. I grabbed you some coffee."

"I see that. Thanks! I'll never turn down coffee."

Victor handed Liam his cup and took a seat as they both began sipping their drinks. The warmth emanating from the cup was soothing to Liam's hand, and it tasted like comfort.

"So, were you sick yesterday?"

"No," Liam responded. He stared at the wall and shook his head back and forth. "I just couldn't make it. I don't know what's going on, but I just didn't have it in me. Just had too much crap swirling around inside me."

Victor nodded. "Well, there's a lot going on. You wanna talk about it?"

"No, I'm alright. Besides, I'm supposed to meet Rachel and some therapist later today, I think I'll have to do enough talking there."

Victor chuckled in agreement. "Yeah, probably."

"I don't know what's going on, but something is really bothering her lately. I don't know. She says it's been going on for a while, but I don't know. Maybe I'm just clueless."

"Well, speaking as a fellow male, you're not the only one."

"Yeah, that is oddly comforting," Liam reflected, laughing quietly to himself. "I just wish I understood what she was talking about. Sometimes it feels like we're speaking different languages," he surmised as he folded his hands behind his head.

"Yeah I get that with Emily sometimes. Sometimes I don't have a clue what she's talking about, and it takes a lot of work to really hear her," he remarked. "Maybe the therapist will be sort of like an interpreter."

"Yeah, that'd be nice."

"Hey, well, I gotta get back," Victor transitioned as he lifted himself out of the chair. "Let's connect tomorrow, compare notes."

"Yeah man, sounds good."

Victor left and closed the door behind him.

Liam sat back in his chair and took a deep breath. The relief of a wrong made right filled his body, and a soft smile appeared on his face.

His phone vibrated and shook on his desk. He leaned forward and unlocked it. He opened his text and found a message from Rachel.

"I'm so glad you decided to come with me. I'll see you soon."

Liam was relieved to hear from Rachel. He has elated that she was still willing to have him, but he feared that he would just screw up again. He locked his phone and returned to his work.

+ + +

A few hours later it was time to wrap up and head to the appointment. Liam's stomach had grown tighter and tighter with each passing minute. As he closed his laptop and packed up, a surge of anxiety flowed through his body. He exited his office. Every step was weighty, as if his feet were trapped in blocks of cement.

He rode the elevator to the bottom floor and headed out to the parking lot. He pressed the unlock button on his key and entered his car. The inside felt warm and cozy from the sunlight, a small comfort compared to the tension within him. He turned the ignition and the engine came to life. As it settled into a quiet hum, Liam turned it off. He felt paralyzed by fear. He laid his head down on the steering wheel. "I don't know if I can do this," he sighed to himself.

+ + +

Rachel arrived at her therapist's office. She took a seat in the waiting room, watching through the window for Liam to appear. She told herself that looking every five seconds was only going to drive her nuts, but she couldn't keep her gaze away from the parking lot.

"Hi Rachel," her therapist Laura greeted her from the hall doorway.

"Hi Laura, how are you?" She inquired with one eye glued to the window.

"I'm good. Are you ready to come back?"

"Well, I'm just waiting for Liam."

"Oh Liam is coming. That's wonderful."

"It is," she said with hesitation, "I'm just afraid he's going to back out."

"Why don't you come on back now. The receptionist can send him back when he gets here."

"Okay."

Laura escorted Rachel down the hall and to the office. Rachel took a seat on the couch while Laura closed the door behind them. She squeezed her arm tightly, trying to release the anxiety. It had been a difficult step to begin therapy, one she was thankful for, but now, adding Liam into the mix was going to be even more challenging. She was glad she invited him, but was still apprehensive about the outcome.

"So, how are you doing today?" Laura inquired.

"I'm okay, just feeling a lot of different things."

"Can you name them?"

"Well, I feel excited that Liam is coming, but worried that he will back out. I'm also nervous about telling him what's been going on with me. Overall, I'm just sad. Sad about what our marriage has become. Sad that we can't seem to have a decent conversation."

Rachel sat quietly for a moment and wiped a few tears from her cheeks.

"It's helpful to be able to identify those feelings," Laura affirmed, "feelings which most people would be experiencing in your situation. And I'm impressed that you've approached Liam and shared what you want from him."

"It has been so hard, and he has been so resistant. I'm shocked he actually said he would come today," Rachel expressed as she glanced at the clock. Liam was now a few minutes late.

"Well we have to remember that you've been on this journey for a few months now. Liam is playing catch up. It can also be particularly difficult for men to talk about these things. It often goes against what they've been taught it means to be a man."

"I know, and his dad fits that stereotype."

"Yes, you've mentioned that. What do you think made Liam change his mind about therapy."

"I honestly don't know. The last time I mentioned it, he shut it down hard."

They continued chatting for a few moments, waiting for Liam to show up. After about ten minutes, Rachel was losing hope.

"I knew he wasn't going to show, I just knew it," she expressed as she shook her head in frustration. "But he left me this beautiful note this morning, and it gave me hope."

"What did the note say?"

Rachel reached into her purse and retrieved the note. She handled it with such care, as if it was a valuable lost artifact. She gently opened it up and took a deep breath. "I'll read it to you: I'm sorry that things have been so difficult lately, and that I've caused you so much pain. I don't really understand what's going on, and I'm not sure how to move forward. But I want to try, because you're my girl. I love you."

A few more tears appeared. "But I guess he's not coming." She folded up the note and slid it back in her purse.

"Well," Laura segued, "I guess we can just … " A knock sounded on the door. "Yes come in."

Liam appeared through the doorway. "Hey babe. Sorry I'm late."

17

—

BILL FELT A NUDGE ON HIS SHOULDER AS HE OPENED his eyes. He was sleeping heavily. The hiking from the day before had exhausted his body. He turned and saw Joshua crouched over him.

"Morning."

"Hey," Bill grunted.

"We're gonna have to head out pretty soon, but I'm gonna go grab some more berries for us before we head out."

"Okay sounds good, I'll try to wake up."

"Alright, be back in a few."

Bill heard Joshua's footsteps get fainter as he walked out into the fog, once again, followed by Rusty. Bill closed his eyes again and turned over onto his side. He wanted to get up, but felt drawn to the ground to rest his eyes for a while longer. He drifted in and out of sleep, and was drawn to a flashing dream of sitting by the river, watching his fishing line rest in the water. He longed to be back there, and the longing only exacerbated his exhaustion.

A few minutes later Bill heard footsteps through some twigs returning to his site.

"That was fast," he informed. He turned over onto his back and opened his eyes. His heart began racing as the dark figure was standing over him, staring down into his very being. Bill froze. He had never been this close to the figure, and never wanted to be. What was more unnerving was that he could now see the eyes. Glowing green eyes. He stared, unable to pull his gaze away. He wanted to run, or fight, but he couldn't move his body. So he laid still, waiting for the figure to speak.

"You should not have come," the figure declared in a hushed tone. "Go back. Go back now."

The figure raised his arms and began hovering over Bill, who could now move and promptly covered his face with his arms. Soon the figure darted into the fog and disappeared. Bill kept his face hidden for several minutes. The memory of the figure's eyes pierced him with despair.

Rusty flew into the site and jumped on Bill, and he screamed in terror. Rusty leapt back and pulled his tail between his legs, shocked by his companion's reaction. Joshua ran in as well to see what was going on.

"Bill, are you okay?"

"Joshua, it was here, standing right above me?"

Joshua lowered down to the ground and took hold of Bill's shoulders. "What was here?"

"The dark figure; he was standing right here, and I could see his eyes. He told me to go back." Bill began shaking his head back and forth. "I knew it. I knew we shouldn't have come. I said this was going to happen."

Joshua sat with Bill for a moment, looking on with compassion. "Bill, you need to listen to me. The darkness cannot hurt you."

"Yes, it can," Bill insisted.

"If it could have hurt you, it would have. But it can't. All it has is lies and threats to produce fear in you. It can't do anything to you that you can't do to yourself. I have walked through the darkness, and I can assure you of that. I can also assure you that one day, you will walk through the darkness as well."

"I want to stay as far away from that thing as I possibly can."

"That is how you used to live, and it helped you for a season. But when the time comes you will face it."

Bill didn't want to argue. It wouldn't get him anywhere anyway. He was in a tough spot. He had no intention of ever facing that darkness, but he was also dependent on his companion.

Bill had been so flustered by the experience that he failed to notice the rabbit that Joshua had brought in.

"That will be lunch," Joshua remarked as he noticed Bill eyeing it.

"Oh I don't want to eat your catch. You'll need that. I'll carry my own weight."

Joshua laughed, which caught Bill off guard and irritated him briefly. "You can carry your weight when your rib gets better. You need to learn to live interdependent with others, Bill. Let people help you out."

"Sorry. I've just been alone for a long time. Not used to having others around."

Joshua nodded his head in agreement. "Yes, that's true. But a lot of that was by design."

"Yes, I suppose that's true as well," Bill admitted. "I've just always had the sense that being alone was good for everyone."

"What do you mean by that?" Joshua dug deeper. Although Bill felt Joshua already knew the answer, he decided to humor him.

"I mean that people just tend to let you down, disappoint you, leave you."

"Yeah, maybe. But maybe you're just as concerned that you will let them down," Joshua proposed.

Bill was silent for a moment and seemed to disregard Joshua's thought. "Well, are we ready to go?"

"Yeah, I think so," Joshua confirmed. "How you feeling today, by the way? Sore?"

"Yeah, but I'll be alright."

"Okay, good. We're gonna hike up most of the day to get to the next ridge, then we'll start our descent."

"Alright, after you."

Joshua proceeded trekking back into the woods, swinging his machete as needed. He was careful to watch out for Rusty, who was sporadic as always, distracted by one stimulus after another. Bill's body was screaming at him more than he wanted to let on. Each step sent a jolt of discomfort through his legs and up his back. The silver lining of it all was that it took some of the attention away from his sore rib.

A few hours had passed when they appeared to be reaching the top of their climb. Joshua suddenly stopped. "Oh, I almost forgot about this."

"Forgot about what?" Bill asked, slightly concerned.

"Come see for yourself."

Bill pushed forward, fighting through a couple branches floating across the path, and arrived next to Joshua. "Wow," Bill breathed out. A huge tract of land had appeared covered with flowered shrubs. It was as if the trees had arranged their own private garden. No color was missing from the display. Bill set his pack down and approached the nearest bushes.

"I've never seen anything so gorgeous," Bill expressed. "What are these?"

"They are called innocents."

"Innocents?"

"Yes, they are some of the first and original plants in these parts, unobstructed by damage or suffering."

"Why have I never seen these before?"

"Over time they can become sparse or hidden. But they can be recovered in a different but often more robust form. You may have in fact seen these before and forgotten."

Bill's eyes locked onto one of the flowers and approached as if in a trance. "Oh, I don't think I could forget seeing one of these."

As he came near the flower, he bent down, stuck his face in it, and took in a deep breath. Suddenly he was shoved backward and his mind was transported. He could hear a young girl running and laughing as a woman playfully chased her. He looked over and saw the girl run behind a swing, leaning on the bar as she caught her breath. They appeared to be behind a long, one story house. The house was grey with blue trim around all the windows. They were surrounded by a tall picket fence.

"William!" the woman called out. "William, come over here."

Bill looked over and realized the woman was talking to him. Her voice calmed his beating heart and soothed his mind. He got up and began reaching out for the woman. He extended his hand and waited for it to be embraced. A swift wind came through and blew the vision away. He was left lying on his back, staring up at Joshua, who was grinning back at him.

"Took a little tumble, did you?" Joshua observed.

Bill bounced up and began wiping himself off, as if bugs were crawling all over him. "What the heck was that?" He demanded.

"That's the powerful effect of the innocents. Their aroma can be intoxicating. So much so that it can transport us into visions of what once was, or of what could be. They give us hints and signposts to things that we are looking for, though we often are not aware of it."

"I don't really understand. I don't remember any of that."

"Well, most people don't, at least not initially. There may well be a time coming where it will all become clear."

Bill shook his head. Everything was so overwhelming, and he was wiped out. "Can we take a break?"

"Actually, I think this is a great place to stop. Let's call it a day, shall we?"

18

"Sorry I'm late," Liam apologized.

"Liam," Rachel said, pleasantly surprised.

"No problem," Laura assured him. "Come on in; have a seat next to your lovely wife."

Liam closed the door and sat down next to Rachel, who gave him a soft kiss on his cheek.

"I'm so glad you could make it, Liam," Laura affirmed.

"Yeah ... me too."

"Well, as you can guess, Rachel has told me a lot about you. You're pretty important to her."

"Well, she is to me too," he said as he turned toward Rachel and smiled.

"I'm sure she is," she agreed.

There was a moment of silence that felt incredibly awkward to Liam. "Look, I don't really know what to do here. I'm just waiting for your cue."

"Liam?" Rachel scolded.

"It's okay; there's no official way to do this, and we want to make sure we are all comfortable to say what is on our minds."

"I'm sorry," Liam apologized again, "This is just so foreign to me. This is not the kind of thing I would normally do."

"It's okay, Liam. Why don't we start with you telling me why you think you and Rachel are here?"

"Well whatever Rachel has told you I'm sure is accurate," Liam answered, trying to be appeasing.

"Well it's not really about accuracy, as if we're looking for some arbitrary facts. We want to get a sense of where both of you are. It's not right or wrong; it just is. I know what Rachel thinks about this, but I want to know what you think so we can see where you both are."

Liam thought for a moment while staring at the ceiling. "I don't really know why we're here, I guess. I know Rachel has said she's not happy with how our marriage is."

"Do you know why that is?"

"Not really. I mean, I feel like I'm pretty much doing the same things I've always done, but I know that she's not really happy with how things are."

"Hmm ... okay. Would you say that you are happy with how things are?"

Liam froze for a second, not wanting to say something wrong or upsetting. "I'm not happy with how Rachel is feeling about things."

"What if I just ask this: Are you happy?"

"I don't really understand. I mean, aren't we here because Rachel's unhappy? I mean, I just want to do whatever I need to make her happy." Liam glanced at Rachel, hoping his altruistic sentiment would bring a smile to her face, but he was disappointed.

"Is that why you're here then? To make Rachel happy."

"Yeah, I mean, that's all I want."

"Hmmm. That's all you want?"

"I don't get it. Isn't that what a woman wants? A man who wants her to be happy?"

"But then what happens to Liam in all of this?"

"Is that really what you think?" Rachel sharply inquired.

Liam looked at her, dumbfounded by the response.

"Rachel, let's give Liam some space here to think and process," Laura advised. Rachel raised her hands, acknowledging Laura's request.

"Liam, what makes you happy?"

"Rachel makes me happy."

"Okay. Anything else?"

Liam sighed as he was growing tired of the pointless questions. "Our kids."

"Okay, what else?"

"You say okay like those answers don't matter."

"It's not that, Liam. It just seems like you're giving me perfunctory answers, the answers you think you're supposed to give."

Liam could feel his body growing tense. "Is there something wrong with trying to make people happy?"

"No, there's not, if that's what you really want. But I don't think Rachel married you to be her jester that caters to her needs and wishes."

Liam lowered his head and ran his fingers through his hair. He was feeling completely lost. "I'm sorry, but I'm really not tracking what you're getting at here."

"I want to be close to you!" Rachel blurted out while leaning forward, gesturing passionately with her hands. "But it seems like all I get is rote responses, like you're trying to follow some script. And then when you're in a rut, and there's no script for you to read from, you just shut down completely." She leaned back against the couch, as if that burst of energy exhausted her. "Sometimes it feels like you don't want anything to do with me. You just follow what you need to do to keep me happy, but we don't do anything real."

Liam crossed his legs and folded his hands together in an instinctive protective stance. He felt vulnerable and afraid of what could happen if he opened his mouth.

"Liam," Laura chimed in, "If it's okay with you, I'd like to explore more of what Rachel is trying to say here, and then come back to you."

Liam nodded his head in compliance.

"Rachel, can you unpack that a little more?"

Rachel took a deep breath, as if she was about to dive into the deep end. "Well, this weekend for example. We went to have dinner with his parents. He's been getting stressed out with work, but he hasn't shared with me what is going on."

"I didn't want to bring you down," Liam commented.

Laura signaled for Liam to give Rachel space to talk. Liam conceded and returned to his protective position.

"Well, we go to his parents' house, and he goes to see his dad. Now, his dad is a huge source of stress for Liam. He seems to always say something that brings Liam down. And yet the stressful situation at work that he wouldn't share with me, he openly shares with his dad. And, as expected, his dad ends up messing with his head."

"I didn't want to bother you," Liam blurted again.

"Bother me! I'm your wife!" Rachel exclaimed. "I care about what's going on in your life, and I want to be a part of it."

The room grew silent for a moment, as if they were giving space for the feelings to enter.

"Rachel, can you tell me how that situation made you feel?"

Rachel began to tense up, and tears began flooding her eyes. "It makes me feel like I don't matter, like I'm not good enough."

Liam felt tears coming to his eyes as well, but he fought to keep them down. He hated seeing Rachel cry. "I'm sorry, I would never want to make you feel like that." He continued to sit with his legs crossed and could not bring himself to look up. "I just don't know what to do."

"Let me give some feedback at this point, Liam," Laura said as she leaned forward and peered in his direction. "Rachel is not a problem to be fixed. You are looking for something to do to fix what hurts in her, but all she wants is for you to share yourself. When you try to fix her, you are not acknowledging her pain, and you are not offering yourself."

Liam squirmed in his seat. "I'm not even sure I know what that means."

"Of course you don't!" Laura chuckled. "That's why you're here."

Liam let out a small smile, relieved at her humor.

"Now, that's all the time we have today. I want you two to reflect on what brought you two together in the first place. I also think it's important for you to do something fun together, so that your relationship isn't just all about hurt and difficult conversations. Find something fun you can do together this week."

They both quietly agreed, collected their things, and exited Laura's office. Liam shuffled his feet against the carpet as they walked out. He opened the door of the building and held it open for Rachel. They wandered down the sidewalk leading to the parking lot.

"Rachel," Liam said as he stopped and pivoted toward her. "I'm sorry I'm not very good at this. I just … "

"Oh babe, that's okay," she caught him off guard by hugging him tight. "You came, and you're trying. That's enough," she affirmed as they shared a deep kiss. She grabbed his hand as she guided him to his car.

19

BILL STOOD AT THE EDGE OF THE RIVER AND THREW IN
his line. His fishing spot was the same as always. He watched his line
bob back and forth in the water. A bird perched on a tree limb several
feet away, its chirps filling the brisk morning air.

Bill's eyes darted open. The bird continued to chirp, no longer in his
dream, but in the new morning around him. Apparently, Joshua had
decided to let him sleep in, as there was no sign of him. Rusty had felt
the need to get more shuteye as well, and was still curled up at Bill's
feet.

Judging by the pile of wood adjacent to him, Joshua had already
prepared for a fire. Bill decided to take the initiative and get the blaze
going.

A few minutes later, Bill could hear rustling in the trees and turned
around to find Joshua emerging from the fog.

"Good morning!" Joshua greeted.

"Morning. How long have you been awake?"

"Oh, probably a couple hours."

"A couple hours? Geez. You can wake me up, you know?"

"Nah, I figured I'd let you rest. Plus, I'm gonna have you take the
lead today, so I wanted you to have your strength."

"Um … what?" Bill replied, not sure he had heard correctly.

"I'm gonna have you lead today. Don't worry, I'll be right there with
you. But you need to learn the art of the journey as well."

"Um … okay," Liam replied, not quite sure that he understood.
He nodded anyway, reluctantly agreeing to Joshua's assessment. Eggs
were on the menu for breakfast this morning. Joshua had scavenged for
some and found enough so they could each have several. Bill's fire was
ready, so Joshua began cooking them.

+ + +

Soon the end of breakfast was signaled as Joshua tossed the last of the food to Rusty. They cleaned up and began packing.

"So how is this going to work?" Bill inquired. "I mean, I have no idea where we're going."

"This kind of journey is an art, not a science. You need to start to learn that process," Joshua explained. "You'll make plenty of mistakes, but that's part of it too."

"But wouldn't it be easier if you just kept leading since you actually know what you're doing?"

"Easier? Yeah, probably, but then how would you learn? This isn't just all about getting to the next phase, it's about learning along the way too."

Bill agreed, but not really. He was just tired of debating. They packed up all their belongings, killed the fire, and started their day of travel.

The first hour of the hike was pretty simple and easy. Bill didn't need to ask many questions. It gave them both a chance to enjoy the scenery and action around them. They noticed lots of critters going about their business. Rabbits jumped across the path, looking for the best plants to snack on. The birds were plentiful and filled the air with their melodies.

Bill noticed a clearing coming up soon.

"How about we take a break up here," he proposed.

"It's up to you," Joshua reminded.

They entered the clearing and plopped their packs on the ground.

"Man, this is gorgeous land," Bill commented.

"Yeah, it really is."

Bill sauntered around a bit to continue exploring the area while Joshua and Rusty both rested on the ground. He gazed up at the trees swaying in the breeze. When he lowered his eyes, he noticed something that hadn't caught his eyes before. The path they were on did not appear to continue. Instead, there were a couple options to the left. One was pretty wide open, the other seemed to be covered with brush and protruding branches.

"Seems pretty obvious which way we should take next," Bill remarked, pointing to the first, open path.

"You think so?"

"Well, yeah. Look at it. It's perfectly clear."

"From what we can see from here, yes, but looks can be deceiving."

"You're joking, right?"

Joshua raised up his hands. "Hey, you're in charge, remember? Why don't you check them both out and see what you think?"

Bill decided to humor Joshua rather than argue with him. He grabbed the machete and approached the second path. He fought his way up for a few yards, and was forced to veer to the right. He soon came to a fork. The option on the left was densely filled with tough branches, so he moved to the option on the right. When he approached, however, he felt a dark presence surrounding him. He jolted around and searched but could see no one. Instead, the darkness seemed to be lurking in a thought: what if I get lost? He turned back and arrived back at the clearing.

"We're not going that way," he announced.

"Okay, it's up to you. Let's get going then."

They retrieved their packs and continued hiking, now up the path that Bill wanted to choose in the first place. He felt very justified in his decision as they traversed the trail. It remained clear and easy. For the first twenty minutes or so, Bill didn't even have to pull out the machete. After that, the area became slightly more populated with brush and fallen branches. Soon after, however, the path began shrinking on them, and Bill was tiring out from swinging the knife back and forth.

"This is exhausting, I don't know how you did this so much before," he commented.

"Well, sometimes a little trimming back is required, but it's not usually as dense as this."

Bill was starting to agree. The path was closing in tighter and tighter, and soon there was nowhere for them to go but through. The machete, however, could not handle cutting through the barrier. Bill, nevertheless, kept chopping and chopping, soon out of frustration rather than progress.

"Damn it! What is going on? This path was so good before."

"As I said before, looks can be deceiving."

"It wasn't just how the paths looked."

"Oh? What else was it?"

"It was something frightening. A dark presence, but inside me, telling me that something bad could happen on the other path. That I could get lost. It looked like there were going to be a lot of twists and turns, and I was just afraid of taking the wrong one."

"Bill, as I told you before, the journey is an art. There is no exact way to do it, no sure way that excludes all chances of failure. But the more you practice, the more you will get a sense for learning the way as you go. But it is virtually impossible to do that if you are ruled by fear."

"But this seemed like such a sure thing."

"Because you assumed that the better path could not include challenges, and definitely not darkness. But as I told you before, darkness sometimes has to be faced to overcome it, and we have to learn what it has to teach us about the way, and about ourselves."

Bill sighed in frustration. "I guess the only way to proceed now is to return to the clearing and to go up the other path."

"That's correct, that is the only way."

"And I guess I'm still leading?"

Joshua grinned back at him. "Correct again."

20

—

It was Saturday afternoon, three days after Liam and Rachel's therapy session. There had been a lightness to their interactions that had not been present for several weeks. Liam was feeling hopeful that things were getting better.

"Daddy, are you ready?" Lizzy asked.

"Yep, let's go."

Rachel was spending most of the day with her parents. She usually visited them once a month as they only lived a couple of hours away. The kids would often go with her, but had opted to stay home this time to attend a friend's party.

"Aaron, are you ready?"

"Yeah, Dad, I'm coming."

Liam was still hoping to connect with his son, but the tension between them was still obviously present. He had a difficult time understanding his own actions toward Aaron. He wanted to get there before he tried to bridge the gap.

They piled in the car and headed for the other side of town. Their neighbors had moved that way a few months earlier and had a couple kids that were around Lizzy and Aaron's age.

"Are you guys excited for the party?"

"Yes! I miss them living next to us!" Lizzy expressed.

"I know, it was nice to have them close. How about you, Aaron, are you excited to see them?"

"Yeah," he replied with no elaboration.

A few minutes later, they were at their destination. The kids hopped out of the car and ran inside. Liam joined them to offer his greetings to their old friends. After a few minutes he returned to the car to complete his mission.

Liam drove to the grocery store to get what he needed for dinner. He wanted to make something romantic, since he and Rachel would be alone, and decided on chicken parmesan. "Can't go wrong with Italian food," he reasoned.

He meandered up and down the isles while repeatedly glancing at his phone to reference the recipe. He tracked down the pasta and sauce, chicken, cheeses and the breadcrumbs. Everything else for the recipe could be found at home.

Liam had cooked on occasion, so the concept was not completely foreign, but it didn't come easy to him either. He was heading up to the check stands when a thought occurred to him. "Maybe I should get something nice to drink as well."

He hunted for the alcohol aisle and spotted a Sangiovese wine. He had read that it paired well with his main dish, so he placed it in his cart and returned to the front of the store.

Liam drove back home and transported his groceries into the house. He entered the house and shut the front door with a kick of his foot. Stumbling into the kitchen, he laid his bags on the floor. It was now 4:00, so he texted Rachel to see when she was heading home. He could see that she read the text right away and began responding.

"I'll be heading home at 5. Should get home around 7. Love you!"

"Love you too!" Liam wrote back.

He looked over the recipe again on his phone. "Okay, three hours, that should be plenty of time," he assured himself. He began unloading the bags and started cooking.

He walked through the process as deliberately as he could, not wanting to mess anything up. There was a bounce to his step tonight. He was quite proud of his plan, and looked forward to seeing the look on Rachel's face. He was glad things were finally starting to move forward.

Three hours and numerous cooking faux pas later, Liam was finishing the last touches on the meal. He looked to the clock to see that he had finished just in time. He sat at the dining room table and fidgeted as he awaited Rachel's arrival.

He glanced at the clock several times, hoping the time would magically proceed faster, but to no avail. His leg raced up and down as it repeatedly tapped on the floor. He decided to wait fifteen minutes before he called to check on her.

That proved to be unnecessary as Rachel's headlights flashed in the window ten minutes later. Liam rushed to the front door to greet her as she made her way up the sidewalk.

"Hey, Babe, I'm glad you're home," he welcomed her as he swung the door open.

"Me too!" She looked at him with confusion. "What's that goofy grin on your face?"

"Come on in and see."

Rachel stepped inside and peered around the corner to see the dining room set with plates, glasses, and two lit candles in the middle.

"Oh, Liam, this is so sweet of you," she exclaimed as she hugged him tight.

"Well, go have a seat," he directed as he pulled off her coat.

Rachel transitioned over to the dining room table. Liam pulled the chair out for her and scooted her in. He opened the bottle and poured the wine into their glasses.

"Ooh, good wine choice," Rachel complimented.

Liam entered the kitchen to present dinner to his wife. He proudly displayed his creation and delivered it to the table. "Tada!" Liam exclaimed.

"Oh, wow," Rachel replied with less enthusiasm than Liam was hoping for. "I can't believe you made this. This must've taken you awhile."

"Yeah, there was a lot of learning on the fly."

"It looks great; you did a good job," she complimented, as she rubbed his arm.

"Thanks babe."

Liam found his seat and began digging in. "So," he began between chews, "how was your day?"

"It was good. Mom and I went shopping for a couple hours. We had a lot of fun. Of course, she tried to buy me too much. I keep telling her she doesn't have to do that. Sometimes it feels like she still sees me like a little kid, you know?"

"Yeah," Liam acknowledged without looking up from his plate.

"Anyway, we grabbed a bite at the food court. I had Chinese food, and Mom had pizza." Rachel waited through a moment of silence before continuing. "How was your day?"

"It was good."

Rachel waited for some elaboration but received none. "What did you do?"

"Not much, went to the store and cooked. Took the kids to the party. That was about it."

Another moment passed by. All that could be heard was chewing and forks scraping against the plates. Liam looked up and noticed Rachel scraping some of the breading off the chicken.

"You don't like it," Liam observed with a disappointed tone.

"Oh no, it's not that," Rachel replied, trying to explain herself. "It's just ... "

"What?"

"It's just that I don't really like parmesan cheese."

Liam's face became flush with embarrassment, "Oh man, I can't believe I forgot about that."

"It's okay, Babe. I really appreciate you working so hard on this, and you did such a good job."

"I'm sorry, I just ... "

"It's okay babe, I really appreciate the thought and all the work you did."

"Okay, well, I really wanted to do something nice for you. I know you're wanting more in our marriage, and I wanted to do something romantic."

"Mm-hmm," she responded, again with much less enthusiasm than Liam hoped for.

They were both quiet through the rest of dinner. There was mostly the pinging of forks against plates and occasional smiles exchanged between them. Rachel went to take her plate to the kitchen.

"I'll get that for you," Liam informed her as he grabbed the plate from her hand.

"Okay, thank you."

"You go relax on the couch."

"Okay," Rachel said quietly as she moved to the living room.

Liam transported the dishes into the kitchen and flipped the hot water on in the sink. He began scrubbing the plates and placing them in the dishwasher. He could hear Rachel bringing up Netflix.

He sensed there was something bothering Rachel, but he was afraid to ask. He methodically performed every cleaning task to postpone broaching the subject with her. He finished putting the food away and washing the pans, and finally joined Rachel on the couch.

For a few moments they sat in silence, staring at the television.

"Do you wanna watch something else?" She asked.

"No this is fine … is something bothering you."

Rachel hesitated for a moment. "I just want to be careful how I say this, because I really do appreciate the dinner you made."

"Okay?"

"But I'm afraid you're still not understanding what I'm asking for."

Liam sighed and grew tense. "Well, I guess I didn't if you're saying that."

"It's just … the big, romantic gestures are great, but that's not what I really need. I need intimacy."

"I guess I don't understand."

"I want to be close to you. Sitting at the dinner table and hardly saying a word doesn't really do it for me."

Liam nodded to acknowledge he was listening, but he didn't understand what Rachel was saying. He felt as if he was in an advanced calculus class, and as was his custom, he refrained from asking a follow up question and risking embarrassment.

Apparently, Rachel could tell that he was struggling, and decided to drop the subject and not risk more tension. She leaned in and held him tight, as though she was bracing for the next bend in their road.

21

BILL PUSHED THROUGH ANOTHER PATCH OF BRUSH AND was stunned to see a prominent light coming through. He lowered to one knee and breathed a sigh of relief.

"Oh my goodness. Thank you. I didn't have much energy left."

Joshua stepped forward and began pushing through the last strips of brush blocking their path. "Let's see what's on the other side." As he knocked some branches down, the light shone ever brighter. "Bill, you're gonna want to see this."

Bill rose to his feet and stood beside Joshua. "That's just ... beautiful," he said, grasping for words.

They appeared to be at the top of a ridge that looked over a vast valley full of vegetation. The trees pierced the sky with power and grace. The scene was breathtaking, but nothing more so than the large body of water that looked to be no more than a few miles away.

"I can't believe it! Look at that lake. That's everything we need, right there!" Bill pointed in disbelief.

"Yep, we're not too far away," Joshua commented.

Bill lunged forward and took several long steps to begin the descent. Suddenly, Bill fell to his knees. His chest grew tight and he strained to breathe. Joshua rushed over and kneeled down, grasping Bill's shoulders in his hands.

"Bill, are you okay? What's going on?"

"It's ... it's hard ... to breathe."

"Okay, let's rest a bit." Joshua helped Bill remove his pack. He stood Bill up and had him lean against a nearby tree.

"I've seen this before, Bill. When people traverse on this journey, sometimes entering a new area can make it hard to breathe. When you're on this journey, even the air can feel different and impact you because you're not used to it."

A look of despair came over Bill's face. "So … I can't … be here? Do we need … to turn back?"

"Well, there's nothing really to turn back to. We would just run into rough patches along the way."

Bill started to look angry and frustrated. Joshua spoke the words written across Bill's face so he could save his breath.

"I know, Bill, not being able to breathe feels like more than just a rough patch, but it will pass. You're adjusting to a new way of life, and that impacts everything. Your mind, your heart, your body. Everything. But right now. You need to calm yourself so your breathing is not labored."

Bill started to let go of the frustration he was feeling. Going from one desperation to another did not feel very comforting. In fact, it felt pretty disorienting. He began to take longer and deeper breaths. After a few minutes, the pain began to subside. He still felt it lurking on the margins, however, and was very careful when he started moving again.

They settled down for the evening. Joshua wanted Bill to have a chance to get used to the air as much as possible before they continued tomorrow. It was going to be slow going for Bill now, and he wanted to avoid any other challenges as much as possible.

Bill rested against his pack as Joshua formed a fire for dinner. Bill watched him, attempting to sort through everything inside of him. He was frustrated by this new wrinkle. He had always considered himself to be fit and in shape. This trip, however, had apparently proved him wrong. The exhaustion of these hikes had ripped apart his sense of self sufficiency, and if he had one shred left, it was gone with his normal breathing patterns. But he couldn't expend much energy being frustrated; he couldn't expend energy doing much of anything.

Joshua hunted down another rabbit and spent the next while preparing and cooking it for dinner. Bill sat and watched him work for a few minutes, stroking the fur on top of Rusty's head. Eventually, he drifted off to sleep, wiped out in every way imaginable.

Joshua nudged him awake a couple hours later.

"Hey, you hungry?"

"Hmm ... um, yeah. I'm starving, actually," he mumbled as he attempted to lift his head up.

After a few moments, and a few sips of water from the canteen, he was sitting fully upright again, ready to partake of Joshua's meal.

"How are you feeling?" Joshua asked while handing Bill his food.

"Um, I'm okay, I guess. I'm just more frustrated than anything, I think."

"Yeah, I can understand that." Joshua sat down across from Bill, and they both began eating.

"I just keep thinking, when is it going to stop, you know? It's just one thing after another. The cabin, the mudslide. These hikes are killing me already, and now I can't even breathe normally."

Joshua nodded in understanding as he chewed his food. "I get that. It's difficult for sure. Your old way of life has washed away, and it really doesn't work anymore. But it's hard to get away from that mode. You're used to it. It feels comfortable. But now you're in a place where you have to learn everything all over again, even the basic, seemingly unchangeable aspects of life now seem up in the air. It's very disorienting."

"Yeah, so what do I do?"

"You just learn to accept it. You learn to sit in the new place and let it do its work on you. It sucks, there's no doubt about it. But it's necessary. And as you move forward, these new ways don't come easy. The things that you used to take for granted, the basic aspects of the way you used to do life, don't work, and you have to learn them from the beginning. It's like learning to walk all over again. You have to be deliberate and intentional about what you do because it feels so foreign at first, but it's getting you ready for something better."

"What's that?"

"Life!" Joshua exclaimed, which startled Rusty from his begging trance. "It's so basic that you miss it unless you're forced to chase after it. It looks the same, but it's not. It's got substance. It's got form. It's meatier. It's like going from mashed baby food to a four course meal. But you have to get ready for it. There's nothing wrong with the air here, Bill. You're just not used to it. That's what the arduous journey is all about."

"I wish I had your enthusiasm."

"You will someday, Bill. You know, there's nothing wrong with how you're feeling right now. It's part of the process. You're frustrated? Well who wouldn't be? I'd be pretty concerned about you if you weren't. It's all part of the process. But someday you will see more clearly, and you won't experience it the same way."

"How will I see more clearly."

"You'll stop judging everything by its appearance. Just like the path that we had to turn back from, but also basic experiences. You have no idea what will come from this journey, from the destruction and the pain, the exhaustion and the difficulties. You'll learn not to judge them so much as bad or good, because you will have seen that amazing growth and vitality comes from even the darkest of nights. In fact, the vast majority of beauty and light comes that way. It's painful now, but you have no idea what could be coming around the corner."

Bill continued eating while reflecting on Joshua's words. He didn't want to admit it, but there was a sense of relief in what Joshua was saying, an optimism that he had not really known before. He let out a soothing sigh and finished his dinner.

22

"I JUST DON'T THINK WE'RE UNDERSTANDING EACH other at all," Rachel answered. She and Liam had met again at Laura's office. They were sitting on the couch, trying to fill in the gaps for her.

"Liam, would you agree with that?" Laura surveyed.

"Yeah, I think that's pretty accurate. I mean, I guess I still don't see that our marriage is struggling as much as Rachel says it is. She says it's been going on for a while, but I don't really understand that."

Rachel let out a deep sigh. "We can't even agree that there's a problem, so obviously he's not hearing me."

Liam sat up quickly, as if something had bit him. "Wait a minute, it can't just be me not hearing."

"What do you mean by that?" Laura probed.

"Well, I mean, isn't it possible that Rachel is making something small into a big deal?"

"Is that really what you think?" Rachel demanded.

"Well, for example," he said as he motioned toward Laura, "the other night I made this romantic candlelight dinner for the two of us. I spent most of the day planning and cooking. But I made chicken parmesan and forgot that she doesn't like parmesan cheese, and that ruined the whole evening for her."

The room sat silent for a few seconds.

"Seriously!" Rachel exclaimed exasperated. "That's really what you took from that night? I told you what my problem was, and it had nothing to do with that. If you would listen and communicate with me ... "

"I am listening to you, I just think maybe you're blowing things out of proportion. I don't think our marriage is really that bad."

The room once again became quiet, and Laura took a deep breath before she chimed in.

"Liam, would you mind giving Rachel and me a minute to speak?"

"What?" Liam exclaimed. He was already feeling like he was on his own in the room, so he didn't like that notion at all. "Aren't we all supposed to be talking here?"

"Yes, absolutely, but I need to make sure I don't overstep my bounds."

Liam hung his head and sighed in reproach. "Fine." He stood up and exited the door.

Laura waited for it to shut before she directed her attention to Rachel.

"This is completely up to you, but I think it might be time to tell Liam about the reason why you initially came to see me."

Rachel held her head in her hands and stared off to the side for a moment. "I don't know. We're so fragile right now. He doesn't get that there's a problem. I just don't understand how he can be so oblivious."

"Well, men often are. I don't mean to stereotype, but they often have a more difficult time with these things. They're just not wired to do relationships the way women are. That's not universally true, of course. But in general, they process things very different."

"Yes, but he's completely disconnected. I'm afraid that this will break him."

"It may be the only thing that wakes him up to what's really going on. But again, it's completely up to you."

Laura remained silent to give Rachel space to reflect.

"I guess it's going to be hard no matter when I do it," Rachel confessed. "Okay, I think I'll tell him."

"Are you sure?"

"Yes, I just need to do it."

"Okay." Laura walked over to the door and peeked through it. "Liam, you can come back in."

Liam followed her back into her office and returned to his seat on the couch. Laura sat back down in her chair.

"Liam," Laura began, "Rachel has something she needs to tell you. It's going to be difficult for her to say, and for you to hear. But she needs you to let her get it out. Can we do that?"

"Yes, of course," Liam replied as concern grew on his face.

Laura motioned to Rachel to begin.

"Liam," Rachel said as her voice shook, "the last year or so has been really tough for me. I've felt really distant from you, and alone. You say that you don't think our marriage has been that bad, but for me, a lot of times it doesn't even feel like we have a marriage. We just feel like two people who happen to live in the same house."

Liam felt every defensive muscle in his body rise up, but fought the urge to fight back. "Okay."

"I guess I didn't realize just how lonely I felt until a few months ago. I went to the Christmas party that Cassandra threw, and I ran into Justin."

"Your ex-boyfriend Justin?" Liam sternly asked.

"Liam, we need to let Rachel get this out," Laura reminded.

Liam threw up his hands and leaned back on the couch.

"Well," Rachel continued, "We got to talking for awhile. You know, catching up. He texted me that week. He asked if we could meet for coffee, and I said yes."

"You're just now telling me this?"

"Please, Liam, just let me finish."

"There's more?"

"After we were done with the coffee, he walked me to my car, and ... he kissed me," Rachel said as she lowered her head in her hands.

"What!"

"And I kissed him back."

"Are you kidding me right now!" Liam yelled as he jumped up from the couch. "You brought me in here just to tell me you hooked up with your ex-boyfriend."

"No, babe, that's all, and I never saw him again. It made me realize I was in a bad place and I needed help."

"This is unbelievable! So you go through all this pretense, and tell me what a terrible husband I've been to you, and all this time you're messing around with your ex?"

"No!" Rachel exclaimed with tears in her eyes. "No, I'm not messing around with anyone. I'm sorry, I know this is hard."

"This is hard, that's all you have to … you know what, I'm done with this. Go back to talking amongst yourselves. This is ridiculous!" Liam shoved the door open and stormed down the hallway.

"Liam! Liam!" Rachel yelled after him. She turned back to Laura while wiping the tears from her cheeks. "What do I do now?"

"We need to let him process this in his own way. I need to remind you again that he is playing catch up. He might need some space."

Rachel collapsed onto the couch and sobbed into her arms. Laura gave her space and waited for a few minutes. Rachel sat up and wiped her face dry.

"I don't know what to do," she lamented.

"This is going to be difficult, but he needs some space. Liam loves you; he just needs to process this. Nothing worthwhile comes without some difficult and trying times. It is dark now for sure, but it's not the end."

Rachel stumbled out to her car, unable to say anything else. She drove off in a daze and arrived home, not remembering how she got there. Liam's car was not in the driveway. As soon as she parked, she pulled out her phone to text him.

"Liam, you don't have to talk to me. I know you're mad and you have every right to be. I just need to know where you are and that you're okay. Please let me know. I love you."

She waited for a few minutes before going in, hoping to hear back from him. She could see him typing for a couple seconds before his response came in. "Parents." She placed her phone back in her purse, grateful that he had responded, but still terrified at what would come next. She took a deep breath before she opened the car door and ventured inside.

23

JOSHUA HELPED BILL CLIMB OVER A LOG IN THEIR WAY. Joshua clamped onto his hand as Bill gingerly stepped over the barrier, and slid down to the other side. They were approaching the end of their hiking day. Bill's breathing continued to be labored, and he still needed assistance.

Even the easier parts of their path were exerting for him. He made sure to walk at a slow pace, not wanting the pain to commence that he had experienced a few nights before. Fortunately, Joshua didn't seem to be bothered by the leisurely pace. Even Rusty had slowed down to remain by his buddy's side.

Bill's body was begging him for a break every step of the way. He felt as though he could lie anywhere on the ground and sleep for weeks. He continued pushing, not wanting to give in. Every once in a while, however, he would wonder how much longer he could do this, and a little more energy was sapped from his body.

The sun was beginning to set, and they were in need of a spot to hunker down for the night.

"Why don't you sit and rest for a few minutes," Joshua advised. "I'll run up ahead and see how far we are from a good stopping point."

"Okay," Bill wholeheartedly agreed. Every bit of rest was a welcomed relief to him at this point.

Bill slowly lowered down and sat against a tree and felt the coarse bark against his back. Rusty nuzzled up close and licked him on his cheek. Rusty had always been a comforting companion, but even more so these days.

The aroma of the cool evening air was beginning to flow around them. The breeze soothed his body, worn and warm from the day's journey. They were going to have very little light to work with unless Joshua found a clearing of some sort. After several minutes, Joshua returned, huffing and puffing from the run.

"I think ... we're gonna have ... to make do here," he expressed between breaths.

"Oh, well that's okay," Bill assured him.

Joshua stood straight up and placed his arms behind his head, attempting to suck in every ounce of air he could. "I'm gonna get some wood. It's cooling down fast."

"Okay. I'm not going anywhere," Bill commented with a grin.

+ + +

Joshua grabbed a stick to stoke the fire a little. He and Bill had just finished cooking and eating dinner, and they were starting to settle down for the night. Joshua poked at the fire a few times and threw the stick into the middle.

"This has been a weird few weeks for me," Bill confessed, thinking out loud.

"Yeah, I would imagine so."

Rusty crawled over to Bill and stretched over his lap, which brought an effortless smile to his face.

"I gotta say though," Bill continued. "It's harder to breathe here, and yet each breath feels better than before. I don't know if that sounds weird or not. It's just like, the air is somehow heavier here, harder to breathe, but I'm getting more from it," Bill explained, hoping he was making sense.

"You're right. Everything about your old life was easier, including the air itself. You didn't really have to be challenged at all."

Bill didn't appreciate that comment. It made him feel weak. Yet, there was some truth to it. "To be honest, I'm not very comfortable with things that are challenging. I mean, I don't mind working, but if it seems too complicated, something in me shys away from it."

"That's a good distinction to make. You do enjoy working. I can attest to that. But you say you shy away from things that seem difficult. Why do you think that is?"

"I don't really know. I mean, I do enjoy hard work, but only if it's in a certain field."

"Let me ask you this: what would happen if you were to take on a challenge and fail."

As that last word came out of Joshua's mouth, Bill could feel his body tense up. The thought of failing at anything felt catastrophic. "I don't know. I don't even like to think about it."

"Maybe that's why you didn't like people coming around," Joshua conjectured.

"I don't like people coming around because they always screw things up," Bill snapped back with more vitriol than he had intended.

"Or maybe you're afraid that you'll screw things up."

Joshua's words hung in the air as Bill tried to make sense of what he was saying.

"I don't think that's true. I mean, I've never been around people long enough to screw things up. I've made sure of that. I've made sure to keep them out."

"Yeah, possibly. Or maybe you've isolated yourself for so long that you began to think that was the only reality. And if you keep people away, nothing is expected of you."

Bill sat quiet for a moment, not sure of how to respond, so he settled on a snarky remark. "I suppose you think that's why I didn't want you to stick around."

"Yeah, maybe."

"You sure it wasn't that I didn't like you?"

Joshua burst out laughing, and Bill followed suit. "Well, like me or not, looks like you're stuck with me, for a while at least."

"Yeah, it could be worse I guess."

"There's going to be a lot more challenges ahead."

"Yeah, that seems like a common theme these days."

"Do you think you have what it takes?"

The question hit a little too close to home for Bill, who was already feeling vulnerable.

"I don't know--if I'm being honest. I mean, I can hardly breathe right now as it is." A deep sadness seemed to erupt within him. "Do you think I have what it takes?" Bill asked, wishing immediately that he hadn't.

"Yeah, I do. You got it. You just don't know it yet. Somewhere along the line you bought into the idea that your cabin life was the only life you were capable of living. That's why it felt so comfortable. It fit the story you were living in."

Bill laid back on the ground, and Joshua followed suit. Bill stared up at the familiar stars in the sky.

"You know, this might sound weird, but I never liked looking up at the stars," Bill admitted.

"Hmm … yeah, that's kinda weird," Joshua responded with a chuckle. "Why's that?"

"They just … they make me feel small, not in control, and I don't like that feeling."

"That's interesting. That's precisely why I do like looking at the stars," Joshua remarked.

"Really? You like that feeling?"

"Oh yes, it reminds me that I'm part of something. I don't have to figure all this out on my own. I am part of a purpose, a mission."

Bill ruminated on that last statement for a few minutes. Most of his energy had been spent just existing and surviving. A purpose seemed far from him. "So what do you think that purpose is?"

"Living out who I was meant to be, and helping others do the same. Helping them see the truth about who they truly are, and to live confidently from that."

"Hmm, so you see an important connection between you and others?"

"Not just me and others, but the whole thing. The whole thing is connected. The whole creation is intimately connected to their creator, and we are all one."

"Hmm, I've never seen things that way. I've always figured we were all pretty isolated,"

"I know, and that's part of why you've fenced yourself in so tightly. It's paradoxical, but the more we see ourselves as a small part of this big purpose and love that we are a part of, the more we feel free to venture out. In other words, when we try to feel big, we feel small. But when we give ourselves to the smallness of who we are in the big picture, we end up feeling bigger as a part of the whole, because it's not just us anymore."

"So you and I are connected?"

"Absolutely. And the more people you encounter who have an impact on you, the bigger your circle of purpose becomes. It helps you realize just how deep you are in all of it."

Bill continued looking up at the stars, and wondered how it was possible that it was all united, and included even him. He shook his head at the shock of it all. "I think that's gonna take some getting used to."

Joshua softly laughed to himself. "It will happen when you least expect it."

24
—

"I NEED TO SEE DR. RAINER," LIAM DEMANDED AS HE
leaned up against the counter.

"I'm sorry sir, but you need to make an appointment," the receptionist replied.

"I don't have time to make an appointment, I need to see her now,"
he looked around and saw that the waiting room was empty. He hoped
this boded well for his chances.

"Sir, that's not how it works," she replied sternly, looking him
squarely in the eyes.

"Is that Mr. Scott?" Laura's voice echoed from behind the reception
area.

"Yes, Dr. Rainer," the secretary answered, keeping her focus locked
on Liam.

"Send him back; it's okay," she assured.

"Okay sir, you can go back," she informed him with a tinge of
attitude.

Liam turned without speaking and entered the hallway leading to
Laura's office, slightly disappointed to have to end the staring contest.
Laura was waiting halfway down the hall. She motioned for Liam to
follow her. "Come on in, Liam."

Liam stormed down in her direction and followed her into her
office.

"Have a seat, Liam," she directed as she shut the door behind them.

"I don't want to have a seat," Liam chided as he paced through the
office. "What the hell are you doing here?"

"Liam, you came to see me."

"No, I mean what kind of a practice are you running? You just have
Rachel lure me in here so she can shatter my life?"

"Liam, I really need you to sit down," she reiterated in a calm voice
that emboldened Liam more.

"I don't want to sit down. I want you to explain to me what the hell I'm supposed to do now."

"We can talk about that, but I need you to sit down first, please."

There was a strength in Laura's eyes that Liam could not deny, so at last he followed her direction. She followed her own advice and sat down in her chair.

"Why don't you tell me how you're feeling right now, Liam."

"Isn't that your job? It's pretty obvious anyway, isn't it?"

"Even if it is, it is helpful for us to verbalize our feelings, so can you start there?"

"I'm pissed off! Obviously," he pointed out, as he rocked back and forth on the couch. "How could she do this to me? This is outrageous! I would never do that to her. And after she went on and on about how I wasn't being a good husband, all this time she was doing this to me."

"Good, what else are you feeling?"

Liam stopped for a moment, trying to figure out how what he had said could in any way be construed as 'good.' "I'm just pissed right now."

Laura paused, letting the pain in the air simmer. "Often, Liam, anger is the surface emotion trying to block out the other emotions that we are less comfortable with. So sit for a moment, be still, and tell me what else is going on inside you."

"No, I'm just angry."

"Liam, trust me. Just sit still."

Liam reluctantly obliged and sat back. He took a few deep breaths and felt the shelter of his anger begin to dissipate. The silence of the room began to build and bombarded his ears. He squirmed in his seat, and the friction of his clothes against the fabric of the couch screamed even louder. His pain began to rise. His mind grew chaotic as uncontrollable thoughts shot from every direction. His stomach became tense, his shoulders tight, and the heat of pain ridden tears began to flood his eyes. He crossed his legs and wrapped his arms around his abdomen, fighting any urge to show weakness in front of this strange woman. His face shook as drops of sorrow began to escape and roll down his face. He was losing every ability he had to fight it back. He struggled to pull them back in, but each gasp gave way to more. His face convulsed with the force of emotion that he could no longer control. He covered his face as he sobbed into his arms.

The minutes crawled by as he sat there, feeling the full force of sorrow that he had long ago determined to never show in front of another human being. He endured there until his tear ducts ran dry, and slowly lifted his head to look across the table. He blinked several times, attempting to clear the blurriness between his eyelids. The face of a compassionate guide revealed itself, and Liam finally spoke.

"I don't know what to do," he acquiesced.

"I know, and for now, that is okay."

"It doesn't feel okay."

"I know that too."

Liam sat with a confusion that he was terrified to accept. "I'm still furious with Rachel."

"Of course you are, and you have every right to be. But at the end of the day, you have to decide what you want. You have to decide if being angry is more important than making things right with Rachel."

Liam stared at the floor, not knowing how to respond.

"The reality is that these kinds of situations, and relationships in general, are complicated. There's nothing simple about them. It's not 'one person did this,' and 'someone else did this.' Yet we often have to start there. Rachel has her part in this, which is vastly more complicated than one bad decision. And you have your part, which is also vastly complex. So at the end of the day, you can choose to stay angry, or you can choose to address the part that you have played, seek to make it right, and find the healing that will help you move forward."

"Are you saying this is my fault? That it's my fault that our marriage is the way it is? It's my fault Rachel did what she did?"

"It's not about fault or blame, it's about wholeness. Rachel is desperate for that wholeness for herself, and she wants it just as badly for you. I think you need to start seeking it for yourself."

"I don't even know where to start."

"Ah, now that *is* my job. I'm here to help you find the next step."

Liam smiled, acknowledging the cleverness of Laura using his own words. "I do want to make things right. I don't know how, but I'm willing to try."

"That's wonderful, Liam. If I were you, I would go tell that to Rachel."

Liam nodded in agreement and stood up from the couch.

"Make an appointment with my receptionist on the way out, and we'll get working on this together."

"Okay, thank you."

Liam exited her office and proceeded down the hall to the exit. He emerged into the waiting room and turned to face the receptionist, a little embarrassed by his outburst earlier.

"Ahem," he cleared his throat, sheepishly trying to get her attention. She looked up, with her facial attitude returning. "Yes?"

"Um, I would like to make an appointment."

She gave him a look that screamed, "Isn't this interesting." He chuckled, and she returned the gesture. "Alright, when would you like to come back?"

+ + +

Liam drove home with a sense of hope that he had rarely known, not only for his marriage, but for something deep inside that he could not yet name. He returned home and entered the front door. Rachel hurried around the corner, and relief fell upon her face.

"Babe, oh my goodness I'm so glad you're home," she expressed as she approached him. Her eyes began to well up. "Honey, I am so sorry. I am so so sorry."

Liam lifted his hands in acceptance of her apology. "I know, Babe, I know. Look, I went and saw Laura again today, and something happened to me. Something broke inside me. And I don't know how to really describe it. But I just want you to know that I want to make things right with you, and I know that there's stuff I need to work on with me. I really do want to do that. I'm probably not gonna do it very well, but I want to try."

Rachel lunged forward and grasped Liam in her arms. "Oh, I love you so much, I love you so much!"

"I love you too, Babe," he affirmed as he squeezed her tight.

25

———

Joshua helped Bill down a small slope. Bill gingerly stepped down, not wanting to elevate his breathing too much. It had been several days since his breathing problems had started, and while the pain was not as pronounced as it had been, his breaths were still labored. Even with Joshua managing his pack, each step felt immense.

Joshua led the way but did not have to cut branches or shrubbery back as he had before, a change that Bill gladly accepted.

For Bill, it felt like they had arrived in this land weeks ago. Normal movements, which were natural to him before, now had to be monitored. He was emotionally and mentally exhausted. He kept questioning how much further he could go.

Joshua looked back and noticed the stress and irritation written across Bill's face. "Time for a break?" he probed.

Bill nodded his head, not wanting to expend anymore breath with a verbal answer. Joshua helped Bill down to the ground and he laid back.

After a few minutes, Bill had caught his breath enough to speak. "How much longer?" he blurted out.

Joshua peered out into the distance. "I'm not sure. This land has some intriguing features. You never really know how close you are to anything. A landmark can seem just a few minutes away and yet remain out of reach. It's a unique area."

"That doesn't make any sense."

"To newcomers it makes no sense. But to those of us who have traversed this territory, it's just something we've come to expect. You usually find what you're looking for in the most surprising moments."

Bill just smiled and nodded to humor Joshua, but he was still cynical. Bill laid his head back and rested his eyes. A gentle breeze caressed his face and took him back to the river. He daydreamed while his mind began to fade.

+ + +

When Bill opened his eyes; he looked over to see Joshua waving his skillet over a fire. The aroma soothed his weary head.

"What are you doing? What happened?"

"You fell asleep," Joshua replied while laughing to himself. "It was still pretty early in the day but I figured you needed the rest?"

"So, it's morning?"

Joshua let out a roaring laugh. "Yep."

"That's crazy. I can't believe I did that." Bill lifted himself up and stretched his body. He could tell his muscles did not appreciate the position he had slept in as they fought his every move.

"Are you hungry?" Joshua inquired.

"Yes, starving," Bill replied as he moved over to the fire and sat across from his travel mate. Joshua retrieved two plates from his pack and divided up the eggs he had found for breakfast.

"Are you feeling any better after all that sleep?"

"Honestly, I still feel about the same. Everything still feels very strained. I think it's going to be another long day," Bill lamented as he attempted to stretch his neck and shoulder muscles.

"Yeah, we've had a lot of those lately, haven't we?"

"Yes. How long can we keep this going?"

Joshua shrugged his shoulders and shook his head. "As long as it takes."

Bill sighed, not appreciating the answer. "I just don't know how much longer I can last. It just seems like it keeps getting worse and worse."

Joshua nodded, trying to let Bill know that he sympathized with him. "Yeah, I get it. I do. You just need to focus on the next leg of the journey, the next hike, the next step even. Don't look ahead, just be present."

"That's easier said than done when the present is pretty miserable."

"Yep," Joshua affirmed while nodding his head again. "But that's also when you are awakened to what's really going on around you.

Everything in you wants to ignore it and just move on, but there's always something to learn if you're paying attention. The pain may not be good, but the way we walk through it can bring out some real beauty."

Bill nodded, pretending he understood, which had become a regular occurrence. The two travelers finished breakfast and Joshua cleaned up. Bill hated feeling helpless, but he knew he needed to save his energy for the next stretch of the journey. He filled the time by calling Rusty over and cuddling with him.

Bill laid back and gazed up into the trees. He allowed the beauty and the serenity of the scene to calm him. As he did, a peace washed over him, something he had not experienced in a long time, if ever. It was a peace deeper than his circumstances, or his ability, but just being engulfed in the present. "Huh," he thought to himself, "maybe Joshua's right."

After several minutes, Joshua sat the packs down, having collected everything that needed to be gathered. "Well, looks like we're ready," he announced.

"Alright, let's go Rusty," Bill directed, patting his loyal companion on his head.

Joshua helped Bill to his feet and then hoisted the packs over his back. They turned around and continued on their journey. Bill scanned the territory ahead. Large trees blocked much of his view. The trail they were to take ventured out a few yards and then took a sharp left turn, concealing the rest of the way. "One step at a time," Bill thought to himself.

They began down the trail and followed the turn. The trek continued to be a steady downgrade, which Bill hoped would descend toward the body of water. They had been traveling for far too long, Bill surmised, not to have arrived there yet. Bill tried to remain patient, as Joshua had advised, but each heavy step and arduous breath made this challenge more difficult.

Bill used the trees to stabilize himself as they continued to tread down the hill. As the day dragged on and the sun rose higher, Bill's clothes became soaked through with sweat. Rusty's tongue hung out the side of his mouth as he panted. Birds sang and chirped all around them, but Bill could hardly concentrate on anything but the strenuous journey.

By mid afternoon, Bill's body was howling at him, begging for relief. "I ... need ... break," he informed Joshua through his exhaustion.

Joshua obliged and tore the packs off his body. They planted themselves on the ground and sought to catch their breath. Bill could feel an all to familiar cramping in his abdomen as he strained to get the oxygen he needed.

"I don't know ... how much longer," he said exasperated.

"I know," Joshua replied, inferring what Bill was saying. "Just catch your breath. We'll wait a little while to get going again."

Joshua brought one of the packs over for Bill to lean back against. Bill seized the opportunity and quickly dozed off.

About a half hour had passed when Bill felt a nudge on his shoulder. "Bill, wake up. We need to get going again."

Bill nodded in compliance and sat up. He felt the weight of his limbs resist him as he sought to get in position to stand up. Joshua grabbed his arms and helped him to his feet. "We gotta keep going a little while longer before we stop for the day."

Bill nodded and waited for Joshua to lift the packs. They proceeded again down the hill, taking care not to slip or slide on the dry, dusty path.

The exhaustion was pummeling Bill. His legs buckled several times, and he scraped his hands trying to keep his balance. He fought with everything he had. He stepped on a large stone that gave way beneath him. He fell, bounced off his rear, and began tumbling down the hill. His momentum lunged him through a bush into an open field, where he landed face down in the grass.

Joshua raced down to find him and knelt down in front of him.

"Bill, are you okay?"

Bill tried to push himself up with his arms, but plopped back down. Joshua helped him roll over and sit up.

"I can't do this. I just can't do it," Bill exclaimed. "I can't get anywhere without straining for a breath. I don't know what to do."

A grin grew across Joshua's face.

"What the hell is so funny!" Bill demanded.

"You're talking normal again," Joshua replied.

Bill placed his hands on his chest and realized he was no longer
straining to breathe. He returned the grin to Joshua, who was now
standing and staring off behind him, eyes wide in excitement. Bill spun
around to find what was grabbing Joshua's attention and was stunned
to see the large body of water within their sight.

"See," Joshua said, "when you least expect it."

26

———

"I'M GLAD YOU CAME BACK," LAURA WELCOMED LIAM. IT had been a week since Liam had broken down in her office. He and Rachel had decided it would be good for him to do some therapy on his own for a while to get some clarity about his own challenges. He adjusted himself on the couch to get comfortable. Laura had some sweet-smelling candles that made him feel cozy.

"Did you think I wasn't going to?"

"Not necessarily, it's just that a lot of people in your situation wouldn't come back."

"Have you had that happen before?"

Laura let out a hearty laugh. "More than you could imagine."

"Well, where do we start?"

"Let's start at the beginning, with your childhood. Tell me about that."

Liam thought for a moment but couldn't come up with anything he figured would be worth talking about, or maybe he just didn't want to. "I don't really know what to say. It was pretty normal I guess."

"Well there's no such thing as a normal anything, Liam. We all have unique experiences, and we all interpret those experiences uniquely." Laura waited for a moment to let that sink in. She saw Liam nod in acceptance and continued. "Let's just start with the basics. Where did you grow up?"

"In Marion."

"Okay, and where did your parents grow up?"

"They grew up in Columbus."

"Okay, and how would you describe your parents? Let's start with your mom."

"My mom? You'll never find a sweeter or more loving person than her. She's a saint as far as I'm concerned. She is the rock of our family, for me and my sister, but also for my dad."

"What did she do for your dad?"

"She just never gave up on him. He's a hard ass, always has been. But she somehow saw something else in him."

"What about you?"

"What?"

"Did you see something else in him?"

Liam paused for a moment. He always had difficulty talking about his dad. He wasn't always fond of him, but he also had a deep sense of loyalty. "I don't know."

"It's just you and me here, Liam. Nothing you say leaves this room. And nothing you say will be used against you, only for you."

Liam took a deep breath before continuing. "I guess all I saw in my dad was a hard ass."

"Mmm, okay. Can you elaborate? What made him a hard ass?"

"There just wasn't any give in him. He didn't take any shit from anyone. He didn't budge on what he expected from you."

"And what was that?"

"What was what?"

"What was it that your dad expected from you?"

Liam thought for a moment, trying to find adequate words. "I guess … he expected me to be like him." Uncomfortable tears again rose to the surface.

"Mmm, yes." Laura took a moment to scribble on her notebook. "Why do you think your dad expected that of you?"

"I mean, I don't know, I guess he just wanted to make me like him. I don't know."

"Well, let's back up a little bit. Why do you think your dad was like that? Why was he such a hard ass?"

"I'm not sure, I guess I've never thought about it that much. I just figure that's who he is."

"Do you know much about his childhood?"

"I know he wasn't very close to his parents."

"Did you know them very well?"

"We saw them a handful of times when I was a kid."

"That's interesting. So they only lived about an hour away, but you only saw them a handful of times?"

"Yeah."

"That's pretty significant."

"Yeah, and to be honest, we only saw them that much because my mom pushed the issue. My dad never wanted to go."

"Do you know why that is?"

Again, Liam felt a sense of loyalty holding him back from speaking up, but fought through it to trust. "I know that my grandpa was not very kind to my dad."

"What does that mean exactly?"

"Well, he beat him. A lot. He was terrible to him. I don't know a lot of details. My dad has never spoken about it to me. But I've heard him and my mom talk about it. My mom has also mentioned some stuff to me. All in all, my grandpa was pretty brutal to him."

"What about your grandma?"

"I think he was pretty brutal to her as well. She just kind of took it and submitted to him."

"I imagine that was pretty difficult for your dad to watch as a kid."

Liam nodded in agreement.

"Are they still alive and married?"

"My grandpa died about ten years ago, but yes, they were still married when he died."

Laura continued scribbling notes on her pad. "Hmm, they stayed married through all of that? That's very sad. And where is your grandmother now?"

"Last I heard, she was in a nursing home."

"Hmm, okay. So you visited them a handful of times. What were those visits like?"

Liam thought for a moment. These were not memories that he visited very often. He had to conduct a thorough search for them. "I remember it being very depressing. Grandpa was always in a terrible mood, and Grandma just seemed sad and lifeless."

"When was the last time you saw them?"

"I think I was around eleven."

"That's an interesting age to see them for the last time. Was there something that happened to make you and your family not visit them again?"

Liam choked up as he returned to the scene in his mind. "I remember … I remember my Grandpa getting physical with Grandma, pushing her against the wall. Something like that. My dad flipped out, and told us all to get in the car. Even my mom. He never ordered my mom around, ever, except for that time. We sat in the car for a few minutes. I remember it must've been summer, because my hair was soaked with sweat. After a few minutes my dad came storming out, and we blew out of there."

"Wow. What happened after that?"

"Well, we just went home. But I heard my parents talking about it later that night. My dad said he would never go back, that he would never allow us to see that again."

It was surreal for Liam to talk about it. He had never spoken about it to anyone, and it almost felt as if someone was speaking through him.

"And you never saw them again either?"

'No. I mean, after a while it almost felt like they didn't exist anymore. We didn't really know them well to begin with anyway."

"How did the rest of your family deal with that?"

"I think my mom finally gave up on trying to mend something between my dad and my grandpa. I don't think my sister really minded much. Actually, if anything, I think she was glad to not go back."

"And where is your sister now?"

"She lives out in California. She's pretty high up in the tech world out there, so she doesn't get to come back here very often."

"And is she older or younger?"

"She's five years younger than me."

Laura wrote some more notes and took a few seconds to ponder. "Okay. Well, it sounds like your dad endured a lot in his childhood, huh?"

"Yeah, I guess he did."

"And he wanted to protect you guys from that."

"Yeah. I mean, my dad has not always been my favorite person. But he has always seemed strong, like the strongest person I have ever known."

"What about you? Are you strong?"

The question made Liam uncomfortable. He took a few moments to ponder before answering. "I don't know. I've never really thought of myself as being very strong."

"Strength comes in many different forms, Liam. I imagine there are many ways in which you are just as strong as your dad is, even if it looks different."

"I don't know. I just have a hard time seeing myself that way."

"Maybe that's something we need to work on, hmm?"

Liam nodded, not really believing in her assertion, but just not to have to press into it too much.

"Well, I think that's all the time we have for today."

27

BILL RAN, SOMETHING HE COULDN'T DO FOR WEEKS. HE ran to the water and, without hesitation or second thought, jumped in. The chill of the water shot through his body and engulfed him. He tumbled around in it, content to be surrounded and embraced.

He screamed for joy as he lunged out of the lake. Rusty ran after him and stopped short of the water and barked voraciously, scolding Bill for having fun without him. Joshua doubled over in laughter, enamored with Bill's spontaneity. It was a trait he had seldom seen before in his friend

Bill jolted out of the water and splashed before he turned toward Joshua. Bill let out a roar that stunned even Rusty. "We made it!" He exclaimed. "I can't believe we finally made it."

"We made it," Joshua echoed through his laughter.

Bill waded through the water to return to the shore. Rusty greeted him by jumping into his arms. Bill fell back and Rusty licked his face. "I know buddy," Bill said as he chuckled, "I'm excited too." Bill sat up and held Rusty on his lap. "I don't know about you, but I'm ready to go fishing," he informed Joshua.

"Sounds good to me," Joshua affirmed.

Bill took a moment to look around, something he had failed to do before his plunge into the water. The scene was breathtaking. Trees peppered the perimeter around the lake, and were backstopped by rolling hills. The grass was bright and lush, and felt like a bed beneath him. There was no fog. In fact, there was no sign of a cloud to be found. Bill let out a soft sigh of relief.

Bill and Joshua prepped their equipment to catch some fish. Bill was able to track down some worms residing underneath a log nearby. He brought a few over to Joshua and finalized their lines. They each found a spot, relatively close to each other, and flung their lines into the water.

Bill was giddy with excitement, a feeling he was not sure he had ever experienced. It had been weeks since he had been able to fish. He wasn't really even concerned with catching any, just the opportunity to cast and gaze upon the water was enough to put a thrill in his heart. He would not turn away a catch, however, and could hardly contain his elation when the first nibbles began.

The catches were coming in fast. It seemed as if the fish were looking for them. Each time someone got a bite, Rusty would run over, carrying on for moral support.

"This is crazy!" Liam exclaimed. "I don't think I've ever done this well."

"I know, this is pretty amazing."

After an hour or so, they had caught quite enough for dinner for the next couple days. They gathered their equipment and fish over by their packs and compared their productivity.

"Wow, those look pretty impressive, Bill," Joshua congratulated.

"Thanks! That may have been the easiest bit of fishing I've ever had," Bill replied, deflecting the compliment.

"Well, do you wanna clean the fish or get the fire going?" Joshua asked.

"I can work on the fire," Bill decided. "I'll go out and find some wood. It's nice to be able to move freely again," he rejoiced, taking an extra deep breath for dramatic effect.

"I bet it is!"

Bill ventured out to a wooded area behind them. The depth of magnificent variety around him was stunning. There were fruit trees and shrubs scattered throughout. He snatched a few blackberries, plopped them in his mouth, and could scarcely contain the taste that burst forth. They had been dropped into a bountiful paradise.

He continued scoping out the area for a few minutes before he found some firewood. He started loading up his arms. As he gathered the pieces, he began to wonder why they had not seen any signs of other people residing in the area. He pondered the unusual observation while he transported the wood back to Joshua.

"Hey, you know what I was realizing?" Bill rhetorically proposed as Joshua came back within sight. "We haven't seen a single other person in this area yet. Doesn't that seem weird? It's such a great location. You'd think it'd be teeming with people."

"I would think you, of all people, would be happy about that," Joshua replied with a grin.

"Very funny. I just mean, you would think there would be a lot of people here with how amazing it is."

"Well, this is the land of Epiphanies. People don't typically stay here for long periods of time," Joshua replied without looking up from the fish he was cleaning.

"You mean you've been here before?"

"Yes, many times. But it never quite seems the same each time I am here."

"And you've never seen people here."

"Oh, I have, but like I said, people don't stay here for very long."

"That's really odd. I'd gladly stay here as long as I could," Bill reflected. Joshua seemed to think nothing of it, so Bill returned into the trees to obtain some more wood.

When Bill came back, Joshua had already finished cleaning the fish and was getting the fire ready. "Wow. You work fast," Bill commented.

"I'm pretty hungry," Joshua giggled.

Bill sat across from Joshua as he placed the prepared fish on the skillet. The sizzle filled the air, as did the aroma. Bill's mouth watered as he watched in anticipation. Rusty sat next to Joshua, patiently awaiting the scraps he knew were coming.

The sun was beginning to set as Joshua finished cooking the last of their haul. The evening was peaceful. The three travelers scarfed down their dinner with great appreciation. Bill found himself full of gratitude, and full of food, a state he had not experienced in some time. He was grateful for the scenery. Grateful for the sustenance. Oddly enough, he was also grateful for the company, something he never imagined would happen.

"This has been a really interesting journey," Bill commented between chewing his food.

Joshua concurred with a methodical nod. "Yes, I should say so."

"Well, and not just all the things we've seen and done and run into. But also, for the way it's affecting me."

"Oh yeah? And how's that?"

"Well, I mean I'm sitting here, eating a meal with another person, and I'm pretty happy with it. Really happy in fact. I never used to want to be around anyone. I built my entire life on that. I never wanted to come to count on another person. I had to depend on myself, and that was it. Yet for the first time that I can remember, I have a friend that has helped me in more ways than I can count. And I guess I feel like I can count on you. That's a weird feeling. But it's good."

Joshua returned his words with a soft and affirming smile and continued eating his dinner.

"I guess I'm just trying to say thank you."

Joshua looked up and locked eyes with Bill. "It's my pleasure."

28

"Go go go! Yes! Woo!" Rachel screamed as she watched Aaron sprint down the basketball court and complete a layup. "Way to go!"

The family had come together to watch Aaron play. Frank and Susie sat behind Liam, Rachel and Lizzy. Aaron had been improving his defense and, in turn, the coach had been giving him more playing time. They were all excited to get to see him play quality minutes.

"He's playing so well!" Rachel commented, as she turned and grinned to the rest of the family.

"He sure is," Grandma Susie affirmed.

They continued watching the pace ebb and flow. It was a close game. The other team jumped out to a fast start and had held the lead most of the game, but Aaron's team had come back to tie it up. Most of the spectators spent a good portion of the first half on the edge of their seat.

Liam glanced up to the game clock to see 3:13 left in the first half. "Anyone want a drink or snack? I want to beat the halftime rush."

"I want some nachos," Lizzy requested.

"That sounds great," Rachel agreed. "Can you get us a couple sodas too?"

"Sure," Liam replied as he leaned in and kissed the top of her head.

"I'll go with you son," Frank informed him.

The two guys scooted over to the aisle and slowly climbed down the bleachers. They walked down the sideline and toward the foyer where the concession items were sold.

"They have good hot dogs here," Frank commented.

"Yeah, I love them too."

They turned the corner and stood in line between a few other over achievers also trying to beat the rush. The buttery smell of the popcorn wafted through the air and filled them with delight. Liam scanned the signs, trying to decide if he wanted anything else.

"So, Son," Frank began. Liam sighed, knowing his dad was about to transition this mundane experience into an uncomfortable conversation. "You never did tell us why you needed to stay the night the other night."

"Nice transition, Dad," Liam thought to himself. "It was nothing Dad. Rachel and I just had a fight. We're good now."

"That's it?"

"Yeah, Dad, it's fine." Liam was firm on not mentioning seeing a counselor to his dad. He knew Frank didn't view that very highly, and he was not in the mood to hear his opinion on the matter.

"I know how it goes, Son. I know marriage can be tough."

"Ugh, I know dad. I know. Everything's tough," Liam remarked, sounding more snarky than he had intended.

"Did I say something?"

"No, Dad, it's fine. I just don't really want to talk about it right now."

"Okay."

A stranger lined behind them and began commenting on the food. "They got some good snacks here, huh?"

"Ugh," Liam thought to himself, "why'd we have to get the talker?"

"They sure do," Frank concurred.

The stranger continued trying to chime in, but much to Liam's relief, they were up next to order their food.

"Hi, what would you guys like?" the concessions worker asked.

"Hello, I need an order of nachos, a hot dog, and two large sodas please," Liam requested, "and whatever he wants," he said as he pointed back to his dad.

As his dad ordered, Liam stared into space and daydreamed about the things he wanted to say to his dad. Words popped up in his mind, words that escaped him whenever he had a chance to speak to his dad. "There are other things to life than being tough. If all you are is tough, then you end up being a jackass to everyone around you." His heart raced as his staged argument carried on in his head.

+ + +

"Lizzy, can you go tell your dad I'd also like some popcorn?" Rachel asked.

"You couldn't have asked him that before?"

"I didn't think of it before. Go please, so you catch him while he's still in line."

"Okay, okay," Lizzy conceded as she hopped down the bleachers.

Rachel watched as Lizzy approached the foyer. "Mom," she began as she turned toward Susie, "I don't know if Liam told you why he stayed with you guys the other night."

"He didn't. But I know my boy."

"I hope you don't … "

"Oh, Sweetie don't worry about that. Marriage is really hard. Trust me, I know. No couple worth their salt makes it through without a few battle wounds."

Rachel's eyes began to well up. Recently, she felt like her wounds were bleeding out. On top of that, ever since Liam had stayed the night over there, a shadow of shame had fallen over her soul, fearing what Susie and Frank might think of her. She felt Susie's arm wrap around her torso and pull her close. "And, let's face it," Susie crooned, "men are clueless."

Rachel giggled, and Susie wrapped her up in warm and affectionate arms. "We love them, but they are clueless."

+ + +

"Anything else, Sir?" The concession's worker double checked.

"Liam," Frank said as he tapped Liam's shoulder.

"What? Oh sorry. No, I think that'll be it," Liam replied as he reached for his wallet.

"Daddy!" Lizzy yelled as she turned the corner. Liam turned his head and locked eyes with her. "Mom wants some popcorn too."

"Okay," Liam yelled back and turned toward the concessions worker. "Sorry about that. I guess we'll need another popcorn."

"No problem. That'll make it eighteen dollars."

Liam pulled cash out of his wallet and paid for the food. After a couple minutes, Liam and his dad were walking back to their seats with arms full. They ascended the bleachers and passed out everyone's items. Liam sat back down and looked up to the scoreboard. Aaron's team was up by three and had the ball with twenty-two seconds until halftime.

"This is a good game," Frank commented.

"It really is," Rachel concurred. "I heard that this team was really good, but we're hanging in there."

Aaron got the ball and drove to the basket, but then passed the ball back out to a teammate on the three-point line, who promptly swished it to add to their lead just before the half ended.

"Yeah!" Rachel screamed with delight. "Way to go." The rest of the family whooped and hollered with her. "That was a great pass!" She exclaimed.

"Yeah, he's really finding his teammates well," Frank echoed.

The two teams returned to their places on the bench and spent the next ten minutes preparing for the second half. In the meantime, the Scott family enjoyed their snacks and continued chatting, except for Liam, who remained quiet throughout.

+ + +

As the second half commenced, the family all braced themselves for more excitement. The other team began with the ball. They brought it down to the other end and passed the ball back and forth, trying to find a good shot. Aaron jumped in front of one of the passes and stole it. He ran down to the other end and laid it up into the basket.

"Woohoo!" the family all screamed in celebration.

Aaron ran back down and rejoined his team on defense. The other team brought the ball down again. One of their players drove near to the free throw line and shot the ball. The ball hit the back of the rim and bounced up. Aaron ran in for the rebound. He jumped off and snatched it in the air but landed on another player's foot. His ankle turned sharply.

He let out an anguished scream as he grabbed his ankle. The referees stopped the game and ran over to check on him. The coach quickly followed suit.

"Oh no!" Rachel exclaimed. "I'm gonna go out there."

"No," Liam responded, "you might embarrass him. He's got the coach. If you're needed, he'll let us know."

Rachel reluctantly agreed, and fought every urge she had to run to the rescue. They watched as the coach worked with Aaron. After a few excruciating minutes, the coach lifted Aaron up and helped him to the bench. He winced in pain each step of the way.

"You got this!" Rachel yelled out in support.

The rest of the crowd in the bleachers applauded, relieved to see Aaron up.

"Tough it out bud," Frank yelled out.

"You can't tough out an injury, Dad," Liam derided.

"I know, I just … "

"Geez, he's hurt dad, can't you see that? Can you ever say anything else?" Liam huffed as he stood up. "I'm gonna go wait for Aaron."

Frank looked to Susie and Rachel with confusion. Liam remained in the foyer for the rest of the game.

29

Bill opened his eyes, but everything appeared blurry. He tried a couple more times, but had to wipe his eyes with his hands to bring any visual clarity. It had been several days since they had arrived. The day before they were fortunate enough to catch a boar and feast on it for dinner.

For perhaps the first time on this entire venture, Bill was up before Joshua. The latter was cuddled up close to the remnants of the fire from the night before. Bill sat up and stretched out his arms. Rusty lay next to him, eyeing Bill's next move. The dog was ready to follow Bill on the inaugural task of the day, although he appeared to prefer that task to be going back to sleep.

Bill rose to his feet and stretched once more. He grabbed his cup and moseyed to the water to get a drink. He was still ecstatic that he once again had this daily opportunity. He dipped the cup in the water and took a sip. It was just as crisp and refreshing as when they first arrived. He peered across the lake; the scene was as gorgeous as ever. He could hear the rejoicing of birds bringing in the morning. These songs were unfamiliar to him; there seemed to be more depth and variety to them. He hoped to catch a glimpse of the winged creatures soon.

The water tasted so fresh, so brisk. He dipped his cup in for a second drink while Rusty tiptoed close enough to get a drink for himself. A couple fish swam in front of Bill, almost daring him to grab his pole. Instead, Bill returned and found his pack. He was ready to explore the area.

Joshua still snoozed away, so Bill tried his best to stealthily gather the items he needed. He grabbed his revolver and tucked it into the back of his pants. He retrieved a smaller pack and filled it with a knife, and some of the boar meat from the night before. He threw a piece to Rusty before zipping up his bag, grabbed the machete, and the two of them marched away.

They ventured around the southern side of the lake. Much of the water was surrounded by tall grass and cattails. Bill weaved in and out of the brush and under the low hanging branches. He cut some of the brush away, but mostly just bobbed and weaved.

A few birds jetted through the trees out across the lake. The sudden flapping startled Bill, and he whipped around to try and catch their breed. They moved so fast he hardly caught a glimpse, but he could see shades of orange and blue beaming off of them. He watched them whirl around from one end of the lake to the other, finally finishing their air dance and vanishing into the trees on the other side.

Bill was so enthralled that he didn't notice Rusty had found his own fixation and was pawing at the ground. Bill finally heard the rustle and turned around to see what had caught Rusty's attention.

Bill was surprised to see Rusty surrounded by what appeared to be an abandoned encampment of some sort. Bill approached to investigate. A tent had fallen over and was half covered by the falling brush. There was also a makeshift fire pit. The discovery confirmed what Bill thought. There had to be others around this area. It was such an idyllic place, it just didn't make any sense that they would be the only ones there. Bill soon continued on his exploration, making a point to revisit the site later to retrieve any useful items.

Bill and Rusty continued trekking around the lake, making their way through the grass and brush. It wasn't long before they stumbled upon a second encampment. They poked around once again to see what they could find. There were no toppled tents at this one, just a fire pit and some logs that had been positioned for people to sit around it. Bill wondered if this was a second site for the people from the previous location, or if it was formed by a different group altogether.

They continued on. Over the next couple of hours they continued to stumble upon a familiar scene. Fire pits, lifeless tents, and even some tools had been left behind. Each time Rusty investigated. Overall, they located at least a dozen of these encampments, each one devoid of people.

Bill was at a loss. He knew others had to be around, and yet they seemed to have all disappeared. Wild thoughts ran through his head. He could not imagine all these people encountering this beautiful land and all deserting it voluntarily. Something must have compelled them to leave. But what? And would it try and force them out too?

Bill continued on while Rusty seemed to be in a crazy mood, running from one bush to another, barely stopping long enough to sniff. Bill scoured the area when he heard a rustling from the brush up ahead. Bill put his hand on the revolver, wanting to be prepared for anything. He saw a stick protruding out of the brush, seeming as if it was marching toward him. A few seconds later, the figure holding the stick emerged from the brush.

The individual was hooded under a brown cloak, and seemed to be wearing a tunic underneath. The person was looking down and was startled to stumble upon Bill.

"Oh, hello," the voice spoke in a higher pitch than Bill had expected.

Rusty heard and ran over to greet the new traveler. The figure pulled off the hood to reveal a strikingly beautiful face. Bill surmised she was of Latin American heritage. She smiled at Bill and rubbed Rusty's head. "Who might you be?" She asked.

"My name is Bill. My friend Joshua and I stumbled upon this area about a week ago, and have been camping on the other side of the lake."

"Oh, it's lovely to meet you. I am Esperanza, keeper of Epiphanies. I'm sorry I have not greeted you previously, I have not been to that side of the lake in a while."

"Of course, that's no problem. We don't mean to intrude on your land. Like I said, we just stumbled here and needed a place to rest."

"Oh you're very welcome to be here. It's been a little while since this land has had visitors. I wondered when the next ones would arrive." She reached up to touch the branch above her head and closed her eyes in concentration, as if the tree was sending her messages.

"If you don't mind me asking, why is there no one else here? I mean, this is such a beautiful land with such a great water source. It seems like this place would be teeming with people."

She finished with the tree before responding. "Well, Epiphanies is not a place where people remain for long."

"Yes, I've heard that, but why? Are there others here who don't want visitors?"

"Oh no, people are always welcome here. But the nature of this land is for no one to stay for good. This land gives people insight, encouragement, and hope. But eventually, they have to continue on their journey. This is not the destination."

"I guess I don't understand. I would never leave this place voluntarily."

"No, of course not, neither did they. But this land becomes less hospitable because it's not meant to be a lasting location. Eventually the fish recoil, the water becomes bitter, and people can no longer survive here. It's meant to help you get to your destination, not to keep you here."

Bill shook his head in disbelief. He was hearing what she was saying, but it did not compute. "That seems pretty fantastical, unbelievable in fact."

"Yes," she affirmed. She gave no elaboration, which elicited a slight scowl from Bill. She then reached into one of her pockets and pulled out some sort of device. "This is for you."

Bill reached out and she placed it in his hand. It had a covered lens on it, as well as a small lever. Bill pressed down on the lever which uncovered the lens. He looked through it, but it simply showed the land around him just as it was.

"Thanks, I think?"

Esperanza chuckled. "That's how most people react to it. It won't seem like much while you are here, but when you go on your way, it will be a great source of encouragement."

"I'm sorry, but I guess I just don't believe you. I don't believe that things will change in the way you have described."

"That's okay. Just hold onto it for now."

Bill complied, not wanting to argue.

"It was lovely to meet you, Bill, I'll be on my way."

"Lovely to meet you as well," Bill replied as he politely nodded to her.

Esperanza replaced her hood over her head and slowly disappeared into the trees.

Bill looked down toward Rusty and scratched his head. "Well, that was kind of weird." Rusty barked in concurrence.

30

____

LIAM CROSSED HIS LEGS TIGHTLY AND FOLDED HIS ARMS. He shook his body as he anticipated Laura emerging through the hall door and calling him back to her office. He had been reluctant to show up this time. He was still reeling from Aaron's basketball game and struggling to grasp what was truly going on. The emotions whirling in him were chipping away at his protective armor. The battle had left him weary and exhausted, and he was uncertain how much more he could handle.

He looked for anything to distract him from his thoughts. The chair he had chosen in the waiting room had an odd squeaking sound each time he leaned forward. He adjusted his weight back and forth in the chair to hear the squeak over and over, getting lost in the repetition.

For a few minutes he stared at the paintings on the wall. He followed that with flipping through the assortment of magazines that seemed to have no common thread at all.

The hall door creaked open and Laura poked her head out. The sound broke Liam out of his trance.

"Liam, ready to come back?" Liam nodded his head and slowly ventured to the door. They quietly moved down the hallway. He stepped across the floor, fighting the impulse to run away. They arrived at the office and entered. "Have a seat," she requested as she closed the door. "So what's on your mind today."

"I don't really know," Liam confessed, as he returned to his seating position. "A lot, I guess. Can't really sort it out."

"Hmm. Okay. Can you decipher how you feel."

Liam thought for a moment with his head facing the ground. He really didn't wanna answer any questions, but he also didn't want to walk out after working just to make it here in the first place. "I guess I'm feeling pretty nervous."

"Okay, are you feeling nervous about anything specific, or just in general?" Laura inquired as she recorded her notes.

"I'm nervous about being here," he replied, staring at the carpet to avoid any eye contact. "Nervous about talking about this stuff, about how I feel."

"Okay. That's really good Liam, and completely normal. Why do you think that makes you nervous?"

Liam thought for a moment, trying to really be honest with himself. "I guess I've always been nervous about sharing my feelings. It's like I think something bad is going to happen if I share them."

"Mmm, yes. I can sense that. What are you afraid is going to happen?"

"I … I don't really know."

"Let's put it as specifically as possible. If right now, you were to share your feelings in this room with me, what are you afraid is going to happen?"

Liam felt more vulnerable than he ever had. Everything in him wanted to bolt out the door now, but he had made a promise to Rachel. "I guess that something I say will make people give up on me. Something I say will make you kick me out."

"Okay. Is it fair to say that you're afraid I will judge and reject you?"

"Yes."

"Liam, can you look at me?" Liam kept staring down. Laura adjusted herself and leaned forward in her chair. "Liam, I would really like you to look at me."

Liam raised his head and met Laura's eyes. His own began to well up as he stared at her.

"Liam, your feelings will never make me judge you or reject you. Never. Remember, I am here for you. Do you feel like you can trust me?"

Liam nodded his head. Part of him sincerely trusted her. Part of him felt that he had no choice but to try.

"I'm just really angry," he blurted out.

"Okay, angry over what?"

"Angry at Rachel for how she has treated me. I mean, I get that I have done things that have been hard on her. I mean. I don't really get what I've done, but I know that's how she feels. But I just can't believe she did that to me. I mean, what the hell? Am I just a pansy for working things out with her? Aren't I just putting up with what she did?"

"Okay, you're angry, and as I said before, you have every right to feel that way. I will point out that anger is often a surface emotion. It often is there to cover up how we're really feeling inside." She gave Liam a moment to let that linger. "You asked if working things out makes you weak. Is that how you feel right now? Do you feel weak?"

"Yes," Liam answered in a hushed tone.

"We spoke last time about how your dad was so strong, but that maybe you didn't feel like you were strong. Do you remember?"

"Yes?" Liam responded with a confused look on his face.

"Have you felt that way most of your life? Felt not strong, or weaker than your father."

"I mean, I don't really know. I'm not sure."

"Did you ever find yourself doing things, hoping that your father would see you succeed."

"Yeah, I guess so. But doesn't every son want to make his father proud of him? I thought that was pretty normal."

"Yes, most sons want their fathers to be proud of them. But there's a difference between acting out of confidence because you know your father is proud of you and acting out of fear that you might not measure up."

Liam shifted his body on the couch. As much as he had difficulty with his dad, he always felt uneasy when someone criticized him. "Look maybe I gave you the wrong impression of my dad. He's tough, but he loves me."

"Liam, I mean no disrespect at all. I'm sure he does love you and did the very best he knew how. But even loving parents can leave us, as children, to develop some unhealthy patterns because of the way we interpret events around us."

"Okay. Yeah I guess there's been times where I've wondered if my dad was proud of me. Wondered if he thought I had what it takes."

"Would you say that you have wondered that often throughout your life?"

Liam started to shake his head but stopped himself. Flashes began to shoot through his mind. Memories of working tirelessly and sensing his father's disapproving eyes watching over him. "Wow. I guess it's happened more than I thought."

"I would imagine that would be the case, given what you've mentioned about your father so far."

"So, I'm still confused. What are you trying to say about all this?"

"I'm suggesting that perhaps this feeling of weakness you're feeling now is not just because of what Rachel has done. Maybe her actions have simply amplified a voice that was already speaking within you."

Liam sat still, trying to respond, but was unable to find any words. He laid his hands to his side and slid down into the couch, as if he had just arrived from a long day. He stared at the floor again, not sure how to proceed.

Laura finally chimed back in. "How are you feeling now?"

"Confused," Liam replied.

"Confused about what, exactly?"

"What to do next. I mean, what do I do with all this anger I have?"

"Sit with it. Not to ruminate and get more angry, but to understand where it's all coming from. I would guess there is a part of you that truly is angry with Rachel, and that's perfectly okay at this point. But perhaps your anger is bigger than just this one incident."

"Like I'm more angry with my dad?"

"Well, there's probably some of that too. But maybe you're angry with yourself too."

Liam was taken aback. He didn't see that coming.

"Let me ask you a question. It's going to be a really hard question. Is that okay?"

Liam tried to brace himself. "Okay."

"Why do you think Rachel did what she did? I don't want you to tell me what you think she thinks, or what you think is the right answer. In your gut, what do you think it was?"

"I ... I don't know. I don't think ... "

"It's okay Liam, I am here to help you."

Liam tried to sit with the pain. It was excruciating. He could feel his body resisting. He took a deep breath and really sat with it. "I guess ... I feel like she's not happy with me. Like ... I'm not good enough."

"Hmm ... yes. That's what I'm talking about. You are angry with yourself. You assume there is something wrong with you, and that's a pretty normal way to feel for someone in your position. But we want to challenge that story. Afterall, if there was something wrong with you, she wouldn't be trying to work things out. You see, you think of yourself as weak, but she obviously doesn't, or else she wouldn't be inviting you onto a path that requires such strength."

Liam smiled as a few tears of relief fell down his face. They continued chatting for a few more minutes until their time was up. Liam drove home afterwards with a sense that a little weight had left his soul.

31

—

BILL WOKE TO THE RUSTLING OF WOOD A FEW FEET AWAY from him. He could see Joshua stirring the area with a stick.

"Sorry to wake you," Joshua greeted him. "It's just so cold this morning." He began to place new wood in the pit to get another fire going.

"That's okay, I don't mind waking up to a fire," Bill replied as he closed his eyes again and rolled over. A few minutes later, when it was clear he wasn't going to fall back asleep, he sat up and drew closer to the fire. The warmth soothed his face.

It had been a couple weeks since Bill had encountered Esperanza. He still did not put much stock in what she had told him, though the fish had seemed to be harder to catch this week. There were lots of explanations for that, however, he told himself. He was determined to make this place his new home, and he pondered the next steps to make that happen.

Joshua had gathered more eggs that he started to cook over the fire.

"I've been thinking, maybe we should start thinking about making a shelter. I mean, in the long run we're gonna want an actual cabin. But just a shelter for now," Bill began.

Joshua concentrated on the eggs and didn't respond.

"What do you think?" Bill asked.

"Bill, I'm not sure that we're gonna be here that much longer."

"What do you mean?"

"Well, you told me about the conversation you had with Esperanza."

"Oh, come on, that's not gonna happen."

"Bill, the fish are already diminishing."

"You really believe that this land is just going to magically change?"

"I've been here before. I don't believe it. I've seen it."

"This is ridiculous. Well, after breakfast, I'm going to start working on a shelter. You can help me if you want."

The two men continued sitting around the fire, waiting for the eggs to cook. Bill held himself tight and nuzzled up close to the fire, continuing to try and defrost from the night chill. He finally got warm, and a few minutes later the eggs were ready to eat.

+ + +

After breakfast Bill grabbed his cup and approached the water to get a drink. Rusty followed behind as he usually did. Bill dipped the cup into the water. He brought it to his mouth and took a drink, but soon spit it out. The water was bitter.

"No," he sighed in desperation. He dipped the cup in again and took another sip, but it was bitter too. "This doesn't make any sense. This water was fine yesterday." He looked over at Joshua, who's face conveyed a deep sense of pity. "Don't look at me like that," he demanded as he pointed his finger toward Joshua. "This isn't happening," he declared as he stomped along the perimeter of the lake.

"Where are you going?"

"I'm going to another part of the lake. Maybe there's just a bad pocket of water here."

Bill marched along the bend of the lake and kept going. His blood pressure was rising as he sought to suppress what he feared to be true. He looked around as he walked along, but the beauty of the scenery failed to lift his spirits. In fact, it only emboldened his rage, as if the bitterness of the water was spreading into his soul.

Before he knew it, he was near where he and Rusty had stumbled upon the first encampment. He turned toward the water and inched closer to dip his cup once again into the lake. He hesitantly brought it toward his lips and took a sip. He spit the water out, turned around, and chucked the cup into the trees.

"Damn it! Come on!"

He fell back onto his rear end and let his head drop into his hands, defeated and hopeless. He sat there for several minutes, furiously panting out his frustration.

"Well hello again" a female voice announced from behind him.

Bill spun around to find Esperanza.

"You scared me; I didn't even hear you."

"You weren't paying attention."

"I didn't believe you before."

"Well, don't feel bad. Nobody ever does. They all just go on their way until they no longer can."

"This just doesn't make any sense."

"No, I suppose from your vantage point, it doesn't."

"But can't you do something? Can't you fix it?"

"You're presuming there's something wrong with it? I assure you, there isn't. I can also assure you that I am simply a steward of this land. I have no power to control how it responds to each visitor. I can only convey the truth of what it is."

"Aaargh," Bill grunted in exasperation.

"Bill, this land has many purposes. One of those purposes is to reveal truths to its visitors, and in many cases, to reveal the truth about the visitors themselves. You don't need to stay in this land to understand the truth about you that it has revealed. In fact, you mustn't stay in order to come to that awareness."

"Yeah? And what truth is that?"

"I can't tell you that. You have to discern it for yourself. Besides, as we've already learned, you wouldn't listen to me anyway."

"Then why are you even here?" Bill asked.

"To let you know that I will be sending you off properly. You cannot make it with the supplies you have. You have not prepared for the next part of the journey, and that is something that I can remedy. You will be leaving tomorrow. Do not leave before I see you in the morning."

Bill remained silent. He was too angry to speak anymore.

"I will see you both then," Esperanza announced as she dismissed herself.

+ + +

Bill arrived back at the camp later that morning. Rusty ran over to jump up on him, but Bill ignored his furry friend's greeting. He tromped over to his pack and punted it as hard as he could. Items from his pack went flying. Joshua came running from the woods. Bill surmised from his armful of berries that he was collecting food for the journey.

"Oh, it's you," Joshua observed as he scanned the result of Bill's anger. "I guess I can assume you didn't find what you were hoping for."

"Apparently it doesn't matter what I was hoping for, or what I want."

"No, I guess sometimes it doesn't, but there's nothing we can do about that now."

"When does this end?" Bill demanded. "Do we just keep going and going?"

"You need to be less concerned about when this ends and more concerned about what you're making of it along the way."

"You sound just like Esperanza," Bill lamented as he threw his arms up in the air.

"I'll take that as a compliment. I take it you saw her when you were out there."

"Yes, and apparently she's going to come visit us before we leave."

"Yeah, she usually does."

"What do you mean?"

"I told you, Bill, I've been here before."

+ + +

The next morning, Bill and Joshua worked on packing up their items to begin their journey. They ate the last of the meat from their catch a few days before. Bill was bent over, feeling the tension in his back as he finished the last of his packing. He saw out of the corner of his eye Joshua standup and turn around.

"Well, look what we have here. Right on time as always." Joshua declared as Esperanza approached. Bill looked up to see her carrying her own pack over one shoulder, and canisters in her other hand. She simultaneously appeared delicate and sturdy, like she was someone who you would want to tuck you in at night, but also to protect you from danger.

"Good morning, Joshua! Did you expect anything less?"

"Of course not."

As Esperanza approached, she laid down her luggage and shared a heartfelt embrace with Joshua.

"So how is your friend doing this morning?"

"Are you talking about me?" Bill demanded.

"He's okay," Joshua answered, ignoring Bill's insistence. "He can be difficult, but I think he'll be okay."

"Well, I've seen some tougher cases, but they turn out alright. I like him," she issued as she winked at Bill. Bill continued getting ready, pretending he didn't care about what she was saying.

"Yeah, me too," Joshua agreed.

"Well, I have what you all need to head out. Here's some dried meat and fish," she informed as she handed him the pack. "And here is some fresh water," she continued as she moved the canisters closer to them.

"Thank you, my dear. It is much appreciated," Joshua replied.

"Well, Bill, it was a pleasure to meet you. Try to enjoy the journey."

All Bill could muster was a slight head nod.

"A joy as always," she said as she faced Joshua.

"Yes, always."

Esperanza turned and left the way she had arrived. Bill pretended not to watch her walk away. He wanted to thank her, wanted to understand why she could be so kind and firm at the same time, but he couldn't bring himself to say anything.

"Well, I suppose we are ready to get going," Joshua concluded as he took one last look around.

Bill scowled back at Joshua. There was so much irritation simmering within him. He wanted to lash out, to make someone as angry as he was, but he knew it would not accomplish anything, or change the reality he was facing. He finally resigned himself to the inevitable. "Let's go."

32

LIAM PRESSED THE BUTTON TO UNLOCK HIS CAR DOOR.
He slid into the driver's seat and roared out of his work assigned parking spot.

His last session with Laura had left a mark. He could not seem
to stop reflecting on a point she had made: "Maybe this feeling of
weakness you're feeling now is not just because of what Rachel has
done. Maybe her actions have simply amplified a voice that was already
speaking within you."

That thought had soaked into Liam's mind, making him feel like
a crazy person. He realized that there were many moments in his life
when he had perceived an attack on his strength and ability, and perhaps much of that came from his own mind.

He reflected on times this occurred in college when a professor tried
to give him advice. He remembered times at work when supervisors
challenged him. But one moment stuck in his mind above all others:
the recent dinner at home when he snapped at Aaron.

Thus, the reason for the trip to pick up his son from school for
a surprise lunch. He was careful to time his arrival to coincide with
Aaron's lunch period. He arrived at the school parking lot in short
order and strolled up to the front doors of the office. He was about
fifteen minutes early, wanting to pull Aaron from class to make sure
they had enough time to eat and talk.

He entered the office and waited at the receptionist's desk. He was
not accustomed to being at his children's school very often as Rachel
was the usual one to take care of any issues that arose there.

"Hello," the receptionist greeted as she ended her phone call. "How
can I help you?"

"Hi. I wanted to pull my son out early to take him out to lunch.
Could you call him down?"

"Sure, no problem. Who is your son?"

"Aaron Scott."

"Oh, well actually he is in with the principal right now."

"Oh, did something happen?"

"He got sent down for disrupting class. I'm sure it's nothing major. We never see him down here."

"Yeah, that's really not like him."

"If you wanna have a seat, he should be done with her in a few minutes. She might want to have a word with you as well since you are here anyway."

"Oh, okay, that's fine."

Liam sat down in one of the chairs across from the receptionist's desk. He was concerned about Aaron's behavior. It was out of character for him to get in any kind of trouble. Aaron was very timid around other kids. If he was in trouble for fighting another student, Liam would almost be proud to see him stick up for himself. Disrupting the class, however, was very odd for a boy who didn't like attention.

Liam heard the principal's door open and saw Aaron exit, followed by Mrs. Davis.

"You can head back to class," she directed.

"Actually Mr. Scott is here to see Aaron," the receptionist chimed in.

"Oh, we didn't call home about this did we? I didn't think it warranted a call."

"No, I just was coming to take my son out during his lunch period," Liam clarified.

"Oh, okay. Well, since you're here anyway, do you care to chat for a few minutes?"

"Umm, sure, no problem. Aaron can you wait here?"

"Umm ... sure," Aaron replied with a confused and concerned look on his face.

"Great, come on into my office," Mrs. Davis directed as she motioned for him to go first.

Liam took a seat across from her desk while Mrs. Davis closed the door behind her.

"It's nice to see you Mr. Scott."

"Yes, you too. Sorry, it's been a while since I've been here."

"Oh it's no problem. I just figured, since you're already here, we could talk about what's going on with Aaron."

"Okay."

"So, he was sent here for disrupting class. It seems that his teacher was asking for his participation. He refused and became very snarky with her. Now, I assure you that I see much worse than that on a daily basis around here, so I'm not overly concerned with that on its own. I am concerned, however, with how different Aaron has been acting lately. He's very irritable and becoming somewhat defiant. Do you have an idea of why that would be?"

Liam was a little embarrassed to go into detail about what he was facing as of late, or the way he had been behaving. He decided to be honest without going into much depth.

"Well, my wife and I are working through some things right now."

"Working through some things? Does that mean there is a separation?"

"No, no, nothing like that. We have just been going to therapy together. We're both trying to work on ourselves so we can, you know, be better. And unfortunately, that has created some tension with us, and I've been more grumpy with Aaron. That's why I came to take him to lunch. I wanted to make up for that and, you know, apologize."

"I see. Do you think he understands what's going on between you and your wife?"

"I'm sure he has some knowledge of it. I know our daughter does, so I'm sure he does as well. I just didn't think it was impacting him that much. I don't know; I guess I'm not doing a very good job."

"Mr. Scott, you are here to make up with your son about, say, lashing out at him, something like that. I can assure you, the fact that you are trying means you're doing just fine. Don't beat yourself up. I just wanted to make sure we had an understanding of what was bothering him. You're a good father, Mr. Scott; I can tell. Now go take your son out to lunch."

Liam used every ounce of energy to avoid getting emotional in front of his son's principal, but hearing her affirmation was touching. "Okay, thank you."

He left the office feeling confident about his next endeavor. He looked over to find Aaron sitting quietly, staring at the floor.

"Are you ready to go?"

Aaron looked up, still appearing confused. "Yeah, sure."

They left the office and wandered toward the car. Liam unlocked it and they both hopped inside.

"Dad, I'm really sorry about today," Liam began as he buckled himself in.

"Don't worry about that, Bud. I honestly was coming to take you out to lunch anyway, it had nothing to do with that."

"Oh, okay. So where are we going?"

"Anywhere you want, just not a sit-down restaurant. That will take too long."

"Can we go to the pizza buffet?"

"That sounds good to me."

Liam pulled out of the parking lot and headed for main street. The buffet downtown was a staple for the Scott family, but the males were particularly fond of it.

"So how's your ankle feeling?"

"It's getting better. So Dad, are you sure you just wanted to eat lunch? You didn't come for what happened at school?"

"No, I didn't even know about it. But there was something I wanted to talk about with you."

Aaron became quiet and tense, like he was bracing himself for an injection.

"I need to tell you … I'm sorry about lashing out at you at the dinner table a few weeks ago. I'm working through a lot of stuff, and I was not in a very good place that night. That's not an excuse. I just need you to know that it wasn't about you."

"It's okay, Dad," Aaron said shaking his head. "I should have known better."

"No, Aaron, it's not okay. You should feel free to joke with me, and if I'm not in the mood for that, there is a much better way for me to communicate that to you than exploding like I did. And I need you to know it wasn't about you. It wasn't your fault."

Aaron looked down and couldn't bring himself to say anything. They had just arrived at the buffet. Liam found a parking spot. He turned off the car and looked over at Aaron. He could see a spot on Aaron's jeans where a tear had fallen. Liam reached over and rested his hand upon Aaron's head.

"I love you son, and I'm so proud of the man you are becoming."

Another tear fell from Aaron's face, but he soon began giggling.

"What's so funny?"

"You don't have very good timing, Dad. You got me all crying right before we're going into a restaurant."

Liam burst out in laughter. "Your mom has said that to me many times. I guess I'm still not very good at it."

"Not really."

"Let's just sit here then until you're ready to go in."

They waited for several minutes, giving Aaron's eyes a chance to dry up. Yet there was no awkward silence, only a father and son glad to be in each other's company.

They exited the car and ambled toward the front door of the buffet. The aroma wafting from the building filled their noses and quickened their pace. There was no line, so soon they were scouring the food lines, finding their favorite slices to pile on their plate. After piling up the pizza to a structurally unsound height, they found a table and began devouring. There was little talking. Their mouths were full but smiling ear to ear. After their pace had slowed down, Liam began speaking again.

"I assume you know that your mom and I have been working through some stuff."

Aaron nodded as he continued chewing his food.

"Has that been bothering you?"

Aaron shrugged his shoulders. "I don't know. I guess."

"Well, I want you to know that your mom and I are going to be okay. Relationships are just hard sometimes, but that can help us grow. And I want you to know you can come talk to us if something is bothering you."

"I just kind of hold it in, I guess. It seems easier."

"Yeah, that's one way I wish you weren't like me. It works for a little bit, but it eventually comes out," Liam explained, lamenting the frequency with which that had been happening to him. "You can talk to us, okay?"

"Okay," Aaron said as he quickly stood up. "I'm going for some more." He scurried over to the buffet line. A smile formed across Liam's face, an effortless smile of accomplishment and gratitude. He stared off into space and soaked it in.

33

—

"I WISH YOU HAD TOLD ME," BILL MUTTERED AS HE AND
Joshua methodically hiked through the woods. It was the third day on
this leg of their journey. Three days since they had left Epiphanies, and
Bill was having a difficult time moving forward.

"Told you what?" Joshua asked.

"I wish you had told me about what was going to happen at
Epiphanies."

Joshua laughed to himself. "I did. But ultimately you needed to
experience Epiphanies and appreciate it for what it is. That was much
more important. Besides, you wouldn't have believed me anyway."

Bill hated to admit it, but Joshua was right. Esperanza had told
him exactly what would happen, but he still didn't believe her. He just
didn't want to.

"I know, you're right, I'm just so disappointed that we couldn't stay."

"You need to remember, Bill, that what you think you want isn't
necessarily what's best for you. Many of the things that you wish for-
-if you knew what would really happen, you would never want them
again."

"I guess, but I still don't understand why we had to leave."

"You weren't meant to stay. No one who travels through Epiphanies
is meant to. But you must hold on to the wisdom it gave, and the hope
it inspired in you."

Bill hung his head. That advice seemed too difficult.

Joshua stopped and turned around to face his friend.

"Bill, pull out the gift Esperanza gave you."

"What gift? Oh, you mean that see-through thing?"

"Yes, where is it?"

"It's in my pack. But what good is that going to do, you just look
through it to see what's around you anyway. I don't get the point of it."

"Just trust me."

Bill sighed and dropped his pack. He searched through it and found the gift.

"Now, open the lens."

Bill sighed once more and pulled the lever to unblock the lens. To his surprise, however, he could clearly see Epiphanies through it.

"Whoa, what the … " he expressed in disbelief.

"This device is to remind you of Epiphanies, but more importantly, to remind you of what Epiphanies gave you, what you experienced there. To remember the realization of knowing you don't have to go it alone, of being able to trust another person. Epiphanies is still with you."

A wave of gratitude came over Bill, and he was no longer so bitter about having to leave. He placed the gift back in his pack and hoisted it back over his shoulders. "Okay, I'm ready to go."

They continued their hike. There was a small ascent that they had to overcome, but it seemed to be moderate, and something they could conquer by the end of the day. Joshua led most of the way. He wielded his machete, but did not have to use it as much as Bill expected.

They zigzagged on a fairly well-established path, grasping at limbs and trunks to keep their balance. As always, Rusty had the easiest go at it, at times simply leaping from one leg of the path to another. Every once in a while, he would look back at his two stragglers with his tongue panting, or scolding them for not keeping up.

"Does he realize he's not in charge here?" Joshua asked, laughing to himself.

"Nope, never have been able to convince him of that," Bill replied.

+ + +

A few hours later they had reached the top of the ascent and were well on their way down the other side. The trek was going much faster than Bill had anticipated. By mid-afternoon they had reached the bottom. They moved inward for a few minutes to find a good place to take a break. They dropped their packs and took turns guzzling from the water that Esperanza had given them. Bill grabbed some of the dried meat and found a log to sit on and rest.

"We're making good progress today," Joshua commented."

"Yeah I think so too. I think … "

Bill stopped as they heard twigs being broken behind them. They turned around to find a child who appeared to be just as surprised to find them. He had straggly hair and dirt all over his face. His clothes were all old and worn. The boy locked eyes with Joshua but did not say a word.

"Hello, my young friend," Joshua greeted him.

A slight smile began forming on the boy's face. He turned and looked at Bill, and a wave of anxiety and fear came over him. He turned and began to run away. Joshua quickly stood up.

"It's okay, Son, have no fear."

The child slowed to a stop and stood in place for a moment, seeming to calculate his options. He turned and looked back at Joshua.

"Come on over here, you're not bothering us," Joshua directed as he motioned with his hands.

The boy took nervous steps back toward them. He took a seat across from them, noticeably closer to Joshua, and refused to look at Bill.

"What are you doing out here?" Joshua asked.

The boy sat and looked at the ground, giving no response.

"Are you hungry? We have some food," Joshua said as he extended some dried meat to the child.

The boy reached out and accepted the food. He took a bite and a slight smile formed on his face.

Bill glared at the child. He had strong animosity toward the boy, though he didn't know why. The boy's sad state stirred up anger and frustration within Bill.

"Do you live in this area?" Joshua continued inquiring.

The child shook his head as he continued nibbling on the meat. "I have a home, but I'm not sure how to get back," the boy finally spoke. "I think I'm lost."

"Well, if you want to tag along with us for a while, you're welcome to. Maybe we can even help you find your home."

"Okay," the boy murmured as he continued eating.

"Okay, sounds good to me," Joshua proclaimed. "You know, this might even be a good place to stop for the day. We're not gonna get much further, and this is a really great spot. I'm gonna go grab some firewood." He handed some more of the meat to the boy. "Here, have some more."

Joshua stood back up and ventured into the woods to track down some wood.

"I'll help you, " Bill announced as he jumped up to follow Joshua.

After they were about thirty yards away, Bill approached Joshua and grabbed his arm.

"What are you thinking?"

"What do you mean?" Joshua asked as he bent down to grab a small log.

"We can't have that kid here."

"Why not?"

"Well, for one, he's going to slow us down."

"Bill, he's a kid. You want to leave him out here all alone?"

"He's made it all this time by himself."

"Bill, he's lost, we can help him."

"That's not what we're out here to do. And how would we have any clue where his house is?"

Joshua turned to look at Bill. "What's going on, Bill? Why are you so against helping this child?"

"I just don't like him. There's something not right about him. He just doesn't belong."

"Bill, he's a child. You need to have some compassion."

Joshua walked to their area and began making a spot to start a fire. Bill followed close behind, unhappy with Joshua's decision.

+ + +

A few hours later they were eating dinner with their new companion, warming themselves around the fire. The child had still hardly
spoken since they had met.

"I guess we haven't actually introduced ourselves have we?" Joshua
spoke up. "My name is Joshua, and this is Bill."

The child continued looking down to the ground. A few more minutes passed by with no words.

"So how old are you, son?" Joshua asked.

The child dug around at the dirt for a moment, but then finally
looked up. "I'm nine ... and my name is Liam."

34

"THERE'S SOMETHING I WANT TO SHARE WITH YOU, BUT I'm pretty nervous about it," Liam began, as he took his spot on the couch in Laura's office.

"Well, that's perfectly normal. And we can go as slow as you need. What's on your mind?"

"Well," Liam continued as he wiped his sweaty hands off on his jeans and gasped for breath, "I've been thinking a lot about what we talked about from the last session. About how maybe I project my own anger and feelings of weakness onto others and end up getting angry at them."

"That's good. What thoughts have come from that?"

"I've started to see how I do that with different people in my life. I've really been seeing how it's come out toward our son."

"That's a good insight, Liam. How have you seen that play out?"

Liam took a moment to really process how to put his thoughts into words. "I guess I take his actions as attacks on my abilities."

"Mmm. Wow. Yes. That's a powerful insight," Laura affirmed. "Perhaps you're looking for the attack, like you're on alert for it."

Liam nodded in agreement. "Yes, I think so." He took a moment to gear up for the next thought. "I think I've realized where a lot of this stems from, like some things that happened with my dad."

"Oh wow. That's a big step. And of course, so is sharing it. Is that what you wanted to share today?"

"Yes, it just feels so silly," Liam confessed, shaking his head, "like it shouldn't have that much power over me."

"That's a judgment statement, Liam. That also involves comparisons to how we perceive other people would handle such things," Laura explained. "Things that happen when we are children--we just can't expect that we would have known how to interpret those experiences adequately. And when we are children, we feel powerless, and many times we are powerless, so the way we handled those experiences was the best we could do to survive."

Laura could see a few silent tears rolling down Liam's face. She waited for a moment before she continued. "Liam, there is nothing wrong or right about how your childhood experiences impacted you. It just is, and there is absolutely no shame in that."

Liam nodded his head as he soaked his tears up with his shirt sleeves. Laura pushed the tissue box closer to him, and he grabbed a couple. He composed himself so he could begin speaking again.

"I was nine years old, starting my first game as a pitcher in little league. I remember the thick humid air covering me like a blanket. I began sweating as soon as I stepped outside that day. I didn't care though. I was so excited about pitching. My dad had been a pitcher when he was younger. He played in high school. Passed up on a college scholarship though because he needed a job. I wanted to be like him though. Pitch like him, you know."

"Of course. Most little boys want to be like their dads."

"My dad caught me just before the game to kinda give me a pep talk with his usual message-be tough. I trotted out to the mound and threw a few practice pitches. I felt good, and was really confident as the first batter came up to the plate. That kid grounded out, and I struck out the second one."

"That was a good start," she affirmed.

"It looked like I was going to strike out the third batter too, but I threw a couple balls. I threw the next one and it was too far over the plate. The kid hit it for a double. I don't know what happened after that. It was like I got nervous or something, and my pitches started going all over the place. I walked the next two kids. I don't think I threw a single strike to them. My coach called timeout and came to check in and calm me down. My next pitch ended being too high. The kid crushed it, but fortunately it went straight to the center fielder. I lucked out, so I still felt like I was losing control of my pitches. Our team didn't do much on offense, so I was back out there pitching before I could catch my breath. And I just had no control. The ball went all over the place. A couple batters got base hits, and I walked a few too. The coach came back and pulled me. He told me not to take it too hard, that everybody has games like that. But I felt like I let everyone down. I walked back to the dugout with my head bowed low. I hung out in the dugout for a moment, but I felt like I was going to cry, so I left there and went to find somewhere secluded. I didn't want to draw attention to myself."

He stopped speaking for a moment to gather himself. Laura just sat patiently, giving Liam the space he needed. "I was trying to find a place to hide, but my dad saw me and charged toward me. I could tell he was angry. He told me not to cry. That crying would never help anything, and I just needed to be tough. I couldn't hold it together, and he got so mad at me. He told me I was embarrassing myself and him, and he just walked away, like he was disgusted with me."

Liam wiped his cheeks as the tears dripped from his eyes. He wasn't sure what else to say. "I've never told anyone about that before."

"Liam, I'm sorry you had to go through that. You were displaying normal emotions, and your dad said it was embarrassing. That sends a powerful message to a child," she said as she displayed compassion in her eyes. "What message did you receive from that encounter? Can you remember how you felt or how you reacted to your dad's words?"

Liam sat and waited, trying to let the memory continue to rise in his mind. Emotions slammed like a powerful ocean wave. "I felt so alone," he reflected. "I felt abandoned and rejected."

"Hmm, yes, of course you did, Liam. That would be a very normal response. What happened after that?"

"I tried to be tough. I pulled all my tears in and walked back to the dugout. I sat there in silence, almost stoic."

"That makes sense. The message you had received was your emotions could get you in trouble."

Liam's eyes grew wide. "Yes! That makes so much sense. That's how I operate now. I don't ever want anyone to see me emotional. I definitely wouldn't want anyone to perceive me as weak. Cause that only gets you in trouble."

"I think that it is also pretty telling that even before this encounter with your father, you didn't feel comfortable showing emotion in the dugout. Perhaps that was because you didn't want to be embarrassed around your teammates and coaches. But maybe you had already got a subtle message from your father that emotions weren't okay. Either way, you already had the impression that it wasn't okay to cry, which is a message a lot of people get, but especially males."

"Yeah, that makes sense."

"So you learned that your emotions can get you in trouble. Would you say you beat yourself up whenever you feel emotional?"

"Yes, all the time. I get really angry and I seclude myself from everyone else."

"So maybe your feelings of abandonment and rejection have more to do than with just your dad."

Liam shot Laura a confused look, "How do you mean?"

"Well, it sounds like perhaps your way of protecting yourself as a child was abandoning yourself. You left that little kid behind, the kid who was real and had real feelings, because he got you in trouble. Punishing yourself made you feel like you had some sense of control. And now, anytime you start to feel those emotions again, you punish yourself again. You are hyper-vigilant against any hint of weakness. And you will lash out against yourself or anyone else who you perceive as seeing your weakness, because you're terrified of what could happen."

"So is that why I lashed out at Aaron? Because I thought he was seeing too deep, or seeing something about myself that I didn't want him to see?"

"Yes, exactly. This is how trauma works in our lives."

"I don't know if I would call it trauma."

"It sounds like it was traumatic for you. Experiences impact people in various ways. We have to validate the way people feel to be able to find healing, and that especially includes children, because they don't know how to handle these kinds of things. They need someone to come along and walk with them through it. But so often, they never get to talk about what is hurting in them. That's part of what we are doing

here. We are giving voice to that child inside you who never had anyone to hear him before."

"Yeah, I guess that makes sense."

"If we don't do the hard work that you are doing right now, all
this stuff ends up coming out in less healthy ways because of how we
respond to trauma. Our fight or flight instinct has us on the lookout
for more trauma, and our defensive mechanisms kick in. So sometimes,
maybe you get mad at yourself as a way to counteract other people getting upset with you. Sort of like--you can't hurt me if I hurt me."

"That sounds pretty dysfunctional."

"It is, but when we are kids, it's all we know, and it's better than
nothing. But when we grow up we have to learn better ways to cope,
because our old ways end up hurting us as well as the people around
us."

Liam smiled and nodded. "I'm really starting to see how true that is
for me. I just wish I could do better."

"That's why you're here. That's why you're doing this work. Not to
do better, per se, but to heal and learn to live from a healthier place.
Then the 'doing better' just begins to come from within you more nat-
urally." Laura paused to look at her watch. "Well, that's it for today."

35

BILL WOKE UP THE NEXT MORNING TO THE SOUND OF laughter. He peaked his eyes open to see Joshua and Liam infatuated with something moving on the ground. Liam had a huge smile on his face as Joshua played with whatever they had found. Bill grew more annoyed as he watched them.

He sat up and tried to get a good look. "What are you guys doing?"

The smile disappeared from Liam's face as he turned to see Bill sitting up.

"Oh, sorry Bill," Joshua replied, "we were just laughing at this little frog over here. He is so cute!" Bill didn't seem to be amused. "Anyway, we were thinking that we probably wanna get going soon."

"We?" Bill responded in a snarky tone.

"Yes, Liam and I."

Bill was beginning to feel like an outsider, and the contempt he had for the child continued to grow.

Bill saw that Liam and Joshua had already eaten breakfast.

"We have some leftover eggs and berries if you want to eat some," Joshua proposed.

"No thanks," Bill scowled. He approached his pack and ate a couple strips of dried meat.

"So Liam, do you have an idea of where your home is?" Joshua asked.

"I think it's on the north end of the valley, but I haven't been able to figure out which way is north, the tree cover is so thick."

"We can help you with that, since we just came down from the mountains?"

"How did you end up out here anyway?" Bill asked rather sharply.

"I was looking for you?" Liam answered.

"What?" Bill said, frustrated by what he perceived to be a nonsense response. "How could you be looking for me? You don't even know me, or know where I was?"

Liam shrugged his shoulders, which irked Bill even more as he shoved his items back into his pack. Joshua gave him a stern look, which caught Bill off guard and urged him to calm himself down.

"So do you have a sense of how far we are from your home?" Joshua continued his query.

"Not really. But I don't think I've been gone that long. The area gets thornier as you get closer to it."

"That'll be fun," Bill thought to himself.

The three pilgrims finished packing up their items and set out for the north. Joshua led and had Liam follow behind him. Bill followed behind them both, which added to his irritation about Liam's presence. Rusty, always one to be fascinated with the latest addition, kept close to Liam.

"So Liam, are there any other landmarks we can keep our eyes open for on the way?" Joshua asked.

"I know there's a creek we'll cross. Other than that, I'm not sure."

"How big is the creek?"

"I was about waist deep in it."

"That'll be nice to find."

As the day proceeded onward, the travelers entered terrain that was becoming rockier. At first the rocks were very small, like gravel. Gradually they grew in size. The travelers' progress slowed as they tip-toed around the obstacles, trying their best to avoid a spill.

Soon they arrived at a small hill. Rusty rushed up it, as though he were trying to impress everyone. Once at the top, he jolted around and urged the other three to hurry up.

"We'll need to be careful here," Joshua instructed.

They began climbing up, bending back and forth to keep their balance. Joshua seemed to have little problem, as did Liam. Bill stayed low, trying his best to avoid tipping over. Once Joshua reached the top, he turned around and offered his hand to help Liam up the last step. He pulled Liam up with an exerting tug.

"There we go," he affirmed as he turned and offered his hand to Bill next.

"I'm fine," Bill responded, waving away Joshua's hand.

"You're almost there," Joshua insisted with his hand still extended.

"I said I'm fine!" Bill snarled.

"Okay, see you up here then," Joshua concluded as he turned and walked away.

Bill grasped the rocks as he pulled himself up, his anger powering him forward. He inched closer to the top and took one last lunge to complete his ascent. He stood doubled over as air shot in and out of his mouth like a cannon. After catching his breath, he looked up to see Joshua and Liam standing with their backs to him, apparently assessing the next leg of the journey. Rusty was pawing at the ground next to them, attempting to catch a critter.

Bill approached and looked down at a hill comparable to the one they just scaled. The rocks seemed to be dissipating more the further he looked. Eventually, his eyes became lost in the trees as they appeared to be more populous as well.

"You ready to continue?" Joshua asked while staring ahead.

"Yes, I'm fine, let's go," Bill insisted.

Joshua took the lead once again, scouting out nooks and crannies where feet could get caught or loose boulders could give way. Rusty showed off his skills once again, passing him easily. Joshua advanced ten feet or so before Liam proceeded to follow him. Bill took his time, not longing to be close to either one of them.

The descent seemed to be going well. Suddenly, Liam screamed in fear as the rock he was standing on moved beneath him. He tried jumping to another one but slipped and slammed his knee into it.

"Liam!" Joshua yelled as he climbed back up to check him out. Tears were streaming down Liam's face as he writhed from the pain. Joshua reached Liam and began examining his leg. "Can I see it?" He asked as he reached out his hand.

Liam nodded in compliance as he tried his best to hold back the tears. Joshua could see where the knee had hit the rock. There was bruising already starting to form.

"Yeah, that looks like it's gonna hurt for a while. Can you bend your leg at all?"

Liam tried to accommodate him, but his leg wouldn't respond. He screamed in pain again.

Bill looked on with impatience and bitterness. The contempt he felt for the child continued to grow. He knew it was not the proper response, but something about Liam bothered him to his core. He did not trust anything about him.

"Okay, well, here's what we need to do then," Joshua continued. "Let's sit here until the pain begins to subside some. Fortunately, the rocks look like they are becoming less prominent, so I'll carry you to the bottom of this hill, and we'll go from there. Maybe the pain will be manageable enough that you can limp your way through. I'm sure we can find a good walking stick out here somewhere among these trees. Sound like a plan?"

Liam nodded in agreement, while Bill just sat silent and refused to speak. He was less and less thrilled with the trajectory of this trip, and he was not going to stay quiet forever.

+ + +

Liam's leg eventually stopped throbbing. He was able to put a little weight on it, but not without a lot of pain.

"Okay, are you ready to try this?" Joshua asked.

"Yes, I will be okay," Liam responded.

"Bill, can you come grab my pack?" Joshua requested.

Bill huffed, stood up, and climbed down to where they were. Joshua lifted Liam over his shoulder and gingerly strode down the hill, careful to keep his balance each step of the way.

Once down the hill, Joshua found a spot to set Liam down against a tree where he could rest. He looked back and saw Bill strolling down the stones. "Bill be careful, we can't afford for two of us to be hurt," he chided.

"Yes, let's all take care of the kid," Bill grumbled to himself.

Joshua grabbed one of the canisters and took a long drink from it. "Well, that was interesting," he commented with a chuckle.

"I'm sorry I made it worse," Liam apologized.

"You have nothing to be sorry for, Liam, it could have happened to any of us, right Bill?"

Bill tried to slyly roll his eyes as he took a sip of the water as well, but he was not as discrete as he had hoped. Joshua scolded him with a look.

"I think we need to stay here for the night," Joshua resumed. "Hopefully you can put a little more weight on that leg tomorrow, Liam."

"We're stopping for the day?" Bill protested. "We have at least five more hours of daylight."

"We need to. Liam needs a chance to let his leg rest. I'm going to go look for some firewood."

"Wait, you can't be serious," Bill chided.

"Bill, he can't walk; what else should we do?" Joshua rhetorically asked as he walked away.

Bill stood in disbelief, flush with frustration and anger. He couldn't think straight, couldn't understand why everything was becoming so difficult and hard fought. He stared at Liam, wondering how hurt he really was, and raged at the weakness personified he was seeing. He lost all patience and stormed into the woods after Joshua.

He trampled down all the branches, leaves, and brush in his way. He stormed through the trees and found his target. "Joshua!" He called out, wanting to tell him off immediately. "Joshua!"

Soon Joshua ran in from the outskirts. "What? What's wrong?"

"What the hell are we doing?"

"What are you talking about?"

"Why the hell are we really staying here?"

"You're still on this?"

"That kid is just slowing us down!"

"Are you serious? What do you want us to do, just leave him out here?"

"He's made it this far on his own, and I don't trust him."

"Bill, he's a little kid, what could you possibly not trust about him?"

"It's just a feeling."

"Bill, this is ridiculous," Joshua concluded as he ventured back to find more fire wood.

Bill trampled off in the other direction.

36

LIAM UNBUTTONED HIS SHIRT TO GET READY FOR BED. The sound of Rachel's toothbrush motor echoed from the bathroom as Liam pulled his pajamas from the dresser. He tossed them on the bed and placed his dirty clothes in the hamper.

His stomach twisted as he heard Rachel finish brushing her teeth. It felt so long since he and Rachel had really connected. As much as he was still angry about what happened between her and her ex-boyfriend, she was still the person he longed to be closest to.

Rachel emerged from the bathroom, brushing her hair as Liam was sliding his pajama pants on. She shot him a soft smile.

"How was your day, Babe?" She asked.

"Um, it was okay," he replied with a slow nod. He tried to keep his eyes down to avoid any further discussion. He felt as though he was at the pool on a summer day. He longed to jump in, but the crisp cold of the water kept him at bay. He kept his eyes down, but he could feel Rachel's eyes piercing through him.

"Are you doing okay?" Rachel asked.

Liam continued looking to the floor. Words seemed to escape him. He felt Rachel approach him. His heartbeat sped up with each step she took closer. He felt her hand grace his cheek and lower to lift his chin.

"Honey, if there's something you need to talk about, you know I'm here to listen, right? I'm not going to get upset with you. I want to know what's going on inside."

Liam looked at her sheepishly. "I'm not very good at this. You know, talking about my thoughts and feelings. I feel like I'm just stumbling around in the dark," he confessed.

"Well, then just follow my voice, okay? There's no right or wrong way to do this. Just say what's going on in your mind."

Liam moved over to the bed and sat down on the edge. Rachel sat next to him. "I think I'm starting to understand what role I've played in this," he began.

"The role you've played in what?" Rachel inquired.

"You know, like how we've got to be where we are. With our marriage, with us needing counseling."

"Oh, okay," Rachel responded, trying to give Liam room to elaborate.

"Laura and I have been talking about my relationship with my dad, and how it may have affected me."

"Oh wow, that's really good, Babe. I wanted to ask you about what happened at Aaron's game, but I wasn't sure if it was something you were ready to talk about."

"Yeah, I just kind of snapped I guess. Working through this stuff has made we aware of how much he has bothered me. My dad is a tough man. I mean, I do believe he loves me and cares about me, but it also seemed like I wasn't good enough for him. Like I wasn't tough enough for him."

"I can see how that could be. Honestly, your dad doesn't seem to think that anyone's tough enough for him."

"Yeah, well, as his son, I felt it all the time." Liam took a moment to catch his breath. He wasn't used to sharing this much with anyone, let alone two people in a short span of time.

"I just never felt like I was good enough for him, like he always looked down on me."

"So what do you think started that all back up again for you? I mean, I feel like something shifted for you at some point, like it got harder or something, because you've been closed off for over a year, at least. Did something happen that stirred it up again?"

Liam tried to reflect on what had caused it. He thought about all that had happened over the last couple years. He remembered getting the promotion from Donald, and how ecstatic he was about it. But something did shift in him. All of a sudden, he remembered a conversation he had with his dad.

"I think I might know what it was?"

"Oh yeah?"

"It was about six months after I got the promotion. I hadn't told my dad about it because I just didn't want him to spoil it. He always has a way of saying something. Or maybe, I just read into what he says because of how our relationship has been. Anyway, I finally told him about it. He was really excited about it, really happy for me. He started talking about how he had worked his way up the ranks at the mechanic's shop, and how we both got promoted, and he said, "Like father, like son." I know it was a proud moment for him, but it just sent a lot of difficult thoughts through my head."

"Like what?"

"I just started thinking, do I want to be like my dad? I mean, I always had a hard time with him, so the thought of being like him was really difficult. I just began noticing a lot of different ways I am like him, like the way I say things, my mannerisms, and it just kept psyching me out."

"I can understand that."

"But I think the thing that was hardest for me was that I just kept thinking--Do I even have what it takes? Am I strong enough to be like my dad? And what if I don't measure up, what is going to happen then? It just got to me. I stopped enjoying my job after that. I didn't like my job for a long time. It just felt like this huge test to see if I had what it took, and I was so afraid that I didn't."

Rachel reached over and swung her arms around him. "Honey, I'm so sorry. I'm sure that was really difficult."

Liam sat for a moment and soaked in Rachel's affection. He was not used to showing this side of himself; being affirmed in that space felt even more foreign. But it also felt good and right.

"I guess in some ways part of me still feels like that kid, and not thinking that I'm good enough. Not just to my dad, but to everyone around me. I guess I'm just so scared of feeling that way that I do everything I can to try to impress, and not show any signs of weakness."

Every time Liam shared more, it seemed as though Rachel squeezed him a little tighter.

"So what I'm trying to say," Liam continued, "is that I can see why you felt so distant from me. I mean, I guess I really didn't give you much, because I didn't really think I had much to offer. And I was afraid that if I gave too much, you'd see through me. You know, see my weaknesses and failures, and want to walk away."

Rachel sat back up. She turned his face toward her own with her hand and looked deep into his eyes. "That would never make me love you less. That would make me love you more. I just want to know you and be close to you. All of you. Your strengths and your weaknesses. Your triumphs and your struggles. And I want to share mine with you. Because then we can really be a team. Celebrate together and cry together. Stand tall and hold each other when we have nothing left."

"I want that too. I really do."

They embraced again and held on tight for several minutes. They continued talking late into the night until Rachel finally thought to look at the time. They finished their nightly routines, slid into bed, and fell asleep in each other's arms.

37

IT HAD BEEN A COUPLE DAYS SINCE LIAM'S FALL ON THE rocks. He was now able to walk on his own again, and they were making some decent progress. Bill continued to be frustrated with Liam's presence, but kept his distance as best as he could. He just wanted to get the kid back to his house so he and Joshua could move on and find a quality place to put down roots.

"I think I can hear some water!" Joshua shouted.

"This area looks pretty familiar," Liam expressed.

Bill dropped his pack in excitement and ran past Joshua. "I hear it too," he confirmed. He continued up a small hill and rose to the top as fast as he could. He stumbled a few times and finally fell near the top. He peered down to see water between the trees. "I can see it!" He yelled out. Bill hadn't believed Liam's claim that water was nearby and was pleasantly surprised to see that he was wrong. His face was beaming with glee. As he continued to scan the area, he saw so much about it that reminded him of his precious river by the cabin.

Joshua and Liam climbed up the hill and caught up to Bill. "I bet there's plenty of fish down there too," Bill conjectured.

"I would imagine so," Joshua concurred. "This looks like a great place to stop for the day."

"Yeah, for the day, right," Bill responded smirked.

Bill went back to retrieve his pack while Joshua helped Liam get down the other side of the hill to the stream. Rusty ran ahead of all of them and began playing in the water. Bill retrieved his pack and made his way to the creek. The hill was steep enough that he had to lean backwards to keep from falling and sliding down face first. As he moved past the trees on the hill, the creek fully revealed itself in all it's breathtaking glory.

"Bill, do you wanna try out your luck with the fish? I'm going to scope out the place and see what food we can scavenge while we're here."

Joshua began walking away. Bill looked over and saw Liam leaning against a nearby log, trying to rest his knee. Bill bolted up and rushed over to catch Joshua.

"Hey, you're just gonna leave me here with the kid?" Bill demanded.

"Yeah. He's not a baby. You don't have to take care of him."

"It's not that. You know it's not that. I don't like the kid. There's something not right about him."

"C'mon Bill. What is it? Really what do you think it is?"

"I don't know, but I'm not staying here with him myself. You're the one who wanted to help him."

"Okay fine, I'll do the fishing, and you can go scavenging."

"Okay fine."

"Just try to gather enough that we can take with us tomorrow," Joshua directed as he began walking back.

"Wait, are you serious?" Bill asked as he stopped Joshua. "You really wanna leave here tomorrow?"

"Of course. We haven't made it to his house yet."

"Joshua, c'mon. We don't even know if he's telling the truth. And we found this creek that could give us everything we need. We need to stay here."

"I'm helping that child, Bill. I'm taking him back home."

Bill was beside himself. "Fine. Go on your own then. I'm staying here."

"Do what you have to do," Joshua conceded.

Joshua returned to the creek while Bill moved out into the perimeter. He began by gathering firewood and transporting it back to the camp. He jetted back out to look for something edible. He used the machete to maneuver through some of the dense areas. As he pushed through, he stopped in his tracks, stunned at the sight before him.

A beautiful peach tree illuminated the foliage around it. It might as well have had a halo hanging over the top of its branches. Bill charged ahead to have a taste of one of the round gifts. He plucked one from the closest branch and sunk his teeth as deep as he could into the fruit. Juice poured down his chin. "Oh my word!" He exclaimed as clearly as he could with a mouth full of decadence.

He finished his treat and gathered as many as he could to bring back to the camp. He turned to head back and tripped over a stick and landed hard on his side. "Aah!" He yelled in pain. Something hurt, worse than just in a normal trip and fall. He turned on his back and felt around to find the pain. He ran his hands up and down his abdomen and felt an object protruding from his side. He looked down to find a sizable thorn that had broken the skin.

"Damn! Thorn my ass! This is a damn spike!" He exclaimed as he pulled the thorn out. Though the thorn had broken the skin, there wasn't a lot of blood. After examining it more, he was satisfied that it would hurt for a few days, but that it would be fine.

He retrieved the peaches he had dropped and gathered some new ones to replace those that were bruised. He made his way back to the camp to reveal the treasure he had found.

"I found a treat for us," Bill announced as he arrived. Rusty ran over and jumped up and down all around him.

"Oh, what do you have there?" Joshua asked, obviously intrigued.

"There's a gorgeous peach tree about fifty yards back that way. I've already sampled one, and it was amazing."

"Sounds great Bill. I've already caught a fish, so maybe we'll be feasting tonight."

Bill set the peaches down in a pile next to his pack. As he was bent over, Liam pointed to his side.

"You're bleeding," Liam advertised.

Joshua turned around and glanced at Bill's side. "Oh Bill, what happened?"

"I'll be fine, I just fell on one of those thorns Liam mentioned. That sucker was huge."

"You need to check it out," Liam advised, "some of those thorns are poisonous."

"Yeah Bill," Joshua agreed as he pulled his pole back and laid it down. "Let me have a look at that."

"I'm fine."

"Bill, I insist. I can have a better look at it than you can since it's on your side."

"Okay fine, if you're gonna keep going on about it."

Joshua walked over and had Bill sit down on a log. Bill lifted the shirt up while Joshua examined it.

"That doesn't look promising. The coloring around it doesn't look good."

"What do you mean?" Bill asked.

"Liam, can you come look at this?" Joshua requested.

"No, I'm fine," Bill inserted, uncomfortable with the idea.

"Bill, this is Liam's area. Maybe he's seen this before. I'm here, just trust me."

Bill reluctantly agreed and Liam approached.

"I have seen this before," Liam said. "This is a dangerous thorn. It's poisonous. The poison moves slowly, but it can shut down your body. We need to get something to counteract the poison."

Bill looked away, frustrated and suspicious of Liam's ability to diagnose anything.

"Is there something around here that will help?" Joshua asked.

"There's a plant that's pretty rare. I haven't seen it in the wild in some time. But I've kept some growing at my home for this reason."

"No!" Bill yelled as he jolted up. "I know where this is going. I said I'm staying here, and I still intend to. I will be fine."

"Bill, that's not a good idea," Joshua replied.

Bill shot Joshua a stern look. "I'm staying."

Joshua raised his hands in surrender. "Look, it's up to you. You can do what you want."

"Oh can I? Can I do what I want? Thanks for the permission," Bill snarked.

Joshua returned to his fishing pole and cast it back into the water. Liam worked on cleaning the first fish that Joshua had caught. Bill returned to the perimeter looking for other food and resources. A pain shot up his side. He stopped to feel it and realized the pain was spreading up his body. He stubbornly continued his search.

38

"HI SWEETIE!" SUSIE SAID AS ELIZABETH APPROACHED her grandparents' front door. It was time for their monthly trip to visit Liam's parents. Elizabeth and Aaron were as excited as they usually were. Rachel and Liam both dreaded the tension that they anticipated around Frank from their interactions at the basketball game.

"Oh, I love seeing you kids!" Susie exclaimed. "How's the ankle feeling?" She asked.

"It's good," Aaron answered. "It was a sprain, so it hurt for a while, but it's getting better."

"I'm sure glad to hear that. Well, go on in. There's some cookies in the kitchen." The two youngsters raced in to find the treats. "How are you, Girlie?"

"I'm doing good mom. It's good to see you," Rachel responded as she wrapped her arms around Susie.

"Aww, it's good to see you too, Sweetie."

Rachel entered the house and Liam inspected his mother's face. He had been concerned with the aftermath of the basketball game. Exhaustion was draped across his mother's eyes, the kind that only his dad's stubbornness could produce.

"You look tired, Mom," Liam remarked.

"Oh I'm fine," she replied, waving her hand through the air as if she was swatting a bug away, "just need some more sleep that's all." She gave Liam a tight hug.

"Dad!" Aaron's voice exclaimed from inside the house.

"Yeah?"

"You wanna play catch out back?"

"Sure! I'll meet you out there." Liam stepped inside. Susie followed and closed the door behind her.

"Mom?"

"Yeah, Dear?"

"What's dad been up to? You know since the game?"

Susie patted him on the back. "Oh we can talk about that later. Go play with your son."

Liam was not too thrilled with that answer, but he decided not to press his mom too much. He ventured out to the back yard where Aaron was waiting with a football.

"Go long," Aaron directed. Liam jogged to the other side of the yard and Aaron launched it to him. The ball sailed over Liam's outstretched hands as he stumbled over to retrieve it.

"You must think I'm pretty tall," Liam chuckled as he tossed the ball back to Aaron. They continued throwing the ball back and forth for the next several minutes. Aaron attempted all kinds of throws, trying to test his dad's catching abilities.

"Do you think Grandpa would want to play with us?"

"Um … " Liam hesitated, "I don't think he's going to be in the mood for that, but you're welcome to ask him."

"Oh, that's okay," Aaron responded, knowing what his dad's hesitation meant.

They tossed the ball around for a few more minutes until Rachel poked her head out. "Aaron, we're about to play Monopoly," she said with a grin, knowing it was Aaron's favorite game.

"Do you mind, Dad?" Aaron asked, not wanting to leave his dad hanging.

"No, go ahead," he replied with a smile.

Aaron ran inside. Liam followed closely behind and found his mom in the kitchen.

"Hey, Mom. That smells great! What are you making?"

"Just some spaghetti sauce," she said as she stirred her concoction.

"So … " Liam said, attempting a transition. "Should I go talk to dad?"

Susie sighed. "You know how your dad is when he's frustrated about something. A complete horse's ass. Talk to him at your own risk is all I'm saying."

"Yeah, I know, Mom. I just don't want him to be upset."

"Don't worry about that. Can't talk sense into him no matter what you do."

"Yep," Liam snickered. "I'll take my chances."

Liam shuffled down to his dad's television room. He could hear the familiar sound of sports echoing down the hall. He entered with caution.

"Hey, Dad."

Frank turned and greeted Liam with an expressionless face. "Oh, hey," he replied with zero enthusiasm.

"What are you watching?" Liam asked.

"Just some game. Couple small schools I've never heard of."

Liam sat and watched for a few minutes. Both men were silent.

"Aaron's ankle is okay," Liam blurted out.

"Okay," Frank barely acknowledged.

"I just figured since we hadn't seen you since the game you might be wondering."

Frank turned his head toward Liam and gave him a stern look. "So are we gonna talk about what the hell happened back there?"

"Look, Dad. I'm sorry I chewed you out. I'm just working through a lot of stuff right now, and it seems like all you ever talk about is being tough, like that's all that matters to life, and it just got to me."

"Well that's because it is all that matters. You wanna make it through life, you gotta be tough. That's the truth. You don't like it? Then you're just gonna make things harder on yourself."

"See this is what I'm talking about, dad. I mean, maybe you've made life harder on yourself by just trying to tough things out all the time."

"Where the hell are you getting this stuff?"

Liam knew going any further was only going to stir the pot faster. He wasn't sure if he could handle it, but he felt he had come too far not to try.

"I've been seeing a therapist, and she … "

"Oh gosh," Frank exclaimed with a condescending laugh. "There's your problem right there."

"I figured you wouldn't appreciate it."

"No I don't. All it does is get you to waste your time and money talking about things you can't do nothing about. Then you come in here whining about your job and your feelings, when it's not gonna change anything."

"So, I just have to be tough, right, Dad? That's your master plan?"

"That's life, that's what I've learned, and I tried to pass it on to you. Maybe it didn't stick."

Liam felt his blood pressure rising fast. "What's that supposed to mean?"

"Nothing."

"I know what it means. You think you're tougher than everyone. Everyone else is just weak. You made that abundantly clear when I was a kid, and a lot of good it did me."

"So what? I wasn't a good father?"

"That's not what I'm saying."

"You have no idea what you're talking about," Frank exclaimed as he stood up from his chair. "You don't know what a bad father is. I can show what one looks like. Go look at my dad. Go look at him. You have no idea."

"I know, Dad; that's not what I'm saying."

"You know what, just leave me alone. Just leave me alone." Frank sat back down and stared at the television.

Liam got up and left the room, but turned back toward his dad once more before he left.

"I just wanted to talk. To share what's going on. I don't know why we can't just do that."

"I've shared with you everything I know. If you don't wanna listen that's your business."

Liam stormed out of the room. He stomped through the hallway and the kitchen, out to the backyard. As he exited the back door, Susie shook her head in dismay. "No one wants to listen."

She finished the sauce and turned off the stove top. She walked out the back door and headed over to the swing where Liam was sitting.

"I know what you're gonna say, Mom," Liam informed as he stared straight ahead.

"I'm not gonna say it, because I don't need to," she responded as she sat down next to him.

"I just don't understand why he's like that. I guess I never have."

"Oh, I know, Honey. I guess I never have either. I mean, I know what he went through as a child, but I figured he would get better with age and soften up a little. It just never happened. Don't get me wrong. He can be caring and sweet, but just in his own gruff way."

"I'd take gruff over what I got."

"Oh yeah? And what did you get?"

"I'm just saying, I wish that just once I could be good enough for him."

"Oh Honey, is that really what you think?"

"That's how it feels."

She wrapped her arm around his back. "That man thinks the world of you. He lights up whenever he knows you're coming. Maybe not today, because he doesn't know what to do with you when you stand up to him. I know it's hard to see, but he has immense respect for you when you do that, but it makes him wonder what he did wrong. He knows he's a huge horse's ass, and he knows at the end of the day he's lucky to have people that will put up with it."

"Then why is he such an asshole?"

"Because he's afraid. He's afraid that he did a bad job as a father. He's afraid that he failed like his dad did."

"But he's nothing like grandpa."

"Well, you and I know that, but for some reason he doesn't see it. He's spent all his life trying to be anything but his dad, but he can't convince himself that he isn't no matter what. Don't let this get you down. Just give him some space, and trust me when I tell you he loves you more than you can imagine."

39

BILL WOKE UP THE NEXT MORNING WITH A DULL ACHE running through his body. His head was covered with sweat and his heart was racing. His pain had awakened him before the other two. He gingerly got up and went to splash some water on his face. Each step was labored. He lowered to his knees, dipped his hands into the river, and brought the water up to his face. The coolness felt soothing, but it did little to relieve the pain he was feeling.

He heard some rustling behind him and turned to see Joshua rising.

"Good morning, Bill. How are you feeling?"

"I'm fine," Bill responded as he had difficulty getting to his feet. "I'm fine, really."

"Have you checked out your side yet?"

"Not yet."

"Let me look at it. I would really feel better if I checked you out one more time."

"Fine, if it'll get you off my back, go ahead."

Joshua moved over to where Bill was standing and directed him to lift up his shirt.

"Oh no!" Joshua exclaimed.

"C'mon, don't try to scare me."

"I'm not, Bill, look at it yourself."

Bill lifted his arm and looked down to his side. Red lines were spreading from the puncture site. His heart began racing even faster.

"Look, Bill, I can't make you do something you don't want to do, but I think it's very dangerous for you to stay here."

Bill nodded his head in agreement, frustrated that it had come to this. It seemed he wasn't suited to be anywhere. Not his cabin, not Epiphanies, and not here. He wondered if he would ever find a place to call home again.

Joshua woke Liam up and informed him of the change of plans. They ate breakfast as quickly as they could, partaking in peaches and leftover fish from the night before. Rusty could tell that Bill was not feeling well. He wouldn't leave his side for a moment.

Joshua pulled Liam aside as they were packing up. "Liam, do you have an idea of how far your place is from here?"

Liam nodded, "It usually takes about a day and a half to get here from my home. But it'll be more like two days with the pace that he's gonna be able to maintain."

"How long will it take that poison to get to him?"

"It works slow. Probably a week or so. But we're gonna be moving, so it'll work through his system a little faster. We need to get to my home as soon as possible."

Once again, Joshua carried both packs to help Bill. Fortunately, the terrain they would be covering was not nearly as rugged as they had traveled on previously. Now, they would simply have a lot of walking to complete.

They set out across the creek and continued heading north. Bill was still frustrated, but tried his best not to focus on that, as it took energy away that he dearly needed for this trip. To make the journey go faster, they determined to take very few breaks. Joshua would periodically hand out food and water to keep all of them sustained.

As the hours dragged on, Bill's pain increased. The sweat poured out of him like a sieve. During the afternoon, as the sun increased the heat around them, his body became weaker and weaker. They ascended a small hill, and Bill fell to one knee and leaned against a tree. Joshua ran back to look after him.

"Bill! Are you okay? Can you make it back up?"

Bill could not respond right away. After a couple moments, he signaled for Joshua to help him to stand, and they continued their walk. Joshua remained with Bill for a while, and allowed Bill to lean on him as they walked. Eventually, Bill was able to walk on his own again and motioned for Joshua to return to his position.

The day grew warmer, and Bill's body was soaked with sweat. As the afternoon dragged on, Bill began to appear delirious. Joshua would often check on him but could not understand the nonsense words Bill was saying. They finally reached a point where Bill could not go any further, and they found a spot to camp for the night.

Joshua laid down the packs and made sure Bill had a good place to rest. He hustled out to find some firewood so he wouldn't have to leave Bill for very long. Meanwhile, Liam worked on making a clean site for the fire. As they were working on their tasks, Bill seemed to be zoned out, when in fact he was beginning to see things around him.

Bill looked up at a tree hanging over them. It looked just like a tree that had stood close to his cabin. Suddenly he was transported to his old home, and he turned his head to see his old cabin standing about fifty yards away. He could hear the burble of his beloved river nearby. Soon, the entire scene was transformed into his old home. He pulled himself up. As Liam focused on his task, Bill stumbled forward, longing to return to his cabin. The door was open, and he could see inside the home he so dearly loved. He reached out his arms as he got closer. Rusty barked behind him, trying to warn Liam. Bill heard the barking, but assumed it came from within the cabin. As Bill came close, Joshua arrived with an armful of firewood. He saw Bill walking away and called out for him. Bill lunged for the cabin, but instead tripped, fell over, and slid down a small hill. He came to a crashing halt at the bottom and cried out in pain.

Liam and Joshua ran over to assess the damage. Joshua rolled him over and Bill writhed in pain.

"Look," Liam directed as he pointed to another thorn that was inserted into Bill's leg.

"Oh no! Another one over here," Joshua announced as he noticed a thorn in Bill's shoulder. "This is not good."

"We really can't afford to stay here overnight," Liam surmised.

"I really don't want to be traveling at night," Joshua confessed, "But we may not have a choice." Joshua leaned over Bill and, grabbing his arms, swung him over his shoulder. "Let's get him back up there and figure out how we're gonna do this."

Joshua carried Bill up to the top and laid him down. He opened his pack and pulled out some rope and cloth. "I can't carry him; I won't be able to move fast enough." He formed the rope into a type of harness that he could tie around Bill. He then manipulated the other end of the rope to tie around his waist. He attached the cloth to Bill's back to protect him from the ground as much as possible.

"Liam, are we getting close to your house? Do you feel like you can get us there now?"

"Yes, I can get us there."

Joshua peered up through the trees and saw the sky growing dim.

"What about at night? If we have a torch to give us some light?"

"I think so. Maybe. There are two trees that form an archway to a path that leads to the house. If we can find that, the rest will be pretty easy."

"Well, we're going to have to try our best. I don't think we have a choice."

Liam nodded in agreement. Joshua swung his pack over his back, with Liam's pack attached to it. Liam would be carrying Bill's pack now. He strained under its weight, but he insisted that he was able.

They continued north, ducking through the trees, and found the smoothest route possible so Joshua could continue dragging Bill. Rusty trotted alongside Bill, clearly concerned and confused. Occasionally, Joshua would have to drop his packs in order to lift Bill over a fallen tree limb or some rough rocks along the way. His muscles screamed as he carried on, leaning forward to gain more leverage.

The daylight continued to diminish, as did the ease of their mission. Before it became too dark, they stopped and formed two torches for them to light their way. Liam's ability to navigate through the terrain became strained as he paused several times to reassess their direction. As the darkness grew thicker, he came to a complete stop.

"I … I'm not sure where to go from here."

"Do you have an idea?"

"I'm pretty sure we need to go this way," he answered as he pointed to the right. "But we might need to go straight too. I'm sorry, it's just really hard to tell with it being so dark."

Joshua laid his pack down and unwrapped the harness from around his waist. He walked over to Liam and knelt to meet him at eye level.

"I'm sorry, I just don't know what to do," Liam insisted.

"You do know, Liam. You just need to trust yourself. Trust your instincts."

"But I mess so many things up, I'm afraid I'm going to mess this up too," he confessed as he looked down to the ground.

"Liam, look at me," Joshua directed. "Look at me, Liam." Liam looked up and met Joshua's eyes. "I am here with you, and I'm not going anywhere, so you don't need to be afraid. Just tell me which way your heart is directing you."

Liam started to speak, but hesitated.

"What is it, just trust your gut."

Liam pointed toward the right. "It's that way. We need to go that way."

"Okay, then we go that way," Joshua concluded as he squeezed Liam's shoulder. He returned to Bill, placed the harness back around his waist, and hoisted the packs over his back. "Let's go."

Liam started up the direction to the right. They made their way up a slight hill that leveled out at the top. They continued on a windy, but relatively smooth trail for about an hour.

Liam froze.

"What is it?" Joshua asked.

"I think I hear something," he whispered back.

As they stood still, Joshua began to hear it too-some rustling in the trees. He laid down his packs and untied the rope from around his waist.

"Stay still," he directed. "I'm gonna grab the revolver out of Bill's pack, just in case we need to scare something away."

He opened up the pack and reached in for the gun. He dragged it out and crouched down, trying to scan the area as best he could. Liam knelt right next to him. Rusty began growling. Joshua pulled him close to keep him quiet. The rustling grew louder. They braced themselves for the unknown.

A deer burst through the tree line about ten feet in front of them and galloped across the path. They both fell backwards, scared out of their minds. After the fear wore off, they laughed hysterically, relieved that it was nothing more dangerous.

"Well, that was fun," Joshua concluded as they stood back up.

"That's one way to put it," Liam commented.

They returned to their traveling positions and continued.

After another hour or so, Liam was getting more concerned. "I hope we haven't missed anything," Liam thought out loud.

"Don't worry about that, we'll just keep going. This is the right way, I trust you."

They persisted on through the night, sluggish and exhausted. Joshua's body was screaming at him, and he had to take a few breaks from dragging his friend across the ground.

After another hour or so, Liam stopped in his tracks.

"What is it?" Joshua asked, concerned there was more commotion in the trees. Liam remained silent, just staring ahead. "Liam, are you okay? What is it?"

"I can't believe it; we found them?"

"Found what?"

"The two trees, the path to the house. We're almost there!"

"Yes! Yes! See, I knew you could do it, Liam!" Joshua exclaimed.

"Wow. I really did," Liam admitted.

40

LIAM'S EYES HESITATED TO OPEN. IT HAD BEEN SEVERAL weeks since the blowup between him and his dad, and everyday had been a chore since then. The pit in his stomach had not subsided, leaving him longing to stay under the covers. He could not tell by the light outside what time it would be, and he was afraid to check his phone in fear that he would need to get up soon. His curiosity got the better of him, and he peaked at his phone. To his dismay, his alarm was only minutes away from going off. He begrudgingly switched off his alarm and swiped the blanket off of his sluggish body.

Rachel sat up and reached out to grab his shoulder. "Hey, Sweetie."

"Hey," Liam responded as briefly as he could. He knew Rachel would want to see how he was doing. As much as he appreciated it, talking about his dad was the last thing he wanted to do.

"How are you doing?" Rachel checked in.

"Not great," Liam admitted.

"I'm sorry. I know it's really hard with your … "

"I'm sorry, Rachel, I really can't talk about that right now. I gotta get ready, and I just can't handle it right now."

"Okay, I understand. Did you want me to make you something for breakfast?"

"No, I'm good, I'll just grab something on the way out."

Liam dragged himself into the bathroom. Thoughts raced through his head. Try as he might, he could not shake them. Part of him wished his dad was right in front of him so he could tell him what a miserable, grumpy old man he was. He was so tired of having to skirt around the real issues with his dad. But as angry and bitter as he was, he could not shake that old familiar feeling that had tagged along with him since childhood: Maybe dad is right about me.

Before he knew it, he was turning the shower off and ready to dry himself with his towel. His mind had been churning so fast that he lost all track of what he was doing.

He hung up his towel and reentered the room to get dressed. Rachel was no longer in bed. He could hear her and the kids laughing together downstairs. As much as he loved to hear them crack up, the thoughts shooting through his mind were clouding everything else around him. As he listened to them, he only felt like an outsider.

He got dressed and scurried down the stairs. His goal was to leave the house as quickly as possible and not have to engage in any conversation beyond pleasantries. He just didn't have the emotional energy, and he was terrified that he was going to snap again.

Rachel and Lizzy were sitting on the couch together. Rachel sipped her coffee while Elizabeth appeared to be going over some notes for school. Aaron shot out from the kitchen and met Liam at the bottom of the stairs.

"Dad!" Aaron exclaimed, "I have to show you this meme; it is hilarious!"

"I can't right now," Liam replied, trying not to let on how grumpy he felt. "I really need to go."

"It's so funny; Daddy," Lizzy reinforced.

"It really is," Rachel echoed.

"Yeah come on, Dad!" Aaron pleaded

"I'm sorry, I really need to go. You can show me tonight."

"Okay," Aaron acquiesced. He was disappointed, but he could also tell that his dad was not in a cheerful mood.

"See you all later," Liam announced as he sneaked out the front door.

Aaron joined Elizabeth and Rachel in the living room and slumped down into the recliner.

"I'm sorry, Buddy," Rachel expressed, attempting to console him. "Your dad's just not having a good morning."

"I know," he acknowledged. "Is it because of what happened with Grandpa?"

"I think so."

"Why is there always so much tension between them," Elizabeth asked.

Rachel patted Elizabeth on the knee. "Sometimes fathers and sons have a hard time getting along. It's something that's happened for a long time."

They sat in silence for a few moments. Rachel continued sipping her coffee, while Elizabeth and Aaron gazed into their phones. Finally, Aaron spoke up, releasing a question that seemed to come from a deep concern.

"So you think me and dad will be like that when I get older?"

"Oh, Sweetie. I'm not gonna lie, relationships are tough, and they don't get any simpler as you get older. But I don't think you guys will be like that. Your dad is working on things to help himself and the rest of us. But it's hard work and it takes time. You need to know that doesn't change the fact that your dad loves you very much. Both of you. And even though he has a hard time showing it, your grandpa really loves your dad too."

+ + +

Rachel arrived at the grocery store later that afternoon. She had looked through the ad earlier that week and saw that they had T-bone steaks on sale. She figured it would be a great way to help cheer Liam up.

Before she exited the car, she decided to shoot him a text to see how his day was going. He had just started to open up to her; she was feeling so much closer to him. She hated to see that fading away, and she was going to do everything she could to prevent that from happening.

"Hey, Babe, I hope your day is going well. I'm sorry you've been feeling so down lately. Please know that you can talk to me about anything. I love you!"

She tossed her phone back in her purse and ventured into the store. It was not very busy, much to her delight. The smell of the bakery caught her attention as soon as she walked in. She grabbed a cart from the collection and pulled out the list she had written earlier. She plotted out her route through the store and began in the produce section, beginning with the green apples, when she heard a familiar voice from behind her.

"Hi, Rachel!"

She turned around to find Laura approaching.

"Hi, Laura! How are you?"

"Oh, I'm doing well, how are you?"

"I'm good, just running some errands."

"Yep, me too. So, what's been going on with you guys?"

"Well, it's been kind of tough lately, with what happened between Liam and his dad last month."

"Oh, I didn't know; that sounds stressful."

"Oh, I figured he would have told you all about it."

"Well, he probably will when he's ready to come see me again."

"Oh … yeah, I'm sure he will," Rachel responded, trying not to sound confused. Liam had been coming home every Monday evening late. He had told Rachel he was still seeing Laura those days, but she was getting the feeling now that maybe that wasn't true.

"Well, give me a call when you want to connect again."

"Okay, I will. Thank you."

Laura turned and walked out of the produce section into the main part of the store. Rachel was feeling concerned and anxious. What was Liam doing every Monday? And why didn't he tell her?

She pushed her cart through the store, not fully there. Thoughts kept bolting through her mind. She tried to focus on her task and look over the list, but she was unsuccessful. A couple times she threw something in the cart without thinking about it.

A few aisles later, she heard her purse buzz. She pulled out her phone to find that Liam had replied to her text. Her heart was racing to have any indication of what was going on with him. She opened the text.

"I love you too. I'm sorry I've been so down. I just don't know how to talk about it. Or maybe it's just that talking about it doesn't seem to do any good. I'm just at a loss right now. I'm sorry if it's making things hard on you."

Sympathy mixed with anger swirled around inside her. "It wouldn't be so hard if you would just talk to me," she told herself as she threw her phone back into her purse. She had worked too hard to move her marriage in the right direction, and she was determined not to let it go backward.

+ + +

Later that afternoon, Rachel received a notification on her phone. She pulled out to see that Liam had texted her.

"Hey, Babe, I'm heading to see Laura, I'll see you at home after that."

She couldn't believe Liam was keeping something from her. She was tired of tip-toeing around the issue. She pulled up the phone tracker app she had for everyone in the family. She pulled up his icon and looked to see where he was. As she zoomed in to get the exact location, she could see that he was at the coffee shop just a few blocks away from the house.

"I need to go out again really quick!" She shouted from the kitchen to get her kids attention.

"Okay, Mom," Lizzy answered from the living room.

"I'll be back soon," she reinforced as she grabbed her keys and headed out to the car.

+ + +

A few minutes later she pulled up to the coffee shop. She could see Liam sitting in the window, sipping a latte by himself. She was furious, but as she looked at him filling time to avoid anyone knowing what was really going on, she was filled with pity. She exited the car and walked toward the front door, less on a rampage, and more on a rescue mission.

She entered the cafe and turned toward his table. He looked up and spotted her. His face turned red with shame and embarrassment. He remained silent as she approached and sat down across from him.

"So, how long have you been ditching therapy?" She began.

He sighed and took another sip of his drink. "Since the thing with my dad."

"I thought we had moved past this kind of stuff," she lamented.

"I just … I just didn't want to disappoint you."

She reached out and grabbed his hand. "Sweetie, I understand how hard this has been for you. You having to take some time from therapy is not going to disappoint me. I just … I just really need you to talk to me and be honest. I've told you from the beginning that's all I've ever wanted. It doesn't matter how clumsy we are at this; we just need to keep connecting. I told you I wanted the whole thing, the bad with the good, remember?"

"I'm so sorry. I shouldn't have kept this from you."

"Thank you," she responded as she continued to hold his hand. "Come on, let's go home."

41

—

"BILL, CAN YOU HEAR ME?" JOSHUA ASKED. HE HAD been sitting over Bill for several minutes, hoping to get a response. Liam stood behind him, watching nervously.

Bill creaked open his eyes. He struggled to remember where he was. For the first time in ages, he was waking up underneath a roof.

"We made it to the house," Joshua answered the confusion written on Bill's face.

Liam moved to the corner, quiet and sullen.

"What happened?" Bill asked. "How did we get here?"

"The poison got worse, and then you fell and got two more thorns stuck in you. Do you remember any of that?"

"No, I don't."

"After the other two thorns, we needed to get here as fast as we could, so I ended up dragging you the rest of the way."

Bill rolled his eyes. "Oh geez, I wish you hadn't had to do that."

"Yeah, I know. But we're here now," Joshua consoled.

Bill sat up on the bed he had been lying on, although calling it a bed would be generous. It appeared to be some sort of old sofa that was flat on the ground. The whole room around him looked worn down and neglected. There were significant holes scattered in all the walls. The paint was peeling all over the place. The ceiling appeared to have some serious water damage as well.

"We're gonna eat breakfast soon. Take your time getting up," Joshua assured him.

Bill continued examining the house. It was a huge eye sore. He looked over the dwelling he was in and realized that most of the windows were cracked as well. Something was off, however, because as much as he was turned off by the house, there was also something extremely familiar about it. He scooted across the floor into what he assumed was the kitchen, although it hardly warranted the word. There was a wood burning stove, however, and Joshua appeared to be cooking some decent sized eggs.

"No hunting for these this morning. Liam has some chickens."

Bill gave a slight head nod, acknowledging that he had heard Joshua. The eggs did look appetizing, especially because he was so hungry. Liam laid out some metal plates on a table behind Bill. He took a seat and Joshua began transferring the cooked eggs to the plates.

The other two sat down as well and started digging in.

"I gather this house has seen better days," Joshua commented while chewing his food.

"Yeah," Liam affirmed, "it's pretty beat up."

"How long has it been like this?" Joshua inquired.

"I'm not sure, at least as long as I can remember."

"Have you ever tried to fix it up?" Bill chimed in.

"I'm sure it would be hard for him to do that, being just a child," Joshua inserted.

"It's not that, it's just that this is the way it has always been, as long as I can remember. And this is the way I deserve it to be," Liam explained.

"What do you mean?" Bill asked.

Liam shrugged his shoulders and continued eating. Bill was becoming frustrated at this recurring response from Liam. "There seems to be a lot of things you don't know."

Liam didn't respond and just kept eating. After a few minutes he finished his food and went outside.

"Bill, I was thinking, it'd be good for us to help Liam fix up this house," Joshua proposed.

"You're kidding right? I told you, I don't want to be around that kid."

"Bill, do you realize that Liam is the reason you're still alive? I may have dragged you here, but he led the way, and he made the ointment to take away the poison."

"Well, I am grateful for that, but … "

"But what more could you ask for? Go take a look around and tell me this isn't a beautiful spot. You have shelter, chickens, and there is even a well out front."

Bill waved his hands in the air, dismissing Joshua's insistence. "I have no intention of staying. But I'll say this: this house is weirdly familiar to me. I can't figure out why though."

"Take a look around; maybe it'll come to you."

"I'll take a look, but that's not changing anything."

Bill stood up from the table. Joshua scooted a cup across the table to Bill. "Take this and get a drink at the well. The water is delicious."

Bill snatched the cup, "I'm thirsty anyway," he insisted. He stepped out the front door and strolled to the well. He didn't want to admit it, but he was overtaken by the beautiful scene around him. The trees were lush and tall. The grass waved obediently with the wind. The house was in the middle of a large clearing that gave plenty of chance to gaze up toward the infinite blue sky. This was quite the location. He wondered, however, why the house had become such an eyesore.

He reached the well and placed his hand on the stone perimeter warming in the morning sun. He leaned over and looked down but could not see to the bottom. He began pulling the rope through the pulley to lift the bucket. After about thirty seconds, he could see the bucket emerging from the darkness. A gust of wind blew his hat off and rattled the bucket, as the trees roared in applause. "Wow, that's pretty impressive." He decided to catch up with his hat later and finish what he was doing. He dipped his cup into the water, lifted it to his parched mouth and took a long sip. "Okay, that is pretty good," he admitted to himself.

After getting enough water, he tied the bucket and went to retrieve his hat. He walked to the right about forty feet and bent down to pick it up. As he stood back up, a fence at the back of the house caught his eye. A fence seemed out of place here in the middle of the woods. He could see a functioning gate to walk through, and he decided to explore behind it.

He sauntered toward the gate and pulled the lever to open it. The lever moved easily, but the gate itself was heavy and stubborn. He finally kicked the bottom, which made it budge just enough for him to proceed into the back yard. He took a few steps until the scene before him bolted his feet to the ground. He could not believe his eyes. It was the exact backyard from the vision that hit him after smelling the innocent flower. It was worn from years of neglect, but the resemblance was unmistakable. There, across the yard, sat the swing from the vision. When he examined the house from this angle, it was clear that it was the same one as well. Emotions swirled through him. His anger and body temperature rose as he considered the ramifications.

He charged back around the house to the front door and stormed in, determined to find answers.

"What is going on here?" He demanded. Liam looked up, but only for a moment. Joshua hurried in from the kitchen to decipher what was happening.

"What's wrong, Bill?"

"Don't play dumb with me! I want to know what is going on here!"

"Bill, I don't know what you're talking about."

"Oh yeah? Well maybe he does," he accused, pointing toward Liam. "I told you from the beginning, I didn't trust him."

"Bill, why don't you calm down and explain what you're talking about."

"Okay, I'll tell you. Do you remember the innocent flower that I smelled that knocked me back?"

"Yes, of course."

"Well, this house is the vision it gave me."

"This house?"

"Yes, this very one. I told you it felt familiar. I went to the back of the house, and it is exactly the same from my vision. There's something going on here. This is my house!"

"Bill, are you sure?"

"I'm positive."

Liam then quietly got up and walked out the front door.

"Where do you think you're going," Bill accosted.

"Bill, you need to calm down."

"Don't tell me to calm down," Bill snapped. He stood in the front doorway and glared at Liam. The child walked nervously toward the tree line and disappeared into the woods.

42

LIAM AND RACHEL DROVE TO THE GROCERY STORE AND pulled into the parking lot. They lucked out and found a spot just a few feet away from the front door.

"Look at that!" Rachel commented.

Liam nodded, but nothing more. It had been about a month since his argument with Frank, and Liam showed no sign of cheering up. It was weighing heavily on Rachel. All she wanted to do was fix him and make him feel better, but she felt helpless. She had asked Liam to go shopping with her at the last minute, and was pleasantly surprised that he had taken her up on the offer.

"Can you grab a cart for me, Babe?" Rachel requested as they meandered up toward the front door.

"Yep," Liam obliged as he veered toward the cart collection.

Liam yanked on the first cart a few times before it released from the rest of the bunch. He wanted to scream at it for being so non-compliant, but he decided against displaying the anger that was stewing inside of him.

Liam composed himself and caught up to Rachel.

"Those things are so jammed sometimes," Rachel consoled.

They approached the door which instinctively opened and beckoned them inside.

"Let me pull up the list," Rachel remarked as she pulled out her phone. "Okay, let's start in the produce section and work our way from there."

Liam was reluctant to follow her lead. He was in a very grumpy mood. He was perturbed by what he perceived to be her bossy attitude, but also didn't have the energy to make any decisions himself.

Rachel led them as she weaved in and out of the produce aisles. She was hoping that Liam would enjoy himself and forget for a moment all that was bothering him. She tried her best not to smother him with care and concern, but it was difficult. She had never seen him quite this down before.

Rachel collected the fruits and vegetables that were on her list. She turned around and pushed her cart to the next few aisles, scanning for needed items while Liam straggled behind. They turned down the aisle with the chips and snacks, and Rachel continued to visually sift through the products.

Liam could tell that Rachel was worried about him, and that she was trying her best to watch out for him. He appreciated it, but he didn't want to be a burden to her or anyone else. He tried to be as helpful as possible while also avoiding conversations involving his dad.

As Rachel looked over the chips, one of Liam's favorite songs came over the speakers in the store. It gave Liam a bolt of energy. He began bobbing his head to it, but pretty soon he was full-fledged dancing and snapping to the music.

Rachel looked over and smiled wide. She loved to see Liam have fun, especially right now. She gave a playful eye roll, which only enticed Liam more. He rhythmically moved toward her and grabbed her hand to draw her into his dance as well. She giggled and played along for a moment. He tried to spin her just as a few other customers walked by. She gave him a flirty slap on the arm. "Okay, okay, you can stop now. You're so embarrassing," she joked amorously.

As soon as Liam heard that word, his whole demeanor changed. The joy left his eyes and he turned and walked to the end of the aisle. Rachel could tell that something she said bothered him, but she was baffled what it could be and why it would impact him so much.

They continued their shopping as Liam grew more distant. The rest of their time at the store felt awkward and forced. Rachel felt as though Liam was becoming angry with her, but she couldn't figure out why. Liam stared into space, and Rachel called him several times as he was oblivious to where they were headed next. In time, she chose to give him space and finished her shopping without bugging him.

"Liam, are you ready to go? I got everything."

Liam snapped up his head, as if he was caught in a trance. "Oh, um … yeah, sure."

They headed up front to check out. Liam mindlessly bagged the groceries as Rachel engaged with the cashier. They walked out to the car and unloaded the bags into the trunk. Liam transferred the cart to the corral. He returned to the car, plopped into the passenger side, and buckled himself in. Rachel left the car in park and seemed to be waiting for something.

"Can you talk to me about it?" she finally asked after an uncomfortable silence.

"Talk about what?" He replied.

"Whatever it is that's bothering you."

"You know what's bothering me, all that stuff with my dad."

"No, I mean what happened in the store. You were goofing and dancing around, and then suddenly you stopped and went back to being down. Did I do something?"

Liam knew what she was talking about, but had a difficult time imagining processing it out loud. "You're gonna think it's stupid."

"Oh, Sweetie, no I won't. I want to know what's going on with you."

Liam just looked ahead; he could not bring himself to talk.

"I wish I could understand why your dad bothers you so much. I mean, I know he's a pain in the ass, but there's something else there that has a hold on you. I just think that if you knew what it was, you could move past it."

Liam continued to stay silent. He knew exactly what it was about his dad, but that didn't seem to make anything better.

"I know it's difficult, Liam. You don't have to tell me now if you can't. Just know that I want to hear what's going on inside you."

Rachel shifted the car into reverse and pulled out of the parking spot. They rolled toward the exit of the lot. They stopped at the streetlight and waited for it to turn green. Liam strived to build up the gumption to speak again.

"It was when you said I was embarrassing," he blurted out.

"What?" Rachel responded, confused by the abrupt admission.

"When you said I was embarrassing in the store; that's what threw me for a loop."

The light turned green and so Rachel proceeded to turn left onto the street.

"I was just playing around with you, I didn't ... "

Liam gestured with his hands. "I know, I know you didn't mean anything."

"Then I don't understand; why did that bug you so much?"

"Because ... " Liam took a moment to continue. "Because my dad said that to me when I was little. He told me I was an embarrassment to him when I was little."

Rachel pulled the car over and turned to look at Liam. "Your dad told you that?"

Tears started forming in Liam's eyes. "It's so stupid. It was such a long time ago."

"That's not stupid, that was a terrible thing for you to have to go through. How old were you?"

"I was nine."

"You were nine! Your dad told his nine-year-old son that he was an embarrassment? Why the hell would he do that?"

Liam was startled by the anger and intensity in Rachel's voice. He had rarely seen her get this worked up about anything. It began to validate the pain and struggle he had felt through all of this.

"I don't know. I guess he thought it was weak to cry."

"Ugh. I hate that macho crap," Rachel declared. They sat silently for a few minutes. Liam couldn't think of what else to say. He was just relieved to be affirmed in his pain. "Are you okay?" She asked as she rested her hand on his leg.

"I think so. It's just weird. Every time I've thought of telling that story, I always doubt how it should affect me. I always think about all the kids who have to go through horrible things with their parents, and I think I'm just making a big deal out of nothing. I half expected you to make fun of me when I told you."

"Babe, I would never do that. You're thinking of it from an adult perspective, but you have to remember that you were a child when it happened, and the impact you feel inside is because of how it felt as a kid. Childhood stuff has a powerful hold on us. The fact that you're still so affected by it should tell you that it is a big deal. In a way, telling yourself it isn't a big deal is kind of like treating yourself like your dad treated you. You know, like you're telling yourself it's not okay to have feelings."

"Wow, you sound like Laura right now," Liam observed with a chuckle.

"I'll take that is a big compliment," she smiled. She reached over and softly touched his cheek. "I love you."

He placed his hand on hers and met her eyes with his. "I love you too."

43

Bill opened his eyes to see Liam and Joshua conversing in the dining room. He had pretended to sleep in to try and eavesdrop on their conversation. He didn't know what was going on, but after yesterday, and seeing Liam disappear into the trees, he knew he had to find a way to ascertain the truth. He focused his hearing to catch each word, hoping to get some clue as to what Liam was up to.

He couldn't hear everything they were saying but picked up on a few words. Liam seemed to be talking about returning to the woods to deliver some sort of object. Joshua seemed to know exactly what he was talking about, which made Bill all the more suspicious. He wasn't sure if he could trust anyone.

Liam grabbed his pack and walked out the front door. Bill kept his eyes open enough to keep an eye on Joshua, who soon returned to the kitchen. Bill saw his chance and snuck toward the door. He peeked his head around to catch a glimpse of where Liam was heading. As he had guessed, Liam was veering toward the same spot in the woods that he had gone to yesterday.

Bill slid out the door and knelt down to wait for Liam to enter the woods and avoid getting spotted. Once Liam was out of sight, Bill sprinted to the tree line that Liam had entered. He could see Liam in the distance. Bill followed far behind, not wanting to draw any attention to himself.

Bill moved from one tree to another, using each one for cover. He continued until there was a long open area where he risked getting sighted. He waited and watched Liam approach a large boulder. Soon Liam disappeared behind it and Bill scurried to hug the rock and peer around the corner.

Bill could see Liam ascending a small hill and decided to stay put until Liam reached the top. For the next few moments Bill remained idle, watching Liam and hearing noises behind him. He looked back several times, wondering if a creature had seen him, or he himself had been followed by Joshua. He whipped his head around the other direction as he heard a rustling in one of the trees adjacent to him. He looked up to find a robin leaving its nest to presumably find some food. "Damn bird," Bill mumbled to himself, trying to slow his heartbeat.

Liam finally reached the top, and Bill proceeded to follow his trail up the hill. He approached the summit and lowered to the ground so he could sneak a peek over the top. He caught the top of Liam's head lowering as he descended into a crevice between some more boulders. He stepped toward the rocks when some twigs snapped to the right of him. He flattened himself to avoid being seen, but instead saw a deer trotting into the distance. Bill shook his head, tired of all the false alarms.

He decided to stay on the ground and crawled on all fours to approach the rocks. He reached the crevice and poked his head through it. He could hear voices, and carefully moved forward. He reached a point where he could look down. His heart stopped as he took in the scene before him. Liam was standing across from none other than the dark figure. Liam slid some small items out of his pocket and handed them to the figure, who placed them inside his robe.

Bill was stunned by what he was seeing. "I knew there was always something off about that kid," he thought to himself. His mind was racing as he attempted to consider all the consequences of what he had witnessed. "That little rat," he continued conversing to himself, "I bet he arranged for the dark figure to drive me out of my house and off the land to keep me away all this time."

Bill leaned forward again, but accidentally pushed some pebbles that fell into the crevice. The dark figure looked up in Bill's direction. Bill fell backwards. He jumped to his feet and raced back the way he had come. As he began down the hill, he stumbled and rolled the rest of the way down. Once at the bottom, he returned to his feet and darted back toward the house.

After a few minutes, Bill emerged from the tree line and hurried to the house. His heart continued to race as he looked behind him, hoping he was far enough ahead of the other two. He flew through the doorway and met Joshua in the house, who was standing next to the dining room table.

"Joshua! Joshua! We have a big problem," he announced.

Joshua turned toward Bill. "What? What's wrong?"

"I followed Liam into the woods. I followed him all the way and I caught him meeting with the dark figure. You know? The one who warned me not to come this way. I think he and Liam are conniving together to keep me away from here. I told you, this is the house from my flashback. This is my house, and they stole it from me!"

Joshua raised his hands to signal Bill to slow down. "Bill, calm down. I'm afraid you don't understand what's going on here."

"Wait ... what?" Bill demanded.

"That's not what's going on."

Bill glared at Joshua in confusion until the realization washed over him. "You know about all this? You know they're working together? You know ... this is my land?"

"Yes."

"So you're in on all of this too?" Bill screamed.

"No one is in on anything. There is not some scheme to hurt you. I told you, the darkness cannot hurt you. But if you are willing, there is much you can learn from it."

Bill pointed at Joshua as he shook with anger. "No more lessons from you. You have played me this whole time." Just then, Bill heard Liam returning from the trees and stormed out to meet him.

"Hey! I saw you. I saw you out there meeting with the dark figure. I know what's going on here."

Liam stood stunned at Bill's aggression, seemingly dumbfounded.

"Don't act stupid. I know what's going on here. I know that you guys forced me out of this house, out of this land, and thought you could keep me away. Well it's not going to happen. I'm staying. This is my land, and I'm not going anywhere!"

Liam spoke up with a shaking voice, "It's our land."

"This ends now," Bill said as he lunged toward the boy.

Suddenly, the dark figure swooped in out of nowhere and stood between Bill and Liam. Bill could not see his face, but he knew the figure was looking at him.

"You will not hurt the boy," the figure hissed. "You will not hurt him again."

Bill looked on stunned and confused. His anger rose back up. "I'm not afraid of you anymore. Keep the kid away from me. I'm fixing up my house. Don't get in my way."

Bill turned and marched back into the house. Joshua signaled for him to stop and listen.

"Save it!" Bill yelled. He entered the house and began searching through the storage room to begin his repairs to the house.

44

RACHEL PULLED UP TO FRANK AND SUSIE'S HOUSE. SHE had grown tired of watching Liam spiral out. She could not stand by and just watch him suffer when there seemed to be an obvious path to resolution.

She slammed the car door behind her and marched up the driveway to the front door. She was about to knock on the door when it suddenly opened. Susie stood there with a confused smile across her face.

"Rachel! Well, this is a surprise. Is everything okay?"

"Hi Mom, everything's fine. I just need to talk to Frank. Is he here?"

Susie's look transformed from confusion to concern. "Yes, he's here. What do you want to talk to him about?"

Rachel was hesitant to answer, as she figured Susie would try to dissuade her. "I need to talk to him about all this crap between him and Liam."

"Honey, that's not for you to get into."

"Mom, I love you, and I mean no disrespect, but that's bullshit. You yourself said they're a bunch of idiots, and I'm tired of sitting back and watching things go as they are."

"Honey, I really wish you wouldn't do this."

"Yeah, well I really wish I didn't have to."

Susie stepped aside and gave Rachel room to pass by. "Okay then, have at it."

Rachel marched through the entryway and down the hall to the television room.

"Frank," she called out.

Frank turned his head to confirm it was Rachel and turned back toward the television. "Hey Rachel, what are you doing here?"

"We need to talk."

Frank took a few seconds to respond as he followed the action on the television. "Talk about what?"

"What do you think? Talk about you and your son."

"Rachel, that's between me and him. You don't need to … "

"No, I do need to, because from where I'm standing there's not much between you and him."

"Okay, c'mon, Rachel, this is not your battle," Frank replied as he got up from his chair to leave the room.

"Sit down!" She yelled at him, surprising even herself.

"Listen, who do you think you're talking to?"

"I'm talking to a stubborn ass about his stubborn ass son."

Frank could see the intensity in her eyes and decided not to fight it. He sat back down and faced the television.

"Turn it off," she said in a matter-of-fact way.

Frank lifted the remote and pressed the power button. He let out a deep sigh and turned toward Rachel. "Fine, what do you want to say?"

Rachel sat down across from him. "Your son is a wreck. He is a wreck because he believes he's not good enough, because he believes that you see him as an embarrassment."

Frank's eyes grew large. "An embarrassment! Where the hell did he get that from?"

"From you."

"From me?" Frank lifted his large hand and pointed a finger toward Rachel. "My son is not an embarrassment. How did he ever get that idea from me?"

"Because you told him that when he was in little league. He was crying one game after he didn't play well, and you told him that he was embarrassing you."

"What? I never said that."

"It was after the first game that he started as a pitcher. He didn't do very well and had to be pulled out of the game early."

Frank stopped for a moment. His face grew grim as he remembered the game that Rachel was referring to. "That was just something I said in the heat of the moment. I didn't mean it. That was so long ago. How could he think that I meant that?"

"That's how kids' minds work. They take that stuff to heart. They think it has everything to do with them."

Frank froze for a moment, but then shook his head in protest. "But he's not a kid now. There's no way that is still impacting him. C'mon. And I was just trying to get him to toughen up, not let things bother him so much. Life was going to chew him up and spit him out if he wasn't more ... "

"Like you?"

"You know what? I'm getting tired of this. Between you and Liam, you'd think I was the most horrible dad ever. I was a good dad. My dad was a bastard. He was a cowardly, no good son of a bitch. He treated my mom and me like trash. That's what a terrible dad looks like. If I hadn't learned to be tough ... " Frank stopped in his tracks. A wave of emotion flashed across his face and disappeared just as fast. He turned away and stared at the wall. "I don't know what would have happened to me if I hadn't learned to be tough, to be strong. I might be dead, or he might be. Who knows? I never wanted my son ever to have to face that same kind of pain, and the only way I knew to do that was to teach him to be as tough as I had to be."

Rachel's posture softened. She leaned forward and let her hand rest on Frank's arm. "I know, Frank. No one is trying to tell you that you're a bad father, because you're not. You did a lot of wonderful things for your kids. You broke the cycle of abuse in your family by refusing to do that to your kids. Frank, I know you're a good dad, and a good person. It's just that even the best of us say or do things we don't intend to, things that hurt the people around us. We all do it sometimes, and we need to set the record straight so that the people we love know how we feel."

Frank sat back in his chair in a posture of resignation. "I don't know how to do that; I never have."

"Well, Liam isn't very good at it either, but he's getting better."

"I don't think it will do any good."

"You sound just like your son."

"Maybe I am a horse's ass. And maybe if I start talking about all this gushy shit, everybody's gonna see how much of a horse's ass I really am."

"Aww, Frank. We already know all that," she replied with a grin. "And yet, we're all still here, because we know that's not the final word on who you are."

Frank waved her off as embarrassment appeared in his cheeks. He sat silent for a moment, just staring ahead toward the television.

Rachel got up and placed her hand on his shoulder. "Just think about it, okay?" She said before she exited the room.

45

Bill woke up early the next morning, fueled by his anger to get moving on the house. He ran out to the well to drink a few cups of water but passed on breakfast so he could get started right away. He returned inside and entered the storage room to take stock of the materials that were available. Many items that lay in the room seemed completely out of place, but then again, so did this house. He decided to start work on patching up the holes that peppered the walls. He took several trips to transport the materials and equipment from the room to the spots where he would need to work. He made as much noise as he could, disregarding the sleeping bodies in the house.

The dark figure, however, was present and alert, not taking his eyes off of Bill. Ever since the blowup at Liam, the dark figure had remained close by, protecting the child from any threats. As far as Bill was concerned, however, everyone here was a threat to him and his mission.

Eventually, as the noise and the daylight grew, Joshua and Liam emerged from their slumber and moved to the kitchen to prepare breakfast. The clanging of pots and pans from the kitchen did little to overcome the sound of Bill's feverish work pace. By the time they had sat down to eat breakfast, Bill had moved the patching materials to most of the holes around the house.

"Bill, you really should eat something," Joshua advised as Bill whizzed past him on one of his trips back to the storage room. Bill ignored his plea and kept on his course.

He started on a crater in one of the bedrooms. It was large and had jagged sides, so he began cutting and scraping to make them even. There was still some considerable debris inside the wall from whatever event had formed the cavity. He reached in to dig the material out, but his mind began spinning. He jerked his hand out and shook his head back to reality. He tried to pull the remains out, but the same thing happened again. He attempted a third time, going as fast as he could.

A few seconds into the process, however, he started feeling weak. He pushed on as much as he could, but his knees began to buckle. "Maybe I need something to eat," he thought to himself. He found his pack and pulled out some of the remaining dry meat he had retained, not wanting to give Joshua the satisfaction of eating any of their breakfast.

He moved back to the bedroom and began working again. He cleaned out the loose material in the wall and finished smoothing out the sides. Grabbing his saw, he cut some plywood out to hold the new drywall piece in place. He cut out a piece of drywall and placed it in the gap. He taped it and proceeded to cover the area with mud. Soon, however, he began feeling weak again. He tried to keep going, but he kept dropping the tool he was using. He felt his hand aching, and he looked down to see it shake.

He stomped out of the room and headed back to the living room, hoping to walk the pain off. When he entered the living room, he saw Liam sitting on the couch. He stopped and pointed at the boy. "This is all your doing. This is all your fault."

The dark figure swooped in and stood between them. "You do not belong here."

Bill dismissed him with his hand and turned to go back to his work. He heard Liam get up and turned to see him holding out his hand to the dark figure, who retrieved another item from Liam, just as he had in the woods. The dark figure placed the item in his robe, just as before. Bill shook his head in derision.

The dark figure exited out the front door and proceeded back into the woods.

Liam pulled a tool of his own out of his pack and moved over to one of the wall cavities in the living room. He began scraping the sides of it when Bill returned to the living room to see what the noise was.

"What do you think you're doing?" Bill demanded.

"I'm helping you fix the house."

"I don't need your help. The house is the way it is because of you anyway."

"I want to help."

"Do what you want then, just don't bother me."

Liam dropped his instrument and walked out of the front door, heading straight for the direction of the dark figure.

"Where are you going now? Off to scheme with the darkness again?"

Liam was silent and continued to walk toward the tree line.

"I'm tired of this," Bill declared. "You guys are not going to mess things up for me anymore."

Bill stormed out the front door and began following Liam, who had vanished into the woods. Bill was catching up, but as he approached the edge, he began to feel weak again. It was different from before, however. It slowed him down, and as he began to step into the trees, he felt like he was fading away. To his astonishment, that was precisely what was happening. As he looked down at his front foot, it was becoming translucent. He extended his hand forward, and it became see through. He jumped back in horror.

He could hear footsteps behind him growing louder. He turned around to find Joshua approaching.

"What is happening to me?" He insisted.

"You are bound to this land; you cannot leave."

"I ... I don't understand."

"You will never be able to leave until you make things right with the child."

"You want me to make things right with him? Have you gone insane? He is the reason for all of this."

"That is how it appears to you. But not for long."

Bill sighed in disgust and trudged back toward the house.

46

LIAM CLICKED SEND FOR AN EMAIL HE HAD BEEN WORK-
ing on and closed his laptop. His work day had been coming to a close.
It had been a productive day. He felt more energized the last few days
since his conversation with Rachel about his dad. It seemed to unclog
some blockage within him.

He was, however, still concerned about his relationship with his
parents. He had not spoken to either of them since their last dinner
and was dreading what it would be like next time. He decided to give
his mom a quick phone call, before heading home, to check in and see
how they were doing. He made sure to call her cell phone to avoid an
ill-timed conversation with his dad.

The phone rang a few times before going to voicemail. Liam felt
tense and nervous. He hated leaving messages, especially when he was
flustered, so he ended the call and proceeded to pack up his things to
head home.

A minute later his cell phone buzzed on the desk and he could see
his mom was calling him back. He snatched up the phone and slid the
green button.

"Hi, Mom."

"Hi, Sweetie, how are you doing?"

"I'm good, how are you?"

"I'm doing good, just working on dinner. What's going on?"

"Oh, I was just checking to see how you guys were?"

"Oh, okay … "

The awkward silence made it clear his mom knew he was calling for
something else.

"How's Dad doing?" Liam finally asked.

"He's okay."

"Is he still upset?"

"I don't even know, to tell you the truth. That conversation with Rachel seemed to do a number on him. He's been pretty distant since then."

"Oh … yeah," Liam responded, pretending to know the event his mom was referencing. He tried his best to subdue his frustration.

"Yeah, I suppose we'll find out one way or another. You know how stubborn he is anyway."

"Yeah I suppose. Well I'll let you get back to dinner mom. Love you."

"Love you too, Sweetie. Talk to you later."

"Okay, bye."

His mind was spinning as to what Rachel would have gone to talk to his dad about, and why she had kept it from him. Suddenly he recalled his conversation with her the other night and considered the possibility that she had gone to talk to his dad about what he had shared. "Oh no, she wouldn't have … "

He shoved the rest of his things in his bag and stormed out of his office. He realized he was walking at a faster pace, but he couldn't stop himself. Anger, fear, and shame all rolled around inside of him. He scurried down the stairs, not wanting to wait for the elevator to open, and headed for his car.

He raced home. His breathing intensified, as did his grip on the steering wheel. He arrived in record time but was disappointed to see Rachel's car missing from the driveway. He went inside and looked at the family calendar. He realized that the kids both had after-school events today, and that Rachel was likely out picking them up. He went upstairs into their bedroom. He waited on the bed, not wanting to cause a commotion with the kids when the three of them returned home.

Liam sat on the bed with his hands folded and his head resting on top of them. He was beginning to be grateful that Rachel was not home when he arrived as he began to calm down and compose himself. He didn't want to explode at her or say something he was going to regret.

After about ten minutes, he heard Rachel's car pulling into the driveway. The front door flew open as the kids raced into the living room to turn on the television.

"Liam?" Rachel called out.

"I'm up here!" he replied.

His stomach tied in knots as he heard Rachel's footsteps up the stairs. He was not used to sharing his feelings and felt as though he had not grown any more adept at it over the last few months. Rachel entered the room and could see the angst on Liam's face.

"What's going on?" She inquired.

"Can you close the door?" He requested.

Rachel closed the door behind her back, keeping her eyes on Liam.

"What's wrong, Babe?" She asked.

Liam took a big breath. "What did you talk to my dad about?"

A wave of embarrassment washed over her face. She could tell that Liam was not happy with her.

"I ... I talked to him about you. I was trying to mend things, make things better."

"I really wish you hadn't done that."

"I'm sorry Liam, I was just ... I didn't want to see you hurting anymore."

"You could have asked me about it."

"I know, it's just that you both are so stubborn and won't talk about this stuff."

"It still should be my call." Liam stood up in front of her. "And what stuff did you talk to him about? Did you tell him about what I talked to you about the other night?"

Rachel stood speechless. She was confronted with the reality of what she had done but couldn't bring herself to acknowledge it. Liam knew that her answer was in the affirmative by the regret in her eyes.

"I can't believe you did that! You told him about the little league game and ... all of it?"

"I'm sorry! I know you were feeling weak and ... "

"So you thought going to talk to my dad behind my back about my stuff would make me feel less weak? Ugh. What were you thinking?"

"I'm so sorry, I was just so angry for you, and for what you had been through. I just hated seeing you hurt so much."

Liam sat back down on the bed and shook his head in dismay. After a moment, Rachel sat down next to him.

"Liam, I am so sorry. I realize I shouldn't have done that. I just ... "

Liam gestured with his hand that he acknowledged what she was saying. "I know why you did it. I get it. But that's not going to help me."

"I understand."

They sat silent as Liam mulled over what was going on inside of him. Deep fear and shame filled his core as he thought about what his dad was thinking of him. He already felt so inferior to his father, and now that his wife had fought his battle, thoughts of insecurity shot through his mind. After a moment Liam slowly stood up. "Well, let's go down and work on dinner."

"Wait," she replied as she stood up and grasped his arm to turn him around. "Are we okay?"

"Yes, we're okay, I just need some time to work through it. There's just too much going on in me right now."

"I understand," Rachel affirmed as he wrapped her arms around him. They shared a long, tight hug, and ventured downstairs.

+ + +

Lizzy grabbed the big spatula in the enchilada dish and served herself some more to eat for dinner. "These are really good, Mom!" She exclaimed.

"Thank you, Sweetie," Rachel replied.

They all worked on their plates for a few moments. Lizzy stared at her father for a while with a puzzled look on her face. "Dad, are you okay?"

"Yeah, I'm fine," he answered unconvincingly.

Lizzy continued looking at him, wondering what was going on.

"Your dad is just," Rachel began. Liam looked up, surprised that Rachel was elaborating. "He's just working through something because I did something kind of inconsiderate."

Liam's eyes grew big as he listened to her.

"What'd you do, Mom?" Lizzy asked.

"Well, that's not really your concern, but suffice it to say we are okay and working through it. People sometimes have to walk through difficult things together, but they end up better on the other side, right Honey?" she finished looking at Liam.

A grateful smile appeared on his face. He was not used to being so vulnerable about what was bothering him. He felt such loyalty and compassion flowing from Rachel's heart. "Yes, yes that's right?" He confirmed.

After dinner, while the kids helped Rachel clean up the table and the dishes, Liam went to his office and shut the door. He pulled out his phone, ready to make a phone call that had been on his mind for weeks. He stared at his black, unlocked phone for a few minutes before he finally swiped the screen and entered his pin. He dialed the phone number and waited for the rings to pass to leave a message.

"Hi, Laura. This is Liam. Um … I'm ready to come back. Call me when you have a chance to set up another appointment. Thanks. Talk to you later."

47

—

BILL HAD AWAKENED EARLY, EAGER TO CONTINUE HIS project. He had been on a rampage, with the house, and with everyone around him. As his body grew weaker, it increased his irritation, as well as his angry determination to get the job done. He had not spoken a word to anyone else in the house for a couple of days and was relieved that his irritable disposition was making them keep their distance.

While working on the hallway, he heard a suspicious sound from one of the bedrooms. He ventured in to find Liam sanding around one of the holes he had repaired.

"What are you doing?" He demanded.

"I'm smoothing the area out," Liam answered.

"Don't touch it! I don't need your help. Stick to your own work," he scolded.

Liam lowered his head and walked back out to the living room. The dark figure glared at Bill, but he didn't care. He was on a mission and that's all that mattered.

Bill returned to the hallway to fill in the large hole in the wall. He filled it and worked to smooth the area. He moved the knife back and forth. Suddenly, however, he was transported into another time. The air swirled and spun him around. He landed on the floor on all fours. He shook his head, trying to make sense of what was happening. Just then, he heard a woman's voice speak.

"Do you want to try one, William?"

Bill looked up and saw the woman from his innocent vision. She was wearing a flowing dress, with an apron tied behind her, and had her back turned to him. She appeared to be lifting baked goods off of a cooking tray and placing them onto a plate.

"William, come over here and see," she directed as she waved him over.

He rose to his feet and stumbled over to her. She turned around and beamed wide at him. She knelt to display the plate of cookies to him. "Don't they look good? Why don't you have a seat at the table. I think I want some milk. How about you?"

Bill nodded in agreement. He walked over to the table to sit down. He still felt like himself, but he was apparently very small. He struggled to climb into the chair on the left side. He watched with anticipation as the woman poured the milk. He could hear the delightful sound of the glasses filling up.

She brought the treat over to the table. He grabbed one and brought it to his salivating mouth. He bit off as big of a chunk of the cookie as he possibly could. It was warm and delicious.

"Mmm," the woman expressed as she took a bite of her own treat.

Bill reached up for some milk, but suddenly heard a crash from behind him. He quickly turned around to see the hole in the hallway had just been knocked out. He turned around to see the reaction on the woman's face, but she was no longer there. The cookies and the glasses were all gone. The house was empty, except for Bill, who was all alone.

Bill opened his eyes to find himself lying on the hallway floor. He looked up to see the work he had just done on the wall. He looked around at his perimeter. No one seemed to have noticed him experience the flashback. He could hear them working away in the living room.

He tried continuing to work on the area and smooth it out, but the flashback had been too disorienting. He decided to walk out to the well and get a drink, hoping the cool water would jolt him back to reality. He pulled the bucket up and dunked his cup into the water. He guzzled it down and let it pour into his stomach as he gazed over the landscape.

He dunked his cup a second time. His body jolted as he heard a loud crash back in the house. He rushed over to find out what was going on. Liam was sitting on the couch, eyes growing wider and wider. Bill looked to the wall by the front door and saw a new hole that had been made. His body began to shake as he turned back toward Liam.

"What did you do?"

"I didn't … " Liam began, but couldn't finish.

"That's it! You've done enough damage here. You useless, good for nothing kid. I hate you!"

Liam's face started convulsing in tears, and he sprinted out the door. Bill's breathing continued to speed up as his anger festered. Joshua marched in the front door.

"What did you do to the child?" Joshua questioned.

"That's what he deserved," he declared as he pointed out the door. "That kid has been nothing but a thorn in my side. He drove me away from my home. And now he's messing up the house even more while I'm trying to fix it. I hate that kid."

"That's not why you hate him, Bill."

"Oh, of course! Because you know everything, right? You always have some lesson to teach me. I know damn well why I hate him."

"You've hated him ever since you met him."

"Damn right!" Bill yelled as he threw his cup across the room. "I knew something was off about him."

"That's not why you hate him."

"Oh yeah? Then why don't you tell me," Bill directed as he pointed at Joshua. "You know everything, so why don't you tell me why I hate that kid."

"Bill, you hate him because you hate yourself. You hate Liam because Liam is you."

Bill stood silent for a moment, trying desperately to disregard what Joshua was saying.

But a wave of flashbacks raced through his head and jolted him. He suddenly remembered details that lay dormant for longer than he knew. In his mind he saw visions of storms rolling in, the house being battered, holes randomly appearing in the walls. But most of all, he saw himself, walking away from the home, leaving Liam behind as he fell apart on the ground.

Bill turned around several times as he sought to get his bearings.

"Liam didn't force you out, Bill. You abandoned him. You abandoned him because you believed everything was his fault. That is why the dark figure exists: to protect Liam from you, especially now, because you're repeating the same cycle again."

Bill felt sick to his stomach as the thoughts continued to swirl in his head. Tears began to form in his eyes, and though he tried with all his might to hold them back, they fought for their freedom and poured out. His legs became weak, and he crumbled into the saving arms of his friend. He squeezed Joshua as tight as he possibly could. Joshua didn't seem to be bothered, but instead returned the gesture.

"I'm so sorry," Bill muttered between his sobs. "I'm so, so sorry." He thought of all the grief he had given Joshua, the lonely life he had lived at the cabin, and the immense pain he had inflicted on Liam. The pain was more than he could bear.

"I know, I know," Joshua assured him.

They continued for what felt like hours. Bill could not bring himself to let go, terrified that if he did, he would never get his friend back. He had acted horribly, had hurt people deeply. There was no logical reason for this man to stick by his side through all of it, and he didn't want it to end.

Eventually, Joshua loosened his grip and backed away so he could look Bill in the eyes.

"Bill, it's going to be okay. I know it may not seem like it, but it's going to be okay."

Bill nodded as he sought to collect himself, trying to trust this man who had never let him down.

"There's a place I need to take you, Bill. Something I need to show you. It won't be easy, but it is necessary. Will you go with me?"

Bill nodded, and Joshua motioned for him to follow him through the front door.

48
—

"IT'S GOOD TO SEE YOU AGAIN, LIAM," LAURA AFFIRMED as Liam took a seat on her couch.

"Thanks, yes it's good to see you too. Sorry I wasn't here for a while."

"It's all part of the process Liam. No apology necessary. So what's been going on? What led you to come back in to see me?"

Liam took a substantial breath and felt like he had a long speech to deliver. "Well, the reason that I stopped coming in was something that happened with my dad."

"Well, I can imagine, based on what you've told me about your relationship with him, that that would have been pretty significant."

"Yes, it definitely was. I wasn't sure what to do with it. I think I just tried to push it down like most other times something has bothered me. I did push it down for a while, but something happened with Rachel last week that kind of made it all come out."

"Oh? What was that?"

"Well, we were out shopping together at the grocery store, and I was just not really responding to anything. I was still so bothered by what happened between me and my dad. But this song came on in the store, and it made me start acting kind of silly. I started dancing, and I got her to dance with me."

"Aww, that sounds like fun."

"Yes it was, for a moment. She got kind of self-conscious when a couple people saw us dancing, and she kind of playfully smacked me and told me I was being embarrassing. I know she didn't mean anything by it, but ... " He stopped mid-sentence, realizing how much it still impacted him.

"Of course, she didn't mean anything by it, but that doesn't mean it won't impact you. Of course, it would. As I recall, your father said something similar to you when you were a child, and it had a strong effect on you."

Liam nodded his head.

"So when she said that, what did it do to you? How did you feel?"

"I felt rejected. I felt alone. I felt like I wasn't good enough. Basically, I felt like I did back when I was a kid."

"Yes, it brings it all back, doesn't it?"

"Yeah."

"So how did you respond?"

"I just got very quiet and distant."

And what did you do with your feelings?"

"What do you mean?"

"Did you allow yourself to feel and acknowledge them? Did you push them down?"

"I definitely pushed them down. I don't like feeling that way."

"No, of course not. Who would?"

They both sat quietly for a moment. Liam waited for Laura to continue speaking, which she soon did.

"Liam, as you're becoming more aware of your tendencies and your feelings, can you look back and see how this may have been a pattern that has occurred often in your life?"

"Umm … can you elaborate on that?"

"Have people said or done things toward you that have left you feeling rejected and alone. And in turn, have you pushed down those feelings and become distant?"

Liam looked up to the ceiling as he sought to recall instances where this had happened.

"Yeah, obviously a lot with my dad. I mean, the little league thing was pretty prominent, but there were a lot of times that what he did really affected me, or I felt really belittled."

"Do you recall particular instances?"

"Yeah. I remember there was a time in fifth grade when I was dealing with a bully at school. My dad kind of made fun of me for it. Like if I was just more like him, I wouldn't have that problem."

"Wow, so he sort of became like a second bully to you then?"

"Yeah, I would say so. He would try to play fight with me a lot, and it just got really rough. It was just another way I didn't feel tough enough for him."

"How did your mom fit into that? Did she ever speak up or stand up for you?"

"Yeah, but it kind of made things worse. She treated me like I was this fragile thing that could be easily broken. It just ended up making me feel way worse."

"So there have been times where people have belittled you, or made you feel less than,

by their words or actions. Occurrences like that can make us more sensitive to our environments or interactions that we have with others."

"What do you mean by that?"

"Well, when something happens that is harmful or threatening to us, our fight or flight kicks in. And that experience gets stored deep within our brain, especially the amygdala, which controls our emotions and fight or flight. What happens is that part of us becomes on the lookout for similar threats because it wants to make sure that never happens again. So, if someone has been cut down and belittled most of their lives, they may be hyper-sensitive to criticism, believing that it is always a threat."

Liam's eyes began to grow large as realizations arrived in his mind.

"Are you connecting some dots?" Laura inquired.

"Yes! This is something that has been a big issue with Rachel and I. She has complained that she feels she can never give me any sort of critique or advice because I become very defensive about it."

"Yes, that is a common scenario in married couples, especially when one or both have experienced being chastised much of their lives, particularly as children. What does it look like for you to become defensive in those moments?"

"It comes out in different ways. Sometimes I will argue with her and explain things away. But I would say that, more often than not, I quietly comply."

"You're quiet with her, but I imagine there's a host of thoughts and words swirling around within you when that happens."

"Yes," Liam replied as he somberly nodded.

"What are some of those thoughts? What are you telling yourself in those moments? Can you think back to a recent time that happened?"

Liam took a deep breath and tried to concentrate. A bizarre energy was flowing through him. He became very nervous and fidgety, and his eyes darted around the room.

"I can see this is challenging for you," Laura sympathized.

"Yes, I can tell there's a part of me that wants to avoid doing this at all cost."

"That's perfectly normal, Liam. We survive so long by avoiding these parts of ourselves, so much so that it feels unimaginable to operate in any other way."

Liam thought back to the conversation he had had with Rachel the other day. "Rachel thinks that I kind of do the same thing to myself that my dad did to me."

"Hmm, in what way?"

"Well, I told her about what happened between me and my dad when I was a kid. She was sympathetic, and frankly, really angry about what my dad did. I told her that when I share that story, with her and with you, I am half expecting you guys to make fun of me, or to tell me to stop making such a big deal out of something that wasn't that serious."

"Yes, that's good insight. That is how your dad may have responded to you if he was in that place again."

"I don't really understand why I do that. I still have a hard time really taking my own stuff seriously."

"Well, it's a defense mechanism. People have lots of ways to cope and protect themselves from things that are too difficult to face, especially when we're kids. And when we don't find healing for those wounds and encounters, those mechanisms remain. The particular one you are describing is called introjection. It is where you sort of take on the part of the person who is hurting you and do it to yourself, because it makes you feel like you have more control over the situation. It's sort of like, if I hurt myself, then it diminishes your ability to hurt me as well."

"Wow, that sounds pretty backwards."

"In a way it is, but we don't have much control when we are kids, so we find whatever way we have of surviving. And it's important to remember that pretty much everyone has defense mechanisms. They might look different in other people, but we all have backward and self-sabotaging ways of dealing with crises in our lives."

Liam just sat in silence, trying to absorb as much as he could.

"These are some of the things we want to work on here, Liam. With that said, for our next session, I would like you to bring in a picture of yourself when you were a child."

"Why?"

"It will be part of the exercise we will do. Do you have a picture you can get from home?"

"Umm, yeah, I'm sure I do."

"Okay, well our time is up. Bring your picture with you next time. For now, try and give yourself space to feel and acknowledge your feelings when they arise. You don't have to dwell on them, but acknowledging them is sort of like when we vent to a friend about something that is bothering us. We don't necessarily need the friend to do anything about it other than to listen to us. When you listen to what your feelings and your body is telling you, you are telling yourself that you are not alone. That's a healthy coping mechanism to have."

"Okay, yeah I'll work on that."

"Okay, good. I'll see you next time then."

49

BILL SHADOWED JOSHUA AS HE WALKED TOWARD THE tree line. Bill felt an unsettledness that was becoming all too familiar, but it was becoming much more intense. He had been confronted with the terrible truth surrounding the connection between him, Liam, and the dark figure. All he could be sure of now was that he could not go on alone, so he willingly followed Joshua wherever he was heading.

As they arrived at the tree line, Bill stopped and reached out his hand, afraid that he was going to fade away again.

Joshua turned back toward him and smiled. "Don't worry. I'm here with you. It will be okay."

They entered in and weaved through trees and brush, Bill doing his best to keep up with his friend. Curiously, Joshua didn't seem to be the slightest bit bothered by the turn of events. As far as Bill could tell, Joshua had been aware of these dynamics from the beginning. As much as Bill instinctively felt ashamed and embarrassed, he was comforted to know that Joshua had known all this about him the entire time, and yet had continually sought after him. Knowing this, Bill was no longer simply following Joshua out of necessity, though he was painfully aware, now more than ever, just how much he needed him.

The chaos in his soul contrasted with the calm scene around them. It had been months since he had experienced an extended peace, and he longed somehow to internalize the contentment of the birds and plants around them.

They continued walking on a path that appeared to be very worn. Wherever they were heading was a frequently visited site. Joshua did not speak a word, and Bill did not feel it was appropriate to ask.

As they drove deeper into the woods, varieties of colors began to emerge in the distance. Bill started to make out different types of flowers. At first, they peppered the perimeter, but soon they covered the sides, as if they were beckoning them forward.

They followed a bend in the path to the left. It wrapped around to the right, and then back to the left as it ascended upwards. Bill gazed up the hill and saw the trees closing to end the path. As they approached, the flowers grew even more prevalent. Bill's eyes scanned upwards and spotted a flowering plant he had seen once before. A breathtaking innocent shrub stood on the right side, at the base of large trees. He slowly walked up to it to take it in when he spotted a tombstone. Joshua stood aside and let him take in the scene. Bill gazed at it stunned and realized it had the same words engraved on it as the one back at the cabin.

Bill turned around and looked at Joshua with confusion "How did this get over here?"

"This is a different one, though it looks exactly the same. You had one, and so did Liam. As you can see, however, Liam's did not end up covered and hidden."

"Did he do all this?" Bill asked as a wave of emotion washed over him.

"Yes, with some help from me. He never stopped thinking about you, never stopped hoping you would return."

Bill fell to his knees while he continued staring at the gravestone. Tears welled up in his eyes. "I can't imagine the pain he must've felt every day. I can't imagine because I don't really know, other than bits and pieces."

"Well, that's partly why I've brought you here Bill." Bill turned around to find Joshua standing next to the innocent shrubbery. "As I recall, you've already experienced the memory inducing power that these flowers possess."

Bill steadily nodded. "I want to know, but I'm afraid of what I'll find."

"It will be difficult to see. But remember, there's nothing you will see that can change how I think of you. I am here with you, and I'm not going anywhere."

Bill stood up and carefully approached the flowers. He remembered the potency that these flowers contained. He looked at Joshua once more, who gave him a reaffirming nod. Bill bent down and took in the aroma.

He was transported back to the house. It looked just as it did in his last flashback. It no longer had the worn down look it had when they had arrived several days earlier. The woman he had seen before was there, making some delicious meal in the kitchen. A young girl played in the living room, while a man sat silently on the couch. Bill was terrified to look at the man. He instinctively knew he was not to be bothered. He tried to read his face but had to look away each time.

A violent wind blew through the house. Bill fell to the ground and covered his head. After a moment, the wind died down, and Bill waited a bit to look up. When he did, he saw Liam standing alone in the living room, his body shaking furiously. Bill walked over to him and laid his hand on Liam's shoulder. Liam spun around and threw his arms around Bill. They embraced for a moment. A palpable sense of loneliness and despair filled the home. There was no sign of the man, the woman, or the little girl, nor any indication of why they had vanished.

A soft wind washed the scene away, and the two appeared again as a powerful storm battered the house. Hail crashed against the exterior, and a branch flew in through the window and sat suspended halfway in it. Bill waved Liam back into the heart of the house, safe from harm. He tried to peek through the front door to get a sense of the storm's power. He could hardly catch a glimpse of the tree line. A gust of wind flew in and shoved him backward and to the ground. The door swung fully open and was nearly ripped off of its hinges. Bill hurried back and returned the door to its closed position, fighting with the wind in the process. He turned around and sat with his back facing the door, the air flying out of his lungs. Liam poked his head around the corner to see if Bill was okay. Bill gestured with his hands to signal that he was fine.

The scene faded away. A vision of Bill returned. He was standing outside the house, nailing boards across the frame of the broken window. As he placed the last board on, some force shoved him off and pushed him on his back onto the ground. He heard a loud crash in the house, and a scream from Liam as he ran outside. Liam refused to speak, but just pointed into the house. Bill ventured inside. He turned the corner to find a large hole in the wall, as well as debris covering the floor just beneath it.

"What happened?" he asked as he turned to look at Liam, who simply shrugged his shoulders. "You don't know what happened?"

"I … I was in the bedroom when I heard it, and I ran out here."

Bill turned back to the hole and stared with confusion. "What is going on here?"

They were quickly transported to another scene, where Bill was at the well, pulling up the bucket to retrieve some water. He watched as Liam walked into the front door of the house, carrying a basketful of eggs from the chickens. A moment later Bill heard another loud crash. He ran inside to find Liam standing next to another hole, this time in the living room.

"What is going on here?" He demanded.

Liam looked toward him in fear.

"Did you do this?"

Liam shook his head as tears began forming. "No, I didn't do anything?"

Bill stormed out of the house with a puff.

Bill was once again caught up in a swirl as he was shifted yet to another scene. He was carrying his pack over his shoulders, walking away from the house. Liam ran after him and grabbed his arm.

"Please, don't go," Liam cried out.

Bill shook him off. "I'm tired of this. This is all your fault," he yelled as he continued walking away. Liam remained, huddled on the ground, sobbing into his hands.

The scene was slowly lifted. Bill opened his eyes and discovered himself lying on the ground. Joshua walked over, knelt down, and placed his hand on his shoulder. Bill reached out and grabbed him to pull him close.

"I'm so sorry," he expressed as he wept into Joshua's chest.

"I know, I know," Joshua assured him, "but for now, there's somewhere else we need to go."

50

The day was closing in on 3:00 PM, and Liam was still having a difficult time getting much done. He had a grave heaviness to him ever since his last session with Laura. A shadow seemed to be covering his every move, and he still could not bring himself to face it. It seemed all his energy for the past several days was simply spent keeping it at bay.

This day had been filled with daydreaming while staring out of the window, and glaring at the blinking cursor on the laptop, expecting words to magically appear. He had taken several walks around the hall, hoping that the movement would jar something loose in him, but to no avail.

A knock on the door jolted him a bit. He had so little energy for this day and was not looking forward to expending any of it on a conversation.

"Come in," he sighed.

Victor poked his head through the door.

"Hey man, how are you doing?"

Liam gave his best head nod and mustered up all his energy. "I'm pretty good, not bad."

Victor brought the rest of his body through the door. He closed the door and slid down into the chair on the other side of the desk. "Really?"

Liam tried to reinforce his earlier answer, but it was clear he was just posing.

"Liam, I've been watching you take walks around the hall all day. I can tell something is bothering you. You don't have to tell me what it is, of course, but I'm happy to listen if you want to talk."

Liam sat silent for a moment. It was clear he couldn't pretend very well with his friend, and he didn't have the energy to do that anyway.

"I'm not really sure, to be honest. I mean, I don't think I've ever felt this way before, or at least I don't remember it anyway. I mean, I've been talking with my therapist and with Rachel about all this stuff, and it's been difficult, but we've been making progress. But now, it's like I've reached this point of no return, and I'm not sure if I can handle it. It's like I've been digging through this tunnel and finding all this stuff. Stuff about my dad, my mom, my childhood, our marriage. I've been digging and digging. But now, I've dug in this place where there is this huge water source, and it is about to burst and completely overwhelm me. I have to hold the rocks in place to keep the wall from bursting open. So it's like I'm stuck. If I let go, I'm going to get swept away."

They both sat quietly for a moment, letting the weight of Liam's words sink in.

"Maybe that's a good thing," Victor chimed in.

"What's a good thing?"

"Maybe it's a good thing if you get swept away."

"What do you mean?" Liam asked, concerned by the sentiment.

"Well, I mean, look at your life. The way you've lived it up until now. I mean, the way you've dealt with your issues and your marriage troubles. You know, the things that you've done that have just ended up shooting you in the foot. Most of the time, we are our own worst enemies, you know? So, what if that got all washed away, and all that was left was the real you. Would that really be such a bad thing?"

Liam sat stunned. The wisdom in his friend's words hung there like a glow. There was hope, but also fear leftover.

"Yeah, that makes sense, but it's still scary as hell."

Victor nodded in affirmation. "The decision I think is the scary part because you're still not entirely sure what you're going to find. It's kind of like when you're a kid, and you think you see something scary in the dark. You're afraid to turn the light on, because you might see the thing you're scared it could be. But most of the time, it ends up being something much less intimidating. So, you could let go of the wall that's holding all the water back, and I suppose there's a chance that you could drown. But you could also end up having the best swim of your life."

"Geez. You talk like you've done this before."

"Well, I never told you this. Haven't really told anyone, but Emily and I had to do our own counseling a few years ago."

"What? Why didn't you say anything?"

"You know how it is. It feels kind of embarrassing sometimes."

"Yeah, I get that." Liam nodded. The room fell silent for a moment. "You know, the whole thing about seeing stuff in the dark. That's not just a kid thing. That happened to me last week," he said with a chuckle.

"Yeah, me too. I just don't like to admit it," Victor echoed while he laughed as well.

"I get what you're saying."

"This is all easier said than done. It's something we constantly have to face. But you're doing good work, Liam. I'm proud of you."

"Thanks man."

Victor nodded and used the arms of the chair to push himself up and exited the office. Liam could still feel the weight within him, but there was a glimmer of hope that there was a way through it.

Liam finished up his day at work. It was not as productive as he would have liked, but he tried to give himself a little grace by acknowledging how hard he had to push today. He exited the building and made his way to the car. He waited for his phone to sync with the car and for his music to begin playing. A song popped up that reminded him of when he and Rachel first began dating. He remembered how alive and adventurous he felt during that time. None of all this crap mattered. He felt freer to be himself. He thought fondly of that time and longed to be that way again. As he daydreamed, he felt a nudge within him, and a subtle message came through in his mind. "Rachel didn't give that to you. She brought it out of you." Liam smiled at the thought but didn't fully understand the ramifications. He pulled out of the parking spot and began driving home.

As he traveled on the highway toward his home exit, the relief of that memory gradually faded, and the weight of his pain reemerged.

He became frustrated with himself, frustrated that he couldn't maintain a sense of peace or relief. As he approached the house, the heaviness grew larger and larger, and his deep sighs became more frequent.

He arrived at home and peeled himself out of the car. He hated feeling like this, especially around his family. He ached to be able to offer something more to them, something more spontaneous and light, but each step up the walkway was labored.

He entered the front door and turned his head to the right to see his family relaxing on the furniture while watching a movie.

"Hi, Sweetie!" Rachel exclaimed.

"Hi, Dad," the kids both said while keeping their focus on the television.

"Hello," Liam responded and smiled as much as he could. He slogged upstairs, not wanting to cause a stir with his melancholy.

He arrived in the bedroom and began taking off his tie and dress shoes. He heard the door open and turned to find Rachel sneaking in with concern on her face.

"Hey, Babe, how was your day," she inquired.

"It was pretty long. I'm glad to be home."

He continued looking down at the floor, fixated on his shoes as he untied them.

"Are you doing okay?" She asked.

"Yeah, I'm okay."

He walked over to the closet to return his shoes to their rightful spot. He continued staring aimlessly into his closet and sighed from the depths.

Rachel walked over, grabbed his arm, and turned him around to face her. She smiled at him. He began to return the gesture, but just couldn't bring it to fruition. Rachel wrapped her arms around him. He placed his arms around her, waiting for the affection to be over. She refused to let go, however. With each sigh, Rachel squeezed a little tighter. Liam tried to wait it out, but something within him rose up. An energy began flowing from her body to his, and back in return. Try as he might, Liam couldn't stop it. Tears began to emerge. He tried his best to conceal them, but it was as if Rachel was squeezing them out of him. Finally, he returned the favor and squeezed her with his arms, and the tears gushed outward. Rachel rubbed his back up and down.

"It's okay," she whispered into his ears. "It's okay."

He lost all his ability to hide and, instead, melted into her.

The heaviness of the day began to subside, and an energy, a hope, an enlivening emerged from within him. He kissed her on the cheek and gave her one last embrace. The message he felt in the car came back to him: "She brings it out of you."

51

JOSHUA LED BILL AWAY FROM THE TOMBSTONE AND IN another direction. Bill had no idea which way was which, but just followed around and through all the trees.

"Where are we going now?" Bill finally spoke up.

"It's time for the next step."

"I still don't understand how Liam is going to even bother listening to me, after all I've put him through," Bill repeated as he grabbed the trees while passing by them.

"Bill, all Liam really wants is for you to stay, for you to not leave when things get tough. It doesn't matter how well you do things while you're here, as long as you stay."

"Do you think he will forgive me?" Bill nervously asked.

"There's no question, he will. But it will take some time to regain that trust and feel comfortable again. That will take a while, but it will be worth it."

Suddenly Bill realized they were heading toward the place he had seen Liam giving the stones to the dark figure.

Bill suddenly stopped. Joshua turned around and looked toward him with compassion.

"What is it?"

"I can't do this. I saw what I did to him. I'm terrible. How am I supposed to be able to do this?"

"You are not terrible, Bill."

"I saw what I did."

"Yes, you did some hurtful things. But that wasn't to show you who you were, that was to show you how you have buried down who you really are. Your identity goes deeper than that. Epiphanies gave you a glimpse."

"That was Epiphanies, though, that wasn't me."

"Bill, Epiphanies can only show you what's true, who you are. Deep down, behind the hiding and running away, you are good, Bill. This is your chance to dare to believe it. I know this is difficult, Bill. I know it is painful. But pushing it aside, keeping it at bay, the pain will only get worse. This is the way to go forward. It's all part of the journey. Trust me."

Bill did all he could to put one foot in front of the other, and they continued. They hiked forward, trekking up the hill that Bill had climbed before. They traversed the rocks and went around a large boulder, down into the meeting area, where Liam and the dark figure were sitting around a table.

The dark figure rose and lifted hands in objection to Bill's presence, but Liam motioned for him to sit down. Joshua and Bill walked over and both took a seat around the table. Bill sat directly across from Liam, who looked only at Joshua.

"Liam," Joshua began, "Bill and I have been conversing over the past couple hours, and Bill has something he would like to say."

Liam struggled to look directly at Bill, but only looked in his direction. The area was silent as everyone waited for Bill to begin speaking.

"Liam, I ... I need to tell you how sorry I am. I'm sorry that I didn't realize what was going on. I've been gone for a long, long time, and had forgotten about everything that happened before, about how I left and hurt you deeply. I need you to know that it's not your fault."

Liam lowered his eyes to the ground and remained silent for a moment. Bill wanted to speak more and convey his regret, but he also wanted to give Liam space, so he waited patiently.

"It is my fault," Liam finally spoke up. "You wouldn't have left if I had not caused so many problems."

"None of that was your fault. I just got scared, scared that I couldn't control anything, scared that if I stayed we were both going to be destroyed. Mostly, I was just scared that I didn't have what it took to stay."

"But if I could have made everything better, you would never have left."

"That's not your responsibility. Sometimes bad things just happen. There's no one to blame. But sometimes, we don't know how to handle that. I didn't know how to handle it. And that's not your fault."

Liam started sobbing into his hands. Bill was overtaken with sympathy. This boy upon whom he had looked down with such contempt, he could now only look upon with a broken heart.

"I'm so sorry for the pain you've gone through, Liam. The pain from all the chaos around us, but mostly for the pain I have caused you. I know that a simple apology is not going to make up for all of that. I know it will take time to earn your trust. But I will stay with you as long as it takes."

Liam began to raise his head. He looked up at Bill and, for the first time, looked him in the eyes. His tears began to dry up, and gradually a smile formed on his face. Bill returned the smile, and suddenly Liam jumped up, ran over to Bill, and leapt into his arms.

"I love you," Liam exclaimed.

"I love you too," Bill replied as he squeezed him tight.

Joshua stood up, and the dark figure followed suit. Liam turned around; he and Bill looked on, awaiting what was coming next.

The dark figure raised a hand and pointed at Bill. "Now you belong here."

He looked over toward Joshua, as though he was awaiting orders. Joshua nodded his head. "It is time."

The dark figure slipped his hand into his robe and pulled out a handful of stones, much like the ones Liam had given him earlier. He gently laid them in a pile on the table.

Bill looked on, confused by the gesture. "What are those?"

"These are the lies of a broken child," Joshua explained.

"I don't understand."

"Look closer."

Bill leaned in and noticed some writing across the stones. He carefully reached over and picked one up. As he brought it close to his eyes, he could see a word more clearly: abandoned.

"These are the lies and stories that Liam believed and that have dominated his existence, but not just his, Bill; yours as well. They are the result of pain unresolved and events misinterpreted."

Bill leaned forward and searched through more of the stones. With each new word, a heaviness pushed into his heart that he had never known, or maybe just didn't want to. Bad. Defective. Problem. Unlovable.

"I can't take this," Bill confessed.

"Yes, you can," Joshua replied, "but you don't have to do it alone. That is why I am here. It is time to face these lies, because only in facing them can you get to the other side. These stones did not always utter lies out of pain and heartache. They once spoke a true word, and if we look deep enough, that original word still resides within them, and still represents reality."

Joshua pulled up his sleeve to reveal something Bill had never noticed: A sizeable scar on his wrist. He retrieved the abandonment stone and held it beneath his scar. Amazingly, a bright beam began forming from the scar and shone on the stone. "Out of the darkness, comes a great light," Joshua announced.

As Bill watched in wonder, abandonment steadily became translucent, and another word began to emerge beneath it. As It did, Joshua announced it with a thunderous tone of authority. "Embraced. The truth of who you are."

Liam sat down next to Bill, and they both looked on in wonder. The dark figure picked one of the stones. "Unlovable," the figure announced as he placed it in Joshua's hand.

Joshua looked deeply into the stone and shone his light on it. Another phrase began to arise. "Eternally accepted. The truth of who you are."

Bill and Liam's eyes both began to water as they fought to keep watching. Occasionally they would look down, overcome by the immensity of it all. Joshua, however, would wait for them to lift their heads up again.

Joshua continued until he had run through all the stones. It was exhilarating and painful all at once. Bill felt overwhelmed by the intensity and wanted to beg Joshua to stop. At the same time, he longed for each new stone to be revealed.

As the last stone was announced, Joshua turned to Liam and held out his hand. Liam solemnly stood and embraced it. Joshua then led him to stand upon the stone table. Liam made it to the top and stood motionless for a moment. Wind blew into the space where they were, and Liam appeared to be swept up in it. He didn't move from the table, however. Instead, it appeared as if a miniature cyclone had wrapped around him. He was engulfed in it, and Bill looked on in wonder.

A flash of light shone from the table, and Bill lowered his eyes in a protective reflex. As he opened them and looked upon the table once more, there was Liam, but only different. Instead of a shy, disheveled boy, there was a beaming, rejuvenated one. Instead of tattered and worn clothing, he was engulfed in new shiny garments. Bill could not believe his eyes.

"This is the image of Liam as he truly is," Joshua announced, "and by extension, you as you truly are."

Bill was startled as he looked to see the dark figure fade into the air and float away.

"This is only the beginning," Joshua announced. Liam and Bill turned to him and waited expectantly for him to elaborate. "We have a house to fix."

52

"So, how have you been?" Laura asked as she sat down in her chair across from Liam.

"I've been okay."

"Yeah? I know our last session was getting difficult for you toward the end. How have you been dealing with that?"

"Well, I've been able to let myself feel a little more, especially with Rachel."

"That's good. That's really good. Do you feel like you're more able to sense the things you are telling yourself?"

"Maybe a little, it's still difficult."

"That's okay. That's perfectly normal. And that's why you're here, and why I asked you to bring a picture of yourself. Did you remember to bring one?"

"Yes," Liam replied as he pulled the picture out of his pocket. He unfolded it and placed it face down on the table between them.

"I see you folded the picture," Laura commented.

"Yeah," Liam responded.

"Do you think that is significant at all?"

"What do you mean?"

"Well, that's not usually how we treat pictures that mean something to us."

"I mean, it's just a picture of me."

"Hmm, it's just a picture of you?"

"Yeah?" Liam responded, looking confused.

"I think maybe that's a telling thing for you to say. If that was an old picture of your wife, or of your kids, would you say, "it's just a picture of them"? Would you fold it up in your pocket like that, as if it had no importance at all? And then place it on the table face down, as if you were ashamed of it?"

"I … I never thought of it like that. Honestly, I didn't even give it a second thought."

"And that's why we're here Liam, to help you recognize what's happening within you."

Liam nodded, but didn't say anything.

"Liam, if it's okay with you, I'd like to go back to that moment in the grocery store with Rachel, the one you told me about last session. I believe she made a remark that really hit home for you. Since that was fairly recent, I think it will be a helpful exercise for us here. Can we do that?"

Liam nodded.

"As I recall, you were dancing and kidding around with each other in the store, and she got a little self-conscious. She made a remark that was meant to be playful, but that really impacted you. What was that remark?"

Liam was a little frustrated. He knew that Laura knew what it was and wasn't sure why she was having him repeat it. He started to say it, but quickly realized how difficult it was to do so. He opened his mouth to try again but couldn't get it out. He sat there for a moment, frustrated at the situation, and at his own inability.

"I know this is hard for you, Liam. Would you like me to say it for you?"

Liam nodded.

"Rachel said, 'You're so embarrassing.'" Laura let the words hang in the air for a moment. "How does that make you feel?"

Liam fought every urge he had to bury his emotions. He was so uncomfortable, but he was tired of hiding. "I feel angry," he finally confessed.

"What are you angry about? With whom are you angry?"

Liam finally had to admit what was really going inside him. He could understand it if he was angry at Rachel, or his dad. But deep down, he knew that wasn't what was really going on inside him. He was ready to start being honest with others, but most importantly, with himself.

"I'm angry at me."

"And why are you angry at you?"

"Because I'm always doing the wrong thing. I'm always screwing things up. I can never do anything right. And I'm angry at how easily I get upset about the smallest things. It seems like anything can set me in a spin." Liam felt himself getting worked up, but he could not stop himself. He had opened the box and couldn't possibly close the lid now.

Laura slowly nodded, validating what Liam was feeling. "Do you tell yourself that often?"

"Yeah, I think so."

"Why do you think you tell yourself that? Is that how you really feel about yourself?"

Liam shrugged his shoulders, more out of discomfort than giving an actual answer.

Laura leaned forward. She grabbed the picture that Liam had brought off himself and turned it over. Liam could see what she was doing but couldn't bring himself to look directly at the photo.

"So you've been able to start to identify how you're feeling about yourself, and what you are saying to yourself. Now, if you can, look at this picture and tell me what you feel."

Liam took a moment to prepare himself. He didn't want to do this, but he wanted to trust Laura. He looked up and saw himself. He was little in the picture, he guessed he was about seven years old. It looked to be a picture of one of his birthdays. He was holding up a gift he had just opened, a teddy bear with a baseball uniform on. As Liam stared at the picture, his anger and frustration continued to grow. Slowly, a sense of contempt began to rise in him as well.

"What are you feeling now?" Laura continued.

"I'm just so angry."

"With whom are you angry?"

"Me. Him. I just feel hatred for myself."

"Sit with that Liam. Why do you feel hatred toward yourself?"

"Because I screwed everything up. I always screw things up. It's like there's something wrong with me. If I could just be better."

"Better how?"

"Better at making my dad proud, better at being a husband and a dad, then I wouldn't screw things up."

"Can you tell me how you would have accomplished that as a child?" She asked.

Liam tried to think of a good response, but none came to mind. "I don't know."

"Because it's an unreasonable thing to expect of a child."

"I just feel like I could have done better."

Laura remained silent for a moment, letting the gravity of Liam's statement rest on them.

"Liam, do me a favor. Open your phone and pull up a picture of your son when he was younger."

"Why?"

"Just humor me, please."

Liam reluctantly pulled his phone out of his pocket and entered the pin to open it. He opened his Facebook account and went to a post that his wife had recently shared of a throwback picture with their son. "Okay, I found one."

"Good, now lay it on the table." Liam laid his phone down so they could both see the picture. "Now if I recall, a while back, Aaron said something to you at the dinner table that rubbed you the wrong way."

"Yes, but he and I worked through that. I let him know that it wasn't about him, and that I shouldn't have responded to him like that."

"But maybe it was about him. Maybe part of your stress lately has been his fault. Maybe he could have been better. And I'm sure there were plenty of times when he was younger when he did things that frustrated or angered you. Maybe he broke something, or maybe he just wouldn't listen. Maybe, he could have done better."

"I see what you're doing?"

"Okay then, you can't have it both ways. You either need to look at this little boy," she explained as she pointed to Aaron, "and tell him that he should have been a better son. Or you need to look at this little boy," she continued by pointing to the picture of Liam, "and tell him that he is okay. That it's okay for little boys to cry. It's okay for little boys to be sad. And tell him that he is loved just the way he is."

Liam shook as he fought to keep his tears back. After a couple minutes, he was able to speak again. "I know what you're telling me is right. I just have such a hard time doing it. I don't know why."

"Just say the words, Liam."

"I can't."

"Why not?"

"Because I don't believe it."

Liam wrapped his hands around his neck and looked down at the ground. He wasn't sure if he had anything left.

"Liam, look at me."

He couldn't bring himself to lift up his head.

"Liam, I really need you to look at me."

After a moment, Liam finally looked up and met Laura's eyes.

"You don't want to say the words because they feel like a lie, and that's the problem. You've believed that you were bad all your life, and that's not going to change overnight. But right now, you need to forget about it not feeling right, and trust what people who care about you say. Rachel doesn't believe you are bad. Your children don't believe you are bad. I'm confident that, as much trouble as you've had with your dad, that both your parents would deny that as well. And I know that you are not bad. So I need you to take a leap, to say the words that you don't feel are right by trusting me. You're okay. You are okay. There's nothing wrong with you. You are okay."

She pointed at Liam's picture of himself, and he took a few moments to compose himself. He breathed deep and looked intently at his picture. Finally, he opened his mouth and said the words, "You are okay." Tears erupted from his eyes. He fell back into the couch and continued sobbing, all while repeating the words, "You are okay."

53

BILL, JOSHUA, AND LIAM WOKE EARLY TO CONTINUE working on the house. It had been a week since the ceremony at the stone table, and each day had been filled with diligent work. There was no obligation, no fulfilling one's responsibilities, only three friends working joyously together on a project near to their hearts.

They woke early but getting up was another story. They had been working as late as possible each day and slept a deep sleep each night. In the mornings, they would enjoy chatting with each other as they soaked in the last few minutes of their cozy sleeping spots.

"I'll go grab some eggs," Liam announced as he finally lifted himself up.

"Aw man, that means we have to get up," Joshua playfully complained.

"I'll go grab some berries," Bill joined in.

"You guys are killing me," Joshua exclaimed.

"Come on, let's go you slacker," Liam joked, and the other two burst out laughing.

Bill set out to the woods to search for some berries. As he had done since the ceremony, he carried the pouch of stones with him. He could not bring himself to let go of them. The experience had been so moving and transformative for him. Every day he pulled them out to gaze at them and look on astonished. It still seemed unreal, impossible even. As he became engulfed by the trees, he pulled the pouch out once again, retrieved a few of the stones from inside, and let them rest in his hand as he looked on amazed.

After a few minutes, he returned them to the bag and began gathering the berries. He filled up his small bucket and returned to the house, overflowing once again with gratefulness and satisfaction.

+ + +

They finished their breakfast amidst much joking and laughter. Before they stood up to begin their work, Joshua stopped them and announced he had something to say.

"I just want to tell you both how much I am enjoying watching you grow and work together. It has been a wonderful thing to watch. I care about you both very deeply, and to see you both growing in love for each other has been remarkable. I am so proud of both of you."

They both sat quietly for a moment, soaking in the impact of Joshua's words.

"I'm not sure what to say," Bill confessed, "other than that I am just so grateful for all of this. I didn't even know what I was missing, but I'm so glad you both have made this possible. It hasn't been an easy journey, but it has been good. Really good."

"I'm so glad you're both here," Liam stated simply and thankfully.

"Well, let's get to work," Joshua proposed.

They cleaned up the table and the kitchen and proceeded to continue working on the house.

Joshua was working on patching up some more holes in the bedrooms. Liam and Bill had been focusing on getting the living room repainted. They pulled open the cans of paint and picked up where they had left off the day before.

"I'm just gonna say it," Bill began as he stood back to look at the wall they finished yesterday. "We're pretty good at this."

"I agree, although I think my side looks better," Liam responded with a chuckle.

"Oh really? Well I guess we'll have to see who wins today," Bill replied with a smile.

They put some finishing touches on the wall from the day before and moved to the next wall. Bill took the right side while Liam began on the left. They gradually worked toward the middle.

"Hey I think you missed a spot," Bill said as he pointed to Liam's side.

"Hey, stick to your side."

Bill turned to dip his brush into the paint and turned around to see a big, out of place, swipe on his side of the wall.

"That doesn't look good at all," Liam laughed.

"Hey, that wasn't me," Bill said as he contributed his own swipe to Liam's side.

Liam responded by brushing paint onto Bill's sleeve.

"Is that how it's gonna be?" Bill laughed.

Liam proceeded to sprint out the front door, giggling all the way. Bill chased after him and they both kept running until they were both exhausted and fell to the ground, gasping for air.

+ + +

Later that day, Bill ambled into one of the bedrooms to grab some more paint and was surprised when he looked at the wall on the left. There was a hole that they had patched up and covered over earlier that week, but all the patch work had fallen onto the floor. He gazed on it confused and called Joshua into the room.

"Yeah Bill, what's going on?"

"Look at this. Isn't this weird? Liam and I worked on this the other day, and it's all fallen off. I don't understand."

"Hmm, well sometimes these types of wounds take a longer time to heal and mend. This may be the very first one in this house. The first one is always the most difficult one to restore."

"Huh. Well should I just work on it again?"

"I think you and Liam need to both work on it again together. I think it will take both of you."

"Well, okay then."

Bill informed Liam of the plan, and they proceeded to patch the hole once more. They spent extra time on it, making sure everything was done well.

"I guess we just wait now, huh?" Liam said.

"Yeah, I guess so." They both returned to the living room to recommence their painting efforts.

After a few hours, the living room was almost complete. They decided to take a break, and Bill walked out to the well to get some water. They pulled the bucket up and dipped their cups in to quench their thirst. As they were drinking, Joshua appeared from the front door and walked out.

"Wow, I leave you guys alone for two seconds," he laughed.

Bill pulled his cup back to avoid spitting the water out. "Hey, we got a lot done."

"Yeah," Liam echoed.

They all shared another laugh, and Joshua brought his cup over as well to join the gathering.

"Do we wanna eat something soon?" Joshua inquired.

"Sounds good to me," Liam answered.

"Me too," Bill agreed. "I think I saw another peach tree out there. I'll go grab some."

"Okay, I'll start cooking up the meat we got yesterday," Joshua announced.

"Okay, sounds good," Bill commented as he began walking out toward the tree line. He headed straight for where he remembered the tree being. When he got out into the trees, he pulled the pouch out and began gazing at the stones again, but he noticed something deeply disturbing. The light in a few of them seemed to be fading, and a hint of the lies was emerging from the background.

"Oh no," Bill lamented. A deep sense of shame came over him. He shoved them back in the pouch and decided not to mention it to anyone.

He spotted the tree and began gathering the peaches for himself and the other two. He traipsed back to the house, distressed by what he had experienced. As he approached the front door, he heard Liam from inside. "Oh no!"

Bill ran in and found Liam in the bedroom staring at the hole in the wall that they had just worked on together. Joshua met them there as well, and they found Liam on the floor, visibly discouraged by what had happened.

"I don't understand," he groaned.

"Apparently this damage is gonna take some extra time and care to make right," Joshua explained.

"This is all my fault," Liam expressed.

Joshua looked over at Bill and directed him with his eyes to comfort Liam. Bill walked over, bent down, and placed his hands on Liam's shoulders.

"It's going to be okay. We're gonna keep at this together."

"But what if it keeps doing this? How long can we keep at it?"

"I told you, as long as it takes. remember?"

Liam nodded his head and, after a moment, stood up and embraced Bill. Joshua squeezed Bill's shoulder. "We're in this together."

54

RACHEL PULLED INTO THE DRIVEWAY FROM HER DOC-
tor's appointment. It was just a routine checkup but was also the perfect opportunity for Liam to surprise her when she got home.

Several weeks had passed since that impactful session with Laura.
The last few sessions had been spent unpacking and processing the
profound truths Liam had discovered. He was finally able to articulate
and ready to share these discoveries with his favorite person.

"You look good, Daddy," Lizzy commented as Liam reached the
bottom of the stairs.

"Thanks, Liz," Liam replied as he paced back and forth. He heard
Rachel approach and flung the door open to greet her. "Hi, Babe!"

"Hi?" Rachel responded, confused by Liam's behavior. "What are
you doing?"

"Just waiting for you."

"Why?"

"Because we have dinner reservations."

"What are you talking about?"

"A date. Go put on that dress I like; we're going fancy tonight."

"Oh wow, okay," she obliged with a smirk on her face. "What about
them?" She asked as she motioned with her eyes toward the two ado-
lescents sinking into the couches.

"I've got it taken care of, don't worry. Now go get dressed."

"Well, okay then," Rachel replied with a big smile.

+ + +

They hopped in the car and pulled out of the driveway. Liam was so
excited he sped off too fast and had to slow down.

Rachel reached over and rubbed his knee. "This is sweet, Liam. Thanks for doing this."

"You're welcome. Thanks for being my date."

They arrived at the restaurant and hunted for a couple minutes to find a parking spot.

"Wait, don't get out yet," Liam directed.

"What? Why?"

"Just wait," Liam replied as he jumped out and scurried around the back of the car.

Rachel chuckled as she saw him approach her side. He opened the door and offered his hand.

"My lady."

"Why, thank you."

Rachel's face was beaming. They seldom went to fancy restaurants, so this was a real treat for them. They strolled toward the front door with Rachel's arm firmly wrapped in Liam's.

Liam swung the door open and ushered Rachel into the foyer. The smell of steak smacked them in the face as soon as they entered. The restaurant was dimly lit and had an intimate ambiance. They were greeted by a young lady standing behind a podium.

"Good evening. Do you have a reservation?"

"Yes, two for Liam."

"Great, right this way," she directed as she motioned for them to follow her.

They followed the greeter around the corner and again to the left. She led them to a comfortable booth where they sat across from each other.

"Would you like to hear the specials?" She asked as she handed them each a menu.

"Sure," Rachel answered with a huge grin.

"Tonight we have lamb chops with mint jelly. We also have a T-bone steak served with steamed vegetables and your choice of a potato."

"Oh, I might want the lamb chops," Rachel conjectured.

Liam smiled back at her, excited to see that she was enjoying herself so much.

"Your waitress will be over soon. Enjoy!"

"Thanks!" Rachel replied.

Liam looked around at the other customers. He liked to get a glimpse of the food on other people's plates.

Soon another young lady arrived at their table.

"Hello, I'm Sarah and I'll be your waitress tonight. Would you like to start off with something to drink?"

"I'll take a beer," Liam replied.

"I'll take a margarita with salt," Rachel requested.

"Okay, sounds good. I'll be back soon."

She left to convey their drink order while Liam and Rachel scoured their menus.

"It's been so long since we've been here," Rachel commented.

"I know, it's been way too long."

"What made you wanna come here?"

"I just wanted to do something special, and I wanted to spend time and chat with you."

"I'm really glad; this is great."

They spent the next few minutes examining their menus and methodically turning the pages. They looked up over their menus and smiled. Liam could see a sparkle in Rachel's eyes that he had not noticed in a while, and it filled his heart with joy.

Sarah returned with their drinks on a platter. "Do you guys need more time to decide?" She inquired as she placed the beverages in front of them.

"I think I am going to go with the lamb chops," Rachel answered.

"Okay great, what kind of potato would you like?"

"I'll take the baked potato. And can I get a side salad as well with thousand island?"

"Of course. And for you sir?"

"I'll take the steak with fries and a salad as well."

"And what kind of dressing?"

"Ranch, please."

"Sounds good, I'll get those orders in for you."

Sarah left them alone again to chat.

"How did it go at the doctor today?" Liam asked.

"Oh fine. Everything looked good. I'm good until next year."

"That's great."

"Yep. How about you? How was your day?"

"It was good. Work went pretty fast. Got a lot done."

"That's good."

They continued chatting and enjoying the feel of the restaurant. They laughed together more than they had in a while. Liam felt a closeness to Rachel that was becoming more common. He was incredibly grateful for that.

They snacked on some delicious bread that Sarah brought out, covering their slices with as much honey butter as possible.

"Liam, I really want to thank you."

"You've already thanked me, Babe. This was my pleasure."

"No, not that. Just … for how you've stepped up for me and you, our marriage, our family. Thank you for fighting for me and doing all the hard work you've done with Laura. I know it's not been easy."

Liam smiled and looked down for a moment. He was taken aback by Rachel's sentiment, and had to take a bit to compose himself.

"Are you okay?" Rachel asked.

"Yeah, it's just really good to hear you say that."

"Well, I mean it. I'm so grateful for you and how hard you've worked."

"It's my pleasure. I would do anything for you."

Rachel returned his smile and reached over to squeeze his hand. They continued gabbing for the next few minutes. Sarah returned later with their salads. They dug into their plates and shared a few more comments. Liam offered a few stupid jokes that brought out Rachel's rolling-eyed laugh each time. They continued enjoying each other's company while they waited for their main dishes.

About fifteen minutes later Sarah returned with the lamb chops and steak.

"This looks so good!" Rachel expressed as she got a glimpse of her dinner

"Yes it does," Liam confirmed.

"Is there anything else I can get for you guys?"

"I think that's it," Liam replied.

"Okay, you both enjoy!"

Sarah left again while Liam and Rachel began enjoying their entrees.

After a few minutes of chewing and nothing else, Liam began talking again.

"I really wanted to share with you about what's been going on with me, you know, in therapy, and what I've been learning about myself."

Rachel stopped what she was doing and gazed back at Liam with her face beaming. "I'd love that."

Liam returned her smile and continued. "Well, Laura and I have been talking about how I can be really sensitive to criticism from others. It can be something some stranger says, or something you or the kids say. She helped me see that the reason is because I tend to be really hard on myself, you know, tear myself down. That's my go to. And so when people give me criticism, it initiates that defense mechanism in me, and I just start being really harsh to myself."

Rachel nodded as she followed along. "That makes sense. We've talked about that too."

"Yeah, I mentioned that to her, and I can see how frustrating it could be for you to feel like you couldn't give me any feedback without me taking it really personally."

"Yeah, but I understand where you were coming from. That's great that you're realizing all this, Babe."

"And she helped me see something else. She helped me see where this all ultimately comes from."

"Your dad, right?"

"In a way, yes, but not ultimately from him. She explained that when parents act out like my dad did, kids assume something is wrong with them, because their world depends on their parents being perfect. If their parents don't know what they're doing, the world would feel too dangerous to the kids."

"Hmm, okay."

"So, when my dad acted like that, I assumed something was wrong with me, and I sort of abandoned myself, because I was causing too much trouble. I stopped being a kid who had feelings and started trying to be the tough kid that my dad wanted me to be. So even though my dad was the one rejecting me in that moment, the real impact came from me abandoning myself. And that's what I've continued to do my whole life. When someone criticizes me, I once again assume something is wrong with me, and I abandon myself by beating myself up and disconnecting from myself and others."

"Wow. I'm really sorry."

"It's okay, because I'm becoming more aware of it and can use tools to work on it."

"Well, I just hate that I've made you feel that way."

"Sweetie, it's not you. This is how I've related to everyone for a long time. It's something I need to work on. I want you to be able to be honest with me."

"I know, I just hate thinking that you feel that way."

"I know. But I'm learning. I'm learning to forgive my dad too. He did what he did because that's all he knew how to do."

Rachel looked down for a moment. She appeared to have something to say, but had trouble getting it out.

"Have you been able to forgive me?" she asked, her voice more vulnerable than usual.

Liam responded with a sympathetic smile. "Of course. I know I was really angry before, but I know that you were in a bad place. I know you would never intentionally hurt me."

Rachel looked down again, not sure how to absorb the grace Liam was offering.

After a moment of silence, Liam continued sharing. "I'm learning to forgive myself too, because abandoning myself was all I knew how to do as a little kid. In some ways, it feels like that little kid is still sitting in that dugout, all alone, just waiting for me to come find him."

Rachel looked up with an ornery grin on her face.

"What? What's that look for?" Liam demanded.

"Let's go get him."

"What?"

"Let's go to the little league field. Go sit where you were sitting. Maybe it will have an impact on you to go back there, especially with how much you've learned about yourself."

Liam thought about it for a moment, and after getting over how odd it sounded, he returned Rachel's smile and agreed.

55

BILL WOKE UP BEFORE THE OTHER TWO. EVEN RUSTY was stuck in a deep sleep and was unphased by Bill's movements. It had been six months since the reconciliation between Bill and Liam, and, along with Joshua, they had made incredible progress on the house. In fact, it was looking like they would be finished within the next week or so. Bill rose up and shuffled through the front door and out to the well for some water. He pulled the bucket up and dipped his cup in. He decided to sit down on the grass next to the well, taking in the beautiful landscape that he had grown to appreciate so much.

He reached into his pocket and pulled out the bag of stones from the ceremony. He pulled one out and ran his thumb over it. The stones continued to be a source of frustration and discouragement. He had been so moved by the truths that were revealed from Joshua's light, but the lies continued to hover in the background of the stones. They were not the dominant feature as they had been before, but they were emerging again, which greatly troubled Bill. He had kept this to himself, however, fearing that he was doing something wrong. He didn't want Joshua or Liam to think less of him.

Bill heard movement behind him and looked back to see Joshua approaching.

"Early riser, huh?" Joshua greeted.

"I don't know about that," Bill replied as he subtly stuffed the bag back in his pocket. "Just got up a few minutes ago."

"Liam and the dog are still out."

"Yeah, I saw that."

Joshua joined Bill on the ground and, for a few minutes, they silently stared out into the trees.

"You know, the house is going to be finished soon."

"Yep, I was just thinking about how fast it's all coming along."

"Are you ready for the next part of the journey?"

Bill looked over confused. "Huh?"

"What? You didn't think this was the end, did you?"

"I guess I should have figured it wasn't with you around."

"There is a difference this time."

"Oh yeah? What's that?"

"This time, there's no circumstances forcing you to go on. This one is up to you."

Bill pondered for a moment, but then shook his head. "No, I can't do it. I can't leave Liam again. I can't do that to him."

"Of course not!" Joshua responded in a whimsical voice. "He would be going with you."

"Oh. I guess that changes things, doesn't it."

"Yeah, I guess it does."

"Do you think he would want to go?"

"I think he wants to go wherever you are going."

"This is such a lovely place. I would hate to leave it."

"Yes, it is. But even the loveliest place can lose its touch when you remain longer than you were intended to stay. Remember what you learned from Epiphanies?"

"Yes, I remember. It makes more sense now. Back then I was just angry."

"Yes, you were," Joshua seconded with a chuckle.

Joshua reached over for Bill's cup and got a drink of water for himself. "Well, speaking of lessons learned, there's one more important lesson you need before we can think of you and Liam venturing out together."

"Oh. Um, okay. What is that?"

"You will see. For now, just follow me."

"Do I need anything?"

"Fortunately, we only need the bag of stones you placed in your pocket."

Bill looked down sheepishly. "Saw that, did you?"

"I'm just giving you a hard time, but we will need them."

They walked out toward the wooded area, but in a direction that Bill had never been before. They walked down a small descent and then ducked underneath a fallen tree. They then proceeded to make so many twists and turns that Bill lost track of where they were.

"I figured we were going back to the stone table," Bill chimed in.

"No, not for this. This lesson is not for Liam. Just for you."

"What? Why?"

"You will soon see."

They made one last turn, and standing there, much to Bill's surprise, was the dark figure.

"I don't understand," Bill professed. "Why is he back?"

"The stones have been a source of confusion for you."

Bill felt a wave of embarrassment. "You know about that?"

"Yes."

"Is he the reason for it?" Bill asked as he pointed to the dark figure.

"No."

"Then it's my fault, then."

"No, Bill. It's time to stop seeking blame. It's time to learn to accept the complicated and ambivalent phenomenon that is reality."

"I don't understand."

"The dark and the light do not always divide into neat and tidy categories. You have to learn to accept the light even when the darkness is present. You must learn to let go, even of that which you think you need to survive, in order to find life."

Just then, the dark figure lifted his staff and slammed it into the ground. It exploded into a thick, black cloud.

"What is happening?"

"I told you, the darkness has much to teach you," Joshua declared as he motioned toward it.

"You want me to go in that thing?" Bill demanded.

"Yes."

"Are you going in?"

"I am already there. You will hear my voice, though it will be challenging at first to hear me. I assure you, I will be with you. Trust me."

Bill stared into Joshua's eyes and could tell he wasn't going to change his mind. His stomach churned as he looked into the darkness. He turned back to Joshua once more, who gave him an affirming nod. Bill paused before stepping forward. At first, the darkness was like a dark fog around him, but soon, he was engulfed. Fear flooded through his body as his breathing increased and his heart rate sped up. He spun around but couldn't see anything. He reached into his pocket to pull out the stones, hoping to gain some light and encouragement from them. The darkness brought out the glow of the words, but the lies continued to seep out. In desperation, Bill cried out.

"Joshua, where are you?"

A faint noise brushed past his ears, but he could not discern what it was. He hunched down and gripped the stones tighter, hoping to squeeze even an ounce of comfort from them, but to no avail. He closed his eyes and covered his head.

He heard the obscure noise once again, but it was becoming clearer. He could now tell that it was Joshua's voice. He could not decipher what he was saying. Bill grasped the stones even tighter, and his hand began to ache. The voice began to become clearer, and amidst the pain and darkness two words emerged: let go.

Let go of what? There was nothing around him to grab. He began to realize that the words were referring to the stones in his hand. "How can I possibly let these go," he demanded. They had been everything to him over the last six months. They were all he had left in this black abyss, but once again the two words were repeated: let go.

He tightened his grip on them. The pain surging through his hands intensified and began spreading up his arms and into his body. No matter, he could still not imagine giving them up. But as his agony increased, he could hear two new words surfacing: trust me.

In an act of faith, he stood and threw the stones up into the abyss. He remained silent for a few seconds. Everything remained black. Every hint of hope and solace vanished from his body. He continued waiting.

Suddenly the stones that he had released burst forth high above him with light and color more magnificent than he could ever imagine. The darkness was overcome and disappeared as quickly as it had appeared. Feet shuffled toward him as Joshua approached.

"Hold out your hand," Joshua instructed.

Bill obliged, and once he did, the stones all dropped back into his possession.

"You must not hold too tightly to such objects, or you will lose sight of what they truly represent. The darkness cannot overcome it. But sometimes the darkness has something to teach you. In this case, to let go in order to find life. It's not all or nothing. It's not darkness or light, it's light that holds you even in the darkness. It's darkness that shows you how you are sabotaging yourself from seeing the light. This is what Liam is not yet ready to hear. You have to help him."

"What if I forget again?" Bill asked.

"Not if, my friend, but when," Joshua chuckled. "You will learn again, and over time, you will become less afraid of the darkness. In fact, you will come to be thankful for it, because of what it continues to teach you. The light encompasses everything, so the darkness can never truly overcome."

Bill took a moment to soak it all in; a wave of hope rose up inside. "Well, I guess it's time to go talk to Liam about the next step," Bill surmised.

"I think you're right."

56

LIAM TURNED INTO THE COMPLEX WITH THE LITTLE league fields. They inched along as they drove on the gravel road leading to the diamonds, stopping several times to check if they had found the right one.

"Is that one it?" Rachel asked as she pointed across Liam's field of vision.

"No, it's a little further down."

They continued driving another few hundred feet.

"There it is," Liam confirmed. He turned left toward the field. The headlights illuminated the fence bordering the outfield.

"It's so small," Rachel commented.

"Well, it is for little league," Liam replied with a chuckle. "It's been so long since I've been here."

They exited the car and approached the field. Rachel took a step on the grass.

"Oh, wait a minute."

"What's wrong?"

"My heel sank into the ground; I'll need to take them off. Come here."

Liam moved next to her so she could lean on him as she took her shoes off.

"Okay, let's go," she directed as she held the straps of her heels in her fingers. "The grass is pretty cold."

"Well come here then," Liam advised. He turned around and got in position for her to ride on his back. "Jump on."

"Okay," she said with a grin. She hopped on his back and wrapped her arms around his neck. "Okay, I'm ready."

Liam marched toward the end of the outfield fence to an opening. He carefully entered through it, not wanting to hit Rachel against anything.

"Which dugout was your team in?"

"We were in the one on the left," he answered as they turned to head toward the dugout.

"Am I getting heavy for you?"

"Is that a trick question?"

"Oh geez, no," she laughed.

"I'm fine. You fit pretty well on my back."

"I'll take that as a compliment."

"That's what it's meant to be."

They soon reached the infield where the ground was dry and dusty.

"I can walk from here," she informed him.

"Okay. But I don't want you to step on anything."

"It's okay, I'll just use my phone to look where I'm walking."

"Okay," Liam complied as he let her down.

Rachel pulled out her phone and used it to illuminate the ground around them. A dust cloud formed around their feet as they proceeded toward the dugout.

As they got closer, Liam slowed down and stretched his hand to touch the chain link fence surrounding the dugout. The metal was cold against his hand. He wrapped his fingers around it and tugged.

"Are you okay?"

"It's just so weird to be here. I've avoided this spot for so long. I always told Aaron that I couldn't coach his team in little league because of work, but I really just couldn't stomach the thought of being in these dugouts. It feels surreal."

Liam looked up and pointed to a spot on the bench. "That's where I was sitting." He moved into the dugout and hesitated before sitting down. He folded his hands in his lap and hung his head.

Rachel entered the dugout as well and sat down next to Liam. She placed her hand below his neck and rubbed his back. "Does it bring back the memories?"

Liam nodded his head. "I can feel how I felt then. It's so ... it's just so strong."

Liam continued looking down. The air cooled as the sound of crickets filled it. They both remained quiet for a moment.

"What would you say to yourself? If your younger self was sitting right here, what would you say to him?"

"I don't know. I know what I would say to some other kid, but being here, it just feels so real. I don't know if I have it in me."

Rachel sat silent for a moment, wanting so badly to flip a switch and make everything okay. As she sat there, reflecting on the pain her husband was feeling, the next best thing came to mind.

"Well, I'll tell you what I would say. If I, as a mother, saw a parent treat their child the way your father did to you, this is what I would say. I would come sit down next to him just like I am with you now. I would tell him, 'I'm so sorry your daddy said those things to you. I'm sure he didn't mean it, and that he's having a bad day. You are not an embarrassment."

Rachel stopped for a moment as a tear fell from Liam's face and soaked the dust beneath it. "It's courageous to show emotion," she continued. "Many people aren't brave enough to do that. Someday that ability will make you an amazing husband and incredible father. And it's okay to have a bad day at something. As long as you get up and try again, you never really fail. But most of all, I'm proud of you."

. With that final sentiment, Liam lost control and sobbed into his arms. Rachel draped her arms around him and squeezed him tight. For the next few moments, Liam allowed himself to soak in what he had always been searching for: affirmation in the deepest reaches of his soul.

+ + +

After the tears dried up, Liam looked into the sparkle of Rachel's eyes that he could still see in the darkness.

"Thank you."

She leaned in for a soft kiss. "You're welcome."

"What do you wanna do now," he inquired.

"Let's lay out on the infield and lookup at the stars."

"Our clothes are gonna get all dirty."

"So? We're not trying to impress anybody."

"Okay."

Rachel stood up and pulled Liam to his feet. They traveled over to the pitching mound, using her phone to make sure there was nothing on the ground to deter them.

"If we're doing this, at least wear my jacket," Liam insisted as he slid it off his arms.

"Oh, alright," she conceded with a chuckle.

They both lowered onto the ground and sprawled out while reaching for each other's hand.

"It's been such a long time since we've done this," she expressed gleefully.

"I know, we used to do it all the time."

"I know, remember in college? We would go to the lake in your truck and lay out in the bed."

"Yeah. To be honest, I never enjoyed it that much, looking at the stars, I mean."

"Really, you seemed to enjoy it."

"Well, I enjoyed lying next to the hot girl I was dating."

"Pfft, whatever. How could you not like looking at the stars?"

"I don't know. I mean, I guess they just made me feel really small and insignificant."

"Well, yeah! That's the point. It's supposed to remind you that you are part of something bigger. That this has been around for a long time before you, and it will be around for a long time after. So, it's not really up to you at the end of the day. You can just be grateful to be part of it."

"Yeah, I never got that. I guess I've spent so much of my life feeling insignificant and trying to find some way to make myself stand out. It's like I was trying to earn my right to exist or something."

"Honey, I'm sorry you felt that way. I guess for me this makes me feel even more significant. I remember going to church when I was a girl, and they talked about how even before God made the universe, he loved us and chose us to be one with him. The whole thing about Jesus was that God was wrapping us in himself. And when I look up at the sky, and think about how vast it is, and that whoever caused all this wanted us to be a part of it, it makes me feel pretty special."

"Huh. I didn't think you liked church that much."

"I'm not really into the structure and the system of it, but I really appreciate that whole message of connectedness to each other and to the source of everything. It made sense to me. It was like I always knew it, but it gave me words for it."

"I guess I never really thought of it that way. I always thought of myself as needing to prove my worth."

Rachel squeezed his hand. "How about now?"

Liam gazed up and let himself relax in the wonder of the infinite scene above them. "I think I'm starting to like this."

57

LIGHT BEGAN BREAKING IN THROUGH THE WINDOW AND illuminating Bill's face. He cracked his eyes open to make sure it was, in fact, morning. He had been awake for a while. He tossed and turned most of the night, partly out of excitement for the next stage of the journey, but also out of profound sadness to leave this place he had grown to love. Unlike his exit from Epiphanies, however, he was not leaving this time with any anger or frustration. He trusted Joshua and looked forward to enjoying his and Liam's company on their trek.

Once again, Bill was awake before Joshua and Liam. Rusty, however, was eager and ready to get moving. He sat beside Bill's head and stared at him, wagging his tail at a rapid pace. Bill decided to get up, wanting to take another look around the beautiful landscape. He snapped up and reached over to scratch Rusty's head. They ventured out through the front door and wandered outside the house.

Rusty was hoping to play and jumped around with excitement. He calmed down as he observed Bill's reminiscent demeanor. Bill walked around the house to the backyard and stared for a while. The flashback from the first innocent he encountered darted through his mind. He smiled effortlessly, grateful for the adventure he had enjoyed since then. He returned to the front of the house and sat down close to the well. Rusty sat down as well and nuzzled up next to him.

+ + +

Liam and Joshua emerged from the cabin. Liam ran over and slid down next to Rusty, who pounced and slobbered all over his face. They all laughed as Joshua stumbled over to their location to take a seat as well.

"It really is beautiful here," Joshua commented.

"Yeah," Bill concurred as he sighed with satisfaction. "I'm gonna miss it."

"Me too," Liam echoed as they cuddled with Rusty.

"What do you guys say? One more breakfast before we leave?" Joshua proposed.

"Sounds great," Bill replied.

"Count me in," Liam answered.

"Great. You guys relax, I'll go get it started."

Joshua stood up and made his way back to the house. Bill turned toward Liam and smiled at the scene of a boy with his dog.

"Are you nervous about leaving?" Bill asked.

"Not really. I'm ready to go. I've been here long enough. I do love it here, but I think I'm ready to go."

"Well, I'm glad you were able to see the house the way it was meant to be before you left."

"Yeah, me too," Liam confirmed as he continued scratching Rusty's head. "So where do you think we're going?"

"I really don't know. I've never really ever known with Joshua. He seems to enjoy it more that way."

They quieted down for a moment. Bill ran his hands over the crisp, morning grass.

"Bill?"

"Yeah, Bud?"

"Do you ever miss your old place? You know, your cabin by the river?"

"Sometimes. Not because it was better, but it was easier sometimes. Everything seemed to make sense, at least for a while."

"Do you ever wish you could go back?"

"I can see how it was helpful for a time. But no, I wouldn't want to go back. Being here with you and Joshua is much better."

"Okay," Liam quickly responded. He jumped up and ran back to the house with Rusty on his heels. Bill spent a few more moments reminiscing before he got up as well and drifted back for breakfast. As he approached the house, the sound of Joshua and Liam enjoying themselves echoed from the kitchen. Another heartfelt smile spread across his face as he entered the front door.

"I think you guys are having too much fun," he greeted them with a grin.

Liam and Joshua both laughed to themselves. Bill took a seat at the table, waiting for breakfast to be ready, which it soon was. The three companions chatted and laughed to themselves like old friends ending a long, satisfying vacation. Bill's heart was full in a way he had never remembered it being full before. Every bite of food, every laugh, every smile was like a jolt of gratitude to his soul. Soon, this would be over, but the sadness was minimal. Instead, he was mostly thankful.

+ + +

Bill and Liam exited the house for the last time, Joshua right behind them. They both stopped and turned to gaze upon the house they had both loved. An invisible force tugged on them to stay and seemed to drain their bodies of the energy to travel forward. After a few tears, Bill wrapped his arm around Liam to comfort him.

"It's harder than I thought," Liam confessed.

"I know, but it will be okay. Come on. Let's get going."

They adjusted their packs for the best balance on their backs and turned back around. They veered toward the tree line across the right side of the house. It was an entry point Bill had not yet explored, and he enjoyed the new sights to behold.

After about an hour, their leisurely hike transitioned into an uphill climb. Joshua led, with Liam in the middle and Bill following behind. This time, however, Bill had no ill feelings about being the last one. He was content to support the other two and provide safety for Liam in case any dangers arose. Per usual, Rusty was on his own agenda, darting back and forth between them.

Joshua stopped for a moment and took a drink from his water canister. "I think," he began between sips, "there should be a place to take a break soon."

"Okay sounds good," Bill yelled from the back.

"You doing okay Liam?" Joshua inquired.

Liam lifted up his thumb. Though he had lived off the land all his life, Liam was not as used to this kind of a hike. He was heavily panting but kept pushing.

Joshua closed his canister and motioned for them to continue. They pushed up the ascent, making each step steady and sure. It was a rough terrain, more so than even Bill was used to. There were large amounts of loose dirt and small rocks that tumbled down beside them. They used the smaller trees to grab and balance themselves as they grew closer to the breaking point.

A few small rocks slid down around them, but one was about a foot in diameter and thundered as it barreled down the hill.

"Watch out!" Joshua shouted.

Joshua sidestepped the small boulder, but Liam was not as quick to move. He leapt to the side and lost his footing. Bill pulled himself toward a tree he had been clinging to and hugged it close as the rock tumbled by, but in the midst of the noise a faint cry from Liam pierced his ears.

Bill swung his head around to analyze the situation. "Liam! Are you okay?"

"I think so," he answered. "I just slammed into this tree and scraped my arm."

Bill raced up to Liam's position. He carefully grabbed Liam's arm and looked it over.

"How bad is it?" Joshua asked from above.

"He's got a pretty good gash in his arm. I'm going to wrap it before we keep going."

"Good idea. I'm going to explore ahead some and see if we have any other big rocks to worry about going forward."

"Okay!"

Bill found a place to lay his pack down without it sliding away. He pulled out his first aid kit and began wrapping Liam's arm. He wound it several times around his arm.

"This is different," Liam chuckled.

"What do you mean?"

"Well, last time I got hurt, you wanted to leave me there."

Bill looked a little sheepish. "Yeah, that was not a good moment."

"It's okay. I'm just glad that we are so much better now."

Bill finished with Liam's arm and tore off the excess wrapping. "Me too," he smiled at Liam.

"You guys doing okay?" Joshua exclaimed.

"Yeah! We're ready to go."

"Okay! It looks like it's clear to the resting point."

"Okay!"

Bill helped Liam to his feet. He pulled his pack back up onto his back, and they continued up toward Joshua.

+ + +

After about an hour, they were coming up on the spot where Joshua wanted to stop. They all dropped their packs, sat down, and leaned against them.

"Well, this has been quite a first day so far," Bill pronounced.

"Yep," Joshua chuckled. "The terrain gets a little smoother going forward from what I remember, but we'll have to decide which path we want to take."

"Which one do you think we should take?" Bill asked.

"Actually, I'd like to leave that up to you."

Bill raised his eyebrows in surprise. "Me? I've never been this way before."

"True, but there are often several ways to take a journey, and many times there isn't one that's best for every occasion. Sometimes different paths are needed at different times for different people."

Bill stood up and walked over toward the tree line where the paths opened. He hesitated for a moment as his nerves began to yell at him. He still was not comfortable taking the lead. There appeared to be three directions they could take. The one on the right looked very smooth, as if it had been traveled often. The one in the middle seemed a little rougher, but it was also wider. The one on the left appeared to be the roughest and seemed to have been very seldom traveled.

Joshua rose up as well and walked over next to Bill.

"So which one will it be?" He asked.

"Honestly, I don't really know. The one over there seems to be the easiest," he conjectured as he pointed to the path on the right. "But I've learned that doesn't always mean it's the best one. I really don't know. I wish you would just decide."

"Well, I'm not going to do that, but can I point something out to you?"

"Sure," Bill sighed, wishing he could just get a straight answer.

"I'm not the only person here you can ask for help."

Bill looked back at Liam, who had his eyes closed and was leaning his head back against his pack. "Liam? But he's never been this way before either."

"No, he hasn't, but Liam has an intuition that you could learn to utilize."

"Intuition? I don't know. I'd rather just have a clear answer."

"I know you would. You have worked so hard to help Liam to trust you again, and you've done an amazing job. But now, it's time for you to learn to trust him too."

Bill stood silent for a moment, nervous about the prospect of trusting a child's judgment. If he was honest with himself, however, he wasn't that thrilled with his judgment either.

"Okay, let's do it. Let's ask him."

Joshua grinned back at Bill. "I think that's an excellent choice."

They sat back down for a while and allowed Liam to get more rest.

58

LIAM SHUT HIS LAPTOP AND REACHED OVER FOR HIS briefcase. Victor wanted the team to wrap up the project they were currently working on, and Liam was close to completing his part. His eyes were growing tired of the backlight from the laptop, and his mind was having trouble focusing.

A knock on the door surprised him. He assumed it would be Victor stopping by to get a status report. Instead, Frank emerged through the doorway.

"Hi son," Frank greeted as he transitioned into the room.

"Dad?" Liam wasn't sure what to say. They had not spoken, much less seen each other, since the awkward dinner at his parents' house a couple months prior. Butterflies played tag in his stomach as he wondered why his dad would come to see him at work. He watched Frank enter the room and sit down across from him. There was something about this man he had known his entire life that he didn't recognize. Instead of a strong, impenetrable exterior, there was a tentative, uncertain man before him. Even his hands appeared to be unsure of what to do with themselves.

"What are you doing here?" Liam asked.

"Well, I haven't seen you in a while. Just wanted to see how you were doing."

"Oh, well I'm doing good. How are you and mom doing?"

"We're doing good," Frank replied with a head bob.

"That's good."

"What are you working on?"

"Just finishing up a pitch we're making to a clothing company."

"Oh, that sounds interesting."

The two shared a moment of awkward silence. Liam could tell by Frank's fidgeting hands and darting eyes that he had something else on his mind.

"Is there something else you wanted to talk about?"

"Son, I've been thinking a lot about what Rachel said when she came to see me."

"Dad, I'm sorry about that. She should have never … "

Frank motioned with his hand to quiet Liam. "No. It was good what she did. She brought up a lot of important things. And so did you; I just didn't listen."

Frank paused for a moment. Liam could tell it was hard for him, so he kept quiet to let him finish.

"I've never been good at talking about this kind of stuff, so just let me get this out."

"Okay."

"I realize I was sometimes hard on you, but I wanted you to be tough because I didn't want you to have to go through the same shit that I did. I don't know how much you remember about my dad."

"I know he wasn't good to you."

"No he wasn't. He was an asshole, to me, to my mom, to everybody. It was a nightmare growing up as his son. He would get drunk and beat me and my mom all the time. The only way I survived was to be tough, stand up for myself. I tried to stand up for my mom, but she just kept defending him and never stood up for me. I was on my own, and I had to be tough to survive. And honestly, that's how I've gotten through life ever since then. That's all I know. And I wanted you to be tough because I didn't want you to have to endure the same shit that I did. But I'm so sorry that I said you were embarrassing. I'm sorry if I did anything else to make you feel like you weren't tough enough. I just wanted to help you, but I can see how it hurt you now."

"It's okay dad."

His dad nodded and smiled, and a wave of relief came over him. His shoulders relaxed and he sat back in the chair. He looked like he wanted to talk more, but it was taking a lot out of him.

"You know what we haven't done in a while?" his father transitioned.

"What's that dad?"

"Go to the baseball field and, you know, hit some balls around."

"Yeah, it has been a long time."

His dad got an ornery grin on his face. "Do you want to?"

Liam's eyes grew big. "Oh man, that sounds like fun. But I don't have my stuff, and I don't have many baseballs."

"Well, I actually went and bought a bunch today. I have a glove and bat in my truck too."

Liam became jittery with excitement. "Okay let's do it!" He exclaimed. He rushed to pull out his phone and called Rachel. The phone rang a couple times before she answered.

"Hey, Babe."

"Hey, I'm gonna be home late tonight."

"Oh, I'm sorry, you gotta work late again?"

"No, actually my dad and I are going to the baseball field to hit some balls."

Rachel was silent for several seconds. "Umm ... what?"

"Yeah, he came to see me at work a few minutes ago, and ... "

"Oh wow, you're serious. Well, that's great sweetie. Have fun!"

"I will! Love you!"

"I love you too!"

Rachel barely got the words out before Liam hung up the phone. He gathered his stuff together as fast as he could, and they scurried down to their vehicles.

+ + +

The boys arrived at the baseball fields about an hour later. Liam was so giddy he could hardly contain himself. He caught himself speeding several times on the way and had to keep slowing down. Rachel had called to point out that he might not want to play in his suit. He begrudgingly agreed and had stopped home on the way to change. Liam pulled up to park behind the backstop, jumped out of the car, and ran over to help his dad get all of the equipment out of the truck.

"I'm really excited about this," Liam told his dad. "I haven't done this in a long time."

"Me either, not since the last time you and I did."

The sky was clear and infinitely blue. Liam's forehead began perspiring. He was grateful that he had stopped at home, not just for the change of clothes, but to grab one of his ball caps and his own glove.

"Do you wanna hit or pitch first," his dad inquired.

"I'll hit."

"Sounds good. We'll see if this arm has anything left," his dad chuckled.

They first grabbed their gloves and threw the ball back and forth to warm up their arms. The sound of the ball smacking the inside of the gloves reverberated through the air. Liam loved hearing that sound, as well as the slight pain that shot through his hand each time he caught the ball

"Dad?" Liam began as he threw the ball back.

"Yeah, Son."

"Do you ever regret not going to play ball in college?"

"Yeah, I do. I mean, I'm happy with how my life turned out, so it's not like I regret that. I just wish I would have taken the chance, really stepped out there, I guess."

"Yeah, that makes sense."

They threw the ball back and forth a few more times, gradually backing up further apart.

"What about you, do you ever regret not playing in college?"

Liam thought about it for a moment, but soon shook his head. "Not really, I guess. I mean, I get what you're saying about stepping out and trying something that is risky, and I think at the time, I was kind of afraid of not being good enough. But I think I've realized that I mostly wanted to play to connect with you. So honestly, this right here is all I ever wanted to get out of baseball."

An easy smile formed on his dad's face. "Yeah, this is good. Well, you ready to start?"

"Yep, let's do it.'

Liam grabbed the bat and strolled over next to the plate. He took several practice swings before he got in his stance. He swiveled his feet and dug into the dirt as his dad began his wind up. The first pitch was a fast ball on the outside of the plate. Liam swung and fouled it back behind the plate. The contact vibrated through the bat and up into his arms.

"Yeah, I think you still got it," Liam laughed.

"Looks like it," his dad echoed.

Liam dug his feet in once again. His dad threw another fastball up and in. Liam got a hold of it and sent it to shallow right field.

"I'm catching up," he insisted.

His dad grabbed another ball and stood on the mound, doubled over as he eyed Liam. "Let's see if I can still do this," he said.

He wound up and threw it much slower this time. It floated towards Liam, but then rotated high over the plate. Liam recognized the spin and stepped in as he swung as hard as he could. The ball popped off of his bat and flew to deep center field. His dad spun around and stared out as the ball fell to the ground.

"That was a good one," his dad complimented.

His dad kept pitching for the next ten minutes or so.

"You ready to switch," Liam asked.

"Sure, sounds good."

Liam walked over toward the mound and handed the bat to his dad. He put on his glove and grabbed one of the balls next to the mound. He tossed the ball up in the air a couple times before positioning his feet.

"Here we go," he narrated as he started his wind up and threw a fastball down and in. His dad swung and missed.

"That was good placement," his dad commended.

Liam set up, threw again, and placed a slider on the outside of the plate. His dad just barely got a piece of it and fouled it out to right field.

"I remember that slider," his dad joked.

They continued and swapped places a couple more times. Their clothes grew dark with sweat. After about an hour, their under-exercised bodies were howling at them to bring it to a conclusion. They gathered all the baseballs and met back at home plate.

As Liam bent down to grab the duffle bag, his dad stopped him and looked him in the eyes.

"Son, I'm really sorry about how I've made you feel."

"It's okay, Dad."

"No, it's not. I need you to know that I am proud to be your father, and I always have been."

Liam looked down toward the ground as he tried to contain the tears that were welling up behind his thankful eyes.

"Thanks, Dad. That … that means a lot. And you know what, I didn't have to deal with the stuff you dealt with … because I had you for a dad."

Frank swung his arm around Liam as they began walking back to their vehicles. Neither of them could stop smiling.

59

LIAM SAT UP AND STRETCHED HIS ARMS AND LEGS. HE rubbed his eyes and continued to wake up from his nap. He stopped suddenly as he noticed Joshua and Bill both smiling at him.

"What?" he said with a grin on his face.

"Nothing. How are you feeling?" Joshua asked.

"I feel pretty good. What's going on?"

"Well, we decided we're going to have you choose the path we take next."

"Really?"

"Yes. Remember how you learned to trust yourself, your instincts, the night we arrived at the house?"

"Yeah, but that was going back to my house. I've never been here before."

"It's still the same process. You know, even when you don't think you do."

"Okay?" Liam responded, not sure if he was trying to convince them or himself.

He stood up and Bill pointed the three options out to him. Liam scanned them for a few minutes. A tightness formed in his chest as the fear of making a mistake washed over him. But soon, he recalled Joshua's previous advice. "Just trust your gut." He looked once more, and let the answer come to him.

"We need to take the middle path," he announced with more confidence than he was expecting.

Joshua and Bill looked at each other and nodded. "Well, that's what we'll do," Bill concluded.

"We have several more hours of daylight, so we should be able to make some good progress on this path," Joshua surmised.

They each hoisted their packs up over their shoulders and moved into the path, with Rusty happily tagging along. The path was fairly rough for the first hour or so. Joshua had to cut back a lot of brush and small branches in their way. When he would get tired from wielding the machete, he would trade places with Bill.

Eventually, the path became much clearer, and they were soon simply strolling along to the east. Their bodies were very thankful for the change in pace. As they continued, the air began to cool down with the evening rolling in. Their warm, perspiring skin was beginning to chill. Soon, they would need to find a place to rest for the night.

Fortunately, they came upon such a place soon after. They all dropped their packs with much relief and plopped on the ground to take a break, sprawling out their weary limbs.

"How much further do you think we have to go," Liam asked.

"I really don't know. It's never the same as it was before. You can just never tell," Joshua explained.

"Well, that doesn't give me much," Liam joked.

"Don't feel bad," Bill chimed in. "He's given me those kinds of answers ever since I met him."

Bill got up to look around the area and see what was available.

"We'll just try to have another productive travel day tomorrow," Joshua concluded.

"Hopefully the path will stay pretty easy," Liam replied.

"I wouldn't count on it," Bill chimed in as he inspected the continuation of the path. He could see a bend coming up that led to a narrow walkway sitting above a long drop.

Liam jumped up to discover what Bill was looking at. He gazed out and saw the narrow stretch. The last bit of energy was sucked out of his body.

"Oh no … we can't do that," Liam exclaimed

"Yeah, I don't know about this, Joshua," Bill echoed.

Joshua stood up and walked over to join his companions. "This is the way we needed to come, difficult stretch or not."

"Are you sure?" Liam asked. "What if I was wrong?"

"Liam, I believe in you, and difficult circumstances aren't going to change that. Let's not psych ourselves out dwelling on it tonight. Let's get a fire going and see if we can get some dinner."

+ + +

Joshua was able to hunt another rabbit and bring it in for their meal. Liam scouted out the area for fruit while Bill prepared the fire. They lounged around the blaze, enjoying the food. Liam and Bill took slow bites as their attention was often diverted to the upcoming path. They struggled to do much of anything the rest of the night, remaining glued to the ground as despair pinned them there. As the sky grew darker, so their eyes grew heavier as they drifted off to sleep.

+ + +

After having a small breakfast the next morning, they gathered their packs and got ready to head out. They approached the exit of the clearing and dreadfully gazed upon the challenge facing them once again. The path wound against rocky ground and was only about three feet wide. It rested above a canyon that looked to be about fifty feet deep. The margin for error was very slim. Even Rusty, who had proudly mastered every landscape they had ventured into this journey, appeared timid and nervous. Their stomachs grew tighter with each second.

They proceeded in their usual order, with Joshua first, Liam in the middle, and Bill in the back. Rusty followed behind them all, having to be constantly coaxed to keep moving forward. They hugged the earth wall bordering the path and tried their best not to look down. They could not tell how long the path was initially, as it bent to the left about a hundred feet ahead.

Bill and Liam made very purposeful steps, often having to remind themselves to breathe. Joshua seemed to be doing just fine, which was not out of the ordinary.

"We're getting close to the bend," Joshua announced. "Everyone doing okay?"

"Uh-huh," Bill quietly answered.

"Yeah," Liam responded.

Joshua peered around the bend and looked back. "Okay, looks like we only have about thirty or forty feet left to go. That's not bad."

The other two nodded, trying not to let their guards down just yet. They rounded the bend and moved toward the end of the narrow path. They tried to focus more on the goal ahead of them, and less on the fall they were desperately trying to avoid, which seemed to be a powerful magnet for their eyes.

As they approached the end, Joshua stepped up the ledge and turned around, ready to help the rest climb up. Liam was next and clamped onto Joshua's arm as he scaled the vertical ground. Bill was ready to go next when Rusty lunged forward and jumped ahead of him.

"Geez, dumb mutt," he expressed.

"Okay Bill, you ready?" Joshua asked.

Bill stepped forward and reached for Joshua's hand. His foot went too far on the outer part of the path, and a portion of the ground gave way. He started to fall when Joshua reached out and grabbed his arm.

"I gotcha. I gotcha," Joshua ensured him.

Bill climbed up as fast as he could and collapsed on the ground, giving his heart a chance to stop trying to escape his chest.

"That was not fun," he sighed as he finally started to calm down.

"No, but we made it," Joshua concluded.

Liam stayed quiet as they prepared to continue on their way.

+ + +

They finished the day by arriving at the base of a large hill. They decided it would be good to tackle the ascent the next morning, so they all dropped their packs and began the evening process of fixing a fire for dinner.

As they sat and relaxed after filling their stomachs, Bill looked over at Liam, concerned with his disposition. Liam had hardly said a word since they had crossed over the canyon.

"Liam, are you doing okay?" Bill asked.

Liam nodded, but Bill didn't buy it.

"You know, you haven't said much since the canyon. Is something bothering you?"

Liam sat still for a moment before speaking. "You almost died today. I chose this path, and you almost died," he lamented with tears forming in his eyes.

"Hey, it's okay. Yeah, it was close there for a second, but I'm okay."

"But what if this isn't even the right path, and I almost got you killed for nothing?"

Bill looked at him with compassion. He looked over at Joshua, who seemed concerned, but also confident in allowing Bill to continue handling the situation.

"You wanna know something I've learned since I've been journeying with Joshua?"

Liam just looked down toward the ground.

"I've learned that you can't judge situations just based on how they look right now. And you can't assume that the right way to go is going to be the easy way. In fact, most of the time, it's not easy at all. But we're here, we're together, and we're gonna keep going, okay?"

Bill scooted over and embraced Liam as a few more tears rolled down his face and dampened Bill's shirt.

+ + +

It was the next morning and they were ready to start their ascent up the hill. Liam remained sullen from the day before, but he did his best to keep moving forward. They started up the hill and were pleased to find that it was smooth. No rocks were present to slip on or fall toward them. The hill was, however, proving to be taller and further up than they had imagined. Halfway through the day, their muscles were burning, and they stopped for a much needed break.

"This did not look so daunting from the bottom," Bill stated the obvious.

"No, it certainly didn't," Joshua concurred.

"I thought for sure we were going to make it over by the end of the day," Liam inserted. "I don't know about that now."

"Well, what do we think?" Joshua asked. "Should we keep going until the next breaking point? It may not be for quite a while."

They all sat quietly for a moment, each waiting for another to speak up. Finally, Bill broke the silence.

"I think we should keep going," Bill proposed. "It will probably make for a long day, but I think we can do it."

Liam nodded his head in agreement, hoping he indeed had the energy to make it the rest of the way. They spent another ten minutes or so resting up for the next challenge. They revitalized their thirsty bodies and continued up the hill.

The hill continued much the same, even but lengthy. Rusty seemed to be losing steam with his tongue dangling out the side of his mouth. They grabbed the small trees around them, not so much to keep themselves steady, but to help pull themselves forward. Several times they took small respites to catch their breath and hydrate. Dusk was soon approaching, and Bill was growing concerned that they did not have enough daylight to make it to the top, or at least to another clearing.

"Woo hoo!" Joshua shouted out in front, startling everyone else in the party.

"What is it?" Bill shouted back.

"We made it! We made it!"

"What? We really made it?" Liam yelled as he leapt in celebration.

"Yes!" Bill screamed.

They all darted forward to see the top. They dropped to the ground and exhaled relief, basking in their triumph.

"I can't believe we made it," Liam expressed

After the initial shock wore off, they sat up and began gazing at their surroundings. Joshua walked over to the edge to take in the view.

"The air feels different up here," Bill commented.

"Yeah, it smells different too," Liam chimed in.

"Guys?" Joshua blurted out.

Bill and Liam both looked over at him, wondering what was grabbing his attention.

"Come over here and see," Joshua directed.

They both jumped up, recognizing the excitement in Joshua's tone. They hurried over and stood by Joshua. There, in the distance and through the trees, was the largest body of water Bill had ever seen. It appeared to have no end in sight. They were overcome with awe and emotion. And in the distance, at the edge of the horizon, the sun lowered into the abyss, creating shades of color Bill had never thought possible. His heart felt as if it was exploding with joy.

"Wow," Liam solemnly observed.

"When we least expect it," Bill uttered as a grateful smile spread across his face.

60

"Good morning sunshine," Victor greeted Liam as he barged into his office. He carried a coffee in each hand. Since their blowout and reconciliation, the two had shared coffee together each Monday morning to start the week. They would sit and chat about the weekend and shoot the breeze for a bit before they started work. It was a ritual they had both grown to appreciate.

"Sorry, Man, I can't stay and talk," Victor blurted out as he handed a coffee to Liam. "I have to run to a meeting."

"Oh really? Dang. What meeting?"

"It's for all the team leads. Also, Donald told me to tell you he wanted to meet with you this morning."

Liam's stomach tightened up. He was not on edge like he had used to be, but the thought of meeting with Donald again was still uncomfortable. He had avoided seeing his boss for the most part ever since the demotion, out of embarrassment. Much of that had subsided recently, however.

"Wait, do you know what it's about?"

"No, do you?"

"No. I mean, I remember him saying that he wanted to put me back in the team lead position after I had worked through stuff. It's funny, I was so angry when he took it away from me, but now I don't really care. I'm really happy doing what I'm doing, and you've been doing a fantastic job."

"Well, I'm up for whatever. I said this was a temporary thing from the start, and as far as I'm concerned, that's still the way it is."

"Well, I guess I'll find out when I see him."

"Yeah. Well, I gotta run. Let me know what happens, okay?"

"Sure, I will."

Victor dashed away to his meeting. Liam took a short sip from his coffee, which still put off a lot of heat radiating through the cup and into his hand. He set it down on his desk, hoping it would cool down by the time he got back. He strolled down the hallway, not knowing what to expect, but much more lighthearted than he expected he would be. Though he was going to his boss's office, he felt as though he were the one with the winning hand. He was not stressing about what position he would have or where he would go. He was satisfied, and confident, two traits that had eluded him for some time.

As he approached Donald's office, Daniel looked up and greeted Liam.

"Good morning Liam, how are you."

"Doing good, and you?"

"I'm good. You can go on in," he directed as he pointed to Donald's office with his eyes.

Liam could barely step inside the office before Donald greeted him. "Liam! Good to see you! It's been a while, huh?"

"Yeah it has. How have you been?" Liam asked as he moved to sit down in the chair across from the desk.

"Oh, don't bother sitting. Let's go grab some coffee, huh?"

"Two coffees in one morning," Liam thought to himself. "This looks like a banner day."

"Okay, sounds good," Liam obliged.

"Great, let's go," Donald directed as he motioned for Liam to go out the door first. "Daniel, when is my next appointment?"

"You are free until 10:30," he answered.

"Great thanks."

Donald and Liam proceeded down the hallway.

"Should I bring anything?" Liam inquired.

"No you don't need anything, I'll drive."

"Okay."

Donald was a very purposeful individual. He always seemed as though he was on a mission, even when they were going to get coffee. There was a reason and a drive to everything he did, so Liam just tried his best to keep up as they hustled down the stairs and toward Donald's car. Donald pressed the unlock button and the car obliged by beeping twice. Liam scurried around to the passenger side of the car and hopped in the front seat.

"So how have you been, Liam?" Donald asked with a forceful tone. He was friendly, but also intense, so even a simple inquiry into your well-being sometimes felt like an interrogation.

"I … I've been pretty good. Been going through a lot of changes, just trying to work through a lot of stuff."

"That's good to hear. And how is your lovely wife? I haven't seen Rachel in quite some time."

"She's doing really well too. To be honest, a lot of the stuff I worked through has either involved her, or she just helped me through it a lot."

"That's great to hear, Liam. I know I wouldn't be where I am today without my wife. I had to work through a lot of stuff too when I was younger. Not that the work ever really stops, but at least as you work on it, you get a feel for some of the patterns. You don't feel completely lost when you go through your issues, even though it can still be painful."

"Wow, I had no idea."

"Yeah, I had a lot of stuff that was eating at me, and I refused to deal with it for a long time, which, of course, made it worse. My dad was an alcoholic when I was little and eventually left my mom and us kids. There's a lot of baggage that comes with that, but I didn't see it. Long story short, I ended up an alcoholic myself."

"I would have never guessed."

They quickly arrived at the coffee shop, which was only a few blocks away. They got out of the car and strolled to the front door. Liam felt a surreal sense of calm around this man that he had previously only seen as a supervisor. Donald's vulnerability was making him more human, more relatable.

"Get whatever you want," Donald directed as he pulled out his wallet.

"Thank you."

"No problem. Happy to do it."

They stood in line, analyzing the menu above the barista's head.

"Can I get a large black americano with a blueberry muffin?" Donald asked.

"Sure thing, and for you, Sir?" the barista inquired as she turned to Liam.

"I'll take a medium vanilla latte and a cinnamon scone."

"Okay, sounds good. That will be $13.50."

Donald handed her his card and paid while Liam waited next to him.

"Here's your receipt," she informed him as she handed it to Donald.

"Thank you."

They moved to a nearby table to wait for their order.

"I've had a complicated relationship with my dad," Liam blurted out, surprised he was sharing so easily.

"Oh, yeah?"

"Yeah, my dad has just always been really hard on me. I know now that he meant well, that he was just giving me what he had to give. And really, he gave me a lot. His dad was horrible to him, and thankfully my dad was nothing like that. But he was still tough on me, and for a long time, I resented him for it. I didn't understand where it was coming from. I assumed he thought I was less than him or didn't have what it takes."

"Yeah, I think that can happen a lot with father-son relationships. But it sounds like you've been able to work through some of that."

"Yeah, thankfully I have. And my dad has really come a long way. He came to see me last week to apologize and try to make things better. It's funny, though. By then, I felt like I had come to an intimate enough understanding of where he was coming from that I didn't need an apology."

"Donald!" A barista called out.

They stood up to grab their items and returned to their table.

"So you said you felt like you didn't need an apology?"

"I knew where his heart was; I knew where he was coming from, you know? He wasn't perfect, but I think he did the best he could with what he had."

Donald lifted his drink for a toast. "Well, here's to hoping our kids think the same about us someday."

Liam raised his drink to return the gesture. "For sure."

They continued chatting for a substantial time, sharing the difficulties they had both faced and the lessons they had learned about themselves and the lives they were living. Liam remained amazed at how comfortable he felt around Donald and was forming a real kinship with him. After about thirty minutes, they finally took a break from their mutual sharing and sat silent for a moment.

"You know, Victor has been doing a fantastic job as the team lead," Donald transitioned.

"I definitely agree. I've enjoyed working on his team."

"Liam, I know when we met a while back, I said I wanted to return you to the team lead position, but I'm thinking that I want to keep Victor in that spot."

Liam took another sip of his latte. "Honestly, I'm totally fine with that. I've been enjoying what I'm doing with him."

"Good, I'm glad you've enjoyed it."

Liam started chuckling to himself.

Donald looked into his eyes with a big smile. "What are you laughing about?"

"It's just kind of funny to me that you would take me out to coffee to tell me that you're keeping things the same as they are."

"Well, I've enjoyed chatting with you."

"Me too."

"But I never said I was keeping things the same way," Donald inserted right before taking another drink.

"But you said Victor was going to stay the team lead."

"Yes, and I would like you to be the assistant director."

Liam stopped in his tracks, his cup in mid-sip.

"Don't look so surprised, Liam."

"But, I don't get it. Why?"

"That's where I've wanted you to be all along. But I saw some of the struggles you were going through personally, and I needed to see that you were willing and courageous enough to face them. If you're gonna be assistant director, you're gonna have a lot of people's fates and livelihoods in your hands. I would never put someone in that position if I wasn't sure they were able to deal with their own demons first."

Liam sat stunned, unable to process what he was hearing. "I ... I don't know what to say."

"Well, if I were you, I would say yes, if you want. And then I would call my wife and tell her the good news."

Suddenly, Liam exploded in hysterical laughter.

"Are you okay, Liam?"

"Yeah," he barely verbalized through the roar, "I'm okay."

"Well, okay then," Donald replied as he continued to offer Liam an inquisitive look.

+ + +

It was approaching 6:30 that evening, and Liam was pulling into his driveway. He had called Rachel to let her know the great news immediately after his meeting with Donald. Being assistant director would mean working much more closely with him. After today's conversation, Liam was excited for that new dynamic. He realized he never would have imagined he would have been ... before today.

Rachel, as expected, was incredibly excited about Liam's new position and told him she couldn't wait to give him a celebratory hug. Liam was just as eager to receive it. In his eagerness to get inside, he almost forgot his laptop bag. He opened the car back up and retrieved it.

He hurried up the path to the door and was surprised to find it locked. He pulled out his keys and opened the door. The house was dim, and no one was in the living room to greet him. He gazed up the stairs but saw no lights up there either. He turned to shut the door behind him and ventured into the kitchen.

"Surprise!" The shouts came from around the corner and behind the table. Liam jumped backed and began laughing at the turn of events.

The kitchen lights turned on, and standing there were Rachel, Aaron, Lizzy, Frank, Suzie, Victor, and the rest of his team from work.

"What did you do?" He playfully demanded as he looked in Rachel's eyes.

"As soon as I got off the phone with you, I called everyone, and we all wanted to give you a proper congratulations."

"Oh my word, you're the best," he declared as he moved forward and wrapped his arms around her.

Lizzy put on some catchy music, and they all began partying. Liam made the rounds and gave everyone a hug, thanking them for their support. Everyone was having a blast, eating pizza, and chatting it up. Liam had almost hugged everyone when he arrived at his parents.

"Oh, I'm so proud of you sweetie," Susie expressed as she embraced him tightly.

"Thanks, Mom!"

"Me too, Son. Very proud," his dad echoed.

"Thanks, Dad," Liam responded as he hugged him.

"Another promotion," his dad commented as he shook his head in astonishment. "Way to go."

"Like father, like son. Right, Dad?" Liam proposed.

His dad gave him a grateful smile. "That's right."

61

IT WAS THE NEXT AFTERNOON AND THE TRAVELERS HAD rushed down toward the ocean faster than they thought possible. Liam and Rusty were running up and down the beach while Joshua and Bill looked on, doubled over in laughter. Bill took his boots off and allowed his feet to sink into the sand.

The boy and the dog continued running around and made their way around a large boulder.

"Whoa!" Liam exclaimed. "You guys have to see this!"

Bill and Joshua ran over and rounded the boulder to see what had grabbed Liam's attention. Lying behind the boulder was a schooner. It was in good shape too, even the sails. They walked over and inspected it thoroughly. Bill hopped inside while Joshua continued to scour the perimeter.

"She looks seaworthy," Joshua commented.

"Yeah, it's pretty amazing."

They gave the boat a thorough inspection, and to Bill's astonishment, it was truly ready to set sail at any moment.

Rusty darted off again, and Liam ran after him.

Bill ran his hand across one of the sails as he looked back at Joshua. "The journey doesn't end, huh?" He said with a smile.

"Nope, the journey never ends."

They returned to find Liam and inform him of the next step.

+ + +

After Rusty had tired Liam out, all four of them sat together on the beach, soaking up the sun. The waves shot mist that cooled their faces.

"I'm starting to get hungry," Bill informed them.

"Me too!" Liam responded.

"I'm gonna try my luck at some fishing," Bill said with a huge grin. He walked back toward the trees and found a couple worms to use for bait. He grabbed his pole from his pack and searched for a good spot, settling on a large rocky area elevated over the water. It jettisoned into the sea to form a peninsula. He threw his line on the right side as he gazed out at the water. He was sure he had never seen anything so breathtaking and was comforted by the immensity of it all.

About an hour later, he was still in the same spot, now sitting down, waiting for a nibble.

"Any takers?" Joshua yelled over to Bill.

"No, not yet."

"Why don't you try casting your line on the other side."

"Umm ... okay," Bill complied, just wanting to humor him.

Bill threw his line in again, and to his astonishment, had a fish tugging on it within a couple minutes.

"I got something!" He yelled.

"Good for you!" Joshua celebrated.

+ + +

That evening, after the night sky had fully arrived, they relaxed around the fire. The warmth soothed their bodies, and the light illuminated their faces.

"So, we're sailing out on the boat tomorrow?" Liam asked.

"Yeah, looks like it." Bill responded. "What do you think about that?"

"It sounds like fun. I'm not sure how Rusty is going to do on the boat, though."

"I need to talk to you two about that," Joshua inserted. "I think Rusty should stay here with me."

Joshua and Liam both jolted their heads up to look at Joshua. Concern scrolled across their faces.

"You're not coming!" Liam demanded.

"I will always be with you. In fact, I have always been with you in ways you haven't recognized. But you will. You will see that my presence never leaves you."

Liam looked at Bill, hoping he would try to dissuade Joshua.

"I don't know if we can do this without you, Joshua."

"Of course you can't, but you will realize that I am with you in a deeper way than I even am right now."

"I don't like this," Liam confessed.

"I know this is difficult, but once again, I must ask you to trust me."

Bill and Liam both sat in silence for several minutes. They knew there was no reason not to trust Joshua. He had led them this far, and if he said he would be with them, then they would believe him as best they could.

They talked all sorts of nonsense the rest of the evening, trying to enjoy the night and take the focus off of what they felt they were losing. There was a sweetness to the evening in the midst of the sadness and apprehension. It was an enjoyment of a journey accomplished, and the anticipation of a new step. They bantered and laughed like the old friends they had become, the old friends they always were.

+ + +

The next morning Bill woke up early and decided to get everything on the boat they would be taking, which wasn't much. He gave it one last inspection and returned to find Joshua cooking some fish over a fresh fire.

"I see you're not wasting any time this morning," Bill observed.

"I should say the same to you," Joshua returned.

Liam was cuddling with Rusty, who was obviously enjoying the attention.

"Well, let's get some food in you guys," Joshua announced.

They cozied up to the fire and all shared the food. Bill and Liam tried their best to enjoy the moment, but a dull anguish flowed through their hearts. They trusted Joshua and what he had told them the night before, but they still mourned the end of an era.

+ + +

The boat was set and ready to sail out; all that was left was the goodbyes.

Liam sprang toward Joshua and clutched him as tightly as he could. "I'm gonna miss you so much. I love you."

"I love you too, Liam. More than you know. Don't worry about anything. I'll look after Rusty and the house."

Liam finally released Joshua, fell down on Rusty, and squeezed him around the neck. Rusty could obviously tell that something was happening, but for the most part, he was still his joyful self.

Bill stepped toward Joshua and embraced him. "I don't know how I can ever thank you. You have done so much for me."

"It was all a delight. I love you, Bill."

"I love you too." Bill stepped back and looked at Joshua with confusion.

"What is it?" Joshua asked.

"I don't understand any of this, how it all happened. I don't really understand who you are."

Joshua let out a lighthearted laugh. "That's okay for now, Bill. You don't need to understand it all. But I will tell you this, if you can hear it: I am life itself. Therefore, it is impossible for me to leave you. You will never be alone."

Bill accepted the answer. He didn't understand, but somehow, he inherently knew it was true.

After a few more hugs and tears shed, Liam hopped into the boat while Bill and Joshua pushed it in. Bill jumped in himself and the two sailors waved back at Joshua for several minutes. Joshua waved back as he crouched down and scratched Rusty's head. He remained on the beach until they were out of sight.

"Well, how about we head home," Joshua asked his canine companion.

They proceeded back into the woods to begin their return journey.

+ + +

A few days later, Joshua and Rusty were almost home. They came upon a path bordered on either side by flowers, a path he had recently traveled with Bill. They strolled up the way, following all the twists and turns until they came near the end. Joshua scanned the area, sauntering up all the way. Rusty sat behind him, curiously observing his friend's behavior. The area looked the same as before, except that there was no tombstone to be found.

They turned to finish their trip back to the house. All the while, Joshua hummed in satisfaction.

62

THE DOORBELL RANG AS LIAM WAS FINISHING UP PACK-ing some snacks. He and Aaron were tagging along with Frank on his motorboat. A long day of fishing was ahead of them. Liam could hardly finish a task as he rushed through every movement he made.

Footsteps filled the hallway as Aaron and Lizzy stampeded for the door.

"Well hi there, sweet peas," Susie smothered affection as the door flew open.

"Hi, Grandma!" The kids yelled in unison.

They lunged forward and embraced Susie.

"Aww, I missed you guys," she doted.

When they finally let her through, Frank stepped forward as well. Aaron lunged forward and embraced him.

"Hi, Grandpa!"

Frank's eyes grew as his eyebrows lifted high. He was not used to this kind of affection from the grandkids. After the shock wore off, he enveloped Aaron with his long arms.

"Well hi, Son, it's good to see you too."

They finished their hug and joined everyone else in the kitchen. The room was buzzing with chatter. While the boys continued to plan their outing, the girls were discussing their day together.

"What time are you boys planning on being back?" Susie asked, with a broad grin.

"We'll probably stay out until dinner time," Frank conjectured.

"Do you all have enough food," Rachel queried.

"I packed quite a bit," Liam responded.

"I got some food in the truck, too," Frank inserted. "What are you girls gonna do?"

"Oh we'll probably go shopping, go out for lunch. Whatever we want," Susie hyped.

Lizzy bounced up and down as Susie spoke.

"Well, someone is excited," Rachel commented.

They all chuckled, which brought a rare shade or red to Lizzy's complexion. "Okay, you guys go now," she responded, trying to deflect the attention.

"Okay, okay," Liam obliged, "We all ready?"

Frank and Aaron responded affirmatively, and they turned toward the front door.

"Bye! Love you!" Rachel shouted as they exited.

"Love you too!" They responded.

Susie waved at them as they piled into the truck and pulled away.

Aaron pressed the radio button and found a station he knew they would all enjoy. They bounced up and down with the truck. The music blared as they all soaked in the anticipation. Every face was beaming.

+ + +

It was afternoon. They had all caught at least one fish, and somehow Aaron had wrangled in four.

The snacks laid out in the middle of the boat, creating a nautical smorgasbord. Their full bellies created a quiet scene as they all gazed out onto their lines flowing with the water.

"Dad?" Aaron spoke up.

"Yeah, Bud." Liam responded.

"I think we should get a dog."

Liam turned his head toward Liam with an amused look on his face. "You know what? I've been thinking the same thing."

Connect with Ben DeLong

✉ delongben49@gmail.com
🅕 @bencdelong
🐦 @DarthBen18

SHAIA-SOPHIA HOUSE

Shaia-Sophia House is a collaborative effort of
Alexander John Shaia and Nora Sophia's passion to
provide a creative home for fresh works from the
great traditions. We begin as a publishing house
with plans to expand soon into various mediums.

www.ShaiaSophiaHouse.com